Broken Places

Books by Sandra Parshall

The Heat of the Moon
Disturbing the Dead
Broken Places

Broken Places

Sandra Parshall

Poisoned Pen Press

Library of Congress Catalog Card Number: 2009931400

ISBN: 9781590586532 Hardcover
        9781590587102 Trade Paperback

Poisoned Pen Press
6962 E. First Ave., Ste. 103
Scottsdale, AZ 85251
www.poisonedpenpress.com
info@poisonedpenpress.com

Printed in the United States of America

For Jerry,
my partner in crime

Acknowledgments

The usual suspects deserve a nod for their help during the writing of this book. My husband Jerry served as proofreader and sounding board, and he never stopped believing I could produce another novel, even when I had doubts and loudly expressed them. Carol Baier and Cat Dubie have been loyal friends, critiquers, and cheerleaders. Every day, I receive an endless supply of support and comradeship from members of the Guppies Chapter of Sisters in Crime. I love them and feel blessed to have their priceless friendship.

My editor, Barbara Peters, provided invaluable advice and direction, and I'm grateful for her help in making the book better. As always, I appreciate the dedication of the Poisoned Pen Press staff and everything they do on behalf of the PPP writers. Special thanks go to Patrick Hoi Yan Cheung for creating an excellent cover for me.

I received information and advice from many people, such as the gang of regulars on the Crime Scene Writers listserv and Dr. D. P. Lyle Jr., and I thank them all. If any errors remain, they are entirely my own.

Many thanks to the real Angie Hogencamp for letting me borrow her name for one of my characters. Marisa Young made a donation to the Malice Domestic charity auction in exchange for the right to give one of my fictional dogs the name Cricket. Two other dogs in this book, Maggie and Lisa, along with the charming guinea pig Mr. Piggles, were named by Meg Born, who made a generous donation to the Bouchercon 2008 charity auction to win the naming rights. The big fluffy cat who belongs to my fictional cartoonist Ben Hern bears the name of Hamilton, who labored long and hard as the store mascot at Creatures 'n' Crooks in Richmond, VA. This wonderful store is closed now, like so many other independents, and Hamilton is living a life of ease in retirement.

Finally, I am grateful to every reader who has taken the time to e-mail me or tell me in person that you have enjoyed my first two books and want to see more. In the end, that is what keeps a writer going: the hope that someone out there will sit down with her book, open it with anticipation, and read it with pleasure.

The world breaks everyone and afterward many are strong at the broken places. But those that will not break it kills.

—Ernest Hemingway
A Farewell to Arms

Chapter One

When Rachel Goddard turned onto Ben Hern's property, she couldn't see the other car barreling toward hers down the long, curving driveway. All she saw up ahead were the massive rhododendrons and trees in summer leaf that formed a screen on both sides. Even Ben's house was invisible from this angle.

Rachel was good-naturedly teasing Holly Turner, her young veterinary assistant. "I've never seen anybody so excited about meeting a dog and a cat. Don't you see enough pets at the clinic every day?"

"I know it's silly." Holly flashed her megawatt smile. "But his cat and dog are like celebrities, bein' in a comic strip and on TV." She paused for a fraction of a second before adding, "It's so excitin' to have somebody famous like Mr. Hern comin' to live right here in Mason County. And to think you grew up with him!"

Rachel glanced at Holly, watched her tuck her black hair behind her ears, change her mind and let it drop against her cheeks again. Acting as if she were on her way to a date and nervous about how she looked. Maybe bringing her along on this house call hadn't been a good idea. "You know, Ben is—"

Holly screamed.

Rachel swung her gaze back to the road, saw the blue car flying around the curve toward them. She wrenched the steering wheel hard to the right. Tires screeching, her SUV bumped off the driveway and crashed into a wall of greenery. Branches cracked, leaves slapped the windshield, Rachel and Holly bounced in their seats.

Rachel floored the brake. When the vehicle stopped, they seemed to be inside a shrub. Big rubbery leaves pressed against the windshield and windows.

"Oh, my god," Rachel gasped. Her heart banged against her ribs, the beat echoing in her temples. She saw everything through a screen of her own auburn hair, fallen forward over her eyes. "Are you all right?"

"Yeah—" Holly paused to gulp. "I'm okay."

Rachel slumped forward against the steering wheel and blew out a long breath. "Was that Cam Taylor?"

"I think so. He went by so fast."

Rachel's mind had snapped a picture as the other car raced past and now produced it in surprising detail—the battered Ford with one front fender a different shade of blue than the rest of the car, the driver's hands clenched around the steering wheel, his hair whipped into a fright wig by the blowback through open windows. "Has he lost his mind? For god's sake, he could have killed us."

With trembling fingers, Rachel pushed her hair out of her eyes. She looked around and tried to orient herself. All she saw was vegetation. She shifted the vehicle into reverse and began backing out slowly.

"Why do you suppose he was here?" Holly asked. "What business would he have with Mr. Hern?"

"Probably the same business he had with you and me. Begging for money. I guess he didn't get it from Ben either." The tires bumped over roots and rocks.

Rachel gave the vehicle more gas. Abruptly it popped free of its leafy trap and lurched back onto the driveway, throwing both of them forward against their seat belts. Holly yelped. Rachel struggled with the steering wheel, couldn't straighten the tires fast enough, and slammed on the brakes just in time to stop the SUV from sailing off the driveway on the other side.

She sat still for a moment, clutching the wheel and willing her heart to slow down. Her mouth was so dry her lips stuck to her teeth.

"Oh, my goodness," Holly said, assessing the mangled rhododendrons from which they'd emerged. "I hope Mr. Hern's not real picky about how his yard looks."

Rachel gave a shaky laugh and shifted into drive. They rounded the broad curve that led to the parking circle outside Ben's Georgian brick house. Rachel pulled in behind Ben's black Jaguar and the little green Volkswagen beetle that belonged to his assistant, Angie Hogencamp.

Rachel couldn't shake the dizzy, helpless sensation of losing control. Her hands were still trembling, her heart still racing when she retrieved her medical bag and acupuncture case from the back seat.

Examining the outside of the vehicle, Holly exclaimed, "Look at your poor car. It's all scratched up."

The hybrid SUV was only a month old, but after the run-in with the rhododendrons its silver paint looked as if a gang of vandals had worked it over with sharp objects. Rachel was too relieved to be safe, though, to care about the car. "It's nothing compared to what could have happened to you and me."

She handed Holly the acupuncture case. *Calm down,* she told herself. She was here to treat an animal in pain, and she didn't have time to indulge a reaction to the near-collision.

She and Holly were mounting the front steps when Ben opened the door and greeted them with a smile. "Hi, Rach—" He broke off, his smile fading, as he glanced from Rachel to Holly and back. "Is something wrong?"

Rachel took a good look at Holly's disheveled hair and dazed expression for the first time and realized she probably appeared equally shaken up. Combing her hair back from her face with her fingers, she told Ben, "Cam Taylor ran us off the driveway. We're both okay, but it would have been nice if he'd stopped to make sure he hadn't killed us."

"Aw, for Christ's sake." Ben inclined his head toward Holly, who stood a foot shorter. "Are you sure you're not hurt?"

Holly bobbed her head. Clutching the acupuncture case to her chest with both arms, she suddenly seemed oblivious to everything but the handsome dark-haired man who stood so close. Holly had met him a couple of times before, when he visited Rachel at the cottage she and Holly shared, but it might take a lot more exposure before his exotic aura wore thin. Females tended to react this way to Benicio Hernandez, the Cuban-American artist who lurked behind the Anglicized tag of Ben Hern, cartoonist. His brooding eyes and sensitive features, combined with well-defined muscles under a black tee shirt, made him look like a model for the cover of a romance novel. Good thing, Rachel thought, that Holly's boyfriend wasn't around to see the rapt expression on the girl's face.

"What on earth did you do to make Taylor take off in such a frenzy?" Rachel asked.

"He got mad because I won't lend him money to bail out his little newspaper. Would you believe he even tried to weasel money out of my mother while she was here?"

Holly found her voice at last. "Mr. Taylor's real stubborn. He's been after me too, tryin' to get some of the money my aunt left me. I don't even have it yet, but he wants me to promise him some of it."

"He asked me too, a few days ago," Rachel said. "He made a very persuasive case, I'll say that for him. The county does need a newspaper, and he's pretty passionate about it. If I'd never seen the paper—But I have seen it, and lately it's started looking like some poor animal that should be put out of its misery."

Ben laughed and dismissed the subject with a wave of his hand. "To hell with Cam Taylor." He turned his smile on Holly. "It's about time you met Sebastian and Hamilton."

"I'm so excited." Holly beamed back at him. "I just love *Furballs*. Are they just like you show them in the comic strip and the TV shows?"

"I think I've caught their personalities. I hope you realize, though, that they can't actually talk."

"Well, I *know* that," Holly said, with a little gust of a laugh.

"They're going to love you," Ben said. "How could they help it?"

Her smile widened beyond the point that seemed physically possible, and Rachel had to restrain herself from rolling her eyes. She could understand other women's reactions to Ben, but she'd known him too long to be fooled by the smooth exterior. She still saw the gawky teenager, too thin for his height, too introverted to mix in groups, happiest when he was alone with his sketch pad or canvas. Although his appearance had changed since they'd grown up as neighbors in Northern Virginia, the person inside was much the same.

"Come on," Ben said. "Sebastian's on the porch with Angie."

As she followed Ben into the house, through the foyer and living room, Rachel experienced the same weird sense of dislocation she felt every time she visited him. He'd bought the house fully furnished from the estate of an elderly woman, and as far as Rachel could see he hadn't changed a thing in the downstairs rooms during the three months he'd lived here. Queen Anne tables, gold-framed mirrors, brocade draperies and upholstery— not exactly Ben's taste. The only alterations he'd made were upstairs, where he'd stripped the master bedroom to essentials and had a wall removed so he could convert two smaller bedrooms into a studio.

Ben ushered them through French doors onto the big screened porch, where his dachshund lay motionless on the floor.

Angie Hogencamp watched over the dog from a green wicker settee. Ben's assistant was a slender young woman with freckles over her cheekbones and brown hair worn in a single braid down her back. "It's awfully hot out here," she said to Rachel, "but this is where Sebastian wants to be. We took him inside and he dragged himself right back out again through the pet door."

"Now he won't even stand up," Ben said. He crouched beside his dog and scratched Sebastian's head.

Placing her medical case on the floor, Rachel knelt and stroked the dog. The remnants of tension over the driveway incident faded as she concentrated on her patient, and her hands once again felt sure and steady. "Hello, love," she murmured. "That old back of yours acting up again?"

Without raising his head, the dog rolled mournful eyes in her direction. Another furry head bumped Rachel's elbow, and she reached around to pat Hamilton, Ben's gray and white Maine coon cat. When the cat turned his attention to Holly, she looked as thrilled as if she were meeting a movie star. She set the acupuncture case on the floor and knelt to pet him.

With Ben looking on like a worried father, Rachel listened to Sebastian's heart and lungs, and gently probed his abdomen to make sure he didn't have a simple bellyache from the rich treats Ben fed him. "His vital signs are normal," she told Ben, returning her stethoscope to her bag. "I'll give him another acupuncture treatment for his back pain and see how he does."

Ben, squeamish about watching the needles go in, turned away and gazed out over the back yard flower garden.

Settling cross-legged on either side of the dog, Rachel and Holly nudged him onto his stomach and stroked him until he relaxed. Rachel tore open a package of long, fine needles, located acupoints with her fingertips, and inserted four needles just under the skin along the dog's spine. With tiny alligator clips, she connected wires to the needles and to the battery-operated electrical stimulator. When she turned on the low-level current, the dog's back rippled but he didn't react otherwise.

"Good boy," Rachel murmured. "Okay, Ben, you can look now."

He did, but winced at the sight of Sebastian with needles protruding from his back like porcupine quills.

"It's not hurting him." Rachel punched in twenty minutes on her pocket timer. "Want me to stick a few needles in you to prove it?"

Angie and Holly laughed at Ben's expression of horror. "Whoa," he said, raising both hands to ward off the threat. "I'll take your word for it."

Just then footfalls sounded on the porch steps, and they all looked around. Cam Taylor stood at the screen door. He rapped on the frame once, then opened the door and stepped onto the porch.

"What the hell?" Ben sprang forward to intercept him. "You can't just walk in here. Why are you back, anyway?"

Rachel said, "Maybe he wants to apologize to Holly and me for endangering our lives."

Taylor ignored her sarcasm and spread his hands as if in supplication. Rachel's eyes were drawn to the stump of the third finger on his right hand, and she wondered briefly, as she had before, how he'd lost it.

"Yes," he said, "I did come back to tell you I'm sorry and make sure you're all right. I'm under a lot of pressure, I've got a lot on my mind. But that's no excuse. Will you accept my apology?"

Rachel hesitated, reluctant to let him off the hook. The man's face was flushed, and half-moons of sweat soaked the underarms of his blue shirt, but his hair, brown shot through with gray, looked as if he'd tried to tame it before he joined them. He gave her a sheepish smile that made him seem boyish and almost handsome.

Rachel sighed. His apology sounded forced, but at least he'd made the effort. "Sure," she said.

"All right, you've apologized," Ben said. "Now you can leave. And don't come back this time."

Sebastian whimpered, probably reacting to Ben's harsh tone. Rachel stroked his head.

"I want to apologize to you too," Taylor said. "I got worked up and I said some things I probably shouldn't have. If you'll just hear me out and take a look at the business plan I've put together—"

"I've already heard your story more than once," Ben said.

"I don't think you've grasped what's at stake here," Taylor said. Rachel heard the strain in his voice as he tried to speak in a calm, measured tone. "We lost the radio station years ago, and if the *Advocate* disappears too, the people of Mason County won't have any source of local news. They won't have anybody to speak for them, to ask the tough questions—"

"Listen to me," Ben said. "One last time: I'm not handing you a check. I don't care what you call it—a loan, an investment— I'm not under any obligation to support you."

"I'm not asking for myself," Taylor protested. A slight edge to his voice and a spark in his eyes, quickly smothered, hinted at the anger he was struggling to control. He gestured at his faded blue shirt and worn khaki pants. "Look at me. Do I look like I care about money? If money meant anything to me personally, I wouldn't even be in Mason County. I care about the people. They depend on the paper to look out for their interests."

"All I know is that you came into my house and started threatening me—"

"Threatening you?" Taylor said with a little laugh. "That's an exaggeration, isn't it? I've just tried to make you see where I stand on…certain things. Things you probably don't want to talk about in front of your friends."

Taylor glanced at Rachel, who regarded the two men with fresh interest. Something was going on here that she couldn't identify, something more than a man asking for a loan that Ben didn't want to give.

Ben's gaze jumped from Rachel to Holly to Angie, and the sudden apprehension in his eyes made Rachel all the more curious about the subtext of his exchange with Taylor.

"I'm through talking to you," Ben said. "You're leaving right now."

He grabbed Taylor's arm and tried to push him out the door. Younger, bigger, and stronger, Ben should have had the advantage, but Taylor caught the door jamb with both hands and held on. His color deepened alarmingly, and Rachel wondered if he had a heart or hypertension problem.

"Ben," she said, "calm down, please. This is ridiculous." She wanted to rise and put herself between the two of them, but Sebastian had begun to tremble and she couldn't abandon him.

Taylor was losing his tenuous self-control. He glared at Ben. "You gave a million dollars to a damned animal shelter, while children right here in Mason County are going hungry—"

"You don't know what you're talking about," Angie exclaimed. She stepped up to face Taylor. "Ben gives a lot of money to help children, but he doesn't brag about what he does the way you do. And he doesn't steal people's money like you stole from my mom and dad."

"*Stole?* I didn't steal anything from—"

"That's enough." Ben pried Taylor loose from the jamb, shouldered the screen door all the way open, and shoved him out onto the steps.

Rachel gasped when Taylor stumbled backward, windmilling his arms for balance. Ben caught him before he fell, and without pausing he propelled Taylor down the steps and into the yard. As they disappeared around the side of the house, Rachel heard Taylor yelling, "If people knew the truth about you, if they knew what you've done—"

Then silence.

Rachel exhaled and willed herself to relax. She'd never seen Taylor act this way before. He had a reputation as a self-righteous do-gooder, but in her few encounters with him she'd found him courteous enough, if exasperatingly persistent. It was Ben's behavior that worried her, though. He had a right to resent being pressured, but seeing him get physical with Taylor scared her a little. What did he mean when he accused Taylor of threatening him? What was it that Ben didn't want to talk about in front of her and Angie and Holly?

Rachel noticed for the first time that Holly, sitting on the other side of Sebastian, looked distraught and on the verge of tears. To break the tension, Rachel grinned and said, "Believe me, not all house calls are this exciting."

Holly managed a weak smile.

Leaning against a post, Angie chewed her bottom lip and watched the yard. When Ben hadn't returned after a couple of minutes, she said, "I guess he's just making sure Cam Taylor really leaves this time."

"I hope so. This little guy needs peace and quiet during his treatment." Rachel was curious about Angie's claim that Taylor had stolen money from her parents, but bringing it up again might provoke another outburst of anger. Stroking one of Sebastian's long ears, Rachel asked, "Are you ever sorry you took this job?"

Angie shook her head. "I love working for Ben. It's the best thing that ever happened to me. I really appreciate you helping me get the job."

"Good. I'm glad to hear that." From time to time, Rachel had wondered whether being here alone with Ben every day was the best thing for Angie, but it was none of her business. She could only hope the young woman was too levelheaded to fall for her boss.

Ten minutes ticked by with no sign of Ben. "Maybe he's in the house," Angie said. "I'll be right back."

Rachel was removing the needles from Sebastian's back when Angie returned. "He's gone," she said, frowning. "His car's not out front."

Strange, Rachel thought. Had Ben followed Taylor beyond the grounds to make sure he didn't come back? That really was going too far, in her opinion. And why would Ben leave without telling anybody?

Rachel expected him to turn up any second as she gave Angie instructions for the dog's care and Holly packed up the equipment, but by the time they left he hadn't returned.

They were on the driveway, headed for the road, when Holly sighed and said, "His house is so beautiful. I can't imagine livin' in a place like that."

Rachel shook her head, bemused. When the court released Holly's windfall inheritance, the legacy would include a house as grand as Ben's, but she'd sworn never to live in it. Too many bad associations. In all seriousness, Holly had suggested the place was haunted by her dead aunt. *Grandma says when somebody dies a bad death in a house, their spirit never leaves it.* For now, Holly seemed content to stay in Rachel's four-room cottage on the McKendrick horse farm, where she'd lived since starting work at Rachel's veterinary clinic months earlier.

Turning onto the road, Rachel wondered again where Ben had gone. Something about this situation gave her the creeps. To distract herself as much as Holly, she said, "I'll tell you a secret—Frank's going to be in *Furballs*, starting about a month from now."

"Oh, wow!" Holly exclaimed. "Frank's gonna be a star!"

Rachel smiled at the thought of her battered one-eared cat, rescued from a Dumpster, transformed into a celebrity. "He'd better not let it go to his head. If he develops a taste for caviar, he's out of luck."

As Rachel drove toward Mountainview, where her vet clinic was located, Holly chattered on about possible storylines for Frank's fictional life. Rachel tried to listen, but she couldn't stop thinking about Ben, and she hoped to see him drive past any minute, on his way home.

Holly's voice trailed off when they approached an old blue car in the middle of the road.

"That's Cam Taylor's car," Rachel said. "Maybe he had a breakdown."

"I sure hope we don't have to give him a ride back to town."

When Rachel pulled up behind the car, she realized it wasn't occupied. The driver's door hung open several inches. "What on earth? Do you see him anywhere?"

They glanced around at the woods on both sides. Nothing but trees.

"He might've gone lookin' for help," Holly said.

"If he has a cell phone, he could have called."

"Maybe he's back in the woods," Holly said, "you know, answerin' a call of nature. But why wouldn't he pull over, instead of…"

Rachel stared at the empty car, the open door, and full-blown dread seized her. She swung around Taylor's car and parked on the gravel berm. "You stay here," she told Holly. "I just want to take a look around."

She got out and jumped over the drainage ditch, her pants legs brushing against the Queen Anne's lace blooming there. A strip of land about ten feet deep, thick with weeds and wildflowers and vines, separated the road from the woods. Spotting a patch of poison ivy, Rachel hesitated to wade farther through the vegetation. She paused, pulled off her sunglasses, and squinted into the gloom under the trees.

A movement snagged her attention. She caught a glimpse of color, no more than a hundred feet in, before it vanished behind a tree. Light blue. The faded shirt Cam Taylor was wearing. Relief washed through her, and she opened her mouth to call out and ask if he was okay, but stopped herself. Of course he was okay. He was probably peeing against a tree and wouldn't welcome her intrusion.

Taylor came into view again—his back, his hair, one gesticulating hand. Although Rachel couldn't see another person, she heard two voices now, rising and falling. Taylor's was the only one she recognized. The other remained so indistinct that she couldn't have said whether it was a man or a woman. Only a few of Taylor's words carried clearly. "…don't have the nerve…dare you." He was arguing with someone. Why here? Why in the woods?

Taylor moved, and she lost sight of him among the trees.

Rachel didn't want to get involved in this. Sliding her sunglasses back on, she turned toward the road and her vehicle.

The crack of a gunshot made her spin around. Another shot rang out. Rachel dropped to her knees, ducked her head and covered it with her arms.

She waited, her heart thudding, her mouth dry. The birds had gone silent. Over the sound of her own raspy breath, she heard a thrashing noise, like somebody running through the undergrowth. A squirrel chittered furiously. Then she heard a car start somewhere in the distance.

A touch on Rachel's shoulder made her flinch.

"You okay?" Holly crouched beside Rachel, her eyes wide with alarm. "Did somebody shoot at you?"

"No, not at me. Get back in the car," Rachel said. "Call 911. Call Tom."

"You call him." Holly stood. "Come on. We need to leave here right now."

Rachel scanned the woods as she rose, trying to pick out the light blue of Taylor's shirt in the forest of green and brown. He could be lying on the ground, bleeding to death. "I think somebody shot Cam Taylor," she said. "I have to see if I can help him."

"No!" Holly gripped Rachel's arm with both hands and tried to pull her away. "You're not goin' in there with somebody that's got a gun!"

Rachel twisted her arm free. "Whoever did it is gone."

"You don't know that. You can't be—"

"I heard him leaving. Holly, go back to the car. Call Tom. Tell him to send an ambulance. Right now!"

Rachel set off into the woods.

The tree canopy closed over her, shutting out the sun. She stuffed her sunglasses into her shirt pocket and pushed on. Slapping aside drooping vines, stumbling over fallen tree branches, she felt like a walking target.

He's gone, she told herself. *The shooter's gone.*

Please, God, let him be gone.

Why hadn't she listened to Holly? She didn't even like Cam Taylor. It was nuts to risk her safety for him.

He's hurt, bleeding; he needs me.

She found Taylor on the ground under an oak tree. He'd collapsed at an odd angle, coming to rest with his right leg twisted under him, his left arm flung up over his face. Blood soaked the front of his shirt.

Feeling exposed and vulnerable, Rachel pivoted in a circle, searching for movement among the trees. She saw no one lurking in the woods, no sign anyone else had been there except for a path of trampled vegetation leading away.

Rachel bent over Taylor, but the stench of fresh blood and feces and urine made her gag and draw back. Flies already buzzed over the body, drawn by the odors. Rachel waved them away. They didn't disperse, but rose to circle above Cam Taylor, waiting, like tiny planes in a holding pattern.

If there was any chance he was alive, that she could help him, she had to try. Holding her breath, Rachel knelt beside him. Pressing her fingertips to one side of his neck, then the other, she searched for a pulse.

He felt warm to her touch, as warm as life, and as still as death.

Chapter Two

Captain Tom Bridger batted a swarm of flies away from the body while Sergeant Dennis Murray crouched and shot a last batch of pictures.

Tom wasn't surprised Cam Taylor had ended up shot to death in the woods. Toss a rock anywhere in Mason County and you'd hit somebody with a grudge against him. Just as many would praise and defend him, though. Few would take the middle ground where Taylor was concerned.

Dennis glanced up at Tom. "What next?"

"Nothing that I can see." Tom pulled a handkerchief from his uniform pocket and mopped a trickle of sweat off his forehead. Humidity and perspiration glued his thick black hair to his scalp like a helmet and made him speculate on whether baldness might be a blessing. "Whoever did this knew how to cover his tracks. It looks like an ambush."

Tom and four other sheriff's deputies had combed the woods and dense undergrowth around the body and found nothing— no spent shells, no fibers, no hairs. The woods lay between two parallel paved roads, with a narrow dirt road through the trees connecting them, and the shooter had left a path of trampled vegetation between the body and the dirt road. That was probably where he'd parked his vehicle, out of sight but close enough for Rachel to hear it leaving. The dry, hard-packed ground hadn't yielded so much as a footprint or tire print. Tom had sent a couple of men to search the pavement and ditches on the far side of the woods, but he'd be surprised if they found anything useful there. Their best hope lay in turning up somebody who'd seen Taylor and his killer on the road. Deputies were already knocking on every door in the area in search of a witness.

Rising, Dennis let the camera drop against his chest on its strap and adjusted his wire-rimmed glasses. "You think it was the cartoonist?"

"We'll start with him, but anybody could have been following Taylor around, waiting for an opportunity. Look, you stay with the body. I'll tell Rachel and Holly they can go for now. No point in keeping them out here."

Tom threaded his way back through the woods, swatting gnats and watching for snakes in the tangle of weeds and vines underfoot. On the road, yellow crime scene tape marked off Taylor's car and the pavement and shoulder around it. A few yards away, Rachel leaned against her vehicle, arms folded and head down.

When she looked up at his approach, her bleak expression made Tom wish he could pull her into his arms, say something that might blunt the horror of what she'd seen. But this wasn't the time or place. He touched her shoulder instead. "How are you doing?"

"I'm fine," Rachel said, a tremor in her voice. "How long does he have to lie in the woods like that, with flies all over him?"

"Gretchen Lauter's on her way. She has to see him before he's moved, but it won't be long." Dr. Lauter, Mason County's part-time medical examiner, had been summoned from the clinic where she saw Medicaid patients on Fridays.

"What an awful way to die. I didn't like Cam Taylor, but I never would have wished this on him."

"I expect to hear a lot of people say the same thing." But at least one person would only be telling a half-truth.

"Do you think somebody was waiting here for him?" Rachel asked. "Flagged him down and made him get out of his car?"

"Possibly," Tom said. "This was a perfect spot for it. There's so little traffic on this road, we probably wouldn't have known about the shooting for hours if you and Holly hadn't come along. But I don't want to start guessing. Right now I need to talk to Hern. He's not back at his house and he's not answering his cell phone. Do you have any idea where he could have disappeared to?"

"He hasn't disa—" Rachel broke off, her eyes widening with sudden alarm. "What if something's happened to him too? If he was following Cam Taylor—"

"We don't have any reason to think anything's happened to Hern. He'll probably turn up anytime now." Tom believed Rachel had given him a truthful account of the argument between Hern and Taylor, but had done it reluctantly, not wanting to make Hern look bad. Or was he imagining that? Tom had been trying to interpret her relationship with Hern, or Hernandez, or whatever his name was, since the man had moved to Mason County three months earlier.

"Why don't you and Holly go home?" he said. "Cancel the rest of your appointments, don't try to go back to work. Somebody'll call you later about coming by headquarters to give your statements. Where'd Holly go, anyway?"

Rachel pointed up the road. Holly and her boyfriend, Deputy Brandon Connelly, walked aimlessly, the sandy-haired young man's arm around her shoulders.

"She's very upset. She didn't see the body, but just knowing what happened and hearing the shots…" Rachel's voice wavered and she covered her face with her hands. "I keep wondering if I could have prevented it somehow."

"None of this is your fault." To hell with propriety. Tom pulled Rachel into a tight hug. Her arms closed around him and she pressed her face against his shoulder. Stroking her silky auburn hair, Tom said, "I'm sorry you had to see him. I know it's hard to get something like that out of your mind."

He felt Rachel draw deep breaths, calming herself. When she pulled back, he kissed her forehead and released her. "Let me get Holly over here. I want to talk to both of you before you leave."

Tom whistled to catch Brandon and Holly's attention, and summoned them with a wave. When they joined him and Rachel, Holly's eyes were puffy from crying, and Tom felt a pang of almost paternal sympathy for the girl. From the day he'd met her he'd had a soft spot for Holly. She was a sweet kid, but aside from that, the two of them were among the few people left in Mason County who were recognizable as Melungeon—mixed race, with skin color showing strains of Native American, possibly black, and Portuguese or Turkish. With their soot-black hair and dusky complexions, they would always stand out in this overwhelmingly white mountain community in southwestern Virginia.

"For now," Tom said, "I don't want either of you to tell anybody what you saw or heard. You didn't hear the shots, you didn't see the body. Tell everybody you were driving along, you saw Taylor's car abandoned on the road but you didn't see him anywhere. You waited to see if he'd show up, and when he didn't, you called 911. Okay?"

Rachel nodded agreement, but Holly asked, "Why do you want us to lie?"

Tom didn't enjoy scaring the girl, but she had to understand the importance of protecting herself. "The killer is still out there, and we don't know who he is."

"Right," Brandon put in, and Tom allowed him to play the voice of authority for his girlfriend. "See, if the killer finds out you were here when the shots were fired, he might think you saw him. He'd be afraid you could identify him."

"Oh," Holly said, her voice falling to a whisper.

"I'll have to let Joanna know that Cam Taylor's dead," Rachel said. "She's been friends with the Taylors a long time."

"Watch what you say," Tom told her, "and ask her not to talk to Meredith Taylor until I've had a chance to get out there." He wanted to be the first to see the new widow's reaction to the news.

Brandon gave Holly a quick kiss before the girl climbed into Rachel's vehicle. Tom opened Rachel's door, but he caught her hand before she got in. "Listen," he said. "I don't want you to talk to Hern about anything that happened today."

Rachel pulled her hand from his. "You can't possibly think Ben killed him."

"I didn't say I did. You're both witnesses to Taylor's behavior and movements before he was killed, and I can't have you discussing what happened and distorting each other's memories. Promise me you won't talk to Hern until I give the all-clear."

She sighed and nodded. "I understand."

A few minutes after they left, Gretchen Lauter arrived in her silver Prius, followed by a hearse from a local funeral home. When she finished with the body, deputies would bag it and load it in the hearse for transport to the state medical examiner's morgue in Roanoke, where the autopsy would be performed.

Gretchen struggled out of her little car, a wince betraying pain in her knees, and banged her head on the door frame. "Crap," she muttered, her fingers feeling through salt-and-pepper curls for the sore spot.

Tom knew better than to say anything, but he had a feeling Gretchen's arthritis made her regret giving up her boat-sized gas guzzler. He busied himself with collecting a body bag from the teenage boy driving the hearse.

"All right," Gretchen said, straightening the hem of her short-sleeved jacket, "where is the poor bastard?"

Tom filled her in as they trekked through the woods. "Two shots to the chest at close range. Right through the heart, looks like. We know the time of death—11:15. But we're keeping that quiet for now." He explained his concern for Rachel and Holly's safety.

When Tom and Gretchen reached Taylor's body, Dennis was flapping his hands in a vain attempt to beat off the buzzing flies.

"Don't waste your energy," Gretchen told him, pulling on latex gloves. "They'll get at him no matter what we do."

She looked down at the dead man for a long moment, and Tom sensed she was making a mental adjustment, reclassifying Cam Taylor from decades-long acquaintance to murder victim. Then she stooped and began a brisk examination, leaning in to study the chest wounds, lifting Taylor's eyelids, prying open his mouth. Tom stood back to distance himself from the urine and feces stench that rose off the corpse like a miasma, intensified by the heat.

"Let's turn him," Gretchen told Tom. Which meant *you* turn him.

Tom rolled the body face-down. "No exit wound."

"The slugs might be lodged in his heart," Gretchen said. "Did you find the casings?"

"No. The shooter cleaned up after himself."

Gretchen stood, grimacing and clutching one knee for a second. "Has Meredith been notified?"

Tom shook his head. "I'll drive out there and tell her."

"I suppose you have to consider her a suspect."

"The spouse is always a suspect."

"Well, I can't believe she had anything to do with this. Are you going to call Lindsay?"

Gretchen's gaze searched Tom's face with a curiosity that made him avert his eyes. "I'll let her mother tell her," he said.

Why hadn't it occurred to him before now that Cam's death would bring the Taylors' daughter back home? Lindsay would stay with her mother through the funeral, at least. Tom hadn't seen Lindsay since the Christmas holidays, and their chance meeting on Main Street in Mountainview had been awkward for both of them. But now her father's murder would be her only concern. Lindsay wouldn't have the time or inclination to think about Tom and their failed romance.

"Hey, boss," Brandon yelled from the road. "Here comes our man."

Tom jogged through the woods as fast as the undergrowth allowed. When he reached the road, Brandon had already stopped Ben Hern in his black Jaguar. Tom took a minute to wipe sweat from his face with his handkerchief before he approached.

Hern had powered down his window and was craning his neck to see up ahead. "What's going on?" he asked Tom.

"You don't know?"

"Know what? Is that Cam Taylor's car? Has there been an accident?"

"Step out of your vehicle, please." Tom rested one hand on the butt of his pistol.

"What? What's happening here?"

"Step out of the vehicle, please. Now."

"Why?"

Tom didn't answer, but met Hern's exasperation with a calm stare.

Finally Hern sighed heavily and cut his engine. Under his breath, he uttered something in Spanish that didn't sound complimentary.

The big man unfolded himself from the low-slung Jaguar with a fluid grace that made Tom think of a powerful cat rising to its feet. Tom couldn't even imagine himself in a car like this, and he'd probably be as awkward getting out of it as Gretchen had been when she'd exited her Prius. But in his early thirties, Tom wouldn't have arthritis to blame.

Hern slammed his door shut. "Are you going to tell me what this is about?"

"Cameron Taylor's body is lying in the woods over there. As far as I can tell right now, you were the last person to see him."

"His body?" Hern's bewildered glance flicked from Taylor's car to the trees. "Are you saying he's dead?"

His confusion seemed genuine enough, Tom thought, but he'd had plenty of time to rehearse what he would say and do when confronted with Taylor's death. Watching Hern's face, Tom said, "He was murdered."

Hern's mouth fell open, and for a few seconds he said nothing. Then he scrubbed a hand across his face and said, "How? Who—"

"Rachel found his car sitting empty on the road and called 911."

Hern winced. "*Ay, Dios mio.* Where is Rachel? Is she upset?"

"Turn around and lean your hands on the vehicle," Tom said.

"Excuse me?"

"I said turn around."

Hern looked so incredulous that Tom expected him to balk. That wouldn't be a problem, with Brandon standing by to help ensure cooperation, but in the end Hern threw up his hands and faced the car. "Go ahead, have your fun, if you think it's necessary."

Tom patted him down, feeling nothing but hard muscle under his black jeans and black tee shirt. The guy was in fantastic shape, probably worked out an hour or two a day. Tom had more than a little trouble seeing him as an artist who made his living—an enviable living—by drawing cartoons about his cat and dog.

Finding no weapon, Tom stepped back. "Where have you been since you left your house?"

"I went for a drive," Hern said with exaggerated patience.

"Did you stop anywhere, talk to anybody?"

"Not a soul."

"Did you see any other vehicles on the road, even from a distance?"

"No."

"Do I have your permission to search your car?"

Again Hern seemed dumbfounded, staring at Tom for a moment without speaking. When he found his voice, he said, "You think I had something to do with this, don't you? You're looking for a murder weapon?"

"I'm just gathering information at this point."

"Well, gather away, Captain." Hern waved a hand at the Jaguar. "You won't find anything."

"Thank you." Tom motioned for Brandon to join them. To Hern's annoyance, he asked Hern to state in Brandon's presence that they had permission for the search.

They did a thorough job, taking ten minutes, but they found nothing. Tom wasn't surprised. He didn't believe Hern was stupid enough to come back with the gun still in his possession. If he'd killed Taylor.

Hern had stood aside during the search, his arms crossed, hostility stewing in his face. "Satisfied?" he said when they slammed the doors closed.

Hern was an arrogant son of a bitch, Tom thought, the kind of person Rachel wouldn't waste time on. Why did she count him as a friend? But then, Tom doubted Hern behaved this way around her. "I understand you had an argument with Taylor this morning," Tom said.

"Who told you that?"

"Is it true?"

"Yes, all right, we had an argument, which he provoked."

"You've only lived in Mason County for three months. How did you develop such a bad relationship with him so fast?"

"We didn't have a *relationship*. He wanted money to save his newspaper."

"Why did he come to you? What made him think you might help him?"

Hern's gaze slid away from Tom's, and he took a moment to answer. "He seemed to believe we had a connection because he knew my mother when they were young, but he didn't mean anything to me and I wasn't going to give him money to throw away."

Hern's hesitation before replying made Tom suspect he was holding something back. "Taylor and his wife were friends of your mother from way back, weren't they? When they were all here working in the poverty program?"

Hern seemed startled that Tom knew this. "I wouldn't say they were friends. My mother was a VISTA volunteer the same time they were, in the late sixties. They all came to Mason County together, but my mother had the good sense to leave when her year was up. They didn't stay in touch."

"Your mother's visiting you now, isn't she?"

"She was. She left this morning."

"Before or after Taylor showed up at your house?"

"What does that mean? You think my *mother* had something to do with this?"

"Just wondering if she knows anything that might be helpful," Tom said. "Did Taylor ask her for money too?"

"Yeah, he did, as a matter of fact, earlier in the week. But he didn't see her today. She was on her way back to D.C. by the time he showed up."

Tom pulled a notebook and pen from his breast pocket. "Would you give me her home and business addresses and phone numbers, please?"

"Aw, come on. You can't be serious."

Tom poised the pen above the paper. "And her cell phone number, so I can reach her on the road."

Hands on hips, arms akimbo, Hern shook his head as if trying to cope with a barely tolerable irritation. At last he rattled off the information Tom wanted. His mother, Karen Richardson Hernandez, was an immigration and civil liberties attorney with an office and an apartment in Washington.

"What kind of car is she driving?" Tom asked.

"Why do you need to know that?"

"What kind of car?" Tom repeated.

Hern muttered something, scrubbed a hand over his mouth and chin, and answered, "A Jaguar, an older one, like mine. But hers is dark blue. Don't ask me what the plate number is, because I couldn't tell you. I have trouble remembering my own."

Tom wrote down everything and stuck the notebook back in his pocket. "I have a lot more questions, so you'll have to come by the Sheriff's Department this afternoon."

Hern's eyes narrowed. "You know, Captain, I don't think so. I'm not going to answer any more questions until I have a lawyer with me."

He turned away without waiting for a response and opened his car door.

"That's your right," Tom said, "but you're making a mistake."

Hern shook his head. "No, I'm not."

Tom was watching him drive away when Gretchen Lauter emerged from the woods, followed by Dennis and a second deputy carrying Taylor between them in the body bag.

Tom had finished here and would leave without a single scrap of physical evidence. All he had to go on were Rachel's story of the argument between Hern and Taylor and Hern's lack of an alibi. Until the M.E. in Roanoke cut the slugs out of Taylor's body, Tom wouldn't even know for sure what kind of gun killed him.

He would question Hern again later, but next he had to talk to Taylor's wife and try to figure out whether she was an innocent grieving widow or a prime suspect.

Chapter Three

Rachel drove up the farm road, past fields where American sad-
dlebred horses of every color grazed in the shade of pecan and oak
trees. She hated bringing news of a murder to this peaceful setting,
dreaded interrupting Joanna's pleasant routine to tell her that her
long-time friend lay dead in the woods a few miles away.

She spotted Joanna in a paddock next to the stable, holding
a young chestnut mare's reins while one of the trainers hefted
a saddle onto the horse's back. Joanna's golden retriever, Nan,
sat outside the rail fence, surrounded by a gaggle of geese that
included Penny, the gray goose Holly had brought to the farm as
a pet and allowed to join the flock. Nan jumped up and wagged
her tail when she saw Rachel and Holly.

Rachel braked and powered down the passenger window.

"Hey, girls," Joanna called. Shading her eyes with one hand,
she walked over to the fence. She'd pulled her strawberry blond
hair back in a ponytail, which might have looked silly on any
other woman in her fifties but suited Joanna's youthful face and
figure. "What are you doing home so early? Playing hooky?"

"I need to talk to you," Rachel said. "It's important. Could
you come over to the house with us?"

Joanna frowned, but she didn't ask any questions. "I'll be
along in a minute."

Rachel drove on to the cottage at the end of the farm road, a
few hundred feet beyond the stable, where she and Holly lived.

Holly, who had been silent since they'd left the murder scene, opened the passenger door but spoke before she got out. "I don't want to talk about what happened. Is it okay if I just go on up to my room?"

"Of course. You don't have to ask my permission. But remember, we have to go in later and give statements. We don't have a choice about that."

Holly screwed up her face as if she were about to burst into tears again. "I should've just told Mr. Taylor I'd give him the money. He was real good to Grandma and me when we had that flood a few years ago. He checked on us every single day, and he was ready to help us get out if we needed to. And now look how I treated him. If I'd promised him the money, then maybe he wouldn't have been over there this morning and he'd still be alive."

"Oh, Holly, you can't blame yourself for—"

Holly jumped out and ran to the house.

As Joanna's SUV pulled into the driveway, Rachel mounted the steps to the front porch to get out of the sun. She wished she could get the image of Cam Taylor's dead body out of her head. She wished she could stop wondering how Ben would explain his absence to Tom.

Ben hadn't killed Taylor. He wouldn't do such a crazy thing. Yet Rachel couldn't shake the fear that Tom would focus on Ben as a suspect.

Joanna let Nan out and pointed toward an oak tree. "Stay there," she ordered. The dog ambled over to the tree and dropped onto her belly in the shade. Joanna paused at the bottom of the steps and looked up at Rachel. "You're scaring me, girl. What's wrong?"

"Let's go in." Rachel still wasn't sure how to break the news.

When they entered the house, her African gray parrot, Cicero, greeted them with a squawk. "Help, help!" Cicero cried. He swooped over to Joanna's shoulder. "Save me! Save me!"

"Oh, sweetie," Joanna crooned to the bird. "What have these mean girls been doing to you?"

"Letting him watch too much TV, that's what," Rachel said. She felt relieved by the distraction and immediately ashamed of her relief. "He picked that up from some cop show, and he's been screaming it ever since. Cicero, go back."

The parrot took wing again and returned to the top of his roomy cage, where he could look out a window at goldfinches on a feeder.

"Let's sit," Rachel said. They settled on the couch with her black and white, one-eared cat, Frank, between them. He yawned, stretched, and presented his head for a scratch from the visitor. Rachel thought of asking Joanna if she wanted something cold to drink, then chided herself for stalling. *Come on, get it over with.* "It's about Cam Taylor—"

"Oh, for crying out loud," Joanna said. "Has he been after Holly again? I asked him to leave her alone."

"He's been murdered," Rachel blurted, then winced at the rawness of the words.

"What?" Joanna's hand paused on the cat's head. "Cam? *Murdered?*"

"I'm sorry. I didn't mean to be so abrupt." Rachel launched into an explanation, using the version of events that Tom had approved.

As Rachel talked, Joanna sank back against the sofa cushion, a hand to her mouth. Tears pooled in her eyes and spilled down her cheeks. "Oh, sweet Jesus, how awful," she murmured. "Poor Cam. Does Tom have any idea who did it?"

"I don't see how he could at this stage."

"Meredith is going to fall apart over this. I should go over there." Joanna started to rise.

"No, no." Rachel caught her arm. "She doesn't know yet. Wait until Tom has a chance to tell her."

Joanna nodded and wiped tears from her cheeks with the back of her hand. "I don't know what Meredith will do without Cam. The newspaper's out of money. She can't keep it going by herself, that's for sure. And Cam was her only family here, she'll be alone now. Lindsay has her own life in Roanoke."

Lindsay. The Taylors' daughter. Cam's death would bring her back to Mason County. Rachel quickly stifled the apprehension the thought stirred up. She couldn't expect Tom to go the rest of his life without ever encountering his ex-girlfriend. He might be seeing a lot of her in the course of the murder investigation. Rachel wouldn't let herself get tied in knots over it.

A distant look had come into Joanna's eyes, as if long past events were playing out in her memory. "I'll never forget the day we all came here. Five of us, four girls and Cam. We trained for VISTA together, and we rode into Mason County on a Trailways bus, ready to shake things up and free the people from the shackles of poverty. Volunteers in Service to America—it sounded so grand, and we thought a few weeks of training in Washington had given us all the answers to Appalachia's problems."

"You were awfully young to be saving the world," Rachel said.

Joanna's little laugh sounded sad, self-mocking. "Lord, what children we were. Hopelessly naive. One of the girls bailed within a month, just couldn't hack it. And I quit and got married way before my year was up. But Cam and Meredith managed to hold onto some of their idealism." Tears filled Joanna's eyes again as she added, "Oh, lord, I feel like a great big chunk of my own history just died."

"I'm so sorry," Rachel said.

Joanna drew a deep breath and wiped her eyes. "Who could have done this?"

"I'm really worried that—" Rachel started, then broke off.

"Worried about what, sweetie?"

"I'm afraid Tom's going to zero in on Ben, just because they had an argument this morning."

Rachel expected Joanna to scoff at the idea of Ben as a killer. Instead, she sighed and said, "Well, it's always a bad idea to fight with somebody who's going to get murdered the same day."

Chapter Four

"So what do you think?" Brandon asked on the drive out to see Meredith Taylor. "Did Ben Hern kill him?"

Passing the entrance to his own small sheep farm, Tom realized he wouldn't get his western boundary fence repaired this weekend after all. And he wouldn't spend much time with Rachel or his nephew Simon until he arrested Cam Taylor's killer. "We don't have any evidence against Hern or anybody else at this point," he told Brandon. "Let's not jump to conclusions."

Brandon, still young and green enough to get excited about a murder case, had been jumping from one conclusion to another since they got in the car. "Well, what about the county supervisors?" he persisted. "Taylor ticked off all of them at one time or another, didn't he? He wrote that story in the paper about Cochran using county property to build his new deck. And he accused Charlie Baier of giving county contracts to his brother-in-law, and he wrote about Ralph—"

"I've already got Dennis looking into all that," Tom said. "The trouble is, it's been about a year since the last of those stories ran in the paper, and none of the supervisors suffered any real damage. Nobody was paying attention to Cam's muckraking anymore except his diehard supporters. Besides, I can personally alibi every one of the supervisors. I was at their meeting this morning, trying to talk them into buying the department a new radio system. That's where I was when I got called out about the shooting."

"Oh, yeah, that's right. Well, maybe one of them hired a killer, or got a relative to take Taylor out. People can hold grudges a long time. And what about his wife? She might've done it, or got somebody to do it."

"Let's hear what she has to say, and see how she reacts to the news." Tom knew he couldn't write Meredith Taylor off as a suspect, but he doubted she was involved. "I think she's going to take it hard. She's always been...I guess fragile is the word. High-strung, sensitive."

"My mom really admires her," Brandon said. "You know, because she tutors kids and teaches grownups how to read and won't let anybody pay her. Mom says she won't even take eggs from people that keep chickens." He paused, then added, "You dated their daughter, right?"

"Yeah," Tom said, "in high school. Meredith used to come to the home games with Lindsay when I was captain of the basketball team. I'd see them up in the stands, and every time I scored, Meredith jumped up and down and screamed louder than anybody else in the place."

"But I thought it was kinda recent that you were dating the daughter. Like last year."

"We got back together for a while." One of the most ill-considered moves of his life, and not one Tom wanted to discuss with the junior deputy. "I've always been friendly with Meredith, but Cam was hard to warm up to. The man didn't know how to relax. I don't think he ever did anything just for fun. He was always working on something, one of his community projects or a story for the paper. I think he felt like he couldn't slow down for a second, he had to keep trying to make a difference."

"Mrs. Taylor sure gave up a lot to stay here with him," Brandon said. "I mean, her family's rich, her dad's a Senator—"

"Was. Senator Abbott died of a stroke last year." Tom turned onto the secondary road that would take them to the Taylor house. This was a hilly area with few places level enough to build on. Trees climbed the mountains on both sides of the pavement. "Meredith actually takes a pretty dim view of the way her family lives. They made a fortune in high-end real estate development up in New York. I've heard Meredith say that if she had their money, she'd give it all away."

As long as Tom had known them, the Taylors had occupied a simple five-room clapboard house—chronically in need of paint—on a quarter acre of land, with a goat pen and a vegetable garden taking up the back yard.

"So she doesn't get any money from her family?" Brandon asked. "She didn't inherit anything when her dad died?"

"Not that I know of." Tom was reluctant to pass on personal details that he knew about only because he'd been close to the Taylors' daughter, but Brandon was part of the investigation and would sooner or later have to hear everything that might be relevant. "Her parents cut her off financially when she married Cam and decided to stay here."

"Trying to make her change her mind?"

Tom swerved to avoid a big chunk of rock that had rolled down onto the pavement from the hillside. "I guess so. Obviously it didn't work."

"So where'd they get the money to buy a newspaper?"

"Meredith's aunt gave it to them. Gave it to Meredith, I ought to say. A lot of people don't realize that the paper is in Meredith's name only."

"No kidding? Hunh. Her husband always acted like it was his baby." Brandon snorted. "I'll bet you anything Taylor married the Senator's daughter thinking he was gonna be set for life."

Tom shook his head. "No, you don't understand Cam. He could rant and rave about the inequitable distribution of wealth until your eyes glazed over, and he wasn't interested in getting rich himself." Tom glanced at Brandon and grinned. "You think it's wrong to marry a woman with money? Have you broken that news to Holly?"

Brandon sighed like a man with a heavy burden to bear. "I tell you, that inheritance is gonna cause more trouble than it's worth. Everybody in the world's lining up to get some of it. A new park, a new wing on the hospital, a new library. And Cam

Taylor was after her too. If Holly paid for everything people are asking her to, she wouldn't have a penny left. But I made her promise not to let anybody talk her into anything."

"Good. Don't let her waste—Jesus Christ, look at that." Up ahead, a plume of smoke rose above the hills. "This is all we need, a forest fire on top of a murder. Call it in, will you?"

While Brandon struggled to get a signal on the radio, Tom accelerated, the cruiser's tires squealing on the sharp twists and turns. He lowered his window and sniffed. The tang of smoke in the air was almost pleasant, not yet overpowering. Maybe the fire was confined to one small area and they could catch it in time. "Can't you get through?"

"No signal." Brandon clicked the call button on the handset repeatedly, but they were hemmed in by mountains on both sides and all he raised was static. Abandoning the effort, he dug his cell phone out of his shirt pocket and pressed a button. "No cell signal either."

"We'll use a land line at the Taylor house," Tom said. "We'll be there in two minutes."

The clapboard house of the Taylors' nearest neighbor came into view on the left. Now that they were closer, Tom realized the smoke was rising above the patch of woods between the two properties.

Brandon leaned forward to take a better look. "I don't think it's the woods on fire. It's something up ahead."

Tom already knew, with a sick certainty, what was burning just out of sight. He sped past the trees, and there it was. Smoke billowed from the rear of the Taylors' house.

Tom swung the car to the side of the road and jolted to a stop.

Meredith's old Plymouth Reliant sat in the gravel driveway, but she was nowhere in sight.

"You think she's still in the house?" Brandon said.

"If she is—" Tom didn't finish the thought. He released his seat belt, jumped out and broke into a run. "Keep trying the radio!" he called back to Brandon.

"Captain!" Brandon yelled after him. "You can't go in there!"

Tom halted twenty feet from the house, his gaze raking the front windows, searching for a face. He saw nothing but gray smoke beyond the glass. He darted around to the back. Smoke spewed from open windows and swirled into the sky. The kitchen door was a solid sheet of fire.

In their pen, half a dozen goats bleated in panic and banged their hooves against the chain link fence.

Tom raced around to the front of the house, up the steps and onto the porch. He grabbed the doorknob, praying the door wasn't locked. It was. Tom beat on it with his palms, yelling, "Mrs. Taylor! You in there? Meredith!"

Brandon charged up the steps. "I finally got through on the radio. Firetruck's coming."

"There's no way they'll get here in time to save the house." Tom could hear the old, dry wood crackle and pop as flames ate into it. "The whole damned thing's going to come down. But if she's in there—I have to go in."

"Captain, I don't think—"

"Stand back." When Brandon hesitated, Tom barked, "That was an order, deputy. Get down in the yard."

"Look, boss, you can't—"

Tom slammed his booted foot against the door. With a loud crack, the wood splintered and part of the door collapsed inward. Smoke poured out, enveloping him. Coughing, Tom kicked at the rest of the door until he had a big enough opening, then he stooped and edged through it.

Smoke stung his eyes and throat and nostrils, and sweat poured down his face. He dragged a handkerchief from a pocket and swiped the perspiration out of his eyes, then clamped the cloth over his nose and mouth. No fire in the front room yet, but the smoke was so dense he couldn't make out the furniture. Toward the rear of the house, leaping flames flashed red and yellow through the murk.

Tom dropped to his knees and crawled a few feet into the room, using one hand while holding the handkerchief over his face with the other. His shoulder slammed against something hard and a spear of pain shot down his arm. Tears streamed from his burning eyes. He could barely see the outline of the coffee table he'd collided with.

He uncovered his face long enough to yell, "Meredith! Where are—" A new odor clogged his nostrils and made him gag. The stench of burning flesh.

"Captain, get out of there!" Brandon called from the porch.

It was too late. If Meredith was in one of the back rooms, she wasn't alive anymore. And he couldn't go blindly into a wall of fire. He had no choice but to retreat.

I'm sorry, Tom thought, envisioning the pretty blond woman who'd cheered for him at basketball games and made hot chocolate for him and her daughter afterward. *I'm so damned sorry.*

Tom was standing in the road with Brandon, watching flames devour the house, when a voice from behind startled him. "Well, I guess I won't have to put up with them no more."

Tom and Brandon swung around. An old badger of a man, low-slung and square-bodied, leaned on a cane and observed the burning house. Satisfaction showed in his little smile and the crinkles of amusement around his eyes.

"Lloyd," Tom said in acknowledgment. "You think this is a good thing?"

Lloyd Wilson's smile broadened. "Good for me. Damned glad to see it."

"That's a callous attitude, even for the likes of you."

Anger lit Wilson's cloudy brown eyes. "Don't preach to me, boy."

Tom stepped closer and leaned into the man's face. "Did you just call me *boy?*"

Wilson shuffled backward a couple of feet, scrubbing a hand over his mouth. "I didn't mean nothin' by it. Your color don't matter to me." He added in a mumble, "You know what it's been like between me and the Taylors."

"I know you're always wasting our time, calling deputies out here to deal with crazy little stuff. Crap that reasonable people could handle just by sitting down and talking."

"Ain't no talkin' to Cam Taylor! Thinks he always knows what's right, he's gotta teach the rest of us how to live. Well, good riddance to him. And them damn stinky goats and that yappin' dog too."

Tom studied Wilson for a moment. "What makes you think you're rid of Cam?"

Wilson flung a hand toward the house. "He can't come back here to live, can he? Look at it. Roof's goin' now."

Tom turned to see the tin roof melting, sagging. With a last *whoosh* the rear wall of the house collapsed in a shower of sparks. A second later the front and side walls crumpled, forcing out a gust of hot, smoky air that Tom felt on his face a hundred feet away. What remained of the roof settled over the wreckage like a twisted shroud.

If we'd gotten here ten minutes earlier, five minutes—

He looked at Lloyd Wilson. "You wouldn't happen to know how this fire started, would you?"

Wilson drew back. "What the hell you accusin' me of?"

"Just answer me."

"Don't you go claimin' I set that fire."

"I'm starting to wonder," Tom said. "You've been telling me how glad you are to be rid of the Taylors."

"You little snot!" Wilson slashed the air with his cane, making Tom flinch to avoid a whack in the head. "I ain't gonna stand here and let you accuse me of god knows what all."

With a huff, Wilson pivoted and limped off down the road to his own place on the other side of the woods.

"What do you think, boss?" Brandon asked as they watched him go. "Would he set somebody's house on fire?"

"I wouldn't put it past him," Tom said. "When my dad was in this job, he was always after Lloyd for one thing or another."

"Her husband being murdered, though—you think the old man could've done that too?"

"I don't know what to think at this point," Tom said. "It's always possible the fire has nothing to do with Cam's death. And it's possible Meredith isn't in the house."

But the sick knot in his gut told him he was looking at phase two of a premeditated double murder.

"He said the Taylors have a dog," Brandon said. "You think it was in the house?"

"No idea," Tom said. "If it's still alive, it might be scared and hiding. Why don't you walk around in the woods and see if you can find it?"

Before the fire truck with an onboard water tank arrived, the remains of the roof had smothered most of the flames. The six volunteer firefighters climbed down from the truck and stood with Tom, watching the glowing embers. In the back yard pen the goats bleated and bawled, probably more hungry than scared now. Brandon returned, without the dog.

"Fire's dying out by itself," said the crew's captain, a middle-aged man with a day's growth of stubble. "But we'll douse it so you can get in there and look for a body."

While the firefighters emptied their water tank on the wreckage, Tom found a bag of goat feed in the shed next to their pen and fed the animals. If Lindsay had lost both parents in one day, he thought, how the hell would he find the words to tell her?

By the time the site had cooled, the county fire chief had shown up to take charge. Tom and the chief used a couple of two-by-fours they found in the shed to lift sections of the melted roof. The nauseating odor of seared flesh grew stronger as they peeled away layers of wreckage. In the area that had been the kitchen, where charred appliances and a wood-burning iron stove still stood, they found what they were looking for.

Her hair was gone, all of her skin and much of her flesh had burned away, and the body had contracted into a fetal position as the fire desiccated the muscles. But the overall size of the remains told Tom this was the corpse of a woman.

Crunching debris underfoot, he moved in for a closer look. The front of the skull, the cheekbones, the jaw had been smashed to fragments.

"The fire didn't do this," Tom said. "She was murdered before the fire started."

Chapter Five

Tom sucked in a deep breath and lifted the receiver of his desk phone. He stared at it a moment, imagining Lindsay's reaction to his gut-wrenching news. How the hell could he drop a bomb like this over the phone? He lowered the receiver back into its cradle.

She had to be told, and quickly. In the time it would take him to drive to Roanoke to talk to her in person, some coworker at the western regional headquarters of the Virginia Crime Lab would make sure she heard that two bodies with her last name were coming in from her home county.

Maybe he wasn't the best person to break the news to her, though, considering their history. He wasn't sure how she felt about him now, but he wouldn't be surprised if she were still angry and resentful. After the accident that killed most of his family, Tom had quit his job as a homicide detective with the Richmond Police Department and moved back to Mason County to be near his nephew Simon, expecting his fiancée to marry him and come with him. Instead, she'd broken off their engagement—and created an opening for Lindsay to step back into his life. He'd been lonely and grieving, and Lindsay loved him and wanted him. He thought she had changed, matured, but eventually her jealousy and insecurity resurfaced. He'd put up with it as long as he could. Their breakup had been a nightmare.

He picked up the plastic evidence bag he'd brought back from the fire. It contained a gold band etched with a leaf design. Meredith's wedding ring. Neither Tom nor Dr. Lauter wanted Lindsay to see her mother's body, and they'd agreed that seeing the ring would help her accept the reality of what had happened. Tom had pulled it off Meredith's finger himself, working it over the blackened skin, ripping off a fingernail in his hurry to be done.

The odor of charred flesh still clung to the back of his nose and throat like a bad taste that couldn't be washed away with any amount of water or coffee.

"Ah, Christ," he groaned, rubbing at his smoke-reddened eyes. He couldn't put it off any longer, and he couldn't dump the job on anybody else. This was his responsibility.

He snatched up the phone and punched in Lindsay's private cell number.

In seconds, he had her on the line. "Well, hey there, stranger," she said, her tone familiar and teasing. "What's up?"

Her friendly tone threw him for a second. She was happy he'd called, reading something personal into it, probably thinking he'd come to his senses and was ready to revive their relationship. He could picture her flipping her long blond hair off one shoulder, flashing her mischievous grin.

Get on with it. "Sorry to interrupt your work."

"Oh, don't worry about that. I'd much rather talk to you than examine a bunch of carpet fibers."

"Look, Lindsay—There's no easy way to say this. I've got bad news."

A brief silence at the other end. Then, "My mom or my dad?"

"I'm afraid it's both."

Tom heard Lindsay's sharp exhalation of breath, as if she'd been punched in the stomach. "Okay," she said, her voice a tremulous whisper. "How bad?"

"As bad as it can be." *Coward. Why can't you just say it?*

"But—What—*Both* of them? Are you telling me they're both *dead*?"

"Yes." Knowing how weak the words were, Tom added, "I'm sorry, Lin."

When she spoke again, her voice gained strength, fueled by anger. "What happened? Was Dad speeding, did he—"

"No. It wasn't a car accident." Tom scribbled meaningless shapes on a notepad, circles and triangles and jagged lines. "They both died this morning, but separately. They weren't together when it happened."

"What? Tommy, that doesn't make any sense."

He couldn't do anything to soften this blow. "Your father was shot to death. Away from home, out on Pogue Hill Road. A while later, your mother—The house burned down, and she was inside at the time. But we believe she was killed before the fire started. We haven't made an arrest yet."

Tom waited for that to sink in. He heard Lindsay breathing, fast and shallow, on the other end of the line. Outside his office door, he heard footsteps and male voices growing louder then fading as people passed in the hall.

"All right," Lindsay said, sounding like her normal, resolute self. "I'll pick up a few things at my apartment and drive down there."

"I don't think you should be driving right now. I'll send a deputy to pick you up."

"That'll take twice as long. I can drive, Tommy. Don't worry about me."

He didn't argue. He knew Lindsay could take care of herself. She had flaws, major ones that drove him crazy, but at her core she was tough.

"Be careful, don't rush," Tom said. She would probably pass the funeral home hearse that had just set off for the crime lab with her parents' bodies inside. He hoped she wouldn't make the connection and turn around to follow it to Roanoke.

He hung up as a knock sounded on the door.

Dennis Murray stuck his head in. "We've got a witness. The guys brought her in. She's waiting to talk to you."

◇◇◇

"You've gotta be kidding me," Tom whispered after he glanced into the conference room and saw who the witness was. He stood in the hallway with Dennis. "Did she actually *see* something, or does she just have a *feeling* about what happened?"

"She says she saw Taylor and Hern together on the road," Dennis whispered back. "Arguing. She's the only witness we've turned up."

Tom sighed and squared his shoulders. "All right. I guess she'll have to do. I just hope she doesn't confuse the issue with a lot of psychic mumbo-jumbo."

He put on a neutral expression before he entered the conference room. The tall, angular black woman turned from the window, where she'd been gazing out at the sun-baked parking lot. Silver threads woven into her flowing red caftan shimmered as she moved.

"Captain Bridger," she said, with a nod and a slight smile. Her hair, coiled on her head in braids, was a mixture of gray and black. "We seem destined to meet under unfortunate circumstances. How are you, now that the turmoil of the winter and spring are long past?"

"Fine, thanks." A gruesome murder case had brought him and Lily Barker together earlier in the year. He pulled a chair out from the conference table and gestured for her to take a seat. "How have you been, Mrs. Barker?"

"I've been quite well, thank you." She settled into the chair and sat stiff-backed, her hands folded over her purse in her lap.

"Glad to hear it."

She added, "Until today."

Tom drew a cup of water from the cooler, placed it on the table in front of her, then sat across from her and pulled his notebook out of his shirt pocket. "Tell me what you saw, and where."

Mrs. Barker pursed her full lips and seemed to gather her thoughts. "I was returning home from Mountainview on Pogue Hill Road. On the stretch adjacent to the Miller farm I came upon Cameron Taylor, whom I know personally, and a tall, handsome man with black hair."

"You can't identify the second man? The *handsome* one?" Tom heard the sarcasm in his voice and wanted to kick himself for it. He hated the petty feelings that Hern—and his long friendship with Rachel—stirred up in him.

Mrs. Barker regarded him with a tilted head and narrowed eyes, giving him the creepy feeling that she could read his mind. Amusement tugged at the corners of her mouth. "He was indeed handsome. Exotic looks. I have never met him, but I have seen his photograph, and I believe he was Benicio Hernandez, the artist, who recently moved here from New York City."

"He calls himself Ben Hern," Tom said. "He's a cartoonist. He draws a comic strip and children's books."

"Oh, the cartoons and all the associated merchandise and television programs and so forth may be the source of his fortune, but under his real name Mr. Hernandez is a serious artist, quite highly regarded."

"You keep up with the art world?" Tom asked. He shouldn't be surprised. Since the day he'd met her, he'd been amazed again and again by the wide range of this working class woman's knowledge and interests.

"To the degree that I'm able to, yes. I'm a bit of an artist myself. Strictly amateur, of course."

"To get back to what you saw," Tom said, "what kind of car was the second man driving?"

She sipped from her water cup before she answered. "He was driving a black Jaguar, which he had parked on the side of the road."

Gotcha, Tom thought. He'd like to hear Hern's reason for neglecting to mention this encounter. The Miller farm was only a couple of miles from the woods where Taylor was shot. "Describe what you saw—where the men were, how they were acting."

"They were both standing in the road, blocking my progress. They were engaged in a furious argument—"

"How do you know that?" Tom interrupted.

"Even from a distance, I had no difficulty discerning the nature of their exchange," Mrs. Barker said. "There was a great deal of gesturing, arm-waving, and at one point Mr. Taylor gave Mr. Hern what I believe is commonly called a one-finger salute."

Tom couldn't stop a short laugh from escaping, but he quickly hid his amusement behind a serious expression. He cleared his throat and asked, "Did you hear what they were saying?"

Smiling a little, pleased that she'd made him laugh, Mrs. Barker went on, "Only a bit. They seemed unaware of my presence, and I knew I had to call attention to myself if I were going to be allowed to pass. I rolled down my window to speak to them, and in that moment I clearly heard Mr. Taylor say to Mr. Hernandez, *You self-satisfied bastard, I could ruin you with what I know. You're going to see the whole story on the front page of the paper.* And then—"

"Whoa, whoa." Tom held up a hand. "You're sure that's what Taylor said?"

"Positive, Captain."

Tom scribbled in the notebook, his mind already racing through possibilities. A threat? Blackmail? He looked up. "What did Hern say to that?"

"He replied—and you'll have to excuse my language, I'm simply repeating what I overheard—he replied, *Fuck you. You're not getting a cent out of me. If you ever come near me again, I'll break your fucking neck.*"

"How did Taylor react?"

"Actually, I decided that would be an excellent time to toot my horn and interrupt their discussion. They both appeared startled to see me there. Mr. Hernandez, or Mr. Hern, if indeed he was Ben Hern, rushed to his vehicle and drove away."

"What direction?" Tom asked.

"He continued north, the direction he and Mr. Taylor had been driving in."

North toward the woods where Taylor had died. But the timing was crucial. "Did Taylor drive off then?"

"Not immediately. He wanted to know how much I had heard. I felt it was wisest to let him believe I'd heard nothing."

"How long was it between the time Hern left and the time Taylor did?"

"Oh…" She considered, furrowing her brow. "Four minutes, five minutes? You see, I deliberately delayed him a bit with inconsequential chatter, because I felt it would be good to prevent him from racing off after the other man. I insisted on telling him in detail about the next organic gardening column I wanted to write for the newspaper if he were able to put out another edition. He was quite impatient with me."

She'd given Hern time to park his car out of sight and get ready to stop Taylor when he came along. In trying to prevent a fight, she might have enabled a murder.

"Captain?" Mrs. Barker leaned forward, her strong-boned face etched with a deep concern that bordered on fear. "I know you have no faith in my…sensitivities, but I would like to say—"

Tom pulled back. "I know you believe you have special insight or perception, but I have to deal with the facts. What you saw, what you heard."

"Yes, of course." She straightened her back, her eyes telling him she was, once more, disappointed by his limitations. "I simply want to warn you that an evil cloud surrounds these people. You will be making a dangerous mistake if you take anything at face value."

Chapter Six

"Why didn't you tell me you heard Taylor threaten Hern?" Tom dropped the transcript of Rachel's full statement on the table in front of her. She'd given the statement to Dennis Murray, but Tom had brought the typed copy to her in the conference room. "Didn't you think I'd want to know about that?"

"I was upset at the murder scene," Rachel said. "I honestly didn't remember Cam saying that until later. I don't think it's important, anyway. He'd been ranting about Ben giving money to animal shelters and not doing enough for poor kids. Do you think he meant something else?"

"Never mind," Tom said. "Just don't hold things back from me. Let me decide what's important. This is ready for you to sign."

Rachel hated the feeling that something was going on she didn't know about, something that made Ben look guilty of murder in Tom's eyes. Trying to get information out of Tom was useless and would only irritate him. She gripped a pen and reminded herself that she'd told the simple truth when she described what happened at Ben's house. She thought she'd made Ben's behavior sound reasonable and normal, but she doubted Tom would see it that way. She wasn't sure *she* saw it that way. Why did Ben pursue Taylor? What happened on the road? Where was Ben when Taylor was shot?

Rachel sighed, signed the statement, and pushed back her chair. "Is Holly finished too?"

"Yeah, she's out front waiting for you. But hold on a minute." As Rachel stood, Tom took her by the shoulders so that she had to look at him. "You know I'm going to be fair, don't you? I'm not trying to railroad this guy."

"Of course I know that," Rachel said. She trusted Tom, didn't she? In the last few months he'd become the most important person in her life. Why would she start doubting his integrity now? "It's just…It's obvious you haven't liked Ben from the minute you met."

Tom let go of her and raked his fingers through his hair, something he did when he was annoyed, impatient, or uncomfortable. Rachel had noticed that his hair got quite a workout every time the subject of Ben Hern came up. "We're too different, I guess. Different worlds. You can't expect us to be buddies." Tom paused before adding, "He doesn't seem like the kind of person you'd warm up to either, to tell you the truth."

"You don't know him," Rachel protested. "You don't know what he's really like."

"So tell me. What is Ben Hern really like?"

Tom was interrogating her now, Rachel realized, collecting information about a suspect. She didn't have to lie. The truth would be enough. "He's a lot like me, actually."

Tom laughed and shook his head. "Not that I've noticed."

"It's true. Even my mother thought so, and she was a psychologist. Ben and I grew up in the same neighborhood in McLean, we're the same age, we went to school together. Both of us have always loved animals. We were both introverts when we were kids, we felt more comfortable with animals than with people. And we both grew up without fathers. We could talk to each other when we didn't think anybody else would understand. Ben was the only real friend I had when I was growing up. I haven't seen much of him the last few years, and I've missed him."

Tom nodded, noncommittal. "Like I told you, I'll be fair-minded. But I'm sure you realize this isn't the time for me to strike up a friendship with the guy."

"No, of course not. You have to keep a professional distance during the investigation. I'd better get out of here and let you work. Is a witness permitted to kiss the chief deputy goodbye?"

"I think we can allow that." Tom pulled her tightly against him.

Rachel circled Tom's waist with her arms, and he kissed her, a deep, lingering kiss that neither of them wanted to end.

"I guess I won't be seeing you tonight after all," she said with a sigh.

He groaned, one hand stroking her back. "Afraid not. This damned case—"

"We'll make up for it." Rachel kissed the hollow of his neck, then raised her lips to his again.

She was beginning to wonder if they could lock the conference room door for a few minutes when she glanced past his shoulder and out the window to the parking lot. A couple of deputies leaned against a patrol car twenty feet from the window, watching the Tom and Rachel show with broad grins. "Uh oh," Rachel said. "We're on display."

Tom shot a look out the window and swore under his breath. They parted reluctantly. "You'd better get out of here," he said, "before we really give them something to talk about." He caressed the back of her neck and didn't drop his hand until they were in the hallway.

Rachel found Holly huddled on the bench in the lobby, her arms wrapped around her waist, her eyes red from fresh tears.

"Come on, kid," Rachel said, "let's blow this joint."

That brought a trace of a smile as Holly stood up.

Rachel was reaching for the door when it swung open and a young woman rushed in. Rachel and Holly quickly stepped aside to avoid being mowed down.

The woman ignored them, her attention fixed on Tom. She looked almost like a teenager in jeans and a tee shirt, with long straight hair the color of a canary's feathers. "Tommy!" she cried. She flung herself forward and threw her arms around his neck.

What was going on here? Rachel wondered. Who was this?

Tom peeled the woman's arms off him and took a step away from her. "Lindsay, this is Rachel Goddard and Holly Turner. Rachel, Holly, this is Lindsay Taylor, Cam and Meredith's daughter."

Rachel had never let herself speculate about Tom's former girlfriend, had never tried to find a photo, but she realized now that she'd formed a mental image of Lindsay and the woman standing before her didn't fit it. She wasn't tall and athletic and outdoorsy. She was shorter than Rachel, much shorter than Tom, and had a delicate bone structure that combined with her loose yellow hair to give a first impression of youth. On closer inspection she looked Tom's age, over thirty.

"It's nice to finally meet you, Rachel," Lindsay said. "I've heard so much about you." She sounded cordial and wore a slight smile, but her cool, frank gaze raked over Rachel as if assessing every attribute and flaw. She ignored Holly.

"Excuse me," Holly said in a tiny voice. "I'm goin' on out to the car."

Rachel wanted to believe Lindsay's rudeness hadn't been deliberate. *Make allowances,* she told herself. *She's had a terrible shock.* She held out a hand to Lindsay. "I wish we didn't have to meet under these circumstances. I'm so sorry about your parents."

Lindsay gave Rachel's hand a quick touch that barely qualified as a shake. "Thank you," she said, her voice falling to a near-whisper.

Lindsay's huge blue eyes swam with unshed tears, but Rachel thought she detected a glint of malice, the kind of look some dogs had when waiting for a victim to come within biting range. *Okay,* Rachel told herself, *I can't expect her to like me.*

"I have to be going. It was nice to meet you."

Tom reached around Rachel and held the door open for her. "Before you go, I meant to ask you—I won't be able to take Simon out to Joanna's place tomorrow for our ride, and I hate to make him miss it. Would you mind picking him up?"

"I'd love to," Rachel said. "I'll give Darla a call when I get home." Simon was Tom's seven-year-old nephew, who'd lived with his maternal grandparents since Tom's brother and sister-in-law had died in an auto accident. He was a great kid and Rachel enjoyed spending time with him.

"Thanks a lot." Tom dropped his voice. "I'll call you later, okay?"

Lindsay's gaze had never left her, but Rachel refused to betray the uneasiness the woman's stare churned up inside her. She couldn't wait to get out of there. "Lindsay," she said with careful courtesy, "I hope we'll see each other again."

"Oh, I'm sure we will."

◇◇◇

When the door swung shut after Rachel, Lindsay said, "She's pretty. Hell, she's beautiful. And she's *here*. That's what I get for being geographically undesirable."

"Lindsay—" Tom shook his head. At a time like this, he couldn't very well say, *Where you live has nothing to do with it.* "Never mind. Let's talk in my office."

He led her down the hall. Inside his office, he shut the door while she dropped into a chair. It didn't seem right to put his desk between them, so he took the other visitor's chair next to her.

"Rachel was the one who found your dad's car sitting empty on the road," he said. "That's what led us to him."

"Really?" Lindsay twisted in her chair to lean closer. "Did she see the shooter?"

"No, she didn't see anything except your father's car."

"Oh." Lindsay slumped back in her chair. "So you don't know any more than you did when you called me?"

"Not really. But I've got crime scene people from the state police out there taking a look, and a couple more at the house, along with a fire investigator. If there's anything to find, they'll find it."

Tears welled in Lindsay's eyes. "I forget for a minute," she said, "then it hits me all over again." She pulled a handkerchief from the pocket of her jeans and mopped her eyes.

Her distress made Tom want to comfort her, but if he touched her she might take it as an invitation to another embrace.

She stuffed the handkerchief back in her pocket. "Where are Mom and Dad? I want to see them."

"They're on their way to Roanoke for autopsy. I signed off on the ID myself. I wanted to get moving as fast as possible." Reaching across his desk, he grabbed the evidence bag that held Meredith's ring. "This is your mother's. I can't let you keep it yet, but I wanted you to see it, for…well, for closure, I guess."

Lindsay fingered the ring through the plastic. "I passed a hearse from Maguire's on my way here. That was them, right? I should've realized." She dropped the bag on his desk and gave him an ironic little smile. "So here we are, Tommy, a couple of orphans."

"I'm sorry, Lin. This is a hell of a thing, both of them at the same time." Tom's parents had died at the same time, along with his brother and sister-in-law. But his family hadn't been murdered. They'd died in a stupid accident that Tom still blamed himself for.

Tears puddled in Lindsay's eyes again. "Holy crap, Tommy, who would do something like this?" She sniffled, blinked away her tears, and tried to smile, but didn't quite bring it off. Laying a hand along his cheek, she said, "I can always depend on you."

That wasn't true, and hearing her say it made him uncomfortable enough to stand up and break contact. "Have you thought about where you'll stay while you're here?"

"I called Joanna from the road, and she said I can stay with her." Lindsay glanced up, met Tom's eyes briefly.

Aw, Christ. Lindsay must have known Rachel was living on Joanna's horse farm. Did she have the presence of mind, after receiving the worst news of her life, to plan a way to put herself in Rachel's path? He didn't have to think about the answer: Of course she did.

"Okay," he said. Maybe Lindsay and Rachel wouldn't run into each other. He might enlist Joanna's help to keep them apart. "I need to ask you some questions, but we can do it later if you don't feel up to it now."

Lindsay shook her head, strands of bright hair brushing her cheeks. Her fair skin seemed paler than usual, and with no makeup except a trace of lipstick she looked young and vulnerable. "Ask your questions," she said. "I know you have to get moving on this. Could I have a cup of coffee, though?"

"Sure." Tom ran a cup from the coffee-maker on a corner table. Black, the way she liked it. When he delivered it to her, she brushed his hand with her fingers. Back behind his desk, he opened his notebook to a blank page and held his pen at the ready. He intended to maintain a professional perspective, treat her like any other relative of murder victims, regardless of how often she tried to cross the line. "Have your parents been having trouble with anybody in particular the last few weeks? Or months? Did they tell you about any unusual incidents?"

"I don't—didn't talk to them on the phone all that much." Lindsay gripped her coffee mug and stared into it. "Actually, I never talked to Dad. It was always Mom. And she'd been so down since her father died that I got depressed every time I talked to her, so…. Now I wish I'd tried harder to help her."

"Your grandfather died almost a year ago," Tom said. "She never got over it?"

"It wasn't just that he died—she wasn't exactly devoted to him. I think she'd been trying all her life to impress him and make him proud of her. She wanted to write the great American novel, you know? Get it published, get on the bestseller list, have everybody raving about it. It was never going to happen, but she couldn't let go of the dream." Lindsay shook her head. "Then the old bastard died."

"And suddenly there was no chance she would ever get his approval."

"Right," Lindsay said. "Then her Aunt Julia died last winter, and that threw her for a loop too. Julia was the only one in the Abbott family who gave a damn about Mom."

"She was the one who lived on a commune when she was young, wasn't she?"

"Yeah, right. She was a hippie before anybody knew what hippies were, but she ended up married to a New York investment broker. Well, anyway, Mom was dragging bottom, with her father and Aunt Julia both dying in the same year, and I just couldn't deal with her depression. I never knew what to say or do. The last time I talked to her was about a month ago."

"When you did talk to her, did she say anything about problems with other people? Do you know of anybody who was mad at your father?"

Lindsay shrugged. "Somebody usually was. You know he's never been afraid of controversy. But the paper's practically dead now, and I don't think he had any other project in the works. You might have to go back awhile to find the last person he ticked off."

Tom only had to go back as far as that morning and Taylor's confrontation with Hern. But he left that aside for the moment. "What about personal grievances? Anything recent you can think of?"

"Well, Mom made a joke about Lloyd Wilson's latest gripe— the goats getting out of their pen and going in his yard and scaring his chickens. It just sounded like more of the same. What's happened to Mom's goats, anyway? Are they okay?"

"They're fine. Still in their pen, and they've got plenty of water and food. Joanna said if you want her to, she'll send a couple of her guys out there in the morning to take them over to the horse farm."

Lindsay nodded, started to sip her coffee, then looked at him in sudden alarm. "What about Cricket? Mom's dog. Was she in the house with Mom when it burned down?"

"We're not sure, but it looks that way. We looked for her, but no luck. It's possible she just got scared and ran off, and she'll turn up okay."

"Poor Cricket," Lindsay murmured.

"So," Tom said, "the situation with Wilson was about the same as always?"

"I was worried it might escalate. That old man's got a mean temper, and I was afraid he'd fly into a rage over some tiny little thing and—I don't know. Do *something*." She frowned. "Is he capable of killing them?"

"I don't know. I'll take a close look at him. Can you think of anything else I ought to check out?"

Lindsay chewed her bottom lip, an old habit when she was concentrating. Tom remembered high school classes when he'd sneaked looks at her, watched her perfect teeth nipping that full lip and felt a jolt of desire that kept him stirred up for the rest of the day.

He dropped his gaze to his notebook.

"Mom told me Dad had an argument with Ben Hern about three months ago, right after he moved here," Lindsay said. "You know, the comic strip guy? His mother was in VISTA with Mom and Dad."

Tom nodded.

"Hern got mad because Dad ran a story about him moving to Mason County. I'm sure you saw it. The antipoverty worker's son moves here and buys a mansion, that kind of thing."

"I remember. What did your mother tell you about it?"

"Hern claimed the story was an invasion of his privacy. Mom said he showed up at the newspaper office the day it ran and shouted at Dad for fifteen minutes. But it's a matter of public record that Hern bought that place, and how much he paid. Mom said Dad apologized anyway." Lindsay added with a wry grin, "You can guess how sincere that was."

"Did you know your father was trying to borrow money from Hern and his mother to keep the paper going?"

"You've got to be kidding."

"No. It's true. I'm wondering, if Hern was already mad at him, why would your father expect him to help out?"

"Mom said they were running out of options. Now I see what she meant. He must have really been desperate. But you say he asked Hern's mother for money too?"

"That's what I hear. Did they stay friendly with her over the years?"

"I don't think so. I never heard her name until her son moved here. Mom was upset about Ben Hern living in Mason County because his mother might visit him."

And so she had, just before Cam and Meredith both turned up dead. "What was that all about?"

"I don't know, I just know Mom didn't like her and it went way back to when they were all in VISTA."

"Then it makes even less sense that your dad would ask her or her son for money. Cam was at Hern's house this morning, and they had a pretty heated argument."

"What?" Lindsay sat forward. "Do you think Ben Hern—"

"I don't know anything yet, and I don't have any answers for you. Just hang in there and try not to jump to conclusions," Tom said, but at the same time he was scribbling a note about looking into Karen Hernandez's background.

"Okay, okay, but it's not easy." Lindsay sighed. "Oh, by the way, Mom had a safe deposit box and she made me co-owner of it in case anything ever…happened to her. I'll let you into it without a warrant if you want to take a look at what's there. Probably nothing of any use, but I thought of it when I was about five miles out of Roanoke, and I went back and got my key."

"Good. Yeah, I want to see the contents. I'll let you know when." Tom stood, tucked the notebook and pen into his shirt pocket. "Why don't you go on out to Joanna's?"

"I'd rather stick around here and follow developments. I won't get underfoot, I promise. I'm a professional too, remember."

Tom shook his head. "There's no way you could be professional in these circumstances. Nobody could. I'm lucky the sheriff hasn't taken me off the case because of the personal connection. I can't let you get too close to the investigation. Go out to Joanna's place and get settled in."

Lindsay didn't argue. She set her mug on the desk and stood, brushing her hair back behind her ears. "Tommy—" As he moved past her toward the door, she caught his hand, making him stop and look down at her. "I wouldn't want anyone else in charge of this case. There's nobody in the world I trust more than you."

Her hand felt cool and fragile in his, and the beseeching look in her eyes strummed a chord of sympathy in his heart. They'd known each other half their lives, been lovers off and on since their teens. He knew she was tough, but she'd lost both her parents today, in horrifying circumstances, and that was enough to break anybody. It had nearly broken him when he'd lost most of his own family. Yet all he could say was, "We'll find out who did this."

Lindsay drew a deep breath and put on her best game face. "I'll let you get on with it. Call me later, okay?"

At the door, she paused. Looking back, she gave him a startling impish grin. "I'm going to enjoy getting to know Rachel. We have *so* much in common."

Chapter Seven

Rachel stretched plastic wrap over the plate of chicken, rice, and green beans Holly had left untouched. She was sliding the plate into the fridge when a knock sounded on the front door.

"Oh, go away," she muttered. Company was the last thing she wanted.

Another knock, this one louder.

Sighing, Rachel headed for the door.

Ben stood on her front porch, hands jammed into his pockets, his whole body thrumming with tension. "I have to talk to you," he said.

Tom had specifically asked her not to discuss the day's events with Ben. What was she supposed to do? Tell her friend to go away and leave her alone? "I've talked about the Taylors more than enough for one day," she said. "I don't want to rehash it all now."

"Please, Rachel. You're the only friend I've got in this place."

She hesitated, weighing Tom's disapproval against Ben's obvious distress. Tom would never know she'd talked to him. She swung the screen door open and let Ben in.

Cicero squawked, "Help! Help! Save me, save me!" from the top of his cage, but he didn't fly to Ben the way he always flew to Tom.

Ben was so wrapped up in his own thoughts that he didn't seem to notice the bird's cries. Instead of taking a seat, he began pacing aimlessly. "Did you know Taylor's wife died today too, and they think she was murdered?"

"Yes, I heard. It's awful."

"I'm going crazy worrying about—" Ben halted and asked in a lowered voice, "Where is Holly? Are we alone?"

"She's upstairs. Sit down, will you? You're making me nervous." What did he have to say that he didn't want Holly to overhear? Rachel took a chair and motioned Ben toward the sofa, where Frank already occupied one cushion.

Ben dropped onto the couch and rubbed the cat's head with his knuckles, but he didn't relax. He seemed to be straining for a light tone when he said, "You're a lucky guy, Frank, getting rescued by this lady." He shot a glance at Rachel. "Remember when we stole Mary right off those people's front steps?"

Displacement activity, Rachel thought. Grabbing at any available diversion to ease his stress. She would play along if it helped him settle down emotionally. "I prefer to think we *saved* her. You did, anyway. I was too terrified of what my mother would do to me if I got caught stealing somebody's kitten."

"I still carry Mary's picture." Ben shifted to pull his wallet from his back pocket. He slid out a photo and passed it to Rachel.

Humoring him, she looked at the beautiful white cat in the picture, then had to smile at the memory. The first time Rachel and Ben had seen her, they were both fourteen years old—and outraged that someone had left the little kitten in a basket on the front steps all day in chilly November. They'd returned after dark to make sure the cat had been taken in out of the cold. But there she was, huddled in the basket while her owners moved about in the warm house. A food dish next to the basket provided proof enough that she was left out all the time. Ben hadn't hesitated for a second. He marched onto the property, swiped the cat, stuck her inside his coat, and took her home with him.

"You gave her a long, happy life." Rachel handed back the picture. She waited until he'd put it away before she said, "Ben, you didn't come over here to talk about our youthful adventure as cat thieves."

He leaned forward, gripping his head with both hands. "I'm sorry I dragged you into this. You and Holly both. That scene this morning, then finding Taylor's car—"

"I'm fine," Rachel said. "And Holly's going to be fine too."

"Well, thank god for that, anyway." His face knotted with anxiety, he met her eyes and blurted, "There was a witness. They've probably found her by now. Christ, I'm screwed. I've got a lawyer coming down from New York, but she can't get here until tomorrow. I'll be lucky if I'm not arrested before then."

Rachel felt as if she'd stepped off solid ground into quicksand. She pushed out her words. "A witness to what?"

Ben's eyes widened when he saw her face. "Aw, shit. What the hell are you thinking? I thought you were the one person I could count on."

"A witness to what, Ben?"

He rose, pivoted away and began pacing again, his fists shoved into his jeans pockets. "Taylor stopped on the road and got out and wouldn't let me pass. We got into an argument, and a woman drove up while we were shouting at each other. She probably heard some of it. I can imagine what your friend Captain Bridger will make of that." He stopped and looked at Rachel. "Can you find out if he's talked to her? Can you get me her name?"

A nasty shiver moved down Rachel's spine. "Her name? Why? Ben, what are you planning to do?"

"Aw, for fuck's sake. I'm not going to *do* anything. I just want to know what I'm up against."

"I can't get information out of the police to pass on to you." Rachel realized she was digging her nails into her palms, and she opened her hands and spread them on her knees. "I shouldn't even be talking to you about this, since I'm a witness too."

"Yeah, I figured you were the one who told Bridger what happened at the house this morning."

"I didn't have a choice. I just told the truth."

"Do you believe I killed Cam Taylor? And his wife too? If you think I'm that crazy, I want to know."

In his eyes Rachel saw anger mixed with fear, confusion, and a desperate need for reassurance. "No," she said, and meant it. "But I'm worried about the way you've been acting. Have you stopped taking your meds?"

He let out a breath, his shoulders slumping. Dropping onto the couch again, he said, "No. I haven't stopped taking the damned drug."

Rachel wasn't sure she believed him. "I know you don't feel as creative when you're on it, but that incident in New York should have convinced you that you can't go without it."

"I said I haven't stopped taking it, and that's the truth." Rachel expected him to blow up at her, but instead he gave her a speculative look and asked, "Are you going to tell your boyfriend what happened in New York if he asks you if I have any history of violent behavior?"

"I don't think that one incident adds up to a history of violent behavior."

"Bridger might think it does. It's just the kind of thing the cops would pounce on if they want to make a case against somebody."

"Yeah," Rachel said with some reluctance. "You're probably right about that, but isn't it better to be upfront about it? So it won't look as if you have some terrible secret to hide?"

"There's something you don't know." Ben rubbed his temples. "Cam Taylor found out what happened in New York, and he knew I made a settlement to avoid criminal charges. He knew that in my position—drawing the strip, doing books for kids, working with animal groups—I could be hurt pretty badly if I looked like a hotheaded bully who attacks people then pays them off. Taylor wanted me to pay *him* off to keep quiet about it. The irony is that after we had that argument on the road, I started thinking it would be easier to give him the money and shut him up. I knew he'd probably keep coming back for more, but I'd almost convinced myself to do it. Then I found out he was dead."

Chapter Eight

Lloyd Wilson's two old mixed-breed hounds pushed up from their resting spots on the porch and circled Tom, sniffing his shoes and pants legs, while their owner peered out through the screen door. Inside the house, a TV blared at top volume.

"What do you want?" Wilson demanded.

Tom raised his voice to overcome Wilson's hearing problem and the TV's racket. "Let me in, Lloyd. We have to talk."

"I got nothin' else to say to you."

"You want me to haul you into headquarters? That's fine with me. Let's go." Tom was already in a foul mood after driving out to Ben Hern's place and getting no answer at the door. He wasn't going to take any crap from Lloyd Wilson.

"Damnation," Wilson muttered. With his lips pressed into a resentful line, he shoved the screen door open.

Tom followed the old man into a hot, stuffy living room where a ceiling fixture cast a murky light. A coffee table held a half-empty glass of tea and a plate smeared with barbecue sauce. Although the house had a tall antenna on the roof, the surrounding mountains nearly defeated it, and the TV facing the couch showed a snowy picture that rolled every few seconds. Alone since his wife's death a few years before, Wilson probably ate his meals with the TV for company. Tom had done the same plenty of times, but at least he had cable.

He snatched the TV remote from the couch and aimed it at the set.

"Hey! I'm watchin' that show," Wilson said.

Interesting choice of programming, Tom thought, eyeing an *Entertainment Tonight* report. "You a big Paris Hilton fan? Or is it her little dog you like?"

Wilson's only reply was a grunt.

"I need all of your attention, Lloyd." Tom pressed the button to turn off the TV set. In the sudden quiet, his ears still rang from its noise. "The sooner we get this over with, the sooner you can get back to your shows. I'll bet you don't want to miss the *Law & Order* rerun tonight."

"That's exactly right. I like watchin' a bunch of cops that know what they're doin'. Makes a nice change." Wilson pointed at the room's only chair. "Sit."

Tom lowered his lanky body into the chair and kept on going as the cushion sank several inches. He pulled himself forward. "Mind if I get a chair from the kitchen?"

Wilson snorted and dropped onto the couch, which appeared to have sturdier springs than the chair. "Suit yourself. Wouldn't want you to be uncomfortable, now would I?"

Tom fetched one of the two chrome-framed dinette chairs from the kitchen, choosing the one that had the fewest cracks in its yellow plastic seat. When he returned to the living room, he placed the chair facing Wilson.

"Now why're you botherin' me?" Wilson said.

"Two reasons." Tom sat down and pulled his notebook and pen from his shirt pocket. "First, you're the Taylors' only close neighbor, and you could have seen something. Second, you've got a long history of trouble with the Taylors. You've made threats against them."

Wilson leapt to his feet. "I never threatened nobody! You tryin' to frame me?"

"I told you I'll be glad to take you to headquarters if you won't talk to me here."

Tom waited, eyes locked on Wilson's. With the TV off, Tom could hear the crickets outside, tuning up for the approaching night, and the rise and fall of the cicadas' early evening chorus. The house felt airless, although the windows stood open.

Wilson broke eye contact first and sat down, waving a hand. "Ask your damn fool questions."

Tom wiped sweat from his upper lip with the heel of his palm. "When was the last time you saw Meredith and Cam Taylor?"

"See 'em every day, drivin' past."

"Did you see both of them this morning?"

"Saw him leavin' early. Not her, though, not today."

"Were you at home all morning?"

"I was, and if you're gonna ask can I prove it, all I can tell you is go ask my hens. Most of the mornin' I was workin' on a new coop I'm buildin' out back."

If that was true, Tom thought, and if Wilson himself hadn't killed the Taylors, he probably wasn't much good as a witness either. He wouldn't have seen anything from his back yard. Tom asked anyway, "Did you see any visitors next door?"

The old man's expression turned cagey, and he cast his eyes heavenward and frowned in mock concentration. "Now, let me see…I'm gettin' on in years, you know. Memory's not what it used to be." He added with a snort, "Like a lotta other things."

"If you saw something over there and refuse to tell me, you're withholding evidence in a murder investigation."

Wilson's gaze swung back to Tom. "Murder? Cam Taylor wasn't nowhere close to here when he got shot. You sayin' the fire's got something to do with him bein' killed?"

Genuine surprise, or a damn good job of acting? Tom cautioned himself not to underestimate Wilson. "Are you telling me you didn't watch everything that went on over there after the fire? You didn't see the hearse?"

All the bravado and contempt drained out of Wilson's face. "I saw a bunch of people comin' and goin' but…I never…You mean the wife?"

"We found her body after the fire was put out."

Wilson flopped against the back of the couch. "Good lord. If I'd have knowed she was in there, I would've—well, I don't know what I could've done. Called for help, at least."

Tom rapped his pen against his pad. "Her car was parked outside the house. Why would you think she wasn't at home?"

Wilson shook his head like a dog trying to throw off a fly. "If she was in the house, she would've run out when the fire started, wouldn't she?"

"If she'd been able to," Tom said. "I think she was already dead by then."

"Sweet Jesus," Wilson murmured. "I had my disagreements with her, but I never…To tell you the truth, I didn't believe she was at home. I thought she went off with that fella, like she does sometimes."

"What fellow? So you did see somebody over there this morning?"

Wilson straightened and shot a resentful look at Tom. "Yeah, I guess I did. Two of 'em, matter of fact. Different cars."

He fell silent again and seemed lost in thought. Tom prodded, "Who, Lloyd? Who was over there? This is important."

"One of 'em was drivin' a fancy car, but I couldn't even tell if it was a man or a woman. It had them windows that look real dark from the outside."

"When? What time?"

"Maybe ten o'clock. But could've been earlier, could've been later."

"How long was the car over there?"

"I don't know, I didn't time it." With a trace of indignation, Wilson added, "I didn't stand around starin' through the trees. I got better things to do than spy on the neighbors."

Not usually, Tom thought. Why the hell did Wilson pick this day to dial back on his snooping? "You said she had two visitors. Do you know who the other one was?"

Wilson snorted. "Ought to. Seen him over there enough times."

A pause without further elaboration.

"Lloyd—"

"Scotty Ragsdale, that's who it was," Wilson said. "You know him, his folks own the hardware store in town. I seen him drive up over there, but I couldn't tell you when he left."

Tom's expectation deflated into disappointment. "Meredith and Scotty have been friends a long time."

"Friends? I guess that's one word for it. Real *close* friends, if you get my drift."

"You have some reason to think it was more than that?"

"I seen 'em kissin' on the mouth one day, right out there in the yard, him with his hands all over her. And he's always over there when Cam Taylor's gone, I guess when he's workin' at the paper. Sometimes they stay at the house, and sometimes Scotty just picks her up and they go off together. He drops her back at the house two or three hours later. You can make whatever you want to out of that."

Oh, man. Would this turn out to be a simple case of jealousy? A triangle involving three volatile personalities was guaranteed to produce trouble sooner or later. "How often have you seen Scotty over there?"

"Two, three times a week."

"Was he there today before the other visitor came, or after?"

"After. I think."

"Did Scotty or the other visitor come back a second time? Was either of them over there right before the fire?"

"Maybe. Maybe not. Like I said, I was busy, I wasn't payin' all that much attention."

"You said the first person drove a fancy car. Did you notice the make?"

"Some kind of a sports car. What're they called, them cars with the cat on the hood?"

"A Jaguar?"

"That's right," Wilson said, nodding, "a Jaguar sports car. Dark-colored. I think it was black, but could've been navy blue. I never was too good with colors."

Ben Hern had said his mother drove a dark blue Jaguar. Had Karen Hernandez visited Meredith before leaving the county? Why would she? Lindsay had said they weren't friends, that her mother disliked Karen Hernandez. Tom hoped he could get her back to Mason County for questioning after the sheriff's department tracked her down. If he had to, he'd drive to Washington to see her.

Right now, though, he was a lot more interested in talking to Scotty Ragsdale.

Chapter Nine

Rachel set a dish of food on the tack room floor for the stable cat, an orange tabby named Ginger, and gave her four kittens a large communal plate. Unable to quiet her worries about Ben and erase the image of Cameron Taylor lying dead in the woods, Rachel had sought solace where she knew she could always find it, with animals who needed her attention. She'd brought vaccine with her. After the cats had eaten, she would scoop them up one by one and give them their shots.

Leaning against the saddle bench in the shadows, watching the kittens' bellies swell as they packed away the food, Rachel wondered if she should keep one or two of the kittens for herself. Frank might enjoy their company.

"Hi there."

Startled, Rachel spun around. Lindsay Taylor stood in the doorway, her blond hair backlit by the early evening sun through the stable's main door. "Hi," Lindsay said again. "You look surprised to see me. Didn't Tommy tell you I'm staying with Joanna?"

Rachel had heard nothing about this. But maybe it hadn't been settled until after she'd seen Tom that afternoon. All she could think of to say was, "I'm glad you have a family friend to stay with."

Lindsay leaned against the door frame and watched the kittens. "They're cute."

"Yes, they are." Rachel turned away, shook out a clean towel she'd brought, and spread it over the scarred wooden table against one wall. From a small zippered case she removed alcohol and cotton balls and the syringes into which she'd already drawn the proper amounts of vaccine.

Silence stretched out. Rachel resisted an urge to look at Lindsay, to examine her more closely. She didn't have to do that to understand why Tom had been attracted to her. Any man would be.

"Do you ride?" Lindsay asked.

"Yes, I do. This is a great place for it." Having fussed with the arrangement of the vaccine syringes as long as she reasonably could, Rachel turned and pinned her gaze on the cats again. Sunlight slanting through the room's single window fell over the little family and made their striped coats gleam like gold. Rachel's skin prickled with awareness of Lindsay's eyes on her.

"Tommy and I used to come out here to ride all the time," Lindsay said. "We helped Joanna saddle-train the young horses. We'd spend practically the whole weekend out here, riding around the hills together, just the two of us."

"Mmm." Was that how it was going to be? Constant reminders that Lindsay shared a past with Tom, had more in common with him than Rachel ever would? She could only hope Lindsay would be gone soon, back to her job in Roanoke, before she could do any damage here. Although Rachel wanted to trust her relationship with Tom, it still felt new and fragile.

"So you found my father's car on the road and called the cops," Lindsay said.

"Yes, that's right." Under normal circumstances, Rachel would offer her condolences again. These weren't normal circumstances. Common courtesy was the most she could offer.

"Are you sure you didn't see or hear anything that could identify the killer?"

"I've given the police a statement about everything that happened."

"Yeah, and I'm wondering if there's something I'm not being told. I have a right to know everything."

"I'm sorry, but you'll have to talk to Tom about the investigation."

Arms crossed, Lindsay watched Rachel with an unnerving intensity. The kittens had emptied their plate and begun their post-meal grooming, dampening their paws with tiny tongues and swiping them over whiskers and mouths. Their mother ate more slowly, savoring her food.

"I've heard about what happened at Ben Hern's house before that," Lindsay said. "How Hern assaulted my father, then went after him when he left."

Rachel was stunned. Tom had promised to be fair. Could he have given Lindsay such a biased account minutes after making that promise? Or had it come from Joanna?

No. Neither of them would have described Ben's behavior that way to Cam Taylor's daughter. Lindsay was distraught over her parents' deaths. She was misinterpreting what she'd heard.

Rachel's impulse was to defend Ben, but she didn't want to start a pointless argument. Letting Lindsay's statements go unanswered, she lifted one of the kittens to the table.

"Six degrees of separation," Lindsay said.

"I beg your pardon?" Rachel focused on the kitten, delivering the tiny amount of vaccine through a fine needle before the animal realized a protest was called for. "Good boy," she murmured.

"You know what they say, that any two people in the world can be connected in six steps. But in our case, it's even less. My grandparents lived in McLean when my grandfather was in the Senate, so my mom spent most of her time there when she was growing up. She came to Mason County as a VISTA with Karen Hernandez. Karen left Mason County, and a few years later she was living in McLean. She had a son, who became your friend. Now you and Ben Hern live in Mason County. And I grew up here. I used to be Tom's girlfriend. Now he's seeing you."

"Small world." Rachel set down the kitten and picked up another.

"You're a long way from home," Lindsay said.

"I like it here." Rachel administered a second injection, set down the kitten and reached for another.

"I can understand why you wanted to move to a place where nobody knew you. I mean, the way your mother died, then that drug addict shooting you."

Rachel looked up sharply, meeting Lindsay's gaze before she could control the impulse. Lindsay's large blue eyes mocked her with an expression of feigned innocence that stirred Rachel's deepest anxieties. Placing the third kitten on the table, she said, "You seem to know a lot about me."

"It's all a matter of public record. It's amazing how much you can find out about people these days."

Good god, what was Lindsay up to? Rachel tried for an off-hand, distracted tone when she asked, "And why would you be searching public records for information about me?"

"I care about Tom. I wanted to know who he's involved with."

What else had Lindsay learned? How deeply into Rachel's past had she probed? Noticing the tremor of her hand when she administered the vaccine, Rachel told herself, *Don't let her get to you. Don't.* She made another kitten swap.

"It's a big change, isn't it?" Lindsay said. "Don't you miss everything?"

"Such as what?" Rachel's mouth had gone dry.

"Restaurants, shopping, museums. This must seem like a real backwater to you. And you don't have any family here either."

"There are compensations."

"Oh? Like what?"

Straightening, with a kitten snuggled against her chest, Rachel met Lindsay's eyes. "Like Tom," she said. "He's more than enough for me."

Rachel saw something shift in Lindsay's face, the pretended innocence fading, replaced by the same hostility Rachel had glimpsed when they'd first met.

Lindsay pushed away from the door frame and said, "I'll be seeing you around, Rachel."

As she watched Lindsay's brisk exit from the stable, dread settled over Rachel like a smothering shroud. Why had she said that? Why had she goaded Lindsay, as if she were claiming Tom as her property?

Lindsay worked in the state crime lab. She probably had access to a staggering amount of information, any database, any old records she wanted to examine. Had Rachel just given her reason to keep digging until she assembled all the bits and pieces that would add up to the truth?

My god, what have I done?

Chapter Ten

Gravel pinged the car's fenders as Tom pulled off the road in front of Scotty Ragsdale's house. "Take it easy," he told Brandon, "and let me do all the talking. Your job is to keep an eye on him and be ready for anything."

The night was dark in the way only a mountain night can be, the moon no more than a dim glow behind looming hills. When Tom killed the cruiser's beams, the single remaining pinprick of light came from a window of Ragsdale's house, a hundred feet back from the road.

"He really take a shot at you one time?" Brandon asked.

"Oh yeah. Almost took the top of my head off. He missed me by a couple of inches. That happened not long after I moved back from Richmond and took this job."

Ragsdale had been cranked up on meth, using his rifle like a broom to whack merchandise off the shelves in his elderly parents' hardware store in Mountainview, making threats one second and begging for help the next. Tom and two other deputies responded to his mother's 911 call. The second Scotty saw the uniforms come through the door, he opened fire. He got away with the assault by agreeing to yet another round of inpatient treatment.

"As far as I know," Tom said, "he's been clean ever since, making a living doing carpentry and refinishing furniture. Really turned his life around. If he's involved in these murders, it's going to be more than his parents can take."

Tom and Brandon approached the house, Maglites trained on the ground in front of them, free hands resting on their holstered Sig Sauers.

A man's shape appeared in the window, then moved away. A moment later the front door opened and Ragsdale's rangy silhouette filled the doorway, his face in shadow.

"Scotty, it's Tom Bridger. I need to talk to you."

"I've got nothing to talk to you about." Ragsdale's voice cracked on the last words. He sagged against the door frame and raised both hands to his face.

"Scotty? What's wrong? Can we help you?"

Ragsdale didn't answer.

"Stay on guard," Tom told Brandon in an undertone. "I don't like the way he's acting." Raising his voice, he said, "Scotty, can we come in? If something's wrong, maybe we can help you."

"Nobody can help me," Ragsdale choked out. He wrapped his arms around his waist and bent over as if in pain. "It's too late."

With Brandon behind him, Tom climbed the steps to the porch.

Ragsdale looked worse than he had in years, his shaggy brown hair sticking out in a dozen directions, his tee shirt soiled down the front and wet under the arms, every wrinkle on his middle-aged face etched deeper by emotional turmoil. His pupils appeared normal. If he'd been high, they'd be the size of dinner plates.

"Come on, Scotty," Tom said. "Let's sit down and talk."

Ragsdale stumbled back into his house and over to the couch. He collapsed onto it and stared into space, a tremor running through his body.

Tom and Brandon both swept their eyes over the living room, looking for accessible weapons. Tom didn't see a gun or knife out in the open, but anything could be hidden under the fast food wrappers on the coffee table. Tom lifted the wrappers, found nothing underneath. Satisfied, he cleared a spot and sat on the table facing Ragsdale. Brandon stood to one side of the couch.

"What's wrong, Scotty? What's bothering you?"

Ragsdale took a deep breath, sat a little straighter. "You know what happened," he said, his voice thick.

"Tell me."

"Meredith—" He broke off, gulped back the rest of his words.

"What about her?"

"Stop playing games with me. I know why you're here."

"Meredith Taylor died today," Tom said. "Is that why you're upset?"

"*Upset?*" Ragsdale shot to his feet and lurched away from the couch. "I feel like I've been hit by a goddamn train."

Wandering the room, Ragsdale stopped to stare at the pile of clothes on an easy chair, moved on to a tall bookcase crammed with hardcovers and paperbacks. He seemed to forget Tom and Brandon were there.

Tom rose and walked over to Ragsdale. "Scotty, come on back and sit down."

When Tom touched his shoulder, Ragsdale flung out an arm and whacked Tom across the chest. "Get off!"

"Hey now!" Brandon barked, bolting toward them.

"It's okay," Tom said. Brandon halted. "Scotty, I want you to sit down."

To Tom's surprise, Ragsdale obeyed and returned to the couch. "Let's get this over with."

Taking his place on the coffee table again, Tom asked, "How did you hear about Meredith?"

Ragsdale's voice came out low and hoarse. "I was in the store—Some people came in, they were talking about it." Not quite meeting Tom's eyes, he added, "I heard there were a couple of witnesses when Cam got shot. That woman vet and the Melungeon girl who works for her. Is that true? How much did they see?"

Tom didn't like the sound of this. Despite his efforts to keep anyone from learning Rachel was on the scene before the shooting, people were already magnifying her role—and Holly's. "I don't know who's spreading that story," he told Ragsdale, "but it's not true."

"You wouldn't tell me if it was. Did somebody say something about me? Is that why you're here?"

Keeping his voice level, Tom asked, "Why would they say something about you? Were you there when Cam was shot?"

"Hell, no. You're not pinning that on me."

"Did you see Meredith today? Did you go over to the Taylor house this morning?"

Ragsdale threw him a defensive look. "No. Somebody says I did, they're lying."

"Why would anybody lie about that?"

"Some people can't stay out of other people's business."

"Are you sure—"

"I'm sure."

Tom watched Ragsdale pull a handkerchief from his pocket, drag it over his face, blow his nose.

"You and Meredith were good friends, weren't you?" Tom asked.

Tears filled Ragsdale's eyes, but he blinked them away. "She's the only person in this whole fucking county that ever treated me with any respect. I probably wouldn't be alive today if it wasn't for her, and I sure as hell wouldn't be clean. She came to see me every week when I was in rehab. That's more than I can say for my own damned family. They dumped me in that hole and forgot about me."

"How long were the two of you friends?"

"Right from the start. When she first came here as a VISTA volunteer."

"But she was a few years older than you, wasn't she?"

Ragsdale stared at his clasped hands dangling between his knees. "She was my sister's friend. I was just a kid, sixteen years old, but she talked to me about writing like she took me seriously. And when Denise died, she was the only person who cared how I felt about losing her. My parents acted like it only happened to *them*. As if I didn't love my sister too."

Denise Ragsdale had died young, before Tom was born, and he knew almost nothing about her. "Yeah, I can see how that would've been rough on you," he said. "So you had ambitions to be a writer? I didn't know that about you."

"Well, you can see what my ambitions amounted to." Ragsdale spread his arms as if displaying himself, the picture of failure. "Meredith was a writer too, and she understood, she didn't laugh at me. She never has. She hasn't been much luckier than I have, but she still believes—still *believed*—in me. She still thought I was gonna make it."

"So you two got together to talk about writing? Read each other's stories?"

Ragsdale seemed lost in thought, or memories, and didn't answer.

"Scotty," Tom said, "were you sleeping with her?"

Ragsdale looked from Tom to Brandon. "You guys—go fuck yourselves. I'm not answering any more questions."

"What happened, Scotty? Did Meredith try to break it off with you? Did she tell you to get lost? Or did Cam find out and raise hell about it?"

"You're not getting shit from me. I don't have to tell you a damned thing."

"Scotty—"

"Get the fuck out of my house and off my property." When Tom didn't respond, Ragsdale yelled in his face, "Get out!"

"All right, calm down, we're leaving. But we'll be back. Count on it."

Chapter Eleven

"Billy Bob! Come here, boy!" Lindsay crouched in the stable yard and clapped her hands. While Rachel held the rear door of her SUV open, Tom's tan and white bulldog plopped out and trotted over to Lindsay, his jowls swinging.

You little traitor, Rachel thought, but instantly felt ashamed of her juvenile reaction. The dog was just greeting somebody he knew. She leaned into the back seat and helped Simon unlock his seat belt. "Watch the drop," she cautioned as the boy started scrambling out. "Want help?"

"Naw, I can do it." Simon jumped down, landing on both feet, and beamed up at Rachel. "See?"

"You're getting bigger every day." He looked so much like Tom, with his thick black hair and olive skin, and Rachel could see that his features would develop the same chiseled strength that made Tom's face striking.

"Hey, Simon, how're you doing?" Lindsay said. She gave the dog a last pat and stood up.

The boy turned shy and uncertain, leaning against Rachel's hip. She placed an arm around his shoulders. "Hi," he said to Lindsay.

"You remember me, don't you?" Lindsay asked, stepping closer, smiling. "Your Uncle Tommy's girlfriend."

Frowning in confusion, Simon glanced up at Rachel.

Oh, for god's sake. Using a little boy to score points was too much. "Not anymore," Rachel murmured, hoping only Simon could hear.

"I remember," Simon said, but he didn't smile and his voice came out small and timid.

Normally Simon bubbled over with friendliness, so Rachel found his reaction odd and intriguing. "Come on," she said, taking him by the hand. "Let's get Mrs. McKendrick and go riding. Come on, Billy Bob."

Lindsay trailed them to the paddock beside the stable. Was she planning to ride with them? Surely, Rachel thought, she had more pressing things to do in the aftermath of her parents' deaths.

Joanna, saddling a chestnut mare while Holly attached the horse's bridle, frowned when she saw Lindsay. "I thought you were going back to the house. Don't you want to be there in case Tom calls with news?"

"He has my cell phone number. I want to go riding too. I need to get out and do something, get my mind off…everything." Lindsay's expression dissolved into sorrow. Tears shone in her eyes.

Joanna shot a *What can I do?* look at Rachel. And that was that. Lindsay saddled a horse for herself. Unless Rachel wanted to sulk and refuse to go riding, an option she couldn't even consider, she had to accept Lindsay's presence.

Lindsay fussed over Simon, insisted on lifting him into the saddle when he wanted to use a stepladder, adjusted his feet in the shortened stirrups. Silently looking on, Rachel saw again the odd expression on the boy's face—distrust? dislike?—and wondered what had caused it.

Holly, who was supposed to ride with them, watched Lindsay smothering Simon with unwelcome attention and announced, "I don't think I feel like ridin' after all."

With Joanna in the lead and Simon behind her, looking tiny on a black mare, they rode the horses up a gentle slope in the shade of oaks and maples. Billy Bob and Nan nosed around in the leaf litter, chased squirrels, and hustled back to the trail when Joanna whistled.

Rachel was aware every second of Lindsay riding behind her, and she could almost feel the woman's eyes boring into her back, but she tried to enjoy the excursion anyway. The day had started with the temperature in the low seventies, and the birds seemed energized by the respite from the heat and humidity. Around her, Rachel heard the throaty songs of cardinals, the *cluck-cluck* of two pileated woodpeckers, the chipping and caroling of a dozen other species.

They'd been on the trail for fifteen minutes when Lindsay trotted her horse alongside Rachel's. With no preamble, she said, "I've heard that Ben Hern's the Howard Hughes of the comic strip world. Is it true he never goes out in public? Is that why you have to go to his house to see his pets?"

Rachel didn't want to gossip about Ben with this woman, but she was wary of saying or doing anything to trigger the vindictiveness she'd detected just under Lindsay's polite surface.

"Ben's reclusiveness is exaggerated," Rachel said. "I go to the house to see his dog because the animal has arthritis, and hauling him into the clinic would be very painful for him."

Lindsay didn't respond to that. Rachel was about to speed up her horse to put some distance between them when Lindsay spoke again, in a mild, conversational tone. "It's really hard for most people to imagine their friends committing a crime like murder. Nobody wants to think their judgment about people is so bad they couldn't see what their friend was capable of. I understand that, I really do. Denial is a natural reaction."

Rachel opened her mouth to answer, then clamped it shut again. *Don't say it. Don't let her get to you.* She slapped her legs lightly against the mare's sides to make the horse speed up.

As Rachel moved ahead, she heard the buzz of a cell phone and her hand automatically went to her shirt pocket. But it was Lindsay's phone. She was a few feet behind now, but Rachel heard her answer.

"Oh, hi, Tommy," Lindsay said, her voice sweet and warm.

Police business, Rachel told herself. She would not slow down, she would not eavesdrop.

Lindsay seemed determined that Rachel would overhear. "Sure, I'll be right in," she told Tom, her voice a little too loud.

"See you soon." Then she called out to Rachel, "Tell Joanna I had to go back. Tommy needs me."

Tommy. Rachel was beginning to hate the nickname. Without looking around, she waved a hand in acknowledgment.

Just police business, she told herself again, but she clenched her teeth and gripped the reins until the leather bit into her palms.

Walking into the conference room behind Toby Willingham, Tom couldn't help noticing the sheriff was listing slightly to the right, like an old hound that was losing its sense of balance. In recent months, the sheriff had lost so much weight that he had to pull his belt tight, bunching up the fabric of his trousers to keep them from dropping around his knees. Willingham was out sick more often than he was on the job, and Tom was more or less running the department. The official story was that the sheriff had a minor heart problem, but his frequent trips to Roanoke suggested something more serious that required a specialist's care.

Tom enjoyed the work, preferred taking the lead, but he felt both frustrated at not having official authority and sad at watching the sheriff, who had been his father's friend, fade into a walking ghost.

Tom and the sheriff took seats at the conference room table, where Dennis Murray and Brandon waited.

Tom paraphrased the preliminary report on Meredith Taylor that he'd pressured the state medical examiner's office to produce. "They won't give us a cause of death until the autopsy's done. The burn pattern on the body is consistent with use of an accelerant. Her hair was burned away, and so was a lot of the flesh on the upper body. The killer might have splashed her with gasoline or kerosene. But they'll have to look at her lungs to determine whether she was still alive when the fire started."

The image of Meredith's blackened, mutilated face rose up in Tom's mind. It was rapidly becoming impossible to think of the corpse as a real woman he had known.

"If the—" Sheriff Willingham broke off and coughed into a handkerchief. Among the alert younger men, he looked exhausted and a decade older than his sixty-three years. He cleared his throat. "If the fire didn't kill her, what did?"

"It looks like a couple of things could have killed her before the fire started. She took a bad beating, for one thing." Tom consulted the report. "Blunt force trauma to the head with multiple fractures of the frontal and lateral regions of the cranium and jaw."

"It sounds personal," Willingham said.

"Like the killer was in a rage," Dennis added.

Willingham sighed and shook his head, then looked at Tom. "Anybody in her family coming? Her parents are both dead now. What about her brother?"

"He's in the Middle East on an official trip. I notified his office so they can get word to him." Meredith's brother now held the Senate seat their father had occupied for forty-plus years. "I wouldn't expect him to show up here, though. I think Lindsay is the only relative who'll care very much about what happened to them."

"What a shame," Willingham said. "You reach anybody in Cam's family?"

"Nobody knows who they are or where they live. Even Lindsay doesn't know anything about them."

"Now that's just plain sad," Willingham said.

"Yeah." Tom had never noticed it bothering Lindsay, though.

"You said two possible causes of death," Dennis put in.

"Right. They found a bullet wound in the back of her skull. We didn't see that ourselves because Gretchen Lauter didn't want to turn her over. She was afraid we couldn't keep the body intact. Anyway, Meredith was shot at least once."

"Man," Brandon said. "Talk about overkill."

"No exit wound, as far as they can tell with all the damage done to the skull," Tom said. "The slug could still be in her brain. Cam's been x-rayed, and the rounds that went into him are lodged in his heart muscle. If we're lucky, we'll get a slug from Meredith too and we'll find out whether the same gun was used on both of them."

The sheriff grunted. "Seems pretty clear they were both killed by the same person. You think the killer went straight from Cam to Meredith? Or was Meredith killed first?"

"We don't know when Meredith died," Tom said, "and her body's in such bad shape, the autopsy probably won't tell us whether she died before or after Cam. Brandon and I got to their house a couple hours after Cam was shot, and the fire had been burning for a while, but not for two hours. One possibility is that Cam was killed first, then Meredith, then the fire was started. Another is that Meredith was killed earlier, the killer left, tracked Cam down and shot him, then went back and started the fire to destroy evidence."

"Going to the house a second time would be a hell of a risk," Dennis said.

"It wouldn't be a problem time-wise, though," Brandon said. "It's just a twenty-minute drive between the two crime scenes. Ragsdale could've done it, easy."

"Didn't Scotty offer you any kind of alibi?" Sheriff Willingham asked, his voice muffled as he wiped his nose with his handkerchief.

"No," Tom said. "And we've already checked with his parents. They didn't see him at all yesterday until he came in the store right before closing."

"Well," Willingham said, "I'd hate to find out Scotty did this. His mom and dad are good, solid people, and they're proud of him for finally straightening himself out."

Tom let that go without comment. He hoped Willingham would go back home after the meeting and leave the investigation to him. The more involved the sheriff became in a case, the more he tended to micro-manage and try to keep Tom from stepping on toes.

"I don't see how Ben Hern could have killed both of them," Brandon said. "Don't we have people saying he was home all morning up to the time he followed Taylor off his property?"

"Not exactly," Tom said. "All we know for sure is that he was at home when Rachel and Holly got there and for a few minutes afterward. We don't know where he was when Cam was shot. I have to talk to his assistant and his mother and find out where he was earlier in the morning. Whether they'll be honest about it is another question."

"You got any opinion about—" the sheriff started, but a wracking cough overtook him. The other men waited for him to recover his voice. "Which one's got the strongest motive? Hern or Scotty?"

"Either of them could have done it," Tom said. "Scotty might have been frustrated over his relationship with Meredith. We've seen that kind of situation turn violent often enough. As for Hern, it sounds like Taylor was threatening him with something. Blackmail's as strong a motive as you could want. And he's stone-walling us. He says his lawyer's coming down from New York, and he won't answer questions until he has representation."

"Hell," Willingham muttered. "All we need is some high-priced lawyer from New York in here running rings around us and the prosecutor."

"Nobody's going to run rings around me," Tom said, annoyed by the suggestion. "If Hern's guilty, we'll find the evidence."

"He's never been arrested in Virginia," Dennis said, "but I haven't heard back about New York yet."

"What's happened to his mother?" Sheriff Willingham asked. "Why can't we locate her?"

"Good question," Tom said. "Her cell phone sends calls directly to voice mail. Her secretary hasn't heard from her. Hern says he can't get in touch with her either. Her car hasn't been spotted."

"Oh, lord." Willingham scrubbed a hand over his face. "Are we looking for a witness or another victim?"

Or the killer? "It doesn't look good," Tom said. "Lloyd Wilson claims he saw a dark-colored Jaguar at the Taylor house yesterday morning. If Hern can prove he was somewhere else, we can probably assume the car was his mother's."

"Maybe all this about Hern and his mother and Ragsdale is just a coincidence," Brandon said. "Taylor floated some projects that were supposed to make money and ended up losing it instead. Maybe somebody's been nursing a grudge for a while and finally decided to act on it."

"He was trying to get a factory built here a few years ago," Dennis said, "and he raised some money to promote that, but nothing came of it. I doubt any one person gave him more than a hundred bucks, though."

"The Hogencamp girl who works for Hern," Tom said, "her dad had a beef with Taylor, and Rachel said she brought it up when Taylor was at Hern's house. She accused him of stealing from her family. Remember that fight we had to break up about a year ago? Taylor landed in the hospital with some pretty bad injuries, and Dave Hogencamp had to be treated in the emergency room. Neither of them filed charges, but we gave both of them citations for disturbing the peace. Maybe Dave decided to finish what he started."

"Aw, now," the sheriff put in, "Dave's a good man. He might lose his temper, but he wouldn't murder two people. He sure wouldn't do something like *that* to a woman." He gestured at the medical examiner's report that described what her killer had done to Meredith.

"I'm going to question him," Tom said.

That brought a sigh and a sad shake of the head from the sheriff, but he didn't object. "Who were Cam and Meredith in touch with recently? Have you got their phone records yet?"

"Just the call log on Cam's cell phone so far," Tom said. "Nothing unusual showed up. Most of his calls were to and from Meredith, when she was at home and he was out. Cam talked a couple of days ago to the guy who used to sell ads for the paper. A two-minute conversation. On the morning he was killed, the only person he talked to was Meredith, calling him from home."

"Could it be two people working together?" Brandon said. "One killed Cam, one killed Meredith and set the fire."

"I'm not ruling anything out," Tom said. "If two people are involved, there's always a chance one of them will slip up and catch our attention."

"Well," the sheriff said, rising, "keep me updated. Tom, you going to the bank this morning?"

"Right." Tom stood. "Lindsay's meeting me here, then I'll head over to see whether Meredith kept any secrets hidden in her safe deposit box."

Chapter Twelve

Tom swung open his office door and stopped in his tracks. Lindsay sat behind his desk, holding a sheet of paper in one hand and wearing the startled expression of an interrupted burglar.

"What the hell are you doing?" Tom marched across the room and snatched the paper from her.

The trapped look gave way to indignation. "I'm trying to get the information you won't give me."

"Lindsay," he said, making an effort to keep his voice down, "you're not going to read the file. You're not going to be part of the investigation. I thought we settled that yesterday." He scooped up the papers she'd spread over his desk and slid them back into the file jacket.

Lindsay stood and crossed her arms. "You've got witnesses. I want to know what they saw and heard. I have a right."

How much had she read? How long had she been sitting here? "Look," Tom said, softening his voice, "what you have a right to is justice for your parents. I'll do my damnedest to give you that. But you have to let me do my job without interference."

"Rachel saw something, didn't she?" Lindsay demanded. "Or heard something. I want to know what it was, Tommy. Why won't you tell me?"

So he'd walked in on her before she had a chance to read Rachel's statement. Maybe her imagination was worse than the simple truth, but Tom would not let the daughter of the victims plow through what little evidence he had.

"I thought you trusted me," he said.

"I do! But—"

"If you're going to interfere, you can forget about going with me to the bank. I'll get a warrant and have the box drilled. If you can't let me do my job, I don't want you there."

Lindsay sighed and squeezed her eyes shut for a moment. When she opened them again, she said, "Okay. All right. You don't have to go to all that trouble. I'll open the box for you, and I'll behave myself. I promise."

Within a few minutes the oblong safe deposit box sat on a table next to the evidence lockbox Tom had brought, and he and Lindsay were left alone in a tiny room next to the bank's vault.

While Tom pulled on latex gloves, Lindsay stood with her gaze riveted on the box and her hands so tightly clasped that her knuckles went white. Since the day before, Tom realized, shock had set in, and the reality of her parents' murders had left Lindsay looking disconnected, as if she couldn't anchor herself in the present.

"You okay?" he asked.

"Yeah, sure." Her voice wobbled. "I'm just really freaked out by all this. It's surreal."

Tom removed two manila envelopes with PHOTOS written on them with black marker, an envelope labeled MARRIAGE/ BIRTH CERTIFICATES, and one labeled ESTATE TRUST. "Would this be the trust your grandfather set up when you were born? It was for you, right?"

Lindsay nodded. "I have a copy too. The payments went to Mom while I was growing up, to help take care of me. A whopping one hundred and fifty dollars a month."

"Are you still getting money from it?"

"Oh, yeah, since I turned eighteen, but I've been sending it to Mom for years. She needed it more than I did. I can't cash out the trust until I'm forty. Dear old granddad was a real control freak."

"At least he cared enough to try to help."

Lindsay expelled a short laugh. "Yeah, sure. My grandmother badgered him into setting it up. Then he felt like he'd done his good deed, so he left Mom out of his will completely."

Tom let the subject drop and moved on. He placed the four envelopes in the lockbox and wrote a description of each item on an evidence log sheet. Returning to the safe deposit box, he picked up a clear plastic CD case. The disc inside had RED MOON written on the label area.

"Any idea what this is?"

"One of my mom's novels. The manuscript file."

"There are some more of them in here," he said. "Four, five, six—there must be nearly a dozen CDs here. Did she write that many books?"

Lindsay nodded and blinked rapidly, fighting back tears. "She kept writing and writing and all she ever got published were stories in the newspaper and a few little articles in a regional magazine. So much wasted effort."

Tom couldn't come up with anything to say. He didn't know what it would take to write a novel, but he knew it wasn't easy, and writing book after book that no one wanted to publish had to be devastating. He placed the CDs in his evidence box and noted them on the log.

"Do you have to take them?"

"I need to verify what's on them. I can't take a chance on missing something relevant to the case."

She exhaled. "Right."

At the bottom of the box Tom found several blue velvet cases of different sizes and shapes, the kind jewelry came in. "Do you recognize these?"

"No." Lindsay's face had suddenly come alive with curiosity.

Tom picked up the longest of the cases, opened it. He and Lindsay stared at a necklace, a broad gold band set with diamonds. Tom whistled. "Is this real?"

Lindsay leaned into him, her eyes on the necklace. "Oh, yeah, it's real. It belonged to Mom's Aunt Julia. But she didn't leave Mom anything in her will. I thought that was really strange at the time because they were so close. I wonder if…I'll bet she gave Mom this stuff before she died. She asked Mom to go see her in New York last fall. That was just a few weeks before Aunt Julia died."

"You didn't know your mother had the jewelry?"

"No."

Tom opened the rest of the jewelry boxes one by one. Diamond rings, bracelets, earrings. A fortune in jewelry. "Why was she keeping it all," he asked, "if she wasn't going to use any of it? Why stash it here? Do you think she was keeping it for you?"

Lindsay laughed, a humorless gust of breath. "As if I'll ever have any reason to wear stuff like this. I don't know why she hung onto it. One thing I'm sure of—Dad didn't know about it. He would have made her sell it all to save the newspaper."

"She cared about the paper too," Tom said. "Seems to me that saving it would have mattered more to her than a lot of jewelry she'd never wear."

"I don't know what to tell you, Tommy, except…She didn't care about the paper the way Dad did. I guess she didn't want to pour any more money into a lost cause. Dad couldn't face the truth, he couldn't give up his dream any more than Mom could give up hers, but I'm sure she knew the newspaper couldn't be saved." Lindsay drew a deep breath and let it out. "If they'd sold the jewelry, they would have been able to start fresh, do something better with their lives."

Tom placed all the jewelry in the evidence box. "I'll keep these under lock and key, and I won't let it get out that we have them."

"There's one more thing." Lindsay pointed into the safe deposit box.

He pulled out another manila envelope. Brown packaging tape secured the flap. He could feel the shape of a CD case inside. Why wasn't it lying loose like the other discs? What had made this one different, special, in Meredith's mind? It couldn't be yet another unsold book.

Tom placed the envelope in the evidence box. "I'll wait and open it back at headquarters."

Chapter Thirteen

Rachel smiled as she listened to Simon in the back seat, solemnly instructing Billy Bob about how to handle a horse, as if the bulldog planned to take up riding. "The most important thing you gotta remember is, you gotta stay cool and show the horse who's the boss. Horses can smell it if you're scared of them. Miss Joanna told me that."

Rachel couldn't let go of her curiosity about Simon's reaction to Lindsay, but she didn't want to spoil his happy mood by asking about it now.

When they pulled into the driveway of Darla and Grady Duncan's rambling Victorian house, Darla rose from a rocker on the porch and came down the steps to greet them. Tall and thin, with light brown hair, she had none of her grandson's striking features. Simon got his looks from the Bridger side of his family.

"Hey, you two," Darla said when Simon and Billy Bob tumbled out of the vehicle. From the grass stains and dirt smudges on her khaki slacks, Rachel guessed that Darla had taken advantage of Simon's absence to get some serious gardening done. "Have fun?"

"Yeah!" Simon ran over to hug her. "And Miss Joanna gave me chocolate cake for lunch."

"But not until after the soup and sandwich," Rachel clarified.

Darla laughed. "Simon always goes straight to the most exciting part of the story."

"Come on." Simon grabbed Rachel's hand. "You have to see Mr. Piggles."

"You run on ahead," Darla told him. "Rachel will catch up."

Simon charged up the front steps and into the house, with Billy Bob in hot pursuit. When Simon was out of earshot, Darla said, "I heard a while ago about that Taylor girl staying with Joanna. I never would've let Simon go over there if I'd known she was there."

"Lindsay had to go into town, so he wasn't around her long," Rachel said as they walked to the house. "I couldn't help noticing that Simon doesn't like her. What's that about?"

"He can see through her. She's a nasty little piece of work. I never could understand why Tom took up with her again. Well, that's behind him now, thank god." Darla paused. "You know, Tom and I have had our problems, but I'm trying to get past that for Simon's sake. I'm glad he found you. You're the best thing that ever happened to him. Don't you let Lindsay Taylor get her claws into him again."

"I'll do everything I can to prevent it." Rachel smiled, but she wondered what she was up against and whether she could trump the years of intimacy Lindsay had shared with Tom.

Inside the house, she climbed the broad, winding stairs to Simon's room. Billy Bob was already stretched out on the rug, eyes drooping. Simon was talking to Mr. Piggles, a butterscotch and white guinea pig who resided in an enormous cage on a table along one wall.

Rachel leaned down to look in at Simon's pet. "Hey, there, Mr. Piggles, how are you today?"

The guinea pig responded by rushing to a corner of the cage and grabbing a tiny plastic bowl in his teeth. Facing Rachel again, he waved the little bowl at her while he squeaked.

"Who could resist that act?" Laughing, Rachel took a peanut from the bag Simon produced and reached through the wires of the cage to drop it into the bowl. Mr. Piggles scurried away and disappeared into a box that served as a private den. "Hey, you could say thanks, at least."

"Rachel?" Simon slipped his small hand into hers.

Rachel looked down into the boy's troubled eyes. His ebullient mood had evaporated. "What is it, Simon? What's wrong?"

"She's not gonna be Uncle Tom's girlfriend again, is she? Lindsay, I mean."

"No," Rachel said. "I promise you that won't happen."

Back at headquarters, Tom logged the items from Meredith's bank box into the evidence register and placed everything except the sealed envelope in the evidence room safe. Checking his watch, he debated whether to take a look at the CD in the envelope now or head out to question Angie Hogencamp and her father. The CD won. He took it into his office.

Waiting for his computer to boot up, Tom sifted through the stack of call-back messages on his desk. Newspapers and TV stations in Washington, New York, Philadelphia, and other big cities wanted more details about the death of Senator Abbott's daughter and her husband. By tomorrow out of town reporters would be on the ground in Mountainview, but for now he didn't have to deal with them. He crumpled the messages into a ball, dropped them in his wastebasket, and tore open the sealed envelope.

The CD he pulled out wasn't labeled. Meredith had set it apart for some reason, but he doubted it would yield information that would lead him to the killer. It probably held nothing more than tax or medical records. Anything he could learn about the Taylors' lives, though, might aid the investigation in unexpected ways.

He was disappointed by what came up on his computer screen—apparently the title page of yet another unsold novel, this one called *Outside Agitators*. What was special about it? Tom clicked to the opening chapter to take a quick look.

Chapter 1: September, 1968

Every fiber of my being thrilled with excitement and anticipation when I stepped off the Trailways bus with Chad and
three other new Vistas in Greenview, a little mountain town in
southwestern Virginia. For the first time in my twenty-one years,
I was free of my parents' supervision and doing something that
demanded selfless courage.

I was beginning to wonder, though, whether we had been
sent by mistake to the wrong place. Greenview didn't look
desperately impoverished. It looked like an ordinary small community, surrounded by mountains dressed in gaudy autumn
colors. But I reminded myself that we wouldn't be working in
town. We were destined for the hills and hollows of the county's
poorest district.

This was real life, and I was ready for it.

The other members of my training class had predicted I
wouldn't even make it this far. *Tourist.* That was what they called
me. They thought I was a little rich girl who wouldn't last a day
without the luxuries of my privileged life. To them I was a naive
child who joined Volunteers in Service to America for my own
amusement, whose ignorance would alienate the people I was
supposed to help. It didn't seem to matter that the others had
grown up in affluent middle-class homes and never experienced
anything more demanding than summer camp. I came from a
wealthy family, so they had to show me I was too pampered to
handle the hard work ahead. I wasn't a *serious person.*

Of course, I realized what the true source of their animosity
was: I was the daughter of a U.S. Senator who supported the
war in Vietnam and denounced protesters as unpatriotic. A lot
of young people thought he was evil, and they despised me for
being his daughter.

Chad, however, treated me with respect. He believed I was
capable of feeling empathy for the poor and helping them make
their lives better. I had fallen in love with him the moment we
met. Lanky and handsome, with shaggy brown hair, blue eyes,

and a charming crooked smile, Chad could have any girl he wanted, but I was the one he chose. He demonstrated his trust by telling me things he had never told anyone. He confessed that he had shot off part of one of his fingers to make himself unfit for military service, and he begged me not to think of him as a coward. Of course I didn't. All I felt was relief that he would never be sent off to be killed in the war.

Chad also confided in me about his family. His parents owned a chain of several loan companies—he said they offered something called "pay day loans"—that made money by charging exorbitant interest on small cash loans and locking working class people into a cycle of debt they couldn't escape. Because no one was at home in the afternoons, he often went to the loan office his mother ran, and he saw the way she manipulated people and drew them deeper into debt. He heard her threaten legal action against people who fell behind in their payments. Those experiences gave birth to Chad's need to help others who are less fortunate. He was deeply ashamed of his parents, and he wanted, in some small way, to make up for the damage they did. He swore me to secrecy because he believed others would hold him responsible for his family's shameful business. He knew I wouldn't judge him for his parents' actions, and he trusted me to honor his confidence.

Chad and I were embarking on a great adventure together. Our future could be anything we wanted to make it.

The man who ran the Marsdon County Community Action Program met us at the bus station and walked us three blocks— almost the full length of Main Street—to the CAP office. He had been a high school social studies teacher before he was hired by the antipoverty program. I expected him to give us a pep talk about the good things we would do during our year in the county. Instead, we sat on metal folding chairs for an hour while the director recited the rules we had to live by. No drinking, not so much as a beer. No loud music. No dating local young men and women. We were forbidden to lend money to the locals. We couldn't discuss Vietnam with anyone, because this was a place where parents were proud to have their sons fight, and die, in their country's wars, and "hippies" were despised. Local politicians regretted allowing the antipoverty program into the county and didn't like young outsiders coming in to work with the poor. If we messed up, we would jeopardize the program and the poor would suffer. We were expected to behave with dignity and to show consideration for the people we worked among.

At the end of the meeting we received keys to the old cars we would use on the job, and we drove single-file behind the CAP director, our caravan making its way out of Greenview and into a foreign land.

The other three girls would live with local families, but I would have a place to myself, and because the CAP director was concerned about my safety, Chad was assigned a house within sight of mine. *Could it get any better than this?* I thought. As we drove, I drank in the beauty of the mountainsides, soaking up the autumn colors that reminded me of the Adirondacks, where my family had a lodge. The sad little houses we passed were mere blotches on the periphery of my vision, and I never looked directly at them.

Only when I saw the one-room shack assigned to me did I start feeling panicky. The place didn't even have running water. In every kind of weather, I would have to use the privy in the back yard and the water pump next to the back door. For heat, I would have to keep wood or coal in the potbellied stove. I stood on the front steps, watching the CAP director drive away, and I wanted to run after him, begging to be rescued.

Then Chad called out from his car, "I'll be over in a few minutes, after I stash my stuff. Hang loose."

I forced myself to smile to show him I wasn't fazed, that I was ready to tackle any challenge. But secretly, I felt ashamed of my weakness.

I can last a year, I told myself as I walked back inside my awful little house. I didn't even have a chair, so I crossed the room, making the floorboards creak with every step, and sat on the iron-frame bed. I looked up at the single bare light bulb that dangled from the ceiling and said a prayer of thanks that I had electricity.

Beneath me, I felt big, solid lumps in the thin mattress. And what was that odor rising off it? *Oh my god! Urine!* I jumped up. At the CAP office, I'd been given two sheets and a pillow case, but I didn't think bed linen would mask the smell.

One year. I would get through this. Chad was with me, and I had my dreams of the future to hold onto. After we fulfilled our commitment to the antipoverty program, Chad would go to law school and I would begin my career as an author. My experiences in Marsdon County were going to be priceless material for the novels I planned to write. I'd brought a thick notebook along to jot down my observations.

One year, I told myself, *then we can get out of this place and start our life together.*

I couldn't have imagined, when I stood in the little house with my suitcases at my feet, what lay ahead for me in Marsdon County, Virginia.

When he reached the end of the chapter, Tom leaned back in his chair, eyes still fixed on the final line. What was this? Bad fiction with a few dashes of reality drawn from Meredith's own past? Or the straight truth with only the names changed? If it was the truth, Meredith hadn't loved her life in Mason County after all—at least not in the beginning. That had been decades ago, before Tom was born, and people could change a lot in that amount of time. But the story was probably ninety-nine percent fiction. It might offer some useful insight into the Taylors' marriage and their relationships with other people, but he doubted it would help him solve their murders.

Tom glanced at his watch, then closed the file and ejected the CD from his computer. He had to question the Hogencamps. The rest of Meredith's tale would have to wait.

Chapter Fourteen

Rachel had only the flimsiest excuse to visit Lloyd Wilson, but it would do. She set off to see him after dropping off Simon and Billy Bob.

She wished she could trust Tom to be fair, to assume Ben was innocent unless proven guilty. But that wasn't Tom's job. His job was to find a killer. He already disliked Ben and viewed him as a suspect, and Lindsay was probably pushing the theory that Ben killed her parents. To her own disappointment, Rachel realized she didn't have much faith in Tom's ability to be objective in this case.

She braked when she saw the roadside mailbox with TAYLOR painted on its side. Yellow crime scene tape drooped along the perimeter of the property, but no one was working the scene now. In the middle of the lot, dwarfed by the mountain that rose behind it, lay the ruins of Cam and Meredith Taylor's house, a pile of ash outlined by a cinderblock foundation.

Rachel had met Mrs. Taylor a couple of times when she'd brought her dog Cricket to the vet clinic, once for routine vaccines and once for a cut on a paw. The wound was minor, but Mrs. Taylor had been distraught, worried about infection and blaming herself for not watching the dog more closely. A little over twenty-four hours ago, Meredith Taylor had lost her life in the fire, and her beloved dog had probably died with her. An image of flames licking at flesh invaded Rachel's head and made her shiver at the horror of it.

What am I doing here? Rachel doubted Lloyd Wilson would tell her anything he hadn't told Tom. But Tom wouldn't reveal what Wilson had seen or heard, and Rachel wanted to know what kind of evidence the police had.

She pulled onto the strip of bare dirt that served as a driveway and parked behind Wilson's pickup truck. His two dogs loped around the side of the house, tails wagging and tongues lolling. Rachel got out and crouched to pet them. Maggie and Lisa were littermates, ten years old now, large brown mutts with suggestions of Labrador in their solid bodies and hints of German shepherd in their erect ears and long muzzles.

"Well, hey there," Wilson called as he hobbled up the side yard toward Rachel. Raising a hand in greeting, he gave her a broad smile that almost made his eyes disappear in the bunched wrinkles around them. "Now how did I rate a house call?"

Rachel rose, returning his smile. "When I realized you live so close to the house that burned down yesterday, I wanted to make sure Maggie's breathing hasn't been affected by the smoke." *You are such a liar.* The dog panted in the heat, and even without a stethoscope Rachel could tell her bronchial passages were clear. "I just want to have a listen, okay? I won't charge you for the visit, since you didn't call me."

"I'd be willing to pay you to come visit me." As soon as he said it, a bright pink flush rose on Wilson's cheeks and he averted his eyes. "I mean—"

"Let me get my bag," Rachel cut in, "and I'll give Maggie a quick exam." She'd always been amused and flattered that this tough old man had a crush on her, and the last thing she wanted to do was embarrass him.

"Now where are my manners?" Wilson said, still a little flustered. "Keepin' you standin' out here in the hot sun. Come on in the house, and I'll give you a nice cold glass of tea. It's sun tea, real smooth, best tea you'll ever drink."

"Oh, thanks, I'd love to have some."

They walked together, the two dogs keeping pace. In the small living room, Wilson steered Rachel away from the easy chair. "Bad springs," he said. "Make yourself comfortable on the couch, and I'll get the tea."

When Rachel sat on the sofa the dogs stationed themselves on either side, a canine chin resting on each of her knees. As she scratched their heads and looked around the room, a deep melancholy ambushed her. This house had never been grand, but she could see it had once been pleasant, perhaps even pretty. An oblong patch of light blue where a picture had been removed showed what the living room walls looked like before they acquired scratches, dents, smears, and grime from fireplace smoke. The braided rug bore so many spots and so much dirt that Rachel couldn't tell what the original colors had been, but she could imagine it as the anchor in a homey, welcoming room. A woman had once lived here. Without her, Rachel guessed, the husband who had outlived her scarcely noticed the deterioration of his home, and wouldn't care if he did.

While Wilson bustled in the kitchen, Rachel went through the motions of examining Maggie, listening to her lungs and heart, checking her eyes for signs of irritation. Nothing out of the ordinary. The second dog shouldered Maggie out of the way and presented herself with an expectant air, so Rachel examined her too.

Wilson returned with a tin tray that held two glasses of tea and a saucer of sugar cookies. Rachel took a glass and sipped. "Mmm. This is delicious."

"Have a cookie." He placed the tray in front of her on the coffee table and took a seat at the opposite end of the couch. "Fresh from the bakery this mornin'."

She reached for one, took a bite. Not-so-fresh from a super-market package was more like it. "It's good."

Wilson smiled and nodded. "How's the dogs?"

"Perfectly fine. Maggie's asthma is very well-controlled. I can tell you're getting her pills into her on schedule."

"Oh, yeah. If I ever let anything happen to these dogs, my wife—" He paused and cleared his throat. "Well, I feel like she's watchin' everything I do for them. These two was her babies."

His voice faded to a near-whisper. "She just barely lived to see them full-grown."

"I'm so sorry." In the silence that followed, Rachel told herself, *Remember why you're here.* "It's terrible what happened to the Taylors. No one's life should end that way."

Wilson dropped his gaze to his gnarled hands, clasped between his knees, and didn't answer.

"I guess you've talked to Captain Bridger about what you saw and heard yesterday."

"Didn't see nor hear much of anything," Wilson said with a shrug. "I told the Bridger boy about seein' Scotty Ragsdale's car over there."

"Scotty Ragsdale? Isn't he the son of the Ragsdales who own the hardware store?"

"Yep. Him and Mrs. Taylor was real close, if you know what I mean."

That was interesting. Rachel didn't know whether to trust Lloyd Wilson's assumptions, but the very existence of Meredith's friendship with another man gave Rachel hope that the relationship had something to do with the Taylor murders.

Wilson went on, "But I seen Scotty's car way before the fire started. Only other thing was that sports car. A Jaguar, that's what it was."

Rachel caught her breath. Ben drove a Jaguar. So did his mother, but she'd left the county hours before the Taylors were killed. At least, that was what everyone believed. "What time did you see the Jaguar? In relation to the fire."

He shook his head. "Bridger asked me that, and I couldn't place it just exactly. Now that I think about it, though, I reckon it was about the same time I heard some hunters shootin' in the woods up the mountain."

"Hunters?" Rachel said. "This time of year?"

"Oh, lord, the time of year don't stop them. I hear shots in the woods all the time. And I heard some that morning—well, one, anyway—and it sounded closer than it ought to be. But that's not out of the ordinary either. Damn fools don't pay a bit of attention to where they're pointin' their guns. Anyway, I brung the dogs indoors. I was afraid them or me might get hit. But I didn't hear any more shots, so after a while I went back out to work on my chicken coop."

"You're sure the shooting was in the woods? Could it have been at the Taylor house?"

He frowned at her. "You sayin' the Taylor woman was shot? How could they tell? I thought if she was all burned up—"

"I haven't heard anything about her being shot." It made sense, though. If the killer hadn't disabled Meredith first, she might have escaped the fire. Maybe the fire was the murderer's attempt to make the death look accidental. "Did you tell Captain Bridger about hearing a shot?"

"No, I don't reckon I did. It just come to me a while ago."

Rachel wiped her damp palms on the knees of her jeans. Was this good for Ben, or bad? Was it possible he had committed these awful crimes? The memory of what she'd seen in the woods popped into her mind, and she blurted, "I was the one who found Cam Taylor's body. Right after he was killed."

Wilson pulled in a sharp breath. "Well, my lord, I didn't hear that part. I'm real sorry you had to see a sight like that."

She'd told Wilson something Tom wanted her to keep quiet about, and she was letting herself get distracted from her purpose in coming here. Pulling herself back on track, she asked, "Can you remember when you heard the gunfire?"

Wilson frowned, considering, then nodded. "I'm pretty sure it was sometime between ten and ten-thirty."

Rachel almost laughed with relief. If Wilson was right about the time, Ben couldn't have been at the Taylor house. He had three people to give him a solid alibi—Angie, Holly, and Rachel herself. But if it wasn't Ben in the Jaguar, then who? Had Ben's mother made a stop at the Taylor house before she left the county?

Chapter Fifteen

When Tom drove up, he spotted Angie in the vegetable garden next to the Hogencamps' small brick house, hacking at the ground with a hoe. He pulled into the driveway on the far side of the house and parked behind Angie's Volkswagen.

She didn't cross the yard to meet him, but stood stiff as a statue among the squash plants, with the hoe in one gloved hand and a bunch of weeds in the other. A shapeless straw hat shaded her face from the sun.

She cut off Tom's greeting. "I think I should call Ben and tell him before I talk to you."

"Come on, Angie. You know better than that." Her father had once been a sheriff's deputy and a cousin of hers currently wore the uniform.

She expelled a small huff. "All right, ask your questions."

"Can we go in and sit down?" Feeling a trickle of sweat down the back of his neck, Tom wished he had a straw hat of his own.

Glancing toward the house, Angie said, "My mother gets upset if anybody besides Dad or my aunt and me comes in the house."

"How's your mom doing?"

Angie shrugged. "It's not like she's going to get well, is it? Her sister stays with her while Dad and I are at work, and she can't tell the difference between my aunt and me anymore. Some days she thinks I'm a complete stranger and starts screaming at me when I come in the room with her."

Good god, Tom thought, *I wouldn't be able to stand it.* What could he say to someone whose relatively young mother was vanishing into the mists of Alzheimer's? He'd seen the two of them together many times, looking like sisters, chattering like best friends on the same wavelength. "If there's ever anything I can do for you—"

"You can leave my boss alone. Ben didn't kill anybody."

Tom spread his hands. "Did I say he did? I'm just trying to trace Cam Taylor's movements before he was shot."

"Yeah, right." Angie flung the handful of weeds into a bucket at her feet. "Like you said, I know better than that."

"What time did you get to Hern's house yesterday morning?"

"Eight-thirty, like I always do, and I'll save you the trouble of asking. Yes, Ben was there. So was his mother. She left around nine o'clock. No, Ben didn't go out. He was at home all morning, up to the time he left to make sure Cam Taylor got off his property."

"All right." Tom noted that Angie was Hern's only alibi for the time between his mother's departure and Rachel and Holly's arrival. "Now tell me what you saw and heard when Taylor was at Hern's house yesterday."

She adjusted her hat, tugging it lower over her eyes before she spoke. "Ben wouldn't let him in the house the first time he showed up. The second time, we were all on the porch and he just barged right in and started his pitch again."

"Hern was pretty ticked off at Taylor, wasn't he?"

"Of course he was. I was mad too. But I guess I shouldn't tell you that. You might accuse *me* of murder next."

"That's a little unfair, isn't it?"

Angie let the hoe drop to the ground and crossed her arms. "Ben's a wonderful man. If it weren't for him, I'd be clerking at the grocery store and making next to nothing and bored out of my mind. Ben pays me a decent salary, he pays for my medical insurance, and he never makes me work late, so I can spend time with Mom and give Dad a little relief. He's one of the best people I've ever known."

She's in love with him, Tom thought. In love with her boss, and determined to protect him. She might lie for Hern even if she believed he had killed Cam Taylor, because she probably thought Taylor deserved it. If she knew of anything in Hern's past that Taylor could have been holding over him, she wasn't likely to share it with Tom. "Yesterday wasn't the first time Taylor went to Hern's house, was it?"

Angie fixed her gaze on a bumblebee crawling around inside a yellow squash blossom. As if begrudging Tom the information, she said, "No. He was there before. And yesterday was the third time this week."

"He was asking for money?"

"Yes. He even tried to get money from Ben's mother. He already knew her because the two of them worked in the poverty program at the same time." Her eyes flicked to Tom, then back to the bee. "You know, I can see Cam Taylor coming here to work with poor people, but looking at Mrs. Hernandez, I couldn't see her doing something like that."

"Oh? Why? What's she like?" If Angie wouldn't talk about one suspect, maybe he could get her to talk about another.

"She drives a Jaguar and I could tell every stitch she had on cost a fortune. She's got a nice haircut, too young-looking for her, a little spiky, you know? And I don't think her hair's naturally that shade of brown. But it was cut just perfectly, you couldn't get a haircut like that in Mountainview. And she wears a ton of jewelry, gold earrings and necklaces and bracelets and this gorgeous ring—" Angie held up a hand and wiggled her fingers. "She said it was a sapphire. I've never seen anything like it in my life."

"What did you think of her? What kind of personality does she have?"

"I like her, I guess." Angie frowned as she considered an unspoken thought.

"But?" Tom prodded. "I get the feeling there's a *but* coming up."

Angie gave a little laugh, as if embarrassed by her obviousness. "She's one of those people who are *too* friendly, you know? Like she's knocking herself out to make you think she's just a regular person and doesn't put herself above you. She wanted me to call her Karen, but I couldn't do that. I mean, I just *met* her, I don't really know her, and she's my boss' mother." She sighed. "Why is it some people are so determined to keep you from showing them any respect?"

Now there was an interesting question, but not one Tom wanted to debate at the moment. "Beats me," he said. "So how did Mrs. Hernandez and Cam Taylor get along?"

"Oh, at first it was a big reunion, big smiles, you know. But it wasn't more than five minutes before he pulled out his so-called business plan and started trying to get money out of her." Angie paused. "I wasn't deliberately eavesdropping or anything."

Tom grinned. "I never thought you were. How did she react when Taylor asked for money?"

"You know..." Angie ducked her head, hiding her face behind the brim of her hat. "I don't mean to criticize her, but I think she was kind of playing with him. He was practically begging, and she was enjoying it. She said—What was it exactly? Something like, *Cam, look around you. The world has changed. You're the only one in it who hasn't.* She made fun of him after he left."

Far from sounding critical, Angie reported this with a clear note of satisfaction.

"What did Taylor say to that?"

"He must have been really desperate, because he kept on talking like she hadn't said it. But he looked like he just swallowed a bug."

"Tell me," Tom said, "did you ever get the feeling that Taylor had some kind of leverage over Ben Hern or his mother?"

"Leverage?" Angie thought about that with a puzzled frown. "No. I don't know what you mean. Is that important?"

"No, no, never mind." Angie wasn't acting as if he was poking around a dangerous subject. Tom was inclined to believe she didn't know that Taylor's request for money was actually a blackmail attempt. "You said Mrs. Hernandez made fun of him. Do you think he deserved to be treated that way?"

Angie looked Tom in the eye. "He deserved a lot worse. He should have been locked up behind bars for stealing from my mom and dad."

"So I guess you're not sorry that he—" Tom broke off when Dave Hogencamp's blue truck pulled up and parked in front of the house.

"Dad's back." Angie turned toward her father with the eager expression of someone about to be rescued from an ordeal.

Dave climbed out of his truck and loped across the yard, looking like a tall, gangly teenager with gray hair and bifocals. A plastic hardware store bag dangled from one hand.

"Hey, Dave," Tom said. "How've you been?"

Dave glanced from Tom to Angie, then down at the hand Tom offered. After a hesitation, he shook hands briefly.

"What's going on here?" Dave demanded. "I hope you're not trying to get my girl involved in that murder case."

"She's one of the people who saw Cam Taylor right before he was killed. You know I have to get her account. And I want to ask you about your dealings with Taylor. You had a serious problem with him in the past."

Dave snorted. "That's one way to put it. He stole eight thousand dollars we couldn't afford to lose. So yeah, I had a *problem* with him."

"Your wife gave him the money," Tom said, regretting the provocation but knowing it was necessary.

Dave's face flushed a mottled red. He thrust the hardware store bag at Angie, letting go too soon and making her fumble to catch it. Through the thin plastic, Tom saw the bag contained a box of slug bait.

"You listen to me," Dave said. "My wife didn't *give* anything to that goddamn thief. He took advantage of a sick woman. He got her to thinking she'd be selfish if she didn't help out her friends in the quilting circle."

"He wanted to sell their quilts through a dealer, something like that?" Tom asked.

"Yeah, right, he was gonna make a fortune for them, selling their homemade quilts for big bucks in places like New York. Folk art, he called it. Rich people would hang them on their walls. All he needed was some money to rent a gallery and hire somebody to run it. He hounded my wife while I was at work, he wore her down until she was too confused to know what she was doing, and he drove her right to the bank to take that money out of savings and hand it over to him. I didn't find out about it for almost a week."

"That's when you realized something was happening to her mind, wasn't it?" Tom asked quietly.

Tom's question brought sudden tears to Dave's eyes, and his face twisted with helpless fury. Angie clutched the hardware bag to her chest, her head bowed and her face hidden.

"He took advantage of a sick woman," Dave repeated. "I wanted to kill the son of a bitch."

"Dad, don't say that," Angie whispered.

"You put him in the hospital," Tom said. "He got your point."

Dave shook his head. "I let him off too easy."

"Did you ever get any of the money back?"

"Not a damn penny. By the time I found out, it was all gone. Handed over to strangers. You know how many of my wife's quilts got sold through that scheme? Exactly one. And she didn't get any damn fortune for it, either."

"Where were you yesterday morning?" Tom asked.

Dave's expression hardened and his eyes turned wary. "I went fishing, if it's any business of yours. I had some comp time coming from the railroad, and I went fishing upriver."

"Anybody with you? Did you see anybody or talk to anybody?"

"I'm not answering any more questions. That's my right."

Tom nodded. "Yes, it is. But if you don't have anything to hide, it's in your best interests to talk to me."

"How the hell would you know what's in my *best interests*? I'm done talking. Now I'm gonna see to my wife." With that, he turned and strode toward the house.

Tom let Dave go. To Angie, he said, "Get him to talk to me, will you?"

"I don't tell my father what to do." Angie pulled the box of slug bait from the bag and tore open the spout. "I'd appreciate it if you'd leave now."

Tom was standing by his cruiser with the door open to release the built-up heat when Dave burst out of the house again. Thinking Dave had changed his mind about talking, Tom waited for him to walk over. But he went no farther than the porch, and he shouted his message to Tom.

"You oughta pin a medal on the man that killed that bastard!"

Chapter Sixteen

In her cramped home office, Joanna McKendrick sat at the desk and motioned for Tom to take the chair beside it. An icy stream of air from a ceiling vent whispered over his head and neck and raised chill bumps on his arms. He seemed destined to either bake or freeze today.

"Lindsay'll be sorry she missed you," Joanna said. "She went to feed the goats."

"How's she doing?"

"She's coping okay. You know how she is." Joanna paused. "I've tried to keep her away from Rachel. If I knew of anybody else who would take her in while she's here, I wouldn't have agreed to let her stay with me."

"I understand that. How does Rachel seem to you? I think she was pretty shaken up yesterday."

"She's fine. She's worried about Ben, though."

"Worried about him?" Tom said. "Why?"

"I think she's afraid you'll rush into charging him with murder."

"I'm not *rushing* to charge anybody." Did Rachel actually think that of him, even after their conversation yesterday? "I'm looking at all the facts."

"And how can I help you with that?"

"You knew the victims longer than anybody else in the county. I'm betting you know things about them that nobody else does."

Joanna swiveled her chair away from him, so the late afternoon sunlight from a window struck her face. Most of the time Tom thought she looked younger than her age, but the strong light emphasized every line on her face and picked up the gray strands among the strawberry blond. "And now you expect me to betray confidences," she said.

"They were murdered, Joanna. This isn't a time to worry about confidences."

She sighed, swiveled to face her desk, and pushed a stack of file folders to one side. "Here, look at this."

Tom rose to look over her shoulder. She pointed to a photograph beneath the thick glass on the desktop. The faded color picture showed four young women and one young man, all of them wearing sweatshirts with college logos.

"That was taken a few days after we got here."

Tom touched a finger to the image of a young Joanna. "You haven't changed a bit."

Joanna gave his arm a light slap. "Flatterer. We were all different people back then. This girl—" She pointed to a pudgy young woman with short curly hair and a morose expression. "—quit and left after two or three weeks. I can't even remember her name. Do you recognize everybody else?"

Three of the girls, including Joanna, had long, straight hair. Tom recognized Meredith, and the young Karen Richardson had the same high cheekbones and dark hair as the woman in Karen Hernandez's current driver's license photo. "My god," he said, "look at Cam."

"Oh, yeah, he was cute. And cocky as hell."

The young Cam matched the description of Chad in Meredith's manuscript: lanky and handsome with shaggy brown hair. Standing with one thumb hooked in a pocket of his jeans and his other hand resting on Meredith's shoulder, Cam grinned at the camera with a confidence that verged on arrogance. The hand in view on Meredith's shoulder was missing most of one finger. Tom had always assumed the injury occurred by accident, but maybe Meredith's account in her manuscript was the truth.

He could easily imagine Cam trading a finger for freedom from the threat of combat.

Tom took his seat again. "I understand why you stayed here—you met a local guy and married him—but I've always wondered why Cam and Meredith stayed. They could have had better lives almost anywhere else."

Joanna ran her fingertips over the glass covering the photo, as if she were physically connecting with the past. "I don't think they ever made a firm decision to stay here. It just worked out that way. When their year in VISTA was up, the director of the Community Action Program offered Cam a job as a special projects coordinator—helping people get bridges and roads repaired, that kind of thing. He wanted to do it, and Meredith wasn't going anywhere without him, so she got a job on the newspaper and stayed too."

"That was when they got married?"

"Yeah. That was kind of sad. Her parents were totally against the marriage. They thought her joining VISTA was a stupid idea, and when she was done they wanted her to come back home and go to graduate school—she'd already been accepted at Georgetown. They definitely weren't impressed with Cam when she took him to meet them, so they weren't about to throw a big wedding for them. They got married in Mason County, with nobody but Dave and me there. And they never left."

"It couldn't have been easy for them," Tom said. "All the disappointments, everything Cam tried that didn't work out."

"You make it sound like everything he did was a failure," Joanna protested. "He accomplished some good things. There are roads in Rocky Branch District that got paved because Cam pushed for it. There are people who'd still be using outhouses if he hadn't worked to get sewer lines extended."

"But—"

"Now wait a minute. You're going to listen to me. You know about the outdoor play that told the history of the Melungeons? Cam got federal funding for that when he was still a VISTA, and Meredith wrote the play."

"And it lasted, what, one summer?" Tom said. "It was pretty bad, from what I've heard. Local people trying to be actors. My dad said it was so amateurish that audiences laughed all the way through it."

"Well, okay," Joanna conceded. "That wasn't a good example, but that was one of Cam's first projects. He did some very worthwhile things after that."

"The antipoverty program didn't last, though," Tom pointed out. "He lost his official status as an advocate for the poor."

"Yeah, that was a disappointment. The local politicians thought at first that the program was just going to bring money into the county and pay for a few public works projects. They didn't like it one bit when they realized federal money was being used to stir up the poor. They wanted the program shut down, and they finally succeeded."

"So Cam was out of a job."

Joanna nodded. "They had to live on what Meredith was making at the paper, and I don't think it was more than minimum wage. But Cam got himself elected to the county board from Rocky Branch District, and he went right on working to help low income people. Until that courthouse crowd found a way to get him off the board."

"They redrew the districts, didn't they? So all the low income voters wouldn't be so concentrated?"

"Right. It was such a damned crooked, self-serving thing to do, and they were so blatant about it. And the courts supported them, for pity's sake. Cam really took that hard. It was just a lucky coincidence that Kip Hardison wanted to sell the paper and retire. They got the money to buy it from Meredith's aunt, and Cam threw himself into it heart and soul."

"Why didn't you help him keep the paper alive?"

Joanna spread her empty hands. "I couldn't. I run this place month to month, and there's never much left over. The rent I get from Rachel is my mad money, if you want to know the truth."

Tom intended to get to the question of Meredith and Scotty's relationship, but first he asked, "Why did Meredith dislike Karen so much?"

For a second Joanna seemed thrown by the change of topic. Then she shrugged. "Karen went after Cam for a while, way back then. She didn't care about him, it was just a game to her. She was bored to death here, and she was just amusing herself. I doubt she even remembers any of that now. But poor Meredith took it very seriously at the time."

"Did the two women see each other while Karen was here this week?"

"No. I suggested we all get together over dinner to reminisce, but neither of them wanted to."

"Okay," Tom said. "Tell me, how long was Meredith involved with Scotty Ragsdale?"

Joanna winced. "Oh, lord. Who'd you hear that from?"

"How much do you know about it?"

She glanced away, twisted a stray wisp of hair around one finger, crossed her legs and uncrossed them. "They were friends for a long time, that's all I know."

Tom raised his eyebrows skeptically.

"It *is* all I'm certain of," Joanna protested. "How should I know what other people do in their private lives?"

"Meredith confided in you, didn't she?"

"Not as much as you seem to think." Joanna sat forward, her expression earnest and pleading. "Look. When Scotty's sister Denise died—it was awful, the poor girl froze to death outdoors in the snow. I wasn't here when it happened, I was back home in Kentucky making plans for my wedding, but I heard all about it. Scotty was just devastated, but his parents didn't have time for him, they were too caught up in their own grief. Meredith sort of took him under her wing. She became a substitute big sister, I guess you could say."

"What did Cam think of their friendship?" Tom asked.

Joanna shrugged. "He certainly didn't see Scotty as a rival, if that's what you're getting at. Cam was sure of Meredith."

"Was Meredith sure of Cam? Were there any other women in the picture? Anybody who might have been jealous or might have a jealous husband?"

"If he ever cheated on Meredith, I never heard even a whisper about it. I know she was worried about that before they got married, and she told him she wouldn't marry him unless he took a vow to always be faithful to her. And he did. He loved her, you know. I never knew anything about Cam's background, but I got the feeling Meredith was different from any girl he'd ever known. She was refined, cultured. Sensitive. He admired that."

If Meredith's description of Cam's family was accurate, Tom could understand his attraction to a girl like Meredith. "Now, let's get back to Scotty."

"Oh, Tom, please don't ask me about that again." Joanna's voice cracked, and she hesitated, letting her gaze roam over the photos of champion horses on the walls. "He was crazy about Meredith. Anybody could see that. He would have done anything for her. And he despised Cam. Do you think the frustration got to be too much for him and he finally broke? Did Scotty kill them both?"

Chapter Seventeen

When Tom walked into Rachel's cottage a few minutes after leaving Joanna, he felt as if he were coming home. Cicero the parrot squawked his crazy cry for help and flew over to land on Tom's shoulder, Frank issued one of his rusty-hinge meows and rubbed against Tom's leg, and Rachel greeted him with a kiss.

If he could come home to Rachel every evening, Tom thought, he'd have everything he wanted out of life.

Holding her with an arm around her waist, he said, "What's up? You know, all you have to do is invite me, you don't have to lure me out here with mysterious promises."

Rachel wriggled out of his embrace. "Let's sit down and talk. After I divest you of the shoulder ornament."

"I don't mind Cicero." Tom turned his head toward the parrot and got a bite on the nose, Cicero's version of a kiss. "Ow!"

Rachel laughed. "Still don't mind him? Cicero, go back." The parrot resisted as he always did, treading on Tom's shoulder and uttering a stream of protesting squeaks. She said more firmly, "Cicero, go back." He flapped away, returning to the top of his big cage by a window.

They were settling on the couch, Frank between them, when Holly stuck her head out of the kitchen. She grinned at Tom, her mood obviously improved since the day before. "Hey, Captain. You want somethin' to eat or drink?"

"Thanks, Holly, but I can't stay long."

"Well, if you change your mind, let me know." She disappeared into the kitchen again.

"Now, finally," Tom said to Rachel. "What's this vital information you've got for me?"

She smoothed her auburn hair back behind her ears the way she often did when she was getting serious. "I went to see Lloyd Wilson this afternoon—"

"What? Why?"

"Because his dogs are my patients. One of them has asthma, and I wanted to make sure she wasn't affected by the smoke from the fire next door."

"Rachel. Come on now. If the dog was sick, wouldn't he call you? Why did you go out there?"

Instead of answering the question, she said, "Lloyd told me he heard a gunshot yesterday morning. He thought it was up on the mountain, but it could have been next door."

Tom frowned. "He didn't say anything to me about hearing gunfire."

"That's why I wanted to tell you. Was Meredith Taylor shot?"

He ignored the question. "Did Wilson say what time he heard it?"

"Between ten and ten-thirty. Tom, Ben was at home then. Holly and I were with him."

"So this is all about constructing an alibi for Ben Hern."

Indignation brought a pink flush to her cheeks. "It's about finding out the truth."

"That's what I'm trying to do. That's my job. I don't need an amateur going around questioning witnesses. You'll do more harm than good."

"Will you talk to Lloyd about it? You can't ignore this."

"Yes, I'll talk to him." Tom got to his feet. "He gets things mixed up, though. He can't keep track of time. He also has a long history of bad blood with the Taylors. He might have his own reasons to create confusion about the facts."

Rachel rose and faced him. "Well, if you think *Lloyd* killed them, Ben's in the clear, right?"

"Aw, for god's sake."

"Go back to work." Rachel waved a hand. "I won't take up any more of your time with my silly theories."

"Rachel—" But her face was a closed door. "Fine. I'll go back to work."

Tom patted Frank's head and left.

◇◇◇

"Help! Help! Save me! Save me!"

Rachel jerked upright in bed, startled awake by the parrot's cries from downstairs. The luminous face on her bedside clock read 12:10. Why was Cicero making such a racket?

She threw back the covers, swung her feet to the floor and pushed them into her slippers.

"Help! Help! Save me! Save me!"

Rachel stopped cold. Cicero cried out that way only when someone other than she and Holly came into the house.

She held her breath and listened. A moment passed in silence. Then she heard Cicero's cry again, followed by a loud crash downstairs. Frank's furry body brushed against her arm as he slid off the bed to hide underneath.

With trembling fingers Rachel found the lamp base and slid her hand upwards along cool ceramic to the switch. The sudden glare made her blink. She grabbed her cell phone from the bedside table and pressed the 911 button.

A young, high-pitched female voice answered. "Mason County 911. What is your emer—"

"Somebody's in my house!" Rachel whispered. "Somebody broke in, they're downstairs."

"Ma'am, what is your name and where are you loca—"

"The McKendrick farm. I'm Rachel Goddard. In the house at the end of the farm road. Hurry! Get somebody out here."

"Yes, ma'am. Now don't hang up."

Rachel heard the dispatcher contacting a patrol car, repeating the information. She held the phone away from her ear, trying to quiet her own harsh breath, listening for sounds from downstairs. Nothing.

"Ma'am? Are you there?"

Rachel brought the receiver back to her ear. "Yes, yes, I'm here."

"A deputy's on the way. He's close by, it'll just be a few minutes. Are you in a safe place?"

"The bedroom."

She heard footsteps downstairs.

"All right, ma'am, don't you leave that room," the dispatcher ordered, sounding like a stern child. "You lock the door and stay right where you are."

The bedroom door—it was standing open so Frank could come and go during the night. Rachel propelled herself off the bed, shut the door as quietly as she could. No lock on it. *What now?* Something to block it.

From downstairs came another crash, the sound of breaking glass.

Cicero squawked, no words, just a scream of fear.

Heavy footfalls. Somebody running through the house.

"Call Tom," Rachel gasped into the phone. "Call Captain Bridger."

"I'm calling Captain Bridger right now," the dispatcher said. "You stay on the line, you hear? Don't you hang up."

Rachel waited for an eternity, listening, hearing nothing. Was Holly awake, terrified and defenseless in the next room? *If he comes up here—*

"Somebody lives with me," Rachel whispered to the dispatcher. "I have to go warn her."

"No! No, ma'am, don't you leave—"

Rachel dropped her hand to her side, reducing the dispatcher's protests to a distant whine.

She opened the bedroom door, quietly, slowly, and came face to face with Holly.

They both yelped. Rachel grabbed Holly's arm, pulled her into the bedroom, closed the door.

"Ma'am?" the dispatcher called. "Ma'am, are you okay? What happened?"

"I heard something," Holly said, her eyes wide. "It woke me up. I smelled—"

"Shh, hush," Rachel whispered. "I called the police."

Holly shook her head. "Listen to me! I smelled gas in the hall, real strong. It's comin' from downstairs."

"Oh my god. Open the windows!"

Rachel shoved one window up while Holly pushed the other open. Warm, humid night air billowed into the room.

Cicero. The thought of her parrot blotted out everything else. Rachel hurried to the door. "The gas will kill Cicero. I have to get him—"

"No!" Holly caught Rachel's arm and held on. "You're not goin' down there! You'll get yourself killed."

"If there's gas downstairs, he—whoever —he can't be down there breathing it. And I heard somebody running a minute ago. He ran out, he's gone."

"You don't know that for sure," Holly said. "Captain Bridger'll kill me if I let you go down there."

"Listen!" Rachel heard a siren, distant but rapidly drawing closer. She pulled her arm from Holly's grasp. "I'm going downstairs."

"Just wait for the deputies."

"Cicero could be dead by then. Roll up the bedspread and block the bottom of the door to keep the gas out."

When Rachel stepped into the hall, the rotten-onion odor of natural gas filled her nostrils and brought on a wave of nausea.

She felt her way down the stairs. *He's gone,* she told herself. *It's safe. He's gone.* Her nightgown was drenched in sweat, but she felt icy cold.

At the bottom of the steps she reached around for the light switch, afraid she would see the intruder standing in front of her. She flipped the switch. The living room was empty.

At first, relief flooded through her, but the smell of gas was strong and she had no time to waste. Cicero might already be dead in his cage, under the night cover. Before she faced that possibility, she had to get air into the house.

She rushed across the room, stepping around an end table that lay on its side, avoiding the jagged shards of glass that had been a lamp, the spilled water from a flower vase, the magazines fanned out on the floor like playing cards.

Edging behind Cicero's cage, she shoved the window up. Now she had to turn off the gas.

She ran into the kitchen. All four burners on the range were turned on and unlit, pouring gas into the air. Rachel grabbed a dish towel from a rack to cover her nose and mouth. Gagging and coughing, she flipped off the burners.

She turned to open the back door and let air in. But the door already stood open a couple of inches.

Rachel backed away. The intruder could still be on the porch. She wouldn't think about that, wouldn't let it scare her upstairs to a locked room. She ran back to Cicero. Yanking off the cage cover, she found the small gray parrot lying motionless on the floor of the cage.

"Oh no. No, no, no." She unlatched the cage and lifted him out. Holding him close, she got the front door locks open and ran outside. She barely heard the siren of the police car coming down the farm road. "Breathe, sweetie, please," she begged, pacing the yard. "Please, Cicero, please don't die."

The limp body twitched and stirred in her hands. His claws groped for something to close around. She gave him one of her fingers.

Sinking to her knees, cradling the bird against her chest, Rachel burst into tears of relief.

Chapter Eighteen

From a quarter mile away on the farm road, Tom saw the flashing lights of police cars, beacons in the ink-black night. An icy fist squeezed his heart.

The 911 dispatcher had wakened him with news of a break-in in progress at Rachel's house. He'd thrown on jeans, tee shirt, and shoes without socks and hurtled along the empty mountain roads, unable to raise a radio signal and connect with the dispatcher or the Blackwood twins. He didn't know what he would find when he reached the horse farm.

A pair of Sheriff's Department cruisers sat outside Rachel's house, their light bars splashing red and blue over the three people on the front porch. The two young blond deputies, twins Keith and Kevin Blackwood, stood talking to Holly.

Tom parked and jogged to the house. "Where's Rachel? Is she all right?"

"She's upstairs makin' sure Frank's okay," Holly said as Tom mounted the steps to the porch. In her pink robe, her shoulders hunched as if she were cold on this hot night, she looked small and vulnerable.

Kevin Blackwood said, "Somebody got into the house—"

"—and turned on the gas on the kitchen range," Kevin finished.

"Somebody tried to kill us!" Holly cried. She clamped a hand over her mouth, stifling a sob.

"Hey, hey, take it easy." Tom patted her shoulder. "You're safe now."

Holly sniffed and wiped her eyes with trembling fingers. The poor kid was scared to death.

"Did you get a look at him?" Tom asked.

She shook her head. "We stayed upstairs until he left. I'm sorry."

The lack of a description would make his job harder, but he sure as hell didn't want to hear that Rachel or Holly had confronted an intruder. "Don't apologize. You did the smart thing."

"We opened all the windows," Kevin said.

"To let the gas out," Keith added.

"Good job," Tom told them. "I'll talk to Rachel before I go over the scene. Stay out here until I'm done inside."

He barreled into the house, nothing on his mind except getting to Rachel, but the mess in the living room brought him up short. He guessed that something had startled the intruder enough to make him stumble around in the dark, crashing into furniture. What had he been looking for in the living room? Maybe nothing. Maybe he'd been on his way upstairs to Rachel and Holly.

"Hey, Tommy."

At the sound of the voice, he jerked his head toward the kitchen doorway. Lindsay stood there, in jeans and a red tee shirt printed with *I'm a detective trapped in a CSI's body.*

"What the hell are you doing in here?" Tom demanded.

"I want to help."

"This is a crime scene. You've got no damned business being in here. What kind of story did you use to get past the Blackwoods?"

"What's the problem?" Lindsay looked mystified. "I can save you some time by collecting prints and trace for you. I'm perfectly well qualified to do that. I'm trying to help out here."

"What have you been doing?" Tom pushed past her into the kitchen. "What have you touched?"

"I haven't touched a thing. I'm not an idiot. I *am* a criminal evidence professional, you know. Why do I have to keep reminding you of that?"

"Then act like one, for god's sake. This is probably connected to your parents' murders. Rachel and Holly are witnesses in that case. You're the daughter of the victims. What the hell makes you think it's acceptable for you to even come in here, much less collect evidence?"

Lindsay's cheeks reddened at the rebuke. "Well, excuse me for trying to help. But I'm not leaving. If this is connected to Mom and Dad's deaths, I want to know what happened here. I want to know what evidence you come up with, and I want to be damned sure nothing is overlooked."

"You don't think the Sheriff's Department is competent to investigate a break-in?"

"I think *you* are, but I've got my doubts about those two little boys out there."

Tom clenched his hands at his sides to keep himself from shaking her. "Those two little boys, as you put it, have been trained in evidence collection procedures, and since they probably heard what you said, I think you've just made a couple of enemies. Now get out of here, and don't expect anybody to let you back in."

Lindsay spun around and marched out. She shoved open the screen door and let it bang shut behind her. Tom followed to make sure she actually left.

The Blackwood twins watched her leave, then shot nervous looks at Tom. "Sorry, Captain," Keith said.

"She showed up and said you sent her," Kevin added. "Man, I feel dumb."

"It won't happen again," Keith said.

"It sure as hell better not happen again. Keep her out of the house, her and anybody else who isn't authorized to be here." Tom noticed Lindsay's car for the first time, parked on the road outside the circle of light around the house. She was headed toward it.

"Mrs. McKendrick's upstairs with Dr. Goddard," Keith said. "She didn't touch anything or walk around downstairs. You want us to make her leave?"

"I'll handle it." Tom crossed the debris field in the living room again and took the steps two at a time.

He found Rachel sitting on her bed in robe and slippers, cradling Cicero in her arms. The parrot nuzzled her chin and neck, his small sounds of distress making Tom think of a frightened, whimpering puppy. The cat, Frank, pressed against Rachel's thigh. Joanna sat beside her.

"Here's Tom, honey," Joanna said.

Rachel didn't look up. She stared at the floor, her face drained of color, her auburn hair draped over one eye.

Tom sat beside Rachel, put an arm around her shoulders and kissed her forehead. "You okay?"

"I'm fine," she said. But her rigid body didn't yield to his embrace.

"Is Cicero all right?"

"Yes."

"Tell me what happened," Tom said, "with as much detail as you can remember."

In a monotone, sounding not at all like herself, Rachel described the events of the night. "Cicero saved our lives," she concluded.

"Yeah, he probably did." Without this scared bird, Rachel could be lying dead in her bed right now. A rush of nausea made Tom's throat close up. He wanted to hold her, feel her warm and alive against him. He tried to pull her closer.

She shrugged off his arm, which surprised Tom and hurt more than a little. Was she still angry about their stupid argument over her visit to Lloyd Wilson? Tom knew he'd been right, but he wished he'd handled it differently.

"This is connected to Cam and Meredith's murders, isn't it?" Joanna said. "The killer's trying to get rid of witnesses."

"Probably. Nothing else makes sense."

"Holly and I didn't see anything," Rachel said, her voice flat. "We don't know anything. Why would anybody come after us?"

"Rumors get around," Tom said. "Every time something's repeated, the facts get changed, and before long the whole story's a fabrication. Look, I want you and Holly out of here, at least for the rest of the night, maybe longer. You can stay at my place as long as you want to."

"No. Thank you, but no." Rachel sounded oddly formal and distant, as if he were a presumptuous acquaintance.

"You have to stay somewhere. This house is a crime scene, and we'll be here for a while."

"The crime scene is downstairs. We'll stay up here. There's no reason we have to leave."

Tom raked his fingers through his hair. How could she be so stubborn under these circumstances? "It's not safe for you to—"

"Tom," Joanna broke in. "Go do your work. Let me talk to Rachel."

He hesitated, but gave in. Maybe Joanna could get through to her. He wanted to touch Rachel, wanted to kiss her, but he held back. "I'll be downstairs if you need me."

He returned to the kitchen. Crouching at the back door, he examined the lock and the wood around it. Rachel had said the intruder left the door standing open. He'd undoubtedly left this way, probably entered this way too. But Tom saw no evidence of a break-in. No damage to the lock, no marks or chips in the wood.

He moved on to check the front door and the windows. They all stood open now to let the gas dissipate, but none of them showed any sign of being forced. Tom didn't believe Rachel would go to bed leaving a door unlocked, but it was possible a window had inadvertently been left unsecured. It was also possible that somebody had gotten hold of extra keys to the house.

He didn't want to interrupt if Joanna was persuading Rachel to leave, but Holly was available for questioning.

Out on the porch, Holly shook her head and told him, "No, sir, we don't ever leave the doors or the windows unlocked at night. Everything was closed and locked up tight before we went to bed."

"All right then." Tom rubbed the tight muscles in the back of his neck. "Your visitor either picked the lock or used a key. Does anyone besides you and Rachel have a key?"

"Nobody but me," Joanna said from the doorway. She stepped out onto the porch. "There's a key to the back door and one to the front door, and only three copies of each. My copies are in my office at the house."

"Then this had to be somebody who could pick locks."

"Both doors have deadbolts that have to be opened with keys from inside and out."

"Aw, hell," Tom muttered. "That's right." Back during the winter, when he'd been concerned for Rachel and Holly's safety, he'd checked out security at the cottage.

He looked to Holly, but she answered his question before he could ask it. "I told you, we locked the doors. With the keys."

"Then we're back where we started," Tom said. "Somebody, somehow, got a key to the back door. As soon as you get back to your place, make sure your keys to this house are still where they're supposed to be, and call and let me know."

"I will," Joanna said, "and I'll get the locks changed tomorrow, if I can find a locksmith who'll work on Sunday. Holly, honey, you go up and get what you need for the night so you can go home with me. I talked Rachel into coming too."

"Now wait a minute," Tom said. Rachel in the same house with Lindsay? "That's not a good idea."

Joanna's eyes met his. "I know what you're thinking, but it's just for the rest of the night. If it doesn't bother Rachel, it shouldn't bother you. We'll go back to my house and go straight to bed. First thing in the morning, Rachel and Holly can come home."

"I don't like it. I'm going to talk to Rachel again."

"Tom, she was very firm about not wanting to stay at your place. Don't be so bossy. Anyway, it looks like my other guest doesn't plan to go back to the house for a while. Give us time to get there and go to bed before you run her off." Joanna nodded toward the road.

Tom looked around. In the shadows, barely visible, Lindsay sat cross-legged on the hood of her car, watching Rachel's house.

Chapter Nineteen

Rachel stretched out on a strange bed in Joanna's house, but when she closed her eyes the drumbeat of panic started in her chest, building to a roar that jolted her out of bed, onto her feet, ready to flee.

But she didn't have to run. She was safe now, wasn't she? She had nothing more to fear.

Frank meowed, the sound oddly muffled. Rachel switched on the bedside lamp and saw a squirming lump under the covers she'd thrown back when she jumped out of bed. She pulled away the top sheet and light blanket. Frank blinked up at her.

"I'm sorry, love," Rachel whispered. She sat on the bed and petted him until he purred.

On the dresser, Cicero was quiet in a small cage, now draped with a towel. He hated that cage, which Rachel used only when moving him from place to place, and he hated being in unfamiliar surroundings, but he'd been unnaturally docile since coming out of his stupor. If the gas had harmed him, Rachel doubted she could reverse the effect. She had to hope he was suffering from stress that would pass once their lives returned to normal.

When would that be? Would life ever return to what it was a few days ago, before the Taylors were killed and their daughter showed up?

She shouldn't have let Joanna talk her into coming here tonight. Joanna had been persuasive and logical, assuring Rachel that she probably wouldn't cross paths with Lindsay in the house, and Rachel felt it would be childish to refuse to spend a few hours under the same roof with her. When she'd put Frank and Cicero in her SUV for the move to Joanna's house, though, the sight of Lindsay in the shadows, perched on her car's hood and watching, had sent a chill through Rachel. Lindsay hated her and wanted her out of Tom's life.

A shocking thought invaded Rachel's head: Maybe it wasn't the Taylors' killer who had tried to murder her and Holly. Maybe it was the Taylors' daughter.

Paranoid. She could never voice such a suspicion out loud. Everybody, including Tom, would think she'd lost her mind. Rachel herself had trouble believing Lindsay would go that far.

I have to get some sleep. I'm not even thinking straight. Rachel switched off the lamp, but she didn't lie down. Joanna's house was silent except for the faint hum of central air conditioning. Joanna had gone back to bed, and Holly had settled on the sofa bed in the den downstairs. Lindsay hadn't returned yet. Was she still at the cottage?

I'm wasting an opportunity, Rachel thought. She might find nothing of interest in Lindsay's room, but then again she might learn whether Lindsay had been systematically collecting information about her.

She found her slippers with her toes and shoved her feet into them. Careful not to make a sound, she opened the bedroom door and peered into the hallway. A nightlight burned at the far end, outside the bathroom, accentuating the pool of darkness surrounding Rachel. Joanna slept in the room directly across the hall. Lindsay's room was next to Rachel's.

She crept into the hallway, holding her breath in anticipation of a creaking floorboard that might give her away. *Paranoid,* she chided herself again. In the unlikely event that Joanna might spring out of bed to demand where Rachel was going, she could always claim to be on her way to the bathroom. Still, she didn't want Joanna to know she was awake and roaming around.

She expected Lindsay's door to be locked and felt a pleasant little shock of surprise when the knob turned freely. In a second she stood inside with the door closed behind her. Lamps burned beside the bed and on the dresser. The bed was made up, the puffy blue comforter still covering it. In the middle of the bed lay a closed laptop computer. Rachel went straight for it.

She figured Lindsay had a password to prevent anyone else from using her computer, but it was worth a try. Prepared to be stymied, Rachel almost laughed aloud when she opened the laptop and found a bright, active screen. Like the rest of Mason County, Joanna's house had only dial-up internet access through the cable TV company, and Lindsay's laptop wasn't plugged in at the moment. The browser history would reveal what sites she'd visited lately, though.

Rachel wasn't surprised by what she learned. Lindsay had visited several law enforcement databases she could access because of her professional position, databases that would give her more information than public records would. She had also been reading old stories from the Washington Post archives. Rachel had no way of knowing, though, exactly what Lindsay had discovered.

Frustrated, Rachel pushed the computer closed. For the first time, a legal pad beside the laptop drew her attention.

Rachel's birth date was scrawled on the pad—not the day she was actually born, but the day she'd celebrated as her birthday since she was a small child. The word MINNESOTA had been printed in block letters, with *Minneapolis? St. Paul?* scribbled under it. Below that, the names of her mother, father, and sister.

Damn her. The snooping, malicious little—Rachel caught herself, told herself that as long as Lindsay stuck to the most obvious aspects of Rachel's background, her prying wouldn't be a threat. Lindsay wasn't the type to stop there, though. She would dig deeper and deeper, in the hope of finding something juicy. Something Rachel didn't want anyone to know.

Outside, a car door slammed.

Rachel shot off the bed and out of the room, through the hallway and into her own room. Leaning against the closed door in the dark, she tried to catch her breath while her galloping heart banged against her ribs.

She heard the faint clicks of the front door opening and closing. A minute later, she heard movement in the hallway, drawing near. Then sudden quiet, and Rachel sensed—she *knew*—that Lindsay had paused outside her door, inches away. Rachel held her breath, waited. Lindsay walked on. Her door made no sound when it opened, but Rachel heard it close.

In the dark, Rachel found her bed and sank onto it. Had Lindsay already learned that no child named Rachel Goddard had been born in Minnesota on the date Rachel claimed as her birthday? What would Lindsay make of it if she discovered all the blank spaces, all the unexplained gaps, in Rachel's past?

Chapter Twenty

The rising sun hadn't yet burned the mist off the mountaintops when Tom parked in the Hogencamp driveway.

"I know you're mad as hell, and so am I, " he told Brandon, "but remember that losing control with a suspect won't get us anywhere. All that does is give *him* control of the situation. Okay?"

Brandon nodded, his mouth a tight line. Tom had phoned him at five a.m., waking him to tell him what happened to Rachel and Holly so there would be no chance of him hearing a garbled account from other sources.

Tom was stepping from the car when Dave Hogencamp flew out the front door of the house and down the steps.

"What the hell do you want now?" Hogencamp yelled. He looked like he hadn't been out of bed long, with his tee shirt hanging loose over his pants, his hair flattened on the left side from being slept on, brown and gray stubble darkening his chin.

"I want to know where you were last night," Tom said.

Brandon slammed the passenger door and watched them across the cruiser's roof.

"Where the hell do you think I was? Right where I am this morning, trying to take care of my wife. I look out the window and here you are again."

"Did you go out at all during the—"

"Dad!" Angie called from the front door. She was still in her robe, and her dark hair spilled over her shoulders. "You've got to help me! She's pulling everything out of the kitchen cabinets and dumping it all on the floor."

From somewhere in the house, Tom heard an incoherent cry that might have been a plea, might have been a scream. Angie darted inside.

"You gonna let me take care of my family," Hogencamp said, "or you gonna make me stand out here answering stupid questions?"

"We need to talk, Dave. Either here or at headquarters."

"Go to hell." Hogencamp hustled back to the house.

Tom took a step forward, then stopped. What good would it do to wade into a family crisis? "Come on," he told Brandon. "We'll catch up with him later."

In the car as they drove away, Brandon asked, "What do you think? He's got a solid motive—what Cam Taylor did to them. But why would he go after Holly and Dr. Goddard? They didn't see anything. If they could I.D. the killer, we would have arrested him by now."

"That makes sense to us," Tom said, "but the rumor's going around that they *did* see something, and the killer wouldn't want to take chances. A man in Dave's situation, with a wife who's totally dependent, might do anything to make sure he can stay with her."

"Or his daughter might do anything to protect her dad and make sure the family doesn't get split apart."

"Yeah." Her father wasn't the only man Angie wanted to protect, though. Her fierce defense of Ben Hern had betrayed feelings that went deeper than the loyalty of an employee. Was Angie capable of trying to kill Rachel and Holly to protect Hern? Tom didn't even have to consider the question. He'd learned a long time ago that most people, if they had a compelling reason, were capable of anything.

◇◇◇

Rachel rose at dawn, hoping to grab a cup of coffee and be out of Joanna's house before Lindsay woke, but by the time she dressed and washed her face she was already too late. Halfway down the stairs, she caught the aroma of fresh coffee. She found Lindsay in the kitchen, fully dressed in jeans and tee shirt, leaning against a counter and sipping from a mug.

"Hey, good morning," Lindsay said when she saw Rachel. She held up her cup. "Want some? Gotta warn you, I make it pretty strong."

"I'll get it." Rachel would have preferred to turn around and walk out, but she didn't want Lindsay to sense her apprehension. She wouldn't sit down, though. After a couple of quick gulps for the caffeine jolt, she'd make her escape. She plucked a mug from a cabinet.

Before she could reach the coffeemaker, Lindsay snatched up the pot. She poured steaming coffee into Rachel's cup. "Tom must be totally baffled," she said as she returned the pot to the hotplate.

Refusing to take the bait, Rachel sipped the coffee. Too bitter to drink. Grimacing, she set her mug on the counter

"I mean," Lindsay went on, "there was no sign of forced entry at your house. I don't suppose you've been handing out keys left and right, and I'm sure you wouldn't leave a door unlocked at night. So…what other explanation could there be?" Her blue eyes widened in disingenuous inquiry.

Rachel stared at Lindsay. *Good god, she's accusing me of making the whole thing up.* She wasn't going to defend herself to Lindsay or stand here debating theories. "I have things to do," she said, and turned to leave.

Joanna appeared in the doorway, yawning. "Oh, my lord," she groaned, "I'm getting too old to stay up half the night. I need caffeine, delivered by IV if possible. Rachel, honey, are you okay? Did you get any sleep?"

"Yes. I'm fine. I was just on my way out."

"Here you go," Lindsay said, handing Joanna a mug of coffee. "Sit down and I'll make breakfast for us."

"Thanks," Joanna said. She told Rachel, "I'll get a locksmith out to the cottage this morning. You tell him what it'll take to make you feel safe. I don't want you to settle for less, okay?"

Rachel smiled and gave Joanna an impulsive hug. "Thank you. And thanks for taking us in."

As Rachel walked down the hall toward the stairs, the door to the den opened and Holly stuck her head out. "Come here a minute," she whispered.

Rachel slipped into the room and Holly closed the door after her. "What's going on?" Rachel asked.

Holly kept her voice low. "I can't *stand* her. I've gotta get away from her. Can we go home now?"

"Absolutely. Let's get our things and go right now."

They moved their few belongings, along with Cicero and Frank, into Rachel's vehicle. Rachel heard Lindsay talking in the kitchen when she quietly pulled the front door shut for the last time.

On the drive to the cottage, Holly burst out, "I'm startin' to think Joanna's not a good judge of people like I thought she was. That woman—Lindsay—She's just—She's…she's *mean.*"

Rachel couldn't help smiling at Holly's limited store of derogatory descriptors. "Let's hope we won't see much more of her."

"I've seen enough already."

"Has she done something I don't know about?" Rachel glanced at Holly to find her face screwed up as if she were about to cry.

Holly's cheeks puffed out when she expelled a noisy breath. "I wasn't gonna say anything to anybody."

"About what?" Rachel braked to let one of Joanna's farmhands drive a pickup truck loaded with hay from the barn to the stable and paddocks across the road. The driver lifted a hand in greeting and Rachel answered with a wave. She prodded Holly, "Tell me what happened."

"I got up real early, and I thought I'd get some cereal."

"And?" Rachel drove on toward the cottage beyond the stable.

"I opened the door to go in the kitchen and there was Lindsay, comin' out of Joanna's office. She was closin' the door real quiet, and she didn't see me at first. Then she turned around and saw me and she got this look on her face, like she just wanted to hit me or somethin'. She talked real low so nobody else could hear her, but she was practically spittin' in my face. She said I was spyin' on her, and if she ever caught me at it again she'd make me sorry. But I wasn't spyin'. I was just goin' to get some cornflakes, and I couldn't help seein' her. And the really weird thing is, she told me I'd better not be gossipin' about her, tellin' people I saw her. I didn't ask her what she was doin' in Joanna's office because she probably would've bit my head off, but her tellin' me to keep quiet about it sure made me curious, you know?"

"I would have been curious too," Rachel said. "Heck, I'm curious *now.*"

Joanna didn't like anyone entering her business office without an invitation. Rachel had always assumed Joanna kept the door locked when she wasn't in the room, but apparently she didn't. What reason did Lindsay have to go in there?

Chapter Twenty-one

"Something tells me we're about to get another warm reception." Tom pulled into Lloyd Wilson's yard.

Like Dave Hogencamp, the old man had seen Tom and Brandon drive up. Flanked by his two big mutts, Wilson hobbled toward them as fast as his arthritic limbs and his cane allowed.

"Dogs look friendly, at least," Brandon said, reaching for the door handle.

"The devil himself could walk into the yard and those two would be drooling all over him, begging to be petted." Tom stepped out and raised a hand in greeting. "Hey, Lloyd. I need to—"

"You're just the man I want to see," Wilson broke in. He sounded excited about something, far from hostile. "I was gonna give you a call this mornin'."

"Oh?" The dogs presented themselves, one on each side of Tom, tails wagging and tongues lolling. He used both hands to pat their heads. "What about?"

"I got it straight in my mind now, what was goin' on over there—" Wilson jerked his head in the direction of the Taylor property on the far side of the woods. "—that mornin' before the fire got started."

While the dogs turned their attention to Brandon, Tom leaned against the cruiser and studied Wilson for any sign that he was mounting a diversion. How he could have gained entry to Rachel's house was a big question, but Tom could easily see him losing his balance and stumbling around the living room in the dark. "Is that right? What's your story now?"

Wilson bristled at that, squaring his hunched shoulders. "It ain't a *story*. It's what happened."

"I'm more interested in where you were last night," Tom said.

"Last night?" Wilson looked baffled. "I was right here at home. Why?"

"Did you have any visitors? Can anybody back you up?"

"Back me up? What are you gettin' at? What happened last night?"

"Somebody tried to kill Rachel Goddard."

"Oh my lord." Wilson's face went pale and he started to sink.

"Hey, watch out!" Brandon yelped. He and Tom grabbed Wilson by the arms to keep him upright.

Clutching his cane, Wilson looked from Tom to Brandon. "Is she all right? Why would anybody want to hurt that sweet young woman?"

"She's fine," Tom said. "We're not sure of the reason, but somebody tried it, there's no doubt about that."

"That's wicked. That's just wicked." Wilson fumbled in a pocket and pulled out a handkerchief that looked as if he'd used it to clean garden tools. Unashamed, he mopped at his teary eyes and wiped his nose.

"What did you want to tell me?" Tom asked.

Stuffing the cloth back in his pocket, Wilson drew a deep breath, steadied himself, and said, "They was both over there at the same time."

"Who? What are you talking about?"

Wilson looked up at Tom. "Scotty Ragsdale's car and that sports car. They was both over there at the Taylor house at the same time, the mornin' Miz Taylor died. And it was around that same time I heard a gunshot."

Tom and Brandon debated all the way to Ragsdale's house, but neither of them could stick to a single side of the argument.

"We have to take Lloyd seriously," Tom said, "because he's the only witness we've got who can put both Ragsdale's car and a Jaguar at the Taylor house that day. On the other hand, he's about as unreliable as they come. We still can't be sure he's right about the time, and the time would tell us whether the Jaguar was Hern's or his mother's."

"Wilson's not even sure it was black or dark blue," Brandon said. "Does it mean anything if one of them was over there the same time as Ragsdale? Can you see Ben Hern or Karen Hernandez teaming up with Ragsdale to kill the Taylors?"

"It's not likely," Tom said, "but even Lloyd's not claiming they *left* at the same time. Ah, hell, this isn't the first story he's come up with. He might tell us something different tomorrow."

"Yeah." Brandon heaved a sigh and fell silent.

"One thing we can believe is that he heard the shot that killed Meredith," Tom said. "When we get a match on the slugs from both her and Cam, we'll know for sure we're not dealing with some weird coincidence."

Scotty Ragsdale didn't answer a knock on his door, but Tom heard the whine of a power tool coming from the back yard. He and Brandon walked around to the shed behind the house. The wide door stood open. Inside, Ragsdale bent over a small chest, his eyes protected by goggles, his gloved hands guiding a power sander across the top of the chest. When he caught sight of Tom and Brandon, he switched off the sander, pushed the goggles to his forehead, and watched the deputies warily as they entered the shed.

"Morning," Tom said. He gave the chest an appraising look. It had been stripped down to bare wood, and curls of apple green paint littered the floor around it. "That's a nice little piece. You refinishing it for somebody?"

"Restoring it," Ragsdale said, his voice flat, his eyes cold with distrust. "Some idiot slapped green paint on it."

Tom nodded. He'd heard that Ragsdale did good work. "How are you holding up? You took Meredith's death pretty hard."

"I'm doing all right."

"Glad to hear it," Tom said. "It's not easy losing a good friend."

Brandon strolled around the shed, checking out the tools, chemicals, and paints on the shelves. Like a rabbit surrounded by foxes, Ragsdale tried to keep an eye on both deputies. Brandon ended up behind Ragsdale, and he nodded to let Tom know he was ready in case the man gave them any trouble. Ragsdale glanced over his shoulder but seemed reluctant to turn his back on Tom.

"What do you want?" Ragsdale asked. "I don't have anything else to tell you."

"You remember Karen Richardson, don't you?"

Ragsdale opened his mouth, closed it, licked his lips. "Who?"

"Come on, Scotty, you know who I mean. She was a VISTA, same time Cam and Meredith were."

Ragsdale rolled his tongue around in his mouth, swallowed, shrugged. "So? What are you asking me about her for?"

"Her name's Karen Hernandez now," Tom said. "She was here visiting her son last week."

Ragsdale didn't respond, and Tom let the silence draw out. A line of sweat popped out on Ragsdale's upper lip, and he wiped it on the sleeve of his tee shirt. "So what? That supposed to mean something to me?"

"How well did you know her back then?"

"I—" Ragsdale paused, yanked off his gloves, bunched them both in one hand. "I didn't really know Karen at all. Just to say hello to."

"She wasn't a friend of your sister like Meredith was?"

"No. They didn't get a—" Ragsdale stopped abruptly and clamped his mouth shut.

"Your sister and Karen didn't get along?" Tom asked. "Why was that?"

"I don't know. Girls. Who the hell understands what goes on between girls?"

Tom smiled. "Yeah, I know what you mean. Did Meredith get along with Karen?"

Ragsdale rubbed the palm of his free hand on his pants leg. "I don't know what you're getting at."

"Were they friends? Meredith and Karen?"

"Yeah, I guess. Sure, why wouldn't they be?"

"Well, then," Tom said, nodding, "if they were old friends, I guess Karen stopped by to see Meredith when she was in the county."

Ragsdale's gaze jumped from one spot to another, landing everywhere except on Tom. He threw a glance over his shoulder at Brandon, who stood behind him with arms crossed. "I don't have any way of knowing who she went to see."

"It's kind of puzzling you'd say that, since you were at Meredith's house when Karen stopped by."

Ragsdale's eyes widened. "What?"

"Your car was seen at the Taylor house at the same time as Karen Hernandez's Jaguar. The morning Meredith died."

"Says who? Who have you been talking to?"

"Anybody driving by would have noticed it," Tom said. "A Jaguar stands out around here. What went on that morning? What did Meredith and Karen have to say to each other after all this time?"

"I don't know anything about it. I wasn't there."

"Your car was there."

"No." Ragsdale shook his head. "No, it wasn't."

"We have a witness, Scotty."

"I don't give a damn what you've got." He might have been aiming for bravado, but his voice wavered like a guilty child's.

"And we have a witness who saw you driving near the McKendrick farm last night," Tom lied, "around the time somebody broke into Rachel Goddard's house and tried to kill her and Holly Turner."

Ragsdale's breath was coming fast and rough now. He backed away from Tom and collided with Brandon. With a startled cry, he stumbled forward again, banged a knee on the chest. "God damn it!" he cried, hopping on one leg and grasping his knee.

"What's going on, Scotty?" Tom asked. "What's your part in this?"

Ragsdale straightened, sweat dripping from his hairline. "I'm not saying another word to you without a lawyer."

"Scotty—"

"You can't ask me any more questions until I get a lawyer. You hear me? I'm done." He still looked scared, but resistance had taken hold in his eyes and voice. "You might as well leave."

Tom hesitated, but he knew when he had to quit. "You'd better go ahead and hire a lawyer soon," he told Ragsdale. "You're going to need one."

As they drove away, Brandon said, "He sure acts guilty."

"But guilty of what?" Tom said. "Did he fire the shots, did he light the fire? I believe he's capable of it, especially if he wanted Meredith to himself and couldn't get her away from Cam.'"

"If I can't have her, nobody can? That kind of thing?"

"Yeah. Maybe what we're seeing now is remorse, and panic over the way things are snowballing."

"What about Hern and his mother?" Brandon asked.

Tom thought about it. "I wonder if Karen Hernandez showing up here could have somehow triggered the Taylor murders. But why, and how it all fits together—I can't see that yet. And I can't even guess whether Karen Hernandez is alive or dead."

By the time they returned to headquarters, a small swarm of journalists occupied a corner of the rear parking lot. They surged forward when they saw Tom pull in.

"Wow," Brandon said, craning his neck to watch the reporters and camera operators trailing the car. "CNN. MSNBC. I wonder if Campbell Brown's here. My mom's a big fan of hers."

Tom parked as close as possible to the back door of the squat cinderblock building, hoping to get inside before he was waylaid, but a dozen journalists surrounded the car before he'd yanked the key from the ignition.

"You gonna make a statement?" Brandon asked. "This is big news, a famous senator's daughter getting murdered. Mom says they've been talking about it on all the cable news stations. Mysterious circumstances and everything."

Tom didn't answer. Putting on what he hoped was a forbidding expression, he shoved his door open, nearly knocking a slick-haired male reporter off his feet. He slammed the door shut behind him and held up both hands to quiet the explosion of questions. "We'll have a statement later in the day."

And exactly what am I going to tell them? he asked himself as he elbowed his way toward the sanctuary of the building. *That this is the third day since the Taylors died and I'm not one damned bit closer to an arrest? That the killer's still around and now he's after Rachel and Holly?*

When Tom and Brandon walked into the squad room, Dennis Murray waved Tom over to his desk.

"Tell me you've found Karen Hernandez," Tom said.

Dennis cupped a palm over the telephone receiver. "Sorry, no luck with that. But somebody from the NYPD's on the line. He's got something for us on Hern."

"Transfer the call to my office."

The cop on the line, Jim O'Neal, turned out to be a booking sergeant at a Manhattan precinct, with an accent Tom had never heard outside of TV and movies. "This guy you're looking at, you know he uses two names?" O'Neal asked.

"Yeah, I know." Tom sat forward, pulling a pad and pen closer. "Benicio Hernandez and Ben Hern."

"Yeah, Hernandez is still his legal name, I hear. Never changed it. I didn't know he was the guy in the funny papers till after it was all over."

Tom heard a squeak like a swivel chair that needed oil. He pictured O'Neal as a grizzled veteran in middle age, spending most of his working day in a chair while he waited to retire.

"Until what was over?" Tom asked.

"We never got all the details because nobody brought charges. Once Hernandez got his lawyer involved, the girl's daddy decided not to put his little darling through the ordeal of making a case. In other words, Hernandez paid him off."

"Whoa," Tom said. He grabbed the pen, poised it above the pad. "What girl? What kind of charges could have been brought?"

"She was a minor. Fifteen, sixteen, I forget which. Her father was threatening to charge Hernandez with statutory rape."

Chapter Twenty-two

Rachel swiped a cloth over the coffee table one last time and turned to survey the living room. "Are we finished?" she asked Holly.

"Yep, we got it all." Holly sat at the bottom of the stairs, holding a filthy cleaning rag. "But it's not right we had to do this. The cops ought to clean up after themselves."

"They're men, Holly. They probably think they did clean up." Although all the surfaces had been wiped down, a layer of black fingerprint powder had remained on everything.

"*Men,*" Holly said.

Rachel collected Holly's cleaning rag and dumped it along with her own in the kitchen trash can. The house looked clean, the living room furniture was back in place, and Frank and Cicero had calmed down as if nothing had happened. The locksmith had installed new locks on both the front and back doors and all the downstairs windows, theoretically rendering the house invulnerable. But the cottage felt like foreign territory to Rachel now, a haven invaded by evil, and she wondered if anything could make her feel safe here again.

She tried to shake off the sense of foreboding. She wanted to change into clean clothes and get outdoors in the sunshine for a while.

Upstairs in her bedroom, Rachel opened the closet and reached for a clean pair of jeans. They weren't on the hook where she'd hung them. Thinking they'd fallen to the floor, she looked down. Not there either. Then denim fabric dangling from the overhead shelf caught her eye. Rachel pulled down the jeans. They'd been wadded up and stuffed onto the shelf.

What the heck?

Frowning, Rachel examined the other clothes in her closet. She always kept them sorted, hanging all the shirts together, all the slacks together, her few dresses and skirts at one end. Now everything was jumbled.

Someone had been in her bedroom while she was gone.

She took a step backward, her fingers crushing the rough fabric of the jeans, and turned in a circle to examine the room. Nothing out of place, nothing missing. She crossed to the dresser and yanked out drawers, examined her small inventory of bracelets and necklaces, found them all there. The condition of her underwear drawer made her pause. She always kept her panties and bras neatly folded, and she couldn't say they looked messy now, but they didn't look quite right, either. Ever so slightly disarranged. Or was she just imagining things? She stood there for a moment, arguing with herself about what to believe, then pushed the drawer shut. She wasn't imagining the confusion in her closet.

Tom must have searched the room, although he'd told her the police wouldn't do anything upstairs. Who else would have come in here?

Lindsay. Now Rachel knew what Lindsay was doing in Joanna's office—returning the keys to the cottage. Joanna had checked when she and Rachel and Holly arrived at the house the night before, and the keys had been where they were supposed to be. Lindsay could have taken them early this morning and gone into the cottage after the police left. Rachel didn't believe Lindsay would go so far as attempted murder, but if she'd seen a chance to snoop she would have grabbed it. Rachel herself had done the same thing when she entered Lindsay's room. But she was trying to protect herself. Lindsay was gathering ammunition.

Rachel pulled her cell phone from her shirt pocket and placed her thumb on the rapid dial button she used for Tom's cell phone number. But she didn't press it. What would she tell him? That Lindsay had come into her bedroom and rearranged her clothes? That sounded crazy.

Rachel sat on the bed, still clutching the jeans. She had no proof that Lindsay had been in this room. Perhaps no one had been here. Maybe she'd disarranged her clothes when she was hastily dressing and gathering things to take with her to Joanna's house.

No. Whether she could prove it or not, someone had searched her bedroom.

Chapter Twenty-three

Sheriff Willingham swung Tom's office door open. "Hern's here, in the conference room." He closed the door behind him. "And his New York lawyer's with him, some pretty young woman. I'm sure she's a lot tougher than she looks."

Tom stood. "She got him here. She must want him to look like he's cooperating."

"Let's talk about this a minute before you go in there," Willingham said. "I know this fellow's an old friend of Dr. Goddard's. If that makes you inclined to go easy on him—"

"It doesn't. He's a murder suspect. I'll treat him like one."

Willingham nodded. "I'll hold you to that. You got any kind of strategy for getting information out of him while his lawyer's sitting right there? He's going to take his cue from her before he answers every question."

"From what I can tell," Tom said, "Hern's pride is a weak spot. He might blow up and let something slip if he thinks I'm ridiculing him, not treating him with respect."

"All right then, try to goad him into losing his temper. Do whatever you have to do. We need some answers, Tom, and we need them soon."

The lawyer who rose when Tom entered the room was indeed young and pretty, a Chinese-American woman with a slender figure and black hair that fell straight and shining to her shoulders. She was no neophyte, though. She met Tom's gaze with the kind of resolve and calm self-confidence he was used to seeing in seasoned lawyers with a long string of victories behind them.

She held out a hand but didn't smile. "Captain Bridger? I'm Jessie Wang. I represent Mr. Hern, and I'm licensed to practice in Virginia as well as New York and several other states."

"Good to meet you." Tom appreciated her firm handshake. Everything about her was understated, professional, from the lightly applied makeup to the trim gray silk suit and black pumps. He wondered if this was the same lawyer who'd handled the payoff to the outraged father in New York.

Tom shifted his gaze to Hern, who slumped in a chair with his arms folded across his chest. "Thanks for coming in."

"My pleasure," Hern said, with heavy sarcasm. He wore a crisp white shirt, the sleeves rolled up over his muscular forearms. "Have you found my mother yet? Do you even care what's happened to her?"

"We're still looking for her."

His attorney placed a hand on Hern's shoulder, a brief touch but enough to make him straighten in his chair and wipe the scowl off his face.

Taking her seat beside Hern, Jessie Wang told Tom, "My client had nothing to do with the deaths of Cameron and Meredith Taylor. He's prepared to cooperate fully in your investigation and do anything he can to help you find their killer."

"I'm glad to hear that." Tom sat across from them and switched on the tape recorder that sat on the table. He recited the date and time and named the people present. Clasping his hands on the tabletop, he looked across at Hern. "Where were you last night a little after midnight?"

Frowning, Hern shot a puzzled look at his lawyer before he replied. "Last night? Why?"

"Just answer the question."

"I was in bed asleep. Why are you asking me about last night?"

"Were you alone?"

This time the lawyer answered. "Yes, Captain, he was alone in his bedroom. I was in the house and awake at that time. I would have heard if he'd left the property."

Tom let it go for now. "Tell me what happened Friday morning, from the time Cameron Taylor showed up at your house until you saw him for the last time."

Hern stared at the whirring tape recorder while he spoke, never looking at Tom. The story he told about Taylor's visit to his house matched Rachel's, Holly's, and Angie's reports in every detail. No openings there for a challenge. When he reached the part about escorting Taylor off the property, Hern halted.

"Go on," Tom said. "What happened on the road?"

Hern glanced at his lawyer. She nodded as if he'd asked her a question.

"I was following him," Hern said, "to make sure he didn't turn around and come back. A couple miles from the house, he stopped his car in the middle of the road and got out."

"Did you stop too?"

"Yes."

"Did you get out?"

"Yes."

Tom waited, but Hern didn't go on. "Why did Taylor stop?"

Hern shifted in his seat. His hands curled into fists on the table, and the muscles in his arms stood out like thick ropes under the skin. "To tell me to go to hell. To start the whole argument up again."

"Why didn't you tell me on Friday that the two of you had another encounter after he left your house?" Tom said. "Why did I have to find that out from a witness?"

Hern stayed silent, his jaw working. Tom could hear his teeth grinding.

"The witness," Tom said, "heard Taylor say he knew a secret that could ruin you if it got out."

"Taylor liked to throw accusations around."

"Oh? I thought he might have been talking about that problem you had in New York."

Hern's eyes met Tom's. He opened his mouth to speak, but Wang touched his arm and he stayed silent.

"Mr. Hern does not have a criminal record, Captain," the lawyer said. "In New York or anywhere else."

Tom addressed his answer to Hern. "If it was on the record, Cam Taylor couldn't have blackmailed you with it. What I heard was that you paid off the girl's father so he wouldn't have you charged with raping his daughter."

Hern jumped to his feet so fast that his chair rocked and fell over behind him, landing on the floor with a clunk. "I'm not sitting still for this crap."

Tom slammed an open hand on the table. "*Sit down.* Remember where you are and who you're talking to."

"Ben," the lawyer said, catching his arm. She spoke quietly, and Tom noted that she seemed neither surprised nor alarmed by her client's behavior. "Sit down, please. Tell Captain Bridger what actually happened."

Hern, his face flushed, glared at Tom while Tom looked back calmly. The silence stretched out for half a minute. Then Hern reached for the chair, yanked it upright, and sat again. "You don't have the whole story."

"I'd like to hear your side of it."

"I never raped anybody. I was painting her."

Tom tried for a slightly incredulous tone when he asked, "You were painting her nude, right? Even though she was a minor?"

"I didn't know she was a minor, and it didn't start out as a nude portrait. One day she just…It was her idea, not mine. The whole thing was her idea. She approached me."

"How did she approach you?"

"She lived with her parents in the same building I lived in. Her father's an executive on Wall Street. The girl started bumping into me in the lobby and the elevator, too often for it to be accidental. She wanted me to paint her. I know a lot of college students, male and female, who make extra money by modeling for art classes, but in this case she wanted to commission a portrait. She couldn't have paid my fee, but she had an interesting face, so I agreed to paint her for a cut rate."

"You thought she was a college student?"

"Yes," Hern said. "She told me she was nineteen, and she looked it. She said she was a sophomore at Columbia." Hern shook his head. "If you saw this girl—I believed she was nineteen."

"How long did the two of you get together for these modeling sessions?"

Hern threw a pleading look at his lawyer, but she nodded. He gave a heavy sigh and said, "A little less than three weeks."

"Then her father found out."

Hern didn't answer. A muscle twitched in his cheek.

"He came after you, and you broke his nose."

"I was defending myself," Hern said. "He invaded my home and attacked me."

"How much did it cost you to make it all go away?"

"Captain Bridger," Jessie Wang said before Hern could answer, "there's something you need to know. Mr. Hern is being treated—"

"No!" Hern broke in. "Don't tell him a damned thing."

"Ben," she said, her voice low and even, "I understand why you don't want to disclose something so personal, but I think it's vital that you give the police this information."

"Oh, for god's sake." Hern twisted in his chair, ran a hand over his face. "It's my business, nobody else's."

Tom waited. What were they talking about? Hern seemed torn, more embarrassed than angry. Obviously the incident with the girl wasn't the only secret Hern was determined to keep hidden.

"I strongly recommend that you tell him," the lawyer said.

"Tell me what?" Tom asked.

Hern's tongue swiped his lips. After a minute of silence, the words gushed out of him. "I'm bipolar and I was off my medication when that happened. The medication fucks up my painting and I hate the way it makes me feel. So I stopped taking it, and I went into a bad manic state—I was working around the clock, I wasn't sleeping, I couldn't slow down. I was literally not in control of myself. That's the condition I was in when all that stuff with the girl happened."

Tom sat back, digesting this in the silence that followed Hern's outburst. He didn't know a lot about bipolar disorder, but he knew it could vary from moderate mood swings to outright psychotic states. Was that what Hern wanted to hide—a serious mental illness? Or did he want to cover up a criminal act committed while he was out of control? Tom sat forward again. "Her father didn't believe it was innocent."

"She told her friends we were sleeping together. She was just trying to impress them, but kids talk, they text and e-mail and post rumors on Facebook, and pretty soon their parents hear about it. So one day I opened my door and her father shoved his way in and socked me in the face. He jumped on me, he was yelling he was going to kill me, and I defended myself." Hern paused, threw Tom a challenging glare. "You'd do the same damned thing if somebody attacked you. Any man would."

"You paid him to forget the whole episode, right?"

Jessie Wang answered before Hern could. "The fact that the man was willing to forget it in exchange for money, and sign an agreement not to disclose the incident publicly, should tell you there was nothing to it."

"Come on, Ms. Wang, I think we both know human nature a little better than that."

"In any case, my client went back on his medication after that incident, and he's been taking it faithfully since then. He also goes to New York once a month to see his doctor."

"But he still can't control his temper," Tom said, "if his behavior toward Cam Taylor the other day is any indication."

"I believe I'm allowed to feel normal anger," Hern said. "Taylor was making a damned nuisance of himself. I had a right to be ticked off."

"Was he threatening to make the incident with the girl and her father public?"

Hern nodded, looking miserable, ashamed. He didn't meet Tom's eyes. "Look, I do children's books. My strip's in newspapers all over the country. I'm on the board of the most respected humane organization in the country. If any of that got out—" He broke off, shaking his head. "The rumors are damaging enough. I don't want it in print."

"How did Taylor hear about it?"

"He told me his wife had relatives in New York City, cousins, an aunt she was close to. That girl's family moves in the same circles as Meredith Taylor's family, and there was some gossip going around—quietly, because nobody wanted to offend the girl's father. I didn't think it would follow me to a place like Mason County. But Cam Taylor said his wife visited her aunt when the woman was sick, and the aunt knew about the connection between my mother and the Taylors, so she filled Mrs. Taylor in on what she'd heard about me. By the time I moved to Mason County, Taylor already knew the story. He must have thought he hit the jackpot when I showed up here."

"Small world," Tom said. "So you had to silence Cam to protect your career."

"No! That's not what I'm saying. I didn't kill him. I didn't kill his wife. I thought—" Hern pinched the bridge of his nose with thumb and forefinger as if he had a headache. "I was hoping Taylor would give up after a while. My mother wanted to intervene, make him drop it, but I told her not to get involved, he'd drop it when he found out I wouldn't give in to his threats. The funny thing is that I ended up deciding she was right. After Taylor and I had that argument, I decided to go ahead and give him the money. But then it was too late."

"How could your mother stop him?" Tom asked. "If Cam was mad at you for refusing to give him money, why would he listen to your mother?"

Hern rubbed a hand over his mouth and chin. "My mother's spent her entire professional career negotiating with idiots, and she's pretty good at getting them to see things her way. I guess she thought she could persuade him."

"A witness saw a dark-colored Jaguar at the Taylor house Friday morning. Your mother must have decided to try her powers of persuasion after all."

The information jolted Hern into sitting bolt upright, his eyes wide. "No. No, she didn't go over there. It couldn't have been her car."

"Was it yours?"

"No! I've never been to the Taylors' house, that day or any other."

"Ben," the lawyer said, laying a hand on his arm.

This time he shook off her touch, refusing to be calmed. "I don't want my mother dragged into this. She has nothing to do with it."

"Did she have any kind of grudge against the Taylors?" Tom asked. "Something that started when they were young?"

"No, for god's sake. My mother is a realist and a pragmatist. She doesn't hold grudges, not even for four weeks, much less four decades. Now I've said all I'm going to say. I'm leaving."

Tom didn't try to stop him when he rose, stalked to the door, and pulled it open. "Jessie?" Hern said. "Let's go."

The lawyer glanced from Hern to Tom and back again. She picked up her big black leather satchel from the floor and swung it onto her shoulder. She plucked a card from an outer pocket of the bag and handed it to Tom. "If you have further questions for my client, please contact me on my cell phone."

"I'm sure I will have further questions."

Hern was already out the door, his heavy footsteps echoing up the hall. His lawyer hurried after him.

Tom fingered the business card as he stood in the conference room doorway, watching them go. How much of what he'd just heard could he believe, and how much was pure bullshit? And why was the subject of his mother enough to send Hern running for the door?

Chapter Twenty-four

Rachel scrambled over the rail fence, a length of rope in one hand, and dropped into the paddock fifteen feet from the snorting billy goat. The animal stamped a hoof and lowered his head, swinging his long, curved horns back and forth. On the far side of the paddock, four young horses bunched together against the fence and whinnied in alarm.

The goat lunged at Rachel.

She heard Holly's strangled little scream from outside the paddock.

Rachel jumped out of the goat's path at the same moment she tossed a loop of rope over his head. He reared, kicking at the rope, and Rachel stumbled and fought to stay on her feet. Digging in her heels, she shouted, "Somebody get in here and help me!"

She took her eyes off the goat long enough to see two young farmhands swing over the fence, both holding lassoes. The goat bolted toward them and one of the men leapt back onto the fence.

"Don't you dare!" Joanna yelled at him. She shoved him off the fence and into the paddock. "I'm ashamed of you. Rope him like a horse!"

The goat swiveled back toward Rachel. Lowering his head, he charged. The farmhands, one on each side, tossed their lassoes around his neck and held on. Caught at the center of a tight triangle, the goat stamped and snarled.

"Just hold your ground—" Rachel gasped a breath. "—let him calm down." Sweat trickled into her eyes, blurring her vision, but she didn't dare take a hand off the rope to wipe it away. The stink of urine and hormones rising off the goat made her gag.

Waiting out the animal's fury, Rachel glanced toward the fence. Holly stood with both hands clamped over her mouth. Joanna had climbed to the top rail, ready to get into the paddock and help if needed. Lindsay looked on, hands stuck in her jeans pockets, face expressionless. And Tom had appeared out of nowhere and stood next to Lindsay.

For a second Tom's eyes connected with Rachel's, he gave her an encouraging grin, and she burst out laughing at the absurdity of the situation. The panting goat tugged at the ropes.

After a few minutes of fighting the restraints, the billy was tired enough to be cooperative. Rachel and the two farmhands led him out of the horse paddock past the four terrified mares. His hooves clacked on the pavement as he trotted down the road to the paddock where Joanna had temporarily installed Meredith Taylor's orphaned herd of five nannies and the billy. Holly had stayed behind to calm the horses, but Joanna, Tom, and Lindsay brought up the rear of the procession.

When the billy returned to his harem, the females rushed to greet him, sniffing his malodorous body and licking his face.

No accounting for a woman's taste in men, Rachel thought. She swung the gate shut.

"A fence like this is not going to hold him," she told Joanna. "He'll be jumping it every day and terrorizing your horses."

Joanna threw up her hands and looked to Lindsay. "They're yours now. What do you plan to do with them?"

"Oh…" Lindsay's shoulders rose and fell in an indifferent shrug. She cocked her head and grinned at Tom. "You want them? You could let them run loose with your sheep. And you'd get some milk out of the deal. I can teach you how to make goat cheese."

Tom shook his head. "I'm not interested in keeping goats."

"Come on, Tommy," Lindsay coaxed. "My mom loved her goats. I'd feel better if I knew they had a good home. Won't you at least think about it?"

"You'll have to find somewhere else for them." Tom's voice had a flatness that, in Rachel's experience, always meant the subject was permanently closed. He turned his back on Lindsay and asked Rachel, "Can you spare a minute, or do you have something else exciting on your schedule?"

"Sure." She had a few things to say to him too.

"Let's walk." Tom gestured toward the field beyond the paddock.

At the same time, Joanna took Lindsay by the arm and said, "Let's go over to the stable and check on that pregnant mare of mine."

Walking into the field, Rachel wiped sweat from her eyes with the back of her hand. "I'm a mess. I think I've even picked up his odor."

Tom grinned and pulled a clean white handkerchief from his pants pocket. "Has anybody told you how cute you are when you're herding goats?"

"Not lately," she said, laughing. She took the handkerchief he offered. "I haven't wrangled livestock since my clinical training with farm animals in vet college."

They strolled through cornflowers and Queen Anne's lace while Rachel blotted perspiration from her face. The shade of a pecan tree up ahead looked inviting.

"Did the locksmith come out and change your locks?" Tom asked.

In an instant the terror of the previous night flooded back, and an involuntary shudder moved through Rachel. "Yes, this morning. Has the report come back on the fingerprints?"

"Yeah, but it didn't give us anything useful. All the prints belong to you and Holly. I'm assuming the intruder wore gloves."

Rachel expected Tom to once more raise the question of whether she'd given out keys to the house, or to suggest that a door had been left open, but he did neither. Instead, he went on,

"I talked to that mob of reporters outside headquarters and told them as clearly as I could that you and Holly didn't see anything Friday and you can't help us identify the killer. I've told everybody in the department to spread the word locally, but I don't know if it'll get through to the one person who needs to hear it. He probably won't believe it anyway. As long as he thinks you might know something, you're going to be in danger."

"Believe me, I'm well aware of that. I won't be able to relax until you've made an arrest." Rachel drew a shaky breath. "At least he can't get into the house again."

"I don't feel good about the two of you staying there at night. Daytime, with other people around, that's one thing, but a bunch of new locks won't keep you safe at night if somebody's determined to get in." Tom placed an arm around her shoulders. "I want to know that you're somewhere safe. Come stay with me. Please."

Rachel stepped away, forcing him to remove his arm. She wished she could sink back into the affectionate relationship with Tom that she loved, but she'd begun to feel as if Lindsay were standing between them all the time. "Holly talked to Brandon early this morning," she said, "and he's going to sleep in our living room every night until—Well, as long as necessary."

Tom nodded. "All right. There might be times when I need him on duty in the evening, but I'll make sure he gets to your place before bedtime."

Reaching the shade of the pecan tree, Rachel halted and faced him. "Do you think this will drag out a long time?"

"I hope not, but…" His grim expression offered no reassurance.

"By the way," Rachel asked, "were you looking for something in my bedroom last night?"

Tom frowned, puzzled. "What do you mean?"

"The room was searched, so I assume you were looking for something. Did you find it?"

"We didn't search your bedroom. You said the intruder never went upstairs."

"I'm pretty sure somebody searched it, between the time I left and the time I went back this morning."

"No, you're mistaken about that. None of us went upstairs after you left. Well, except to use the bathroom, I guess."

Had she imagined it all—the disorder in her closet, the jeans that weren't where she'd left them, the subtle signs that her underwear drawer had been searched? For the last few hours she'd debated the question with herself, but she kept coming back to the same certainty. "No, I'm not mistaken. Somebody went through my closet and my dresser drawers."

This wasn't her Tom she was talking to. This was a blank-faced cop who betrayed no hint of his reaction to what Rachel was saying. "Do you think something was stolen? Do you want to file a complaint against one of my people?"

"No, of course not," Rachel said. "Nothing's missing, as far as I can tell. I can't imagine either of the Blackwood twins going through my underwear."

"You think it was me?"

"I—No. If you say you didn't, of course I believe you, but—" She knew this might backfire on her, but she blundered on anyway. "Joanna says there aren't any other keys except the ones she keeps in her office, so I have to wonder who has easy access to her office."

"If nothing was stolen, I'm not sure what you want me to do."

Stung by his indifference, Rachel said, "I guess there's nothing you can do." Wanting to get away from him before he challenged her again, she turned to leave.

"Wait a minute."

Rachel looked back at him.

"I don't want to believe this," Tom said, "but I'm beginning to wonder if you've been hiding things from me."

Rachel went cold through and through. What had Lindsay told him? What had she found out? "Hiding things?" Her voice sounded weak. "I don't know what you're talking about."

"Ben Hern's legal problem in New York. Did you know about it?"

Relief that he wasn't talking about her own past almost overwhelmed her concern for Ben. "He lost his temper," she said with a shrug. "He got into a fight with some guy and bloodied his nose. So what?"

"Why didn't you tell me?"

The disappointment in his eyes shamed her. She wanted to say something that would erase that look, but she was not going to apologize for protecting Ben. "Is it really important? How many men do you know who have done something like that?"

Tom didn't answer, but his face tightened as if he were struggling to hold his temper in check. He wouldn't take anything she said seriously. Rachel felt herself retreating into that closed-off space where she was invulnerable to anyone's emotional demands.

"I was afraid you would use it against him," she said, hearing her voice go cool and even. "I can see I was right."

She walked away before he could answer.

Chapter Twenty-five

Watching Rachel go, Tom wondered whether she knew the whole story about Ben Hern and the girl in New York. If she did, and she'd chosen to withhold the information from Tom, he would feel doubly betrayed. Not only had she given her trust and friendship to a man who didn't deserve it, but at the same time she didn't believe Tom was capable of doing his job professionally and impartially.

Her maddeningly indirect tale of her bedroom being searched was more proof that she didn't respect or trust Tom. Why hadn't she come right out and accused Lindsay of snooping, instead of dancing around the idea? Because she thought Tom wouldn't treat it seriously? Or because it wasn't true? Ordinarily, Tom took everything Rachel said at face value, believed her without hesitation, but now he was starting to doubt her judgment and her honesty.

He strode off toward the stable in search of Joanna. He found her in a double stall, brushing the mane of a heavily pregnant chestnut mare while Lindsay looked on. Fresh straw on the floor gave off a sweet, clean fragrance.

When Joanna saw Tom, she paused with brush in hand. "Is everything okay?"

"Lindsay, will you step outside?" Tom said. "I want to talk to Joanna alone."

"Wow," Lindsay said, "somebody's in a bad mood."

That's all I need, more crap from you. "Will you step outside?"

She gave him a tight little smile. "Sure. I'll get out of your way."

She pushed open the stall door and walked out of the stable.

Tom, watching Lindsay cross the road toward the barn, considered the possibility that she had gone into Rachel's house early that morning after the crime scene was processed and everybody left. He knew she wouldn't hesitate to do it if she believed she had reason. But she had no reason that Tom could see—except a jealous desire to find out more about the woman who had replaced her in Tom's life.

Joanna broke into his thoughts. "Bad mood doesn't quite cover it. You look ready to throttle somebody."

"Sorry." The stable was hot even with a ventilation fan stirring the air, and Tom reached in his pocket for his handkerchief so he could mop the sweat off his forehead. Then he remembered Rachel had the handkerchief. "Your set of keys to Rachel's new locks—Be sure you put them where nobody can get to them, okay?"

"I'm way ahead of you. They're already in my safe."

"How many people know the combination?"

"My lawyer and me, nobody else." Joanna resumed brushing, pulling the bristles through the horse's mane with enough force to make the animal snort and stamp. "Easy, girl, easy," she crooned, stroking the mare's head.

"Look," Tom said, "I need to follow up on a few things with you. I want to know everything you can remember about Cam and Meredith's relationship with Karen Hernandez."

Joanna had gone still, watching him with apprehensive eyes. "I thought you were focusing on Scotty Ragsdale. You can't possibly think Karen had something to do with the murders. That's laughable, Tom."

Tom saw a ripple of tension move down the horse's back in response to Joanna's sharp tone. "Let me decide that," he said.

"But why on earth would she…?"

"That's what I'm trying to find out," Tom said, forcing himself to be patient. "Will you tell me what I need to know?"

Joanna released a long sigh. "All right. Can I get my work done while we talk? There's a mess in the tack room that's been there since the kids' riding class yesterday afternoon." When Tom agreed, she gave the horse's flank a light tap. "Go on, Marcella. Finish your dinner."

The mare shuffled over to a bin attached to a wall and dipped her head into it. When she started chewing, Tom caught the aroma of fresh oats.

He and Joanna walked down the wide center corridor past empty stalls and into the tack room. A pile of orange tabby kittens, sleeping on a blanket in a corner, didn't stir when they came in.

"I can't believe the mess they leave things in after riding class," Joanna said, crossing to a wooden table that held a jumble of halters and bridles.

Tom, leaning against the table, prompted, "Karen Hernandez and the Taylors?"

"I don't know what you want to hear. It's been forty years, for heaven's sake. How could these murders be related to anything that happened that long ago? People don't hold grudges that long."

"What kind of grudge would Karen have against the Taylors?"

"I didn't say she had a grudge! I just meant that even if she did, how could it possibly lead to murder?"

"You told me Karen tried to take Cam away from Meredith. I want to hear more about that."

Joanna's shoulders slumped and her hands stilled, fingers enmeshed in the leather straps of the halters. "Meredith loved Cam from the first second she laid eyes on him. And I believe he loved her. Karen...like I told you before, she was bored. The VISTAs were outsiders, we weren't supposed to get personally involved with any of the local people. That's why I quit early. The CAP director found out I was seeing Dave McKendrick and he gave me an ultimatum, stay away from Dave or leave VISTA. I told Dave and he said to hell with it, quit now and let's get married."

Tom steered her back to the subject. "You were talking about Karen and the Taylors."

Joanna worked on the tangled straps and buckles of two halters but didn't seem to be having any success in separating them. "I've already told you everything I know. Karen was just having fun."

"Did she ever sleep with Cam?" Tom said.

Giving up on the halters, Joanna tossed them back onto the table. "No, I'm pretty sure she didn't. She just about drove Meredith crazy, though, while she was trying."

Tom picked up the halters she hadn't been able to separate and started working on them. "Meredith got what she wanted—she married Cam."

"Yes, of course she did. So what's the point in digging up all that old stuff? It has no bearing on the present."

Tom handed her the two halters, now separated, and she hung them on pegs. "Do you know if Karen and the Taylors had any contact at all over the years between then and now?"

"I'm positive they didn't. And I'm sure Karen never gave another thought to Cam after she left here. She went back to Georgetown for her second year of law school, then she married Jorge Hernandez. He was a young Cuban doctor, an immigrant from a rich family, and I swear, he was the best-looking thing. I went to their wedding. It didn't last, but Karen was crazy about him when she married him. Cam never meant anything to her."

"Did she talk to you about the Taylors while she was here visiting her son last week?"

Joanna shrugged. "Just briefly."

"Did she seem to be having any problems with them? Current problems, I mean. Any disagreements?"

"What? No. Well, she did say Cam had asked her for money. But she laughed that off. I don't think it particularly bothered her. Why would it?"

Joanna apparently didn't know about the blackmail attempt. Tom didn't want to press her further and end up revealing what could have been Karen Hernandez's motive for murdering the Taylors.

He found Lindsay outside on a bench, directly under the open tack room window.

"Aw, Christ," Tom said. He could kick himself for not realizing she would find a way to listen in on his conversation with Joanna. "How long have you been sitting here?"

"A couple of minutes." Lindsay looked up and gave him a wry grin. "I didn't learn anything new."

Tom sat on the bench beside her. "Tell me something," he said. "Did you go to Rachel's house early this morning?"

She shifted to face him, her blue eyes placid. "No. Why would I?"

"Rachel thinks somebody went into the cottage when she wasn't there and searched her bedroom."

"Tommy," Lindsay said, outrage bringing a blush of pink to her cheeks, "is she claiming I was in her house? Is she accusing me of stealing something?"

Lindsay's face was a perfect picture of wronged innocence, but Tom knew how easy it was for her to assume that expression. "No," he said, "nothing's missing. She hasn't accused you of anything."

"But she somehow managed to make you suspicious enough that you're sitting here asking me about it."

"It's not as if you aren't capable of it."

"Tommy!"

"Look, I'm not going to argue with you. Just remember that I'm watching you."

The eruption of anger and self-defense he expected didn't come. Lindsay was silent a moment, eyes downcast. Then she touched his knee for a second, quickly withdrew her hand, and said, "I want to ask you something, and please don't get angry at me."

Oh god. Now what? Tom looked at her, waiting.

"How well do you know Rachel? How much do you really know about her?"

"I'm not going to discuss Rachel with you." He rose to leave.

"Tommy, wait a minute," Lindsay said. "Please."

Against his better judgment, he paused.

"You may not want to hear this," she said, "but I have an obligation to give you my professional opinion. I don't believe there was an intruder in that house last night. I think somebody who lives there left the gas on and the back door open."

Chapter Twenty-six

"It's like Karen Hernandez just vanished," Dennis Murray told Tom back at headquarters. Seated in front of Tom's desk, Dennis pulled off his wire-rimmed glasses, held them up to the light, and used a handkerchief to clean the lenses. "No sightings of her car, nobody at her apartment—I got the DC cops to send somebody over there and check—and her cell phone hasn't been used since Friday afternoon."

"Afternoon?" Tom asked. "That was after both the Taylors were killed. Who did she call?"

"That's the most interesting part of all this," Dennis said. "She called the Taylors' number at home. She was about forty-five miles northeast of here at the time. The call didn't go through, of course. By then the house and everything in it was burned to the ground."

"Hunh." Tom swiveled his chair to face the windows. The sun hung low in the sky, and the billowing clouds glowed pink and gold. "If she really did make the call, she could have been setting up an alibi for herself. If somebody killed her, he might have been trying to throw us off by making it look like she was still alive."

"Her secretary hasn't heard from her. But there's an important meeting on her schedule for Monday morning. We'll see if she shows up. Meanwhile, we've got the bulletin out on her car."

Tom nodded. Waiting patiently wasn't one of his talents, but they were doing all they could to find Karen Hernandez. He swiveled to face Dennis again. "Why don't you go home? Spend some time with your kids before the weekend's over."

After Dennis left, Tom walked down the hall to the evidence room and removed Meredith Taylor's manuscript CD from the safe. Now that Tom knew Cam had been blackmailing Ben Hern, he saw Hern as a stronger suspect than ever, but the danger to her son also gave Karen a solid motive. Whatever her outward reaction had been, Tom didn't believe for a second that a mother who loved her child would laugh off a threat to ruin his career and an attempt to extort money from him.

Joanna's description of the youthful rivalry between Meredith and Karen made him wonder if Meredith had included it in her book. Although decades had passed with no contact, the past might shed some light on the way Karen and the Taylors interacted when they'd met again.

Back in his office, with the CD file open on his computer screen, he clicked to chapter two. Not much of interest there, just descriptions of the way Mason County's poor lived and a scene where the VISTAs talked about plans and priorities and plotted to work around the restrictions imposed on them by local politicians and the directors of the Community Action Program itself. The character named Chad came across as Joanna had described the young Cam Taylor: energetic, enthusiastic, full of ideas, a natural leader. Magnetic. At that point, the narrator—Meredith, Tom assumed—thought everything was perfect between her and Chad. The chapter ended with an overwritten love scene that made sex on a lumpy mattress sound like a romp in paradise. *I fell asleep in his arms,* Meredith had written, *knowing that I could face anything, endure any hardship, with Chad at my side.*

Tom kept going, skimming over the narrator's homesickness, her guilt about secretly receiving money from her mother and aunt when the VISTAs were supposed to live on their small government stipends and experience poverty as the "target group" did.

"Target group?" Tom muttered. He was astonished by the vanity of these young, naive outsiders who thought they were fit to tell grown men and women how to live.

He quickly spotted the character who represented Joanna. Another character, a local girl called Donna who became involved in plans for the outdoor play about the Melungeons, might be Denise Ragsdale, Scotty's doomed older sister.

Having never met the other VISTAs, Tom wasn't sure at first which character was supposed to be Karen Hernandez—Karen Richardson back then. By chapter four, though, Meredith mentioned that the girl named Celia had taken a break between her first and second years of law school to spend a year in VISTA. Celia, tall, pretty, and dark-haired, was the only budding lawyer mentioned, so Tom tagged her as Karen. A little farther into the book, he came upon a scene in which the four VISTAs ate dinner at the home of a Community Action Program employee. After the meal, they talked into the night and danced to the rock music that the local radio station never played.

Wondering where Chad had gone, I walked into the kitchen. The sight that greeted me made me feel as if I was dropping into a deep, dark pit. Celia was leaning against the refrigerator door with her arms wrapped around Chad's neck. He had his hands under her skirt, cupping her buttocks and pulling her against him. I could see their tongues moving in and out of each other's mouths as they kissed.

I must have made some sound, because Chad looked around at me. I was so shocked that I ran out the back door, wanting nothing more than to get in my car and drive until I was far away from there.

Chad ran after me and caught up with me before I could get into the car. "Hey," he said. He wrapped his arms around me from behind. "Slow down, let me explain."

He tried to make me turn around, but I couldn't face him. At the same time, I couldn't break away from him. I felt like a prisoner in his arms, and so ashamed of my weakness.

"Celia doesn't mean anything to me," he whispered in my ear. "You're the only one I love."

"Then why—" I felt like I was choking. I couldn't stop myself from crying, and I was humiliated to let him see me like that. "Why were you—"

"She came on to me," he said, "and I had a moment of weakness. Forgive me? Please?"

He went on that way, sounding so contrite that he wore down my resistance in no more than a few minutes. I wanted to believe him. I wanted to be convinced it would never happen again.

We went back to my house together, and Chad made love to me slowly and sweetly, and I tried to cleanse my mind of the scene I had come upon earlier.

Tom closed the file and removed the CD from the computer. He would read more later, but right now he didn't have the stomach for it. The manuscript might be disguised as fiction, but it felt real, and reading the account of Meredith's youthful humiliation at the hands of the man she later married felt like voyeurism.

Did any of this relate to the murders, or was he just wasting time reading it? The big question was whether Karen Hernandez, a respected attorney with everything to lose, would commit double murder because her son was being blackmailed. Most people were capable of impulsive acts of violence if they were pushed hard enough. Maybe she hadn't gone to the Taylor house with murder in mind, but Tom could see how an argument might have escalated out of control. But how could she have found Cam and killed him? Ben Hern was the only one who had known exactly where Cam was.

Caught up in his thoughts, Tom took the CD back to the evidence room and locked it in the safe.

The incident at Rachel's house the night before raised a whole new set of questions. It made sense to assume that the person who had tried to kill Rachel and Holly was the same one who murdered the Taylors and that he was trying to eliminate witnesses. Lindsay, though, wanted Tom to believe Rachel had staged the entire thing.

Recognizing that Lindsay was motivated by jealousy, he should probably discount everything she said. And yet—Tom had examined the doors and windows at Rachel's house himself, and he hadn't seen the slightest sign of a break-in. If he hadn't known Rachel personally, all his instincts as a cop would have made him suspect immediately that the incident was staged.

How well did he really know Rachel? She didn't like to talk about her family, especially her dead parents, so he'd learned next to nothing about her background. She had a maddening habit of withdrawing emotionally, the way she had after the break-in and today when they were arguing. Every relationship had trouble spots, but Rachel's silence about her past was a lot bigger than a bump in the road. Why, though, would she fake something like an attempt to kill her and Holly? Purely to draw suspicion away from Ben Hern?

Tom didn't know. He couldn't be certain what Rachel was thinking and feeling and he couldn't predict what she would do.

Lindsay, on the other hand, was a known quantity. He could see her stealing a key from Joanna's office and poking around in Rachel's house. It was the kind of thing she might do out of jealousy. But she would never own up to it.

This petty squabbling between the two women was a distraction he didn't need. Until he uncovered the whole truth, the only safe assumption was that the person who murdered the Taylors had also tried to kill Rachel and Holly. The killer was still nearby and posed an imminent danger to anyone in his way.

Chapter Twenty-seven

"Dr. Goddard?" A young woman with a bright red smile rose from a chair in the animal hospital's waiting area and rushed toward Rachel.

Behind her, a man wielded a professional video camera with a cable news network's logo.

Rachel groaned inwardly. It was barely eight o'clock on Monday morning and she and Holly had just walked through the door, ready to begin the work day. The sight of a reporter coming at her made her want to turn around and walk right back out again.

"May I have a minute of your time?" the reporter asked.

Rachel had seen her on TV, and it felt weird to see her in the flesh, dressed in a stylish pants suit, with her dark hair falling to her shoulders in sculpted waves. Rachel couldn't help staring at the woman's vividly painted lips and unnaturally white teeth.

She gave Holly a hand signal to move on, out of the reporter's range. "I don't have any information to give you about the Taylors," she told the woman. "I didn't see or hear anything."

The reporter's smile died like a light being switched off, replaced in an instant by an expression of deep sympathy. "This must be a difficult experience, losing both Mr. and Mrs. Taylor in such horrifying circumstances."

Was the camera running? Rachel couldn't be sure, but the lens was aimed at her, so she assumed it was recording. "I'm sure it's a terrible time for their family and friends," she said, "and my sympathy goes out to them, but I barely knew either of them. Now if you'll excuse me, I have to get to work."

Rachel walked away, but the reporter and camera man stayed with her. "You found Mr. Taylor's body in the woods, didn't you?"

Rachel stopped and looked at the reporter. "Where did you hear that?"

"From many different sources. Although Captain Bridger discounted it, most local people believe you're a key witness in the case. Some say that you might be able to identify the killer. I've also heard that you had a break-in at your house Saturday night, and it might be connect—"

"It's not true," Rachel said. "I didn't see the killer. I can't identify him. Now I'd appreciate it if the two of you left the building."

She strode past the main desk, where Shannon, the young receptionist, stood transfixed by the sight of the celebrity journalist. Inside her office, Rachel closed the door and leaned against it.

Why were people spreading that story? Didn't they realize they were endangering both her and Holly? Was that what they wanted—more violence?

Now she had to worry about what the reporter would say on the air. The truth didn't matter, denials counted for nothing. If a newscaster said on national television that Rachel might have seen the killer, everybody would believe it.

She pulled on her white lab coat, determined to concentrate on work and put everything else out of her mind. She and Holly were safe here, and tonight they would be secure at home, with all the doors and windows bolted and Brandon bedding down on the couch as he had the night before. They were going to be all right, and Tom would find and arrest the Taylors' killer soon.

Rachel and the two other vets on duty had back-to-back appointments all morning, and she quickly immersed herself in the work she loved. She was at the front desk saying goodbye to an exuberant collie pup and his owner when Shannon told her she had a personal call.

"Take a message," Rachel said. "I'll call back at lunchtime."

"She's kind of insisting." Shannon made an apologetic face. "She says to tell you it's Janet Shaw."

The name startled Rachel. Janet was the business manager at the animal hospital where she used to work. Why would she be calling?

"I'll take it." Rachel hurried into her office and grabbed the receiver of her desk phone. "Janet? Hi. How are you?"

"Fine, thanks, but I just had a weird phone call about you."

"What? Who was it?"

"Some woman who wanted information about you. She said she was with the Virginia Crime Lab and it had to do with a murder investigation."

For a second Rachel was too stunned to respond. Lindsay. Who else could it have been? The woman had gone off the deep end. "Did she give you her name?"

"Johnson. Ann Johnson."

"Yeah, right," Rachel muttered. To Janet she said, "That's not her real name and she had no right to call you. What did you tell her?"

"I didn't tell her a damned thing. But get this—she *threatened* me. Said I'd be in a lot of trouble if I withheld information. I told her if anybody wanted to ask me questions they'd have to show up in person and produce a subpoena."

"Thank you," Rachel said.

"Can I ask you what's going on? Does this have something to do with that politician's daughter who was murdered down there?"

"It's a long story," Rachel said. "But, really, the woman who called you was just snooping. Nobody's investigating me. If she calls again, please don't talk to her, and please let me know about it. Okay?"

"Sure." Janet paused. "This sounds pretty wacky, Rachel."

Rachel sighed. *You ought to try it from my vantage point.* "Don't worry about it. I'm sorry you were bothered, but thanks for calling. Take care."

Rachel hung up, buffeted by a storm of anger and frustration. This was too much. This went beyond simple jealousy and curiosity. If Lindsay discovered certain key pieces of information about Rachel's background and refused to stay quiet, she could bring a world of hurt to people Rachel wanted to protect. She had to find a way to stop Lindsay.

Chapter Twenty-eight

Tom knew something was wrong as soon as he saw Lloyd Wilson's two dogs. Instead of trotting over to greet Tom and Brandon when the cruiser pulled into the driveway, the dogs huddled together against the front door of Wilson's house. No sign of the old man, but his truck sat in the driveway.

Uneasy, but not sure why, Tom got out and stood looking at the dogs. The shrill song of cicadas in the nearby woods rose and fell, rose and fell.

Tom had come out here to get Wilson and take him back to headquarters to give a written statement about the cars he'd seen at the Taylor house the morning of the murders, as well as his many sightings of Scotty Ragsdale's car in the past. He hadn't called in advance because Wilson was contrary enough to disappear if he decided he didn't want to get any further involved. Tom had brought Brandon along in case he needed any help in overcoming Wilson's objections.

Brandon asked quietly, "Something feel off to you?"

"Yeah." Tom unsnapped his holster, drew his pistol. "Go around back. I'll try the front door."

Tom advanced slowly. Brandon trotted around the side of the house.

The dogs started whining when Tom approached. As he mounted the steps, they scrambled to their feet, nails scraping the planks. They pressed against each other, their eyes on Tom, their tails tucked between their legs.

"Hey, girls," Tom whispered. "What's wrong? You know me. It's okay."

They erupted into sharp, loud barks.

"Hush," Tom said. "Hush now. Quiet down."

The dogs went on barking, not at Tom but at the door. When one threw back her head and began to howl, the other joined in.

Jesus Christ. Anybody in the house was already aware that visitors had arrived. He had to act fast.

He wrenched open the screen door, grabbed the knob of the main door. Unlocked. He threw the door open, raised his pistol in a two-handed grip and stepped inside. Across the living room, a man appeared in the kitchen doorway, gun raised and aimed at Tom. Jolted, his heart thudding, Tom tightened his finger on the trigger. A split-second later he realized it was Brandon looking back at him.

Tom pulled in a deep steadying breath. At the same moment, something on the floor to his right caught his eye. "Aw, Christ," he groaned. The crumpled body of Lloyd Wilson lay wedged between couch and table. "God damn it all."

Wilson was face-down, one arm under his body, the other spread into a pool of blood beneath the table. Crouching, Tom felt the old man's neck for a pulse, then looked up at Brandon and shook his head. Wilson hadn't been dead long. The body had barely begun to cool, and the spilled blood still had the sheen of liquid.

The dogs howled at the screen door. Tom rose and closed the main door. He tried his cell phone, couldn't get a signal, and went to the kitchen to use Wilson's telephone to summon Dr. Lauter and Dennis Murray.

The dogs bayed nonstop from the porch. When he finished his call, Tom checked their bowls in a corner of the kitchen and found a smear of canned food in the bottom of each. He touched a finger to it. It felt fresh and moist.

"The dogs were fed sometime in the last couple of hours," Tom said. He grabbed a dish towel from a counter and wiped his finger clean. "Lloyd was shot after they finished eating. Damn it, I wish I'd gotten his statement down on paper two days ago, even if I had doubts about it. Now all we have are my notes on what he told me."

Tom retrieved his crime scene kit from the trunk of the cruiser, but he didn't want to do anything inside the house until Gretchen Lauter had seen the body. He and Brandon settled on the steps to wait. The two dogs pushed against them, whining.

"What are we going to do about his animals?" Brandon asked. He scratched and patted one of the dogs. "We can't just leave them here."

"Lloyd's sister lives down the road." Tom gave his attention to the other dog. "I think they got them from her when they were puppies. She'll probably be willing to take them. The chickens too."

"Somebody's sure trying hard to get rid of all the witnesses," Brandon said.

"The fact that Lloyd saw the cars at the Taylor house Friday morning points us toward two people—three, actually, since we're not sure whether he saw Hern's car or his mother's. I told Dennis to have somebody pick up Ben Hern and take him back to headquarters for questioning. After we get things underway here, you and I are going to take these dogs over to Lloyd's sister and break the news to her. Then we'll pick up Scotty Ragsdale and take him in for a talk."

"What about Hern's mother?"

"We'll keep looking for her," Tom said. "She's either in this mess up to her eyeballs or she's lying dead somewhere."

Chapter Twenty-nine

Under the merciless summer sun, Scotty Ragsdale was chopping firewood. Tom and Brandon rounded the side of the house and stood watching as Ragsdale raised an ax and brought it down on a thick circle of tree trunk. The wood didn't split. The ax blade lodged deep inside it.

"Goddammit, goddammit, goddammit," Ragsdale muttered. He yanked on the ax handle, worked it back and forth. When it broke free, Ragsdale staggered backward. Sweat poured down his face, and his soaked tee shirt clung to his body as if he'd just climbed out of a pool. He wobbled on his feet when he approached the chunk of wood again.

"Oh, man," Brandon whispered. "He's flying."

Removing his sunglasses and tucking them into the pocket of his uniform shirt, Tom answered quietly, "Yeah, he's high on something. If it's meth, he might do almost anything. Be careful. Don't let him get anywhere near your gun."

What had driven Scotty back to drugs after he'd been clean for years? Grief for Meredith? Or guilt over killing her?

Ragsdale heard their footsteps and spun around, eyes wide. His dilated pupils had reduced his irises to narrow rings of brown. "What're you doing, sneaking up on me?" he demanded. "Huh? Spying on me."

Tom raised both hands, palms out. "We need you to come with us to headquarters so we can ask you a few questions. Just calm down—"

"*Calm down?*" Ragsdale raised the ax to shoulder height and advanced on them. "You tell me to calm down, when—when—" He seemed to lose the train of thought. He shook his head hard as if to clear it. Finally he sputtered, "*You* calm down. I'm not going anywhere."

"All right," Tom said, keeping his voice quiet and even. "We can talk here. Wouldn't you like to go in the house and cool off, have something cold to drink?"

"Cold. Yeah." Ragsdale nodded. "Winter coming on. Gotta get my logs cut." He turned back to the chopping block.

"Scotty," Tom said, "look at me. Listen to me. I need to ask you about Lloyd Wilson. Did you see Lloyd this morning?"

Ragsdale whirled to face Tom, brandishing the ax. "Don't you say that name to me. I don't want to hear that name. You understand me?"

"Take it easy, Scotty. We need to talk about this."

"Talk, talk, talk, that's all it's ever been." Ragsdale's eyes lost focus, as if he'd turned his attention to some inward vision. "I should've known it would never happen."

"What, Scotty?" Tom asked. "What wouldn't happen?"

"San Francisco."

"San Francisco? What do you mean?" Tom watched the ax come down, inch by inch, as if pulled by its own weight. Brandon had edged away and was slowly coming up behind Ragsdale. "What was going to happen in San Francisco?"

"Nothing," Ragsdale spat out, his face contorted with disgust. "I should've known. It was just a—a dream. Fantasy."

Brandon was close enough to grab Ragsdale if the man went for Tom with the ax.

"Were you and Meredith planning to go to San Francisco together?" Tom asked. "Was that your dream?"

Tears filled Ragsdale's eyes and overflowed, mixing with sweat on his cheeks and dripping off his chin. "Dreams never come true. Not for losers like us."

"Scotty—"

"I see you sneaking up on me!" Ragsdale spun around and swung the ax at Brandon. Brandon jumped back and the blade missed him by a couple of inches.

Tom tackled Ragsdale from behind. He looped his own arms around Ragsdale's elbows and jerked the man's arms back hard, hoping pain would make him let go of the ax. It didn't work. Ragsdale twisted left and right, trying to shake Tom off. Tom held on and rode with it. The ax swung from Ragsdale's hand, back and forth, the cutting edge grazing Tom's pants leg.

With a roar of fury, Ragsdale bent over and bucked like a horse, trying to pitch Tom to the ground. He lost his balance and collapsed with Tom still on his back.

Ragsdale pushed and squirmed under Tom's weight. Holding him down with a knee in his back, Tom forced Ragsdale's arms straight out to the sides in the dirt. One hand still gripped the ax.

"You son of a bitch, get off me!" Ragsdale shouted.

Panting, Tom ordered Brandon, "Grab the damned thing. I can't hold him for long."

Brandon slammed his boot heel down on the hand that held the ax. Ragsdale screamed and released his grip. Brandon snatched the ax and flung it onto the back porch of the house, far out of reach.

Robbed of his weapon, Ragsdale seemed to find fresh energy in rage. He pushed and rolled, and before Tom could regain control Ragsdale's fist flew up and smashed into his face. Tom felt a shock of pain and blood spurted from his nose. "Damn it, Scotty," he gasped, "now you're making me mad."

Brandon caught one arm, Tom the other, and they pinned Ragsdale face down in the dirt again. Tom sat on his back, jerked his hands together and cuffed them. Blood poured unchecked from Tom's nose onto Ragsdale's hands and back, soaking into his shirt. "You're under arrest," Tom said, "for assaulting a police officer."

After Tom finished reading him his rights, they hauled him up. Before he was even steady on his own feet Ragsdale started kicking at their ankles and legs. His foot connected with Tom's shin and Tom stumbled backward, his leg threatening to fold under him. He righted himself and he and Brandon pushed Ragsdale forward, around the house toward the cruiser out front.

"I've got rights!" Ragsdale ranted. "You can't do this!"

Tom couldn't breathe through his nose, and blood ran into his open mouth with every gulp of air. A pulsing pain made him want to shut his eyes against the sun. His damned nose was broken, he'd bet on it. Blood streaked and spotted the front of his brown uniform.

"You okay?" Brandon asked as they approached the car.

"Yeah," Tom grunted. He spat blood into the dirt.

"You need to—"

Ragsdale swung his head sideways and butted Brandon's chin. Brandon staggered and Ragsdale almost slipped free of his grip, but Tom still had a firm hold on Ragsdale's other arm. After the surprise of the blow, Brandon recovered and the two of them maneuvered Ragsdale to the car.

Even with his hands cuffed behind him, getting Ragsdale into the back seat felt like trying to cram an octopus into a bucket. He kicked, nipped at their hands, spat in their faces.

"You'll pay for this!" Ragsdale yelled when they finally shoved him in the car.

"Aw, shut up," Tom said, and slammed the door.

Chapter Thirty

A couple of hours later, Tom sat at his desk with an ice pack pressed to his nose. His left eye had turned a lurid blend of red and purple, but the ER doctor had stopped most of the bleeding from his nostrils. Tom had changed into a shirt and jeans he kept in his locker at headquarters, and the sheriff's secretary had taken the soiled uniform down the block to the cleaners.

Dennis Murray rapped on the open office door and walked in. Peering at Tom's face, he said, "You sure you don't need a splint on that nose?"

"It's cracked across the bridge, but it's not displaced. The doctor said there's no point in a splint. What have you got for me?"

Dennis took a seat in front of the desk. "Lloyd Wilson's body's on its way to Roanoke. I didn't find any casings at the scene. And this just came in."

Dennis handed Tom a fax. Lowering the ice pack, Tom read the autopsy report on Cameron Taylor. Two slugs removed from his heart muscle had been fired by a .22 pistol.

"They took a slug out of Meredith's brain," Dennis said. "Both the Taylors were killed with the same gun. They'll have Meredith's complete autopsy report sometime tomorrow."

Tom dropped the stapled sheets on his desk and returned the ice pack to his aching nose. "I'll be surprised if Lloyd wasn't killed with the same gun."

"Right. By the way, while you were gone I checked on Mrs. Barker, made sure nobody's bothered her. She went on quite a bit about the evil she senses floating around Mason County, but she's not getting any vibrations, or whatever she gets, about the killer coming after her."

"Oh, well, that's a load off my mind," Tom said. "But I hope you reminded her to keep her doors locked at night."

"Yep. I also heard this morning that some people out in Rocky Branch District are calling a citizens' meeting at the school for tomorrow night. A lot of those people have been involved with the Taylors since they came here with the poverty program, and Cam was a crusading hero to them."

"I guess they think we should have solved the murders by now," Tom said. "Having a meeting won't hurry things along."

"What I heard was that people are sure Ben Hern killed the Taylors, and we're tiptoeing around him because he's rich and famous."

"Aw, for god's sake," Tom said. "If I had one piece of solid evidence against him, he'd be locked up."

"The sheriff expects you to go to the meeting and calm everybody down."

"Great," Tom said. "After everybody finds out there's been another murder, they'll be ready to lynch me."

Dennis grinned. "Hey, I'll go along as your bodyguard if you want me to." Turning serious again, he went on, "I checked on Dave Hogencamp's whereabouts, and he's been at work since around five this morning, according to his supervisor. Out of the county, in fact, moving some coal cars. His daughter's the one without an alibi. She didn't go to work at Hern's place today, says her aunt had a doctor's appointment and couldn't stay with Mrs. Hogencamp, so Angie had to stay home."

"And her mother's not much of a witness to back her up."

"What now?" Dennis asked. "Hern's been waiting in the conference room for a while, and he's getting pretty cranky. I had to talk him out of leaving."

"His lawyer still with him?"

"No. She went back to New York because of another case. He said she's coming back later in the week, though."

"I'll talk to him now." Tom dropped the ice pack on the desk and pushed to his feet, setting off an explosion of pain in his head. He stood still for a minute to let it die down a little before he walked to the conference room.

Hern was on his feet, pacing. "It's about time," he burst out when Tom entered. "I've been stuck in this room for hours. I don't have to put up with this. I'm trying to cooperate, but I can walk out anytime—" He broke off, taking in the sight of Tom's face. "What the hell happened to you?"

"Walked into a door," Tom said. "Sit down."

Hern yanked out a chair, dropped into it, and folded his arms across his chest. "I don't suppose you have any news for me about my mother."

Tom took a seat across from him. "No. I gather you haven't been in touch with her since I talked to you yesterday."

Hern's mask of hostility slipped, revealing his underlying anxiety. He sat forward, fists clenched on the table. "I haven't heard from her and I can't find her. She's not at home, and she didn't go to her office today. My mother blowing off an important meeting—" He shook his head. "It doesn't happen."

"Wherever she is," Tom said, "she's well hidden."

"She's not hiding, damn it, she's *missing.* I know something's happened to her." Hern scrubbed his hands over his face. "Aw, hell, what's the point? At least you're looking for her, and that's all I care about."

"Are you sure she didn't go to the Taylor house Friday morning?""

"Yes, I'm sure. How many times do I have to say it? And I wasn't there either. Your witness made a mistake."

"What have you been doing since I saw you yesterday?" Tom asked.

"I went home. I ate dinner with my lawyer. I worked all evening. This morning I had breakfast with Jessie at seven. She left right afterward. She had to get back to New York because she's due in court tomorrow and has to prepare. After she left, I worked until one of your men showed up and told me it was *urgent* that I come in to headquarters. I've been sitting here wasting time ever since."

"Did you see or talk to anybody between the time your lawyer left and the deputy arrived at your house?"

"I talked to Angie on the phone around eight. Why are you asking me about this morning? Has something happened? Can't you be straight with me for a change?"

"There's been another murder," Tom said.

Hern groaned. "Who?"

"Lloyd Wilson, the Taylors' closest neighbor."

"Captain, I wouldn't have known the man if I'd passed him on the street. Why in god's name would I kill him?"

"He was the witness who saw a Jaguar at the Taylor house Friday," Tom said. "So there's no one who can verify your whereabouts this morning?"

Hern swore and shook his head. Then he stood. "If you're not arresting me, I'm leaving."

Tom didn't try to stop him. "Keep yourself available. And let me know if you hear from your mother."

When he was gone, Tom considered his options.

If Karen Hernandez was another victim, why had the killer hidden her body but not the others? And where was her car? It was a distinctive vehicle, not easy to hide, but by now it might be in a hundred pieces in some chop shop.

He was getting nowhere.

He stared down at his hands, fingers splayed on the tabletop. Rough from working around his sheep farm without gloves, they bore a few nicks suffered in a wrestling match with a barbed wire fence that a neighbor's cows had knocked down. Had Rachel ever cringed inwardly at the touch of these country man's hands? Ben Hern had an artist's hands, strong but smooth, his fingers long like Tom's but more refined. Elegant.

The dull pain around his nose and eyes had intensified to a steady throb in the short time he'd been without the ice pack. Rising, he wished he could go back to his office, sit quietly for a while and let the cold numb his face. But he had another stop to make first.

◇◇◇

Tom walked through the passageway between Sheriff's Department headquarters, nodded to the jailer at his desk, and entered the cell block. He found Sheriff Willingham standing outside Scotty Ragsdale's cell with Ragsdale's elderly parents. The prisoner sat on his bunk with his head in his hands. In place of his dirty jeans and bloodied tee shirt, he wore a standard blaze orange jumpsuit with MASON COUNTY JAIL INMATE stamped on the back in black letters.

Irma Ragsdale, a little woman in a green smock she wore at the hardware store, turned on Tom the second she saw him. "What is our son locked up for? He hasn't done a thing. He ought to be in a hospital, not a jail cell."

Tom glanced at the sheriff, who shrugged and spread his hands in a helpless gesture.

"Scotty's under arrest for assaulting two police officers," Tom said. He thought it was probably obvious that he'd been one of them.

"But you provoked him into it! Why were you bothering him in the first?"

"Irma," her husband said, "let's just find out what we have to do. There's no point in declaring war over this. He's using meth again, anybody can see that." Carl Ragsdale, an older version of his son in looks, tried to take his wife's arm but she shook him off.

"I want him moved to the hospital, right now," she said.

"If he needs medical care, he'll have it," Sheriff Willingham assured her. "But I believe he'll be okay with us while the—whatever—works its way out of his system. We'll keep a close eye on him."

"I'm right here!" Ragsdale roared from the cell, making all of them flinch in surprise. He rose and slammed his open palms against the bars. "Stop talking about me like I'm not here, like I'm deaf, dumb and blind."

"How are you feeling, Scotty?" Tom asked.

"How the hell do you think I feel?"

"When was your last hit?"

"I'm not admitting anything to you."

"I'd just like to know when you might be clear-headed enough to answer some questions."

"Go to hell. I've got nothing to say to you."

"All right then. I guess we'll both have to wait until you have a change of mind." To Scotty's parents, Tom said, "He's staying here, at least until his bail hearing, and that's not going to be today. The jailer will keep a close watch on him and get him help if he needs it. God knows I don't want anything to happen to him. I need some straight answers from him."

Irma Ragsdale's face knotted with frustration and sorrow. "He didn't kill those people, Tom. He's my boy, I ought to know what's in his heart. He hasn't got it in him to hurt anybody." Her tear-filled eyes flicked to Tom's bruised face. "Except when...But he'd never *kill* anybody. I'd stake my own life on that."

"Come on now, Irma." Her husband put an arm around her and gently turned her toward the door. "He'll be safe and sound here tonight. We'll see how things look in the morning."

"See ya!" Ragsdale yelled after them. "Thanks for nothing! Again."

His mother sobbed as her husband led her from the cell block.

Sheriff Willingham sighed, looked at Ragsdale, then at Tom. He started to speak but changed his mind and instead shook his head and walked out. Tom understood how helpless Willingham must feel. The sheriff had known the older Ragsdales most of his life, had always been friendly with them, but they had a worthless son and he couldn't do a damned thing to change that.

When Willingham was gone, Ragsdale reached out and tried to grab Tom's arm. Tom never got close enough to a cell to let a prisoner touch him, and Ragsdale's fingers closed on air. "Please," he said, his tone turning desperate. "I've gotta get out of here now. I've got things to do. I can't stay here tonight."

"You don't have a choice, Scotty. Now accept it and settle down."

Ragsdale crumpled against the bars and began to sob, open-mouthed, tears and mucus dripping from his chin. Watching him, Tom realized he'd have to order a suicide watch at least through the night.

Was this the killer who had managed to take three lives without leaving any evidence behind? Was he capable of killing a woman he'd loved?

Tom felt sure Scotty played some part in the crimes, but he couldn't believe he was looking at the entire answer to the puzzle. Something else was out there, just beyond sight, waiting for him to focus his eyes in the right direction.

Chapter Thirty-one

Rachel steeled herself for an argument when she walked into Tom's office at the end of the work day. She had to tell him what Lindsay was up to, but he'd been so angry with her the last time they'd talked that she wasn't sure he would listen now.

At the sight of his battered face, she momentarily forgot all about Lindsay.

"What happened?" she exclaimed. His olive complexion couldn't hide the bruising around one eye and across his nose. "Did you have an accident?"

"I'm fine," he said, his words clipped and cool. "But I'm very busy, so—"

"Tom, give me a minute, please." She wouldn't nag him to tell her how he'd been hurt, but she was going to say what she came here to say. She was reluctant to jump right into it, though. Taking a seat facing his desk, she said, "I was shocked when I heard about Lloyd Wilson. Is there anything I can do? What's happened to his dogs and chickens?"

"His sister has them."

"Good," Rachel said. "That's good." Tom was giving her the minimum number of words required, and he looked at her as if she were an unwelcome stranger. "I know you're busy with Lloyd's death on top of everything else, but there's something I have to talk to you about."

Tom waited, his face impassive.

If she blurted this out she'd make matters worse. Maybe she should let him draw his own conclusions. "I found out earlier today that a woman from the state crime lab called the clinic where I worked in McLean, asking a lot of questions about me."

Rachel saw the quick narrowing of Tom's eyes.

"The woman said her name was Ann Johnson," she went on. "I didn't think the crime lab did that kind of thing, gathering background information about people, and there's no reason for them to be interested in me anyway. So I called Roanoke and asked to speak to Ann Johnson. They told me no one by that name works there."

Now Rachel waited, watching Tom's face. His eyes slid away from hers and a muscle twitched in his cheek. She would not allow herself to speak again, however long he took to respond.

At last he said, "You think it was Lindsay." A flat statement, not a question.

She met his gaze, telling herself she was the one in the right and she had nothing to apologize for. "Yes, I do. She's been prying into my background. Now she's lying and misusing her professional position to get information about me."

"Why would she do that?"

"Tom—" How had things gone so wrong between them that he could turn such cold eyes on her? "I think she's trying to find something she can use to drive a wedge between us."

"She doesn't have to bother. You've done a pretty good job of that yourself."

Rachel knew her face betrayed how deeply his words wounded her, and she struggled to get her emotions under control. "I'm sorry. That's not what I wanted."

"You know," Tom said, "there have been times when I thought about doing a background check on you myself."

"What?" Rachel said, unable to raise her voice above a whisper. "Why?"

"Why? Is that a serious question? You've told me next to nothing about yourself. You won't talk about your family. If I get anywhere near that subject, you practically panic."

"No, I don't." *Yes, I do.* Everything he said was true. "Tom, I just—"

"You change the subject, you try to distract me, you won't answer questions. You do everything you can to avoid telling me anything about yourself. My life's an open book to you, but you've never been honest with me, you've always been secretive."

"I'm sorry, I—"

"Ben Hern, he's just one example. If he's such a dear old friend, why is it I never heard a word about him until he suddenly showed up in Mason County? Then I was supposed to accept him, no questions asked."

Tears stung Rachel's eyes and she blinked to get rid of them. She would not let him make her cry. Feeling trapped, she lashed out. "Yes, there are some things I don't like to talk about. What does that have to do with Lindsay? How does that justify her calling people I used to work with and telling lies and making threats?"

"What threats?"

"She told the person she talked to that she *had* to answer questions about me and would be in a lot of trouble if she refused. None of which is true."

"Aw, for god's sake."

Tom rubbed at the bruise between his eyes and winced at his own touch. Rachel stifled a rush of concern. He didn't want her sympathy. He would probably never want anything from her again.

Tom stood abruptly. "I've got three murders to solve. I don't have time for this crap. Whatever's going on between you and Lindsay, handle it yourselves. Don't put me in the middle of it."

It was happening because he was already in the middle. Couldn't he see that? Was he blind to everything Lindsay did? Rachel said nothing, but rose and walked out of his office, feeling foolish and utterly alone.

"God damn it," Tom muttered when Rachel was gone. What else would go wrong before this day was over? Pressing the cold pack to his face, he realized it had long ago reached room temperature.

He flung it into the wastebasket. He grabbed another instant cold pack from the desk drawer where he'd stowed them and squeezed it hard to release the crystals, giving in to a brief fantasy of strangling Lindsay.

What the hell did Lindsay think she was doing? If her bosses found out about it, she'd either be suspended or fired outright, and Tom was willing to bet Rachel was too ticked off to let the incident go unreported. He understood how she felt. But damn it, Rachel's behavior was driving him crazy too.

He pressed the new cold pack to his swollen eye and the bridge of his nose.

During the drive home, with Holly's inconsequential chatter as background noise, Rachel carried on a silent debate with herself about the dangers of confronting Lindsay. If Lindsay smelled fear, rather than simple anger over her prying, she would be intrigued and gratified, and more determined than ever to mine Rachel's past for information to use against her. But how could Rachel stand back and do nothing, hoping Lindsay would lose interest before she uncovered anything harmful? She had to stand up to this woman.

Damned if I do, damned if I don't.

Overwhelmed by frustration, Rachel groaned aloud.

"What's the matter?" Holly asked.

Rachel sighed. "I'll drop you at the house, then I have to go to Joanna's and take care of something."

A few minutes later, she walked into Joanna's kitchen. The room was redolent of garlic and onion, oregano and tomatoes.

Joanna looked around from the range, where she was stirring something in a pot. "Hey, sweetie. What's up?"

Lindsay, washing lettuce at the sink, gave Rachel a dismissive glance and returned to her task.

"I need to talk to you, Lindsay," Rachel said to her back.

Lindsay's shoulders rose and fell in a shrug but she didn't turn. "So talk."

"Can we do this privately?"

"I'm busy right now."

"Well, I can leave the room," Joanna said.

"No," Lindsay said. "I can't imagine what Rachel has to say that you can't hear."

All right, if that's how you want it. Stepping closer to her, Rachel said, "I don't appreciate you calling the place I used to work and asking questions about me."

"What?" Lindsay spun around, her expression a mixture of incredulity and amusement. "What on earth are you talking about?"

Aware of Joanna looking on in slack-jawed surprise, Rachel felt her face flush. "You called this morning, you gave a phony name, and you told the animal hospital's business manager she'd get in trouble if she didn't tell you what you wanted to know."

Lindsay threw a wide-eyed *Can you believe this?* look at Joanna, then gave Rachel a sad little frown. "Rachel, I'm sorry, but I'm afraid you're not making any sense."

"You know exactly what I'm talking about." This was a mistake. She shouldn't have barged in here and confronted Lindsay, but it was too late to retreat.

"You said someone called and gave a phony name?" Lindsay asked. "So you're not claiming that someone using *my* name is making phone calls about you. And in that case, what makes you so certain it was me?"

"I'm not going to argue with your lies," Rachel said. "I just want you to realize that I know what you're doing."

She walked out at a measured pace, wanting to run but refusing to flee like a coward. Outside, though, she allowed herself to run to her vehicle.

After starting the engine she sat gripping the steering wheel. She felt sick. She felt like banging her head against a wall. She felt like screaming at Lindsay and Tom and herself for all the wrong steps that had led to this moment.

Chapter Thirty-two

Ben thrust a crumpled sheet of paper at Rachel, then began pacing her living room, his shoulders hunched and fists stuffed into his jeans pockets. "I found it in my mailbox when I finally got home after wasting the whole day at the Sheriff's Department."

Rachel and Holly, seated on the sofa, read the hand-printed note together.

YOU'LL PAY FOR WHAT YOU DID. CAM AND MEREDITH WERE WORTH A THOUSAND OF YOU. YOU WON'T GET AWAY WITH IT. WE KNOW HOW TO DEAL WITH SCUM LIKE YOU.

"Oh, no." Rachel dropped the note on the coffee table, not wanting to touch it for another second. "Did you report this?"

Ben gave a bitter laugh. "Report it to who? Tom Bridger, who believes I'm a murderer? You really think he'd do anything about it?"

Maybe not, Rachel thought, surprised that she could imagine Tom shirking his duty. "It's a death threat. At least it sounds like one to me."

"How can people be so mean?" Holly looked up at Ben. "What if somebody breaks into your house and tries to hurt you?"

"I guess I'll find out whether my alarm system was a worthwhile investment."

"You can't just let it go," Rachel said. "I really am worried about you."

"I'm worried about all of us." Ben slumped into a chair, his long legs stretched in front of him. "I'm going out of my mind worrying about my mother, and I can't get Bridger to see that something's happened to her. He probably thinks she's part of a conspiracy with me, like the two of us killed the Taylors together." He looked at Rachel. "And I'm worried about you. Why didn't you tell me you had a break-in Saturday night? Is it true somebody turned on the gas? Why didn't you call me?"

"You have enough on your mind." His handsome face had taken on a haggard, haunted appearance and she doubted he'd slept through a single night since the Taylors were killed. She hoped he'd been taking his medication regularly. "We're safe now. New locks, and Brandon Connelly's sleeping here. His Sheriff's Department car parked out front should be an effective deterrent."

"Do you know about the meeting tomorrow night?" Ben asked. "Angie warned me about it. Sounds like all the Taylors' supporters are getting together to decide how to dispose of the evil outsider, meaning me. What do you think they'll do? Tar and feather me, or just string me up and get it over with?"

Holly gave a little cry of distress.

"Don't make sick jokes," Rachel said.

"Who says I'm joking?" Ben sat forward. "Do you know who's behind it? Lindsay Taylor. Angie told me she's been stirring people up, telling them I killed her parents and she's afraid I'll get away with it just because I've got money."

Rachel wished she could doubt that report, but after what she'd seen of Lindsay's behavior, she believed it immediately.

"Well, that doesn't surprise me one little bit," Holly said. "That Lindsay is like some nasty little bug that keeps buzzin' around and won't go away. I wish I could stomp on her."

That made Ben laugh. "I'd like to see that."

Rachel couldn't summon any amusement. "Lindsay might as well accuse Tom of not doing his job. I'm surprised he'd put up with that. Of course, if he asked her about it, she'd deny she was doing it."

"Is she giving you a hard time because you're a friend of mine?" Ben asked.

"That's part of it, but she has other reasons too."

"She thinks she's gonna get Captain Bridger back," Holly volunteered. "Like *that's* gonna happen."

"I'm afraid she's already turned him against me."

"No!" Holly protested.

"It's true. I think our relationship is over." Speaking the words, admitting the reality of her break with Tom, brought on a crushing sadness. "Now I just want Lindsay to leave me alone."

Ben frowned. "Exactly what has she done?"

How could she explain her fear of Lindsay's prying? Neither Ben nor Holly had any idea what kind of family secrets were hidden in Rachel's past. "It's been mostly little stuff. Insults and innuendoes. Nasty but probably hard for anybody to see as dangerous. But it's getting worse." She told him about the call to the animal hospital in McLean.

"Why would she be stupid enough to say she was with the crime lab?" Ben asked. "No matter what name she used, that's going to point to her."

"Exactly," Rachel said. "She can say that she *wouldn't* have been stupid enough to mention the crime lab, therefore it couldn't have been her. It had to be somebody else, or—"

"Or you made it up. *Dios mio.* She's a clever little bitch. And dangerous as hell." Ben pushed his thick black hair off his forehead, but it flopped back when he lowered his hand. "What a mess. We've got a cold-blooded killer who's after the two of you, I'm a murder suspect, and Lindsay Taylor's out to get both of us. Man, to think I moved out here to get away from stress."

Rachel managed a tired smile. "You and me both."

"At least you know there's nothing in your background she can dig up that would hurt you."

Holly said, "She can't dig up anything bad about *either one* of you, because you've never done anything bad."

This spirited and naive defense silenced both Rachel and Ben.

Ben's morose expression made Rachel wonder whether he had told her the whole story of his legal problem in New York or withheld something from her. Was there more to it? Something scandalous? If so, and Cam Taylor had found out, Ben's motive for stopping Taylor's blackmail attempt would be stronger than it appeared at first. And if Cam had known a damaging secret about Ben, Cam's daughter might know too. Lindsay wouldn't hesitate to blow it out of proportion and use it to incite a mob to go after Ben.

Rachel couldn't ask Ben about this in front of Holly. What right did she have, in any case, to demand that he reveal his secrets to her, when she had never shared hers with him?

"Yes, Lindsay's dangerous," she said. *To both of us.*

Long past dinnertime, Tom made a cold ham and cheese sandwich and ate it standing in his kitchen. The relentless pain around his nose and eyes had spread, and now his head felt like an over-inflated balloon ready to explode. He wanted to toss down a pain pill and collapse into bed, but first he intended to read more of Meredith's manuscript. Something was going on in this case that he either didn't know about yet or didn't understand. If the answer lay in the past, he hoped Meredith had included it in her fictionalized account. Whether he would recognize it when he came across it was another question.

Billy Bob scarfed down his own meal and topped it with a long slurpy drink that nearly emptied his water bowl. After refilling the bowl, Tom grabbed the case containing the CD from the kitchen table. "Come on, boy," he said to his dog. "Let's go read a novel."

Billy Bob trotted alongside him down the hall to the home office that had once belonged to John Bridger, Tom's father. The only sound in the house was the click of the bulldog's nails on the floor.

When Tom's relationship with Rachel had begun back in January, he'd been pathetically optimistic, imagining a wedding within a few months. Rachel's presence would bring this quiet house to life again, and before long they'd have a couple of kids running around the place. The problem with that dream was that Rachel didn't share it. They'd become intimate physically, but she kept her heart and mind locked away, out of his reach.

Lindsay, he knew, imagined herself living here as his wife, the mother of his children. She apparently still clung to the hope that Tom would come back to her if Rachel were out of the picture. But even if he'd lost Rachel, he wouldn't make the mistake of getting involved with Lindsay again.

He sat at the desk in the office and booted up his computer. Dwelling on what had happened with Rachel was pointless. A waste of emotional and mental energy when he needed to be sharp and get this damned case closed before anybody else ended up dead. But the realization that his relationship with Rachel was probably over sat in his mind like a boulder that he would have to work around.

Billy Bob settled on the floor with a deep sigh and closed his eyes. Tom opened Meredith's file and clicked through to the spot where he'd stopped reading the day before. The narrator, the young Meredith, had just caught Chad—Cam—kissing Celia, who was apparently meant to be Karen Richardson, now Hernandez. Tom expected to read about consequences, turmoil in the VISTA ranks, escalating hostility between Meredith and Karen. Instead, the story focused for several chapters on Cam's pet project, an outdoor drama about the history of the Melungeons in Appalachia. Charged with writing the play script, Meredith had interviewed Melungeon residents of the county, some of whom Tom recognized from her descriptions. Cam was busy with production and recruiting local people for the project.

Karen/Celia was still around, still making Meredith uneasy. But the local girl named Donna had quickly become a bigger problem. Although she wasn't Melungeon, Chad/Cam chose her for a starring role in the play.

Meredith had written:

Donna was shameless—brazen. She placed herself in Chad's path at every opportunity, and she was always taking him off to a corner to have a private talk. When she looked at him, anybody could see that she wanted him. She was his to take anytime he liked.

Interesting, Tom thought. He was sure that Donna was Scotty Ragsdale's older sister, Denise. Meredith hadn't bothered to alter the fact that her parents owned the county's only hardware and lumber store. Tom hadn't heard of any friction between Meredith and Denise, though. Scotty said they were friends. Maybe this conflict over Chad/Cam was something Meredith invented to give her story more tension. Tom reminded himself that he was reading a novel, not an autobiography, despite the similarities to Meredith's real life.

Leaning back in his chair, he pressed a hand to his aching forehead. He'd hoped to get all the way through the manuscript tonight, but he could see that wasn't going to happen. Pain pills and sleep were all he wanted. A night of rest and recuperation would help him see the evidence more clearly.

Chapter Thirty-three

Tom leaned against the wall opposite the cell and watched Scotty Ragsdale pick at the lavish breakfast his mother had brought in. Pancakes doused with syrup, half a dozen slices of bacon, scrambled eggs, two biscuits, a thermos of homemade coffee. The aromas made Tom's mouth water—his breakfast had consisted of a bowl of cold cereal and a cup of coffee that he'd brewed too weak—but Ragsdale seemed unmoved by the bounty on his plate. After a few bites of the eggs he set the tray aside on his bunk.

"No appetite?" Tom asked.

Ragsdale shook his head. "My mouth tastes like a toilet bowl." He glanced at Tom and winced. "Holy shit. Did I do that to you?"

"Oh, yeah. And you socked Brandon Connelly in the jaw. With your head. Remember any of that?"

"A little. It's pretty vague."

"Do you remember going to Lloyd Wilson's place yesterday morning?"

"Wilson?" Ragsdale's gaze connected with Tom's for a second, then flicked away, as an expression of pure horror came over his face. He sounded breathless when he spoke again. "What happened at his place?"

"He's dead. Shot at close range."

Ragsdale hung his head, gripping it with both hands. "And you think I did it."

"Did you?"

"I don't remem—No. No." He shook his head vigorously.

"Maybe your memory will improve after you've been here a while longer."

Ragsdale shoved himself to his feet and stepped over to the bars. "Listen, Tom, I need to get out of here. It's important. I've got—" He paused and seemed to search for a word. "Commitments."

"When you get out is up to the judge. I can tell you the prosecutor's going to ask for a high bail when you're arraigned, and I think the judge will go along."

Ragsdale was nodding impatiently. "When's my arraignment?"

"Tomorrow."

"*Tomorrow?* I can't stay here another night!"

"You don't have a choice, Scotty. If you've got work lined up, it'll have to wait."

Grasping two of the bars, Ragsdale leaned his forehead against them and closed his eyes. He whispered, speaking to himself, "It'll be all right. It'll be all right."

Tom was about to press on with more questions when Dennis Murray flung open the door into the cell block. "Hey, Tom, come here," the sergeant said, with a wave of his hand. "Something's come up."

A cold dread descended on Tom. What now? *Please, God, not another killing.*

They moved into the jailer's office before Dennis spoke. "We got a call from Matt Dolan." Dolan was sheriff in a neighboring county. "They found Karen Hernandez's car."

Ninety minutes later, Tom followed Sheriff Matt Dolan along a narrow trail into the pine woods, with Dennis and Brandon bringing up the rear. The forest birds had fallen silent, but cicadas kept up a steady drone.

Dolan, a burly ex-Marine with a gray crewcut, said over his shoulder, "It's just lucky those two hikers felt like they had to report it. Most people wouldn't have bothered." He chuckled. "I could name a few that would've tried to salvage it. We don't see many Jaguars free for the taking. But they'd need a crane to lift it out of that ravine."

Tom swatted away a cloud of gnats. "Have your people found any evidence on the scene since you called us?"

"Naw, I didn't let my deputies go down there tramping around. All I did was check to make sure nobody was in the vehicle. I didn't even open a door. If there's anything to find, the State Police techs'll spot it. They oughta be here any time now."

Driving a car into the woods along this path couldn't have been easy, Tom thought as he pushed aside a low-hanging branch. About two hundred yards in, they came to the lip of a ravine. "There it is," Dolan said.

They stood in a splash of sunlight, looking down the slope on the Jaguar that had come to rest at the bottom. The vehicle had landed upright, its nose shoved into a scraggly holly bush. Most of the car was covered with pine branches in an obvious attempt to hide it. The sight stirred a deep sense of foreboding in Tom. He could have been moving in the wrong direction on this case since day one.

Dolan lunged and stumbled down the slope like a drunken bear. Tom descended more slowly, letting his feet slide when they wanted to but somehow staying upright. Brandon and Dennis edged down the embankment after him.

While Dennis moved around the Jaguar with the camera, Tom and Brandon remained in place but scanned the ground for evidence. A hundred feet away, a jostling horde of turkey vultures tore at a deer carcass. Grunting and hissing, they seemed too occupied with their meal to mind the humans nearby. A dozen crows, denied places at the feast, protested from the skeleton of a dead tree.

"I don't see a damned thing," Tom muttered.

"Been so long since we had rain," Dolan remarked, "the ground won't even take a footprint."

"What do you think?" Brandon asked Tom.

"I think we need to pop the trunk." Tom asked Dolan, "You have any objection?"

"Not a one," Dolan said. "I've got a crowbar in my truck. Be right back."

As Dolan climbed back out of the ravine, Brandon said, "You think Mrs. Hernandez is in the trunk? Maybe she just abandoned the car because it's too easy to spot."

Tom shook his head. "First of all, how would she even know this ravine was here? And look at the size of some of these branches. It would have taken a lot of effort to haul them down here and throw them over the car. Then she'd have to get out of the area on foot. I think two people did this, and they left in a second vehicle."

"Hey, Tom," Dennis said, "come look at this."

Tom joined him on the driver's side of the car. The window was uncovered, the large branch that had hidden it pulled aside and dropped on the ground. Dennis pointed, and Tom leaned close to peer through the window. The glass had a skim of condensation on the inside, but Tom spotted what had caught Dennis' attention. One section of the steering wheel bore a brownish-red stain—as if it had been gripped by a bloody hand.

"Let's hope it's not just dirt," Tom said. "But either way, we might get prints."

This situation was looking crazier by the minute. If the stain was blood, whose blood was it? Why would anybody be careless enough to leave a bloody hand print behind?

He moved around to the rear of the car, leaned close to the trunk, sniffed deeply. He picked up the odor of decomposition, but it was wafting over from the dead deer. The Jaguar was a luxury vehicle, and the trunk, like every other opening, would be well-sealed.

"Here we go," Dolan called from the top of the slope, holding up a crowbar. They waited for him to descend. "Now then," he said when he joined them, "let's see what's in there."

Tom tried to keep his impatience in check as Dolan fussed with the crowbar, searching for the right angle to force the lock. When Dolan got the bar into position and pressed down on it, Tom held his breath, almost convinced by now that they would find Karen Hernandez's decomposing body inside. The lid flew open.

The trunk was spotless, and empty except for an emergency jack and a set of jumper cables.

Chapter Thirty-four

"Oh, Rachel, please don't." Joanna emerged from the empty stall and faced Rachel in the stable's wide center aisle. She held a bucket filled with fragrant grains she was distributing to all the stalls before the horses were brought in for the night. "What's the point of listening to a bunch of ignorant people bitch about the police? They don't understand what a murder investigation involves. All they'll be doing is venting their frustration."

"If anybody there believes I saw the killer," Rachel said, "I want to set them straight."

"Oh, dear lord, you're going to stand up and speak?"

"Only if I have to. And I want to hear what they say about Ben."

Joanna groaned. "Honey, you're not Ben's protector and defender. You don't have to fight this battle for him. That's his lawyer's job."

Rachel didn't want to argue, so she let that pass. "I was hoping you'd come with me."

"Oh no." Joanna shook her head. "I couldn't hold my temper in check. I'd probably start a riot. And I really do wish you wouldn't go."

"I'll be okay." Rachel paused. "Did you know that Lindsay is the one who talked her parents' supporters into having this meeting?"

Joanna swung open the door to another stall. "I figured as much. She's been on the phone a lot, and she's been out and about, seeing people. Well, maybe it'll backfire on her. Tom's going to have a fit when he realizes she's behind it."

The sky was still bright when Rachel set off, but the sinking sun splashed streaks of purple and gold over the clouds above the hills. Within an hour full darkness would descend. If the meeting were being held deep in Rocky Branch District, Rachel would have skipped it rather than venture into that alien territory alone at night, but the consolidated middle school straddled the district's boundary.

She had imagined, feared, a huge turnout, with hundreds of people screaming for Ben's arrest, but she was relieved to find no more than three dozen vehicles in the school's parking lot. Six Sheriff's Department cruisers lined up nose to tail along one edge of the lot, and two cable TV trucks sat near the building's entrance.

A few people stood talking in small groups outside the door, but Rachel didn't know any of them and she didn't acknowledge their stares on her way in.

When she reached the auditorium, she immediately spotted Lindsay in the first row, shaking hands and speaking with the people who formed a small crowd before her. One woman after another leaned to kiss Lindsay's cheek. Playing the role of the grieving daughter to the hilt, Rachel thought. She had no idea how much sadness Lindsay actually felt over the deaths of her parents. It was possible that she viewed it as an opportunity for gain rather than as a loss.

About fifty adults and a handful of adolescents had gathered in the auditorium. Several teenage boys talked and laughed at the back of the room. Half a dozen deputies, including Brandon and the Blackwood twins, stood along the side walls. The press swarmed the area between seats and stage with their notebooks and cameras at the ready, probably excited that something they could tape for TV was finally about to happen.

Rachel took a seat several rows behind Lindsay. On the stage, Tom inclined his head to listen to Sheriff Willingham. They weren't looking at the audience, and Rachel doubted Tom had seen her come in. Even from a distance, his swollen, discolored eye and nose looked awful. Brandon had come to the cottage the night before with a black and blue jaw, and he'd told Rachel and Holly the story of Scotty Ragsdale's arrest. Tom should be at home, taking time to heal, but he'd probably been working with little rest since—*Stop it,* Rachel told herself. *He doesn't want your concern.*

Tom stood stiff and grim-faced beside the sheriff while the last of the arrivals trickled in and the crowd settled down. For a second Rachel thought Tom's eyes connected with hers, and she quickly looked away.

A plump, white-haired man in a short-sleeved shirt opened the meeting with a prayer. "Dear Lord," he intoned in a deep, resonant voice that was made for preaching, "we beseech thee to welcome our friends Cameron and Meredith into your loving presence and grant them eternal peace. We beg you to extend your loving hand to their daughter and bless her in her time of loss."

Cameras whirred, focused on the speaker from the floor in front of the stage. At the mention of Lindsay, all of them swung around and trained their lenses on her. She kept her head bowed, her pale hair falling forward over her cheeks. Murmurs of "amen" rose from the crowd.

The man at the podium concluded his prayer and launched into a speech. "Many years ago, two young people came to our community with the intention of giving one year of their lives in service to the poorest, the most needy, among us." His voice swelled with emotion. "Little did any of us know that they would devote the rest of their lives to that service, and they would give of themselves without regret or expectation of repayment. Many of us can point to the ways our own lives are better because of Cameron and Meredith. They were our champions. They stood by our sides through many battles, and when we wearied they fought on alone."

One person's pest is another's hero, Rachel thought. She was willing to believe the Taylors had done some good, although

Cam's methods also made enemies. What had the Taylors' home life been like? What had they done to produce such a scheming, ruthless daughter?

"Now a monster has come among us," the speaker went on, "and taken these dear friends from us. That monster remains right here in our peaceful community. We must not relax our vigilance. We must hold our families and neighbors close and let our love form a barrier against the darkest side of humanity. With God's help we will crush the invader."

"Amen!" the crowd answered.

Rachel cringed at this outrageous attempt to whip up fear and suspicion, although she had to concede the truth behind the over-wrought warning. She was as frightened by the murders as anyone in the room, and she wouldn't feel safe until the killer was caught. But these people were looking for an easy answer, and she wasn't sure any of them had the patience to wait for the truth to emerge.

Some of the women present were weeping by the time the white-haired man called on Sheriff Willingham for an update on the investigation. Willingham fiddled with the microphone, loosing a screech of feedback, while cameras pointed at him. He cleared his throat and said, "I want to assure the community that we're working on this twenty-four hours a day, and we won't rest until we've got the killer in custody. My chief deputy is with me tonight, Captain Tom Bridger. A lot of you know Tom, and you knew his dad, John Bridger, a fine man who grew up in this part of the county. Tom's heading up the day-to-day operations in this investigation, so I'm going to let him take your questions."

Tom didn't have a chance to open his mouth before a woman called out, "Why won't you tell us more details about what happened to Cam and Meredith and their next door neighbor? How are we supposed to protect ourselves if we don't know what we're dealing with?"

Tom cleared his throat. "We don't have any reason to think the general public is in danger. We believe the motive in these murders was personal. We're following several leads, and we hope—"

"Was Meredith raped?" An elderly man had risen from his seat in the third row to ask the question. "I heard she was raped and tortured and mutilated. Is that true?"

Good grief, Rachel thought. Why did people need to embroider an already horrific murder with sensational fantasies? She had to admire Tom for staying cool in the face of such stupidity.

He gripped the sides of the podium and answered in a calm voice. "We have no reason to think a sexual assault took place. I can't comment on Mrs. Taylor's injuries or the cause of death until we get the autopsy report."

The man next to Lindsay in the front row stood next. Although Rachel could only see his back, she recognized Beck Rasey, who had recently brought his four hunting dogs to the free rabies clinic she'd conducted in this area. Tall, with reddish brown hair and a florid complexion, he looked like a typical former athlete losing the battle with flab. Rachel remembered him because he'd lost his temper when she told him all his dogs badly needed to have their teeth cleaned. In so many words, he'd declared that Rachel was trying to scam him out of a big chunk of money.

Rasey told Tom, "I think you ought to be honest with the citizens of this county and just admit you're running around in circles. You're not any closer to making an arrest than the day the Taylors died."

"Beck—" Tom started.

"You know who did it. Why don't you lock him up?"

"Beck," Tom said, his tone sharper now, "if we had enough evidence to arrest anybody, we would have done it already. We're looking at every possibility. We—"

"You've got an eyewitness," Rasey said. Shouts of agreement rose from the crowd. "What's the matter? Can't you make your girlfriend tell you the truth?"

To a chorus of hoots and laughter, Rasey turned and pointed at Rachel.

She felt her face go hot, and then she was on her feet. "I *have* told the truth. I wish I knew more, but I don't. I did not see the killer. I don't know any more than I've already told the Sheriff's Department. I want this person caught as much as you do."

She sat down, knowing Tom's eyes were on her, refusing to look back at him. Her gaze settled on Lindsay, who had shifted in her seat and was watching Rachel with an innocent expression on her face. Rachel felt like slapping her and was grateful for the distance between them.

"We're satisfied that Dr. Goddard has told us everything she knows," Tom said from the stage. "She didn't see anything that would help us identify the killer. Beck, if you'll sit down and listen, I'll finish filling all of you in about the investigation."

Rasey stayed on his feet. "We all know the *celebrity* living in our county is a friend of hers," he said, spitting out *celebrity* as if it were a bad taste.

Rachel wondered if Lindsay had written this guy's script.

"Beck, will you sit down and listen to me?" Tom said.

Ignoring Tom, Rasey swept the crowd with his gaze. "Did y'all know that artist, the Cuban guy that got rich drawing cartoons, he likes to paint pictures of young girls without any clothes on? God knows what else he does with them."

Rachel heard gasps all around her. For a moment she was stunned, then she told herself Rasey was inventing things, throwing out any wild thought that popped into his head.

Tom hustled down the steps from the stage. The sheriff replaced him at the microphone and tried to make himself heard, but Rasey was on a roll and couldn't be drowned out.

"That's the real reason he had to leave New York City." Rasey shouted. "He got caught with a girl, her daddy caught them and tried to protect his daughter, and that so-called artist beat the girl's father so bad the man landed in the hospital."

Tom grabbed his arm, but Rasey shook him off and stepped away. The deputies along the walls moved forward.

"Cam and Meredith found out the whole story," Rasey went on. "They got worried he was gonna do the same thing to our girls here in Mason County. And look what happened."

"No, no," Rachel muttered. Her heart thudding, she pushed herself to her feet again. "That's not true. It's a lie."

When she saw the ugly curl of Rasey's mouth she knew she'd invited disaster.

"Don't you call me a liar," he said. "You think I don't know about you? You let your own mother die right in front of you. You've got medical training, but you stood by and let your mother bleed to death—*then* you called 911."

The words hit Rachel like a punch to the chest. She gasped for breath, and the buzz of voices filled her head and overwhelmed her. She stumbled past knees and feet toward the aisle. She had to get out of here. As she ran up the aisle to the door, she thought she heard Tom calling her name, but the only clear voice was the sheriff's booming over the sound system. "This meeting is over. Deputies, clear the room."

Rachel leaned on the panic bar and shoved the door open, then she was outside in the muggy night air.

Tom elbowed through the crowd and out the door. Rachel stood in the parking lot in the eerie yellow glow of the mercury vapor lights, surrounded by half a dozen teenage boys. Tom recognized most of the boys, all of them troublemakers, and the worst of the bunch was Beck Rasey's son Pete, a bulked-up high school football player.

Pete advanced on Rachel, but she stood her ground. He lowered his face to hers.

Rage propelled Tom forward. He shoved a couple of boys out of his way, grabbed Pete's arms and jerked them backward. The boy yelped in surprise. Pinning Pete's arms behind him, Tom spun him around, marched him six feet to the nearest car and slammed him face down across the hood.

Pete struggled futilely and shouted, "Get your hands off me, you fucking asshole!"

Tom pulled the boy's arms higher, making him yowl with pain. "What did you call me? Say that again, you little punk, and you'll spend the next month in a cell."

"Like hell he will," Beck Rasey shouted. He jogged toward them. "Take your hands off my son."

"Back off," Tom warned.

"You gonna make me, hotshot?" He kept coming. Pete's friends, emboldened, closed ranks with Rasey.

Tom planted a hand between Pete's shoulders, leaned on it to keep the boy where he was, and drew his pistol with his free hand. He leveled the gun at the father. He heard squeals and cursing and realized a crowd had gathered. "You're interfering with an officer of the law. Back off."

Reporters and cameramen edged closer, but Tom was too damned mad to care.

Rasey took a couple more daring steps before he stopped. The boys pulled up short behind him. He glared at Tom, his face working with fury and hatred. "You better keep that gun with you every minute from now on, deputy. You're gonna need it."

At that moment, Sheriff Willingham arrived on the scene with Brandon, the Blackwood twins, and three more deputies. "Beck," Willingham said, "did I hear you threaten my chief deputy?"

Tom holstered his gun. He yanked Pete upright. The boy tried to squirm free, but Tom had an iron grip on his arm. "Beck seems to think it's okay if this punk he raised goes around picking on innocent women."

"Innocent?" Pete sneered. "She's helping a murderer—"

"Shut up!" Willingham ordered, shaking a finger in Pete's face. "God in heaven. If you were my son I'd be ashamed to claim you." He rounded on Beck Rasey. "What you did in there was a pure disgrace. Now you take your boy home and see if both of you can learn how to act like civilized human beings. You stay away from Dr. Goddard and you stay away from Ben Hern. If I hear about either one of you bothering anybody ever again, you're going to be in real trouble."

Tom shoved Pete toward his father. "Get out of here, both of you."

As Rasey and his son stalked off, the crowd scattered to their cars and trucks. The reporters advanced on Tom.

"Stay away from me," he said, holding up a hand to stop them. "I've got nothing to say to you." All he cared about was Rachel. Where had she disappeared to?

He found her leaning against her vehicle, her face in her hands. He touched her shoulder. "Come on, let me take you home. Brandon can follow us in your car."

Rachel pulled away from him. "No, thank you," she said in a stiff voice. "I'll be fine on my own."

"Like you have been so far?" Tom said, the words falling out of his mouth before he had time to consider their effect.

Rachel looked at him as if he were a stranger who'd forced his loathsome attentions on her. "Lindsay's been feeding these people lies about Ben," she said, "and telling them they have to take things into their own hands. And filling them in about me while she's at it."

For a second Tom's mind refused to focus on that last piece of information, and instead grabbed hold of what she'd said about Hern. He had to make Rachel see the truth. "They're not lies. It's true, what happened in New York. I got the story straight from a cop who was there. Hern can't deny it."

Rachel wasn't listening. "I don't think you give a damn what Lindsay does. I'm sick of her. I'm sick of both of you. I wish I'd never set foot in this godforsaken place." She wrenched open the door of her vehicle and climbed in.

"Rachel, damn it, will you just calm down and listen to me?"

Still holding the door open, Rachel said, "Why don't you ask your nephew about Lindsay? Haven't you ever wondered why he can't stand being around her?"

Tom opened his mouth to speak, but Rachel slammed the door in his face.

Chapter Thirty-five

Was that Tom following her in a police car or another deputy he'd assigned to play guardian? On this dark road, Rachel couldn't tell who was behind the wheel. As long as he didn't try to stop her, she would ignore him and go about her business—which didn't include going straight home.

She couldn't let this night pass without talking to Ben. She was willing to allow him his secrets, but if he'd hidden something as scandalous as a relationship with an underage girl from her while she was going around defending him, he owed her an explanation and she was damned well going to get one.

The Sheriff's Department cruiser stayed with her as she drove toward Ben's property, then up his long driveway.

"Oh, great," Rachel muttered when she pulled into the parking area in front of the house. Angie Hogencamp's green VW beetle sat behind Ben's Jaguar in the bright arc of the security lights. Rachel didn't want anybody else around when she confronted Ben.

On second thought, maybe it wasn't a bad idea for Angie to hear this. She had a right to know the truth about the man she worked for.

When Rachel stepped out of her vehicle, the air felt electric, making her skin tingle, and the swaying trees warned of a coming storm. Thunder rumbled in the distance. She slammed her door and waited to see who was driving the cruiser that pulled in behind her vehicle.

Brandon, not Tom. Okay, she could handle Brandon.

When he opened his door, Rachel said, "Why don't you go on to my house and keep Holly company? I might be here a while."

"The captain told me to stick with you all the way home. He's really worried about those nut cases at the meeting. They might come after you."

"Right," Rachel said. "I guess it would make the Sheriff's Department look bad if anything happened to me."

"I don't think that's the only reason the captain's worried," Brandon said.

Brandon's reproachful look gave her a twinge of guilt. Rachel sighed. It wasn't fair to put poor Brandon on the spot by venting her frustration with his boss. Starting up the steps, she said, "I hope you don't mind waiting."

Ben opened the door just as she was about to press a thumb to the bell. "I saw you drive up," he said. He frowned at Brandon. "Why do you have a cop with you?"

Rachel marched past him into the foyer and waited until he'd closed the door. She assumed Angie was within earshot, although she didn't see her in the living room off to the right. "I got blindsided at that meeting tonight. Somebody stood up and said you left New York because you were sleeping with an underage girl and her father found out. Is it true?"

"Aw, shit," Ben groaned. "Why did you go to that damned meeting?"

"Answer my question, please. Is it true? Is that what Cam Taylor was really trying to blackmail you with?"

"I'm sorry you got caught up in this. I should have told you, but I was ashamed of the whole business, and I wasn't sure you'd understand—" He broke off and shook his head.

"You didn't think I'd understand if you told me you were sleeping with a minor? Well, yeah, I guess you were right. I do have a little trouble understanding that."

"Come on, Rachel, don't you even want to hear my side of—"

"It's not true!" Angie exclaimed, striding up the hall from the back of the house. "You'll never make me believe something like that." When she reached them, she turned a pleading look on Ben. "It isn't true, is it? It's just some wild story Cam Taylor made up?"

Both women waited for Ben's answer. Hands on his hips, he stared at the floor. *Deny it, please deny it,* Rachel begged silently. *Convince me it's not true.*

Gesturing toward the living room, Ben said, "Let's sit down and I'll tell you both what really happened."

Tom sped along the mountain roads, reminding himself every few minutes to slow down before he lost control and wrapped the cruiser around a tree. He heard the growl of thunder coming closer, and he looked up to see streaks of lightning against tumbled dark clouds. Since the night his parents, brother, and sister-in-law had died in a crash during a thunderstorm, Tom had tried to avoid being on the road when a storm broke, but unless he turned toward home right now, he was going to get caught this time.

He kept going. He had to inform Ben Hern that his mother's car had turned up. So far the department had kept a lid on the news, but it would leak before long. Hern should hear it from Tom first.

After seeing Hern, he had to track down Lindsay and get it through that thick head of hers that he wasn't going to put up with her scheming. What in god's name did she think she was doing when she got that mob together and turned them on Rachel? And on him and the Sheriff's Department into the bargain. Didn't she see how explosive, how dangerous, a situation she had created with her meddling?

Tom had gone looking for Lindsay after Rachel left the school where the meeting was held, but he couldn't find her in the dispersing crowd. She knew him well enough to get out of his way, and she'd probably taken off while he was dealing with that gang of punks. He'd catch up with her later. And after Rachel had a chance to calm down, he'd see her and try to apologize, for whatever good it would do. He had a sick knot in the pit of his stomach when he thought of losing her. Despite his doubts and all his unanswered questions, he knew he loved her, and he couldn't stand by and watch her walk out of his life.

As he drove up Hern's driveway, flashes of lightning illuminated the treetops. The storm would break any minute, and if he was lucky it would slacken off before he was on the road again. He expected to be here a while, dealing with an outburst of fury and recrimination from Hern.

What he didn't expect was Rachel's car, sitting outside Hern's house. What the hell was she doing here? Had she come running right over here to give Hern a report about the meeting?

A department cruiser sat behind Rachel's vehicle, and Brandon leaned against the cruiser's fender. He spoke as soon as Tom got out. "You told me to stick with her all the way home. I couldn't stop her from taking a detour."

Tom slammed his car door. Angie Hogencamp's VW beetle was here too. One more person to give Hern backup against Tom. "Wait for her. I don't want her driving without protection."

A gust of wind thrashed the trees, tearing loose a flurry of pine needles that swirled down around Tom and Brandon. Lightning threw a stark blaze across towering clouds, then the sky went black again. Tom's skin suddenly felt damp, and the hairs on his arms stood up. "Come inside with me," he told Brandon. "I don't want you sitting out here with all this lightning around."

Hern answered the door and groaned aloud when he saw Tom. "Have you come to arrest me, or just haul me in for more interrogation?"

"I need to talk to you," Tom said.

"Can't it wait until morning?"

"No." Tom edged past him, brushing Hern's shoulder, and Brandon followed. "This can't wait. You need to hear it now."

For a minute Hern stood gripping the door handle as if debating whether to shut the door and accept their presence or keep trying to get rid of them. A blast of wind found the opening and flung pine needles over the foyer's parquet floor. Hern closed the door. "All right," he said. "What's so damned urgent?"

Without an invitation, Tom strode into the living room with Brandon behind him. Rachel sat on one end of the sofa, Angie on the other. Angie folded her arms and pinned hostile eyes on Tom. Rachel studied her fingernails.

"I hope you won't mind if I don't ask you to sit down and stay awhile," Hern said.

"I won't stay a second longer than I have to." Tom sat in a chair opposite the sofa. Brandon remained standing near the door, with his hands clasped behind his back. Glancing around at the heavy draperies and upholstery, the furniture that looked like well-maintained antiques, Tom was surprised to find such a curiously old-fashioned room in the home of a young man.

His gaze settled on the big, longhaired cat that occupied the chair to his right. Tom recognized the animal as Hamilton, the cat in Hern's comic strip. The cat stared back at him, unblinking.

Returning his attention to Hern, Tom said, "I came to tell you that your mother's car was found this morning. At the bottom of a ravine about fifty miles from here."

Tom watched the shock waves move over Hern's face, bringing surprise, confusion, and finally a realization of what the news meant. "My mother—Did you—Was she—" He wobbled as if his legs were giving way.

Brandon sprang forward, but Rachel and Angie reached Hern first. One on each side, they guided him to the sofa. He collapsed onto it, his face slack with dread. "Tell me everything," he said in a hoarse croak.

"We haven't located your mother. There were no personal items in the car. But it is definitely her car."

"Oh, god," Hern moaned. He slumped forward, clutching his head in his hands. "I knew it. I knew something had happened to her."

Angie leaned close to whisper. Rachel stroked Hern's hair once, like a mother calming a child, then placed an arm around his shoulders. At the sight of these intimate, caring gestures, Tom's gut twisted with jealousy.

Thunder rumbled overhead, and lightning flared in the windows like flashbulbs every few seconds.

"Let's not jump to conclusions." Hern's reaction looked sincere, Tom had to admit. That kind of raw emotion, the overwhelming sense of loss that felt like being flayed alive, was something Tom remembered all too well. He'd never met anyone who could fake it convincingly.

Hern's head came up, his face animated by sudden hope. "You said it was at the bottom of a ravine? You mean it went off the road? She could have walked away—"

"The ravine isn't next to the road. It can only be reached by a track through the woods. The car was driven in there and rolled over the edge into the ravine. Then somebody tried to hide it by dragging tree branches over it." Tom paused. "Big, heavy branches dragged down from the woods. Unless she was a bodybuilder, I don't think she could have done it alone. If she was injured, it would have been out of the question."

No one spoke. When Tom thought Hern had absorbed the implications of the situation, he said, "I have to ask you what your mother's blood type is."

"Her blood—Oh, no."

Rachel asked quietly, "You found blood in the car?"

"Not much, just a smear," Tom answered without looking at her. To Hern, he said, "Do you know your mother's blood type?"

"It's A positive," Hern said, his voice thick, his eyes swimming with unshed tears. "Is that what you found in the car?"

Tom pulled in a breath, let it out. "Yes, it is."

Hern made a strangled sound in the back of his throat and buried his face in his hands.

"There's enough for a DNA test if you'll give us a sample for comparison," Tom said. "You don't have to give blood. Just go over to Dr. Gretchen Lauter's office first thing in the morning and they'll do a cheek swab."

He expected Hern to object to this intrusion, but instead he dropped his hands and nodded.

"DNA will take a while," Tom said. "A week, at least—"

Thunder cracked directly overhead, making Tom wince. Lightning lit the windows. The big cat shot off its chair and galloped out of the room. In the next instant rain poured from the sky like a river breaking through a dam. It beat against the window panes. The walls around Tom's memories fell away, and he had a dizzying sensation of spinning, sliding out of control. He heard again the crunch and screech of metal as a massive tree flattened his parents' van.

Trying to drag himself back to the present, he drew a deep breath to slow his racing heart and gripped the chair arms to keep the others from seeing his hands shake. But Rachel saw. When he met her eyes, she looked back with sympathetic understanding.

Ben Hern, oblivious to Tom's struggle, seemed to be fighting to gain control of his own emotions but failing completely. Tears ran down his face. "She's dead," he choked out. "My mother's dead."

For a crazy moment Tom heard an echo of his own voice, when he woke up in the ER after the accident. *They're dead? They're all dead?*

"Whoever killed the Taylors," Hern said, "they killed her too."

Concentrate. Tom yanked his attention back to the distraught man sitting across from him. "Don't jump to conclusions. We don't know that anything has happened to your mother. Just let us do our jobs and we'll get the answers you need."

Hern swiped at his wet cheeks with the back of a hand. "If I'd never come here, she wouldn't have either. She never would have seen the Taylors again, and she'd still be alive."

"Was something going on between them that you haven't told me about?" Tom asked. "Did she go to the Taylor house Friday morning? You need to be honest with me now."

Hern shook his head. "None of that matters now. If she's gone, nothing matters anymore."

"*Everything* matters," Tom said. "Look, if you want me to find out who did this, you'll stop obstructing the investigation."

"Leave him alone!" Angie cried. "Can't you see you're just making it worse?"

Out of patience, Tom turned on her. "I've got a few questions for you too. How is it you just happened to take a day off from work on the same day the Taylors' neighbor was killed?"

Outrage flooded her face. "First my boss, then my father, now me. You think we were all in it together?"

"This is crazy," Hern protested. "Angie couldn't hurt a fly."

"Really, Tom," Rachel said, "you can't be serious."

Tom ignored Rachel's scolding and said to Angie, "Your father had a very good motive to kill the Taylors. And you'd do anything to protect him, wouldn't you? You knew Lloyd Wilson might have seen something—"

"That's enough!" Rachel cried. "Stop this right now."

"I'm doing my job, Rachel." Tom rose and looked down at Hern. "When you're ready to cooperate and help us find your mother, let me know."

He walked out, signaling Brandon to stay. He was soaking wet by the time he reached his car and set off in the blinding rain.

Chapter Thirty-six

"Do you want something to eat?" Rachel asked Ben. "Did you have dinner?"

He shook his head. "I'm not hungry."

Angie reacted the way Rachel hoped she would. Rising from the sofa, she said, "Well, I'm going to bring you something anyway. You need to eat."

With Angie on her way to the kitchen, Rachel had only Brandon to worry about. He leaned against a wall in the foyer, looking casual and a little bored, but he never took his eyes off Rachel and Ben.

She spoke to Ben in a whisper. "Let's go out on the porch where we can talk privately."

"There's nothing to talk about," Ben said, his voice loud enough to make Brandon snap to attention.

"Keep your voice down." Rachel raised a hand to assure Brandon everything was okay. "Come on."

She stood and waited until Ben heaved a sigh and rose too. "We're just going on the porch for a minute," she told Brandon. "I'll be right back in, okay?"

Brandon didn't look happy, but he nodded agreement.

Rain pounded the porch roof, drowning out the night sounds of crickets and frogs. A firefly, taking refuge from the storm, clung to the outside of the screen and blinked off and on, off and on.

Although security lights illuminated the yard beyond, the porch was dark, and Rachel could barely make out Ben's features when he faced her. "I know you feel like you've been hit by a truck," she said. "I'm so sorry, Ben."

"I hope to god they'll find her alive somewhere," he said. "I have to keep hoping she's alive."

"I'm hoping for that too," Rachel said. "You know I am. But— Ben, is there something you're not telling Tom? You think your mother did go to the Taylor house Friday morning, don't you?"

Rachel heard the scratchy sound of his hand scraping over a day's growth of chin stubble. "I'm pretty sure she did, yeah."

"Why can't you tell Tom that?"

"She wanted to pay off the Taylors, give them a big chunk of money, but I was afraid she'd just make the whole situation worse. Cam would've kept coming back for more. I'd never be rid of him. But I guess she tried it anyway. That had to be her car the neighbor saw."

"She wasn't doing anything illegal," Rachel said. "Why not tell Tom?"

Ben inhaled a shaky breath. "If she's still alive, I'm not going to help the police pin the murders on her."

"What?" None of this seemed quite real to Rachel. But the murders were real. She had touched Cam Taylor's dead body. "Ben, do you think your mother could have killed the Taylors?"

She braced for an explosion of anger over the question. It didn't come.

Ben answered in a subdued voice. "She was furious about Cam trying to blackmail me. She didn't let him see how mad she was, she laughed it off when she was talking to him, and she didn't let Angie see it, but she was...*enraged.* She's always had a temper, but I've never seen her that mad before. She was storming around here, saying she could kill Cam, who the hell did he think he was, she could throttle him with her bare hands—"

"Oh, Ben, that's the kind of thing a lot of people say when they're angry. It doesn't mean she did it."

"Tom Bridger would think that was exactly what it meant. And I don't know what to think. I don't want to believe she's dead—but if she's alive, where is she? What reason would she have to hide if she didn't do anything wrong?"

They stood side by side at the screen, damp wind blowing against their faces. Rachel knew what it was like to suspect a parent was capable of something unspeakable, and she wished she could erase that suspicion from Ben's mind. But she also knew how it felt to lose a parent, and she understood why he would rather believe his mother was a fugitive than accept that she had been murdered. Now that Karen Hernandez's car had been found, Rachel felt certain she was dead, and she couldn't produce any soothing words that would help Ben.

"I lied earlier," he said. "I lied to you and Angie."

His admission brought a stab of disappointment. Ben had been utterly convincing when he'd poured out his version of what happened in New York. "Are you saying that you—"

"Yes." In the dark she heard Ben breathe in, breathe out. "I had sex with the underage girl who was posing for me. But it only happened three times, and I swear, at first I thought she was nineteen."

"So you went on…seeing her after you found out she was a minor?"

"I don't have an excuse, except that I was crazy and out of control. I'm ashamed of it. I never wanted you to know."

Rachel swallowed to push down the bile that soured her throat. Ben had sex with an underage girl and bought his way clear of criminal charges. Cam Taylor had known the whole truth, and his wife had probably known too. Of course Ben feared them. Of course his mother had been afraid for her son.

Rachel had heard a lot of theories about the Taylors' murders in the last few days, but she'd heard of no one with a stronger motive than Ben Hern and Karen Hernandez.

Abandoning the idea of confronting Lindsay right away, Tom turned toward home. He tried to shut everything else out of his mind and concentrate on navigating the flooded road, but he couldn't stop himself from reliving every minute he'd spent in Hern's house.

Tom had a gut feeling that Karen Hernandez was dead, she'd died the same day the Taylors did, but her son wasn't sure, and he was withholding something, probably to protect her. The way Rachel blindly supported and protected Hern infuriated Tom.

Lightning flashed and thunder sounded in the same instant, jolting Tom out of his thoughts and forcing his attention back to the road. He could swear the heart of the storm stayed directly above him all the way home. It made him feel like that woeful character with the unpronounceable name who trudged through the old L'il Abner comic strip with a black cloud perpetually hovering over his head.

Tom had left lights on at home for Billy Bob, and as he approached the white clapboard farmhouse the windows shone bright and welcoming in the storm. He'd always hated coming home to a dark house. Something seemed wrong, though. He was sure he hadn't left the upstairs lights on too, but now his bedroom window was lit up. Frowning, he turned into the driveway. Then he spotted Lindsay's car parked at the end, next to the house. Had she broken in?

"God damn it," he muttered. He parked behind her car, stepped into the rain, and charged up the front walk to the shelter of the porch. In the light cast by a fixture next to the door, he sorted through his keys, but before he could find the right one, Lindsay opened the door. Billy Bob stood beside her, wagging his tail.

"Oh, you're soaking wet!" Lindsay exclaimed. "You poor thing."

Tom pushed past her and slammed the door shut. "How did you get in here? If you broke a window—"

"Of course I didn't break a window. Why would you think something like that? You need a towel. I'll get you one."

Lindsay turned to head off down the hall, but Tom grabbed her arm and spun her back around to face him. "How did you get in here?"

"I used my key, of course." She pulled her arm free.

"You don't *have* a key. You gave it back to me, remember?"

"Well…" She shrugged and wrinkled her nose, giving him an apologetic half-smile. "I gave back the original, but I've still got a copy I had made."

"Why did you have a copy made?"

"You know, in case I lost my keys. You remember how I was always losing keys and Mom had to make sure we had extras. It's just second nature to me by now, to make a copy of everything." She added, "I didn't realize I still had it until tonight. It's not as if I deliberately held onto it."

"I want it," Tom said. He unbuckled his gun belt and stowed it on the shelf in the hall closet. "If you've got any more copies, I want those too."

Lindsay's silence made him turn to look at her, and he found her watching him with tear-filled eyes. "I can't believe how hateful you're being to me," she said.

"And I can't believe some of the things you've been doing," Tom shot back. "I thought I knew what you're capable of, but you've really outdone yourself in the last few days."

"I don't know what you're talking about!" she cried, sounding more wounded than angry.

"What the hell were you thinking when you encouraged that lynch mob?"

"Lynch mob? Now I *really* don't know what you're talking about."

"That meeting was your idea, wasn't it?"

Lindsay shook her head. "No. No, it wasn't. They asked me to be there, but it was not my idea. Is it so hard for you to believe that people loved my parents enough to want their killer caught?"

"And you're happy to point a finger at the person *you* want to see arrested."

"Are you saying Ben Hern isn't at the top of your suspect list?"

"Whether he's a suspect or not is beside the point. I don't have enough evidence to arrest anybody, and I'm not letting a mob push me into doing the wrong thing. You, of all people, ought to know how crazy it would be to move ahead without solid evidence."

"I don't control those people," Lindsay protested. "I don't tell them what to say or do."

"No? Where did Beck Rasey get that stuff about Rachel?"

Lindsay's blue eyes sparked with fury, and her voice trembled when she said, "It all comes back to Rachel, doesn't it? If you listen to her, you won't be able to tell the difference between the truth and a lie. Her whole life is a lie."

"Give me a break, Lindsay. I'm not stupid, I can see what you're up to."

"Tommy, you have to listen to me, you need to know."

He raised his hands. "I've heard enough from you."

"Just listen to what I've found out about her. To begin with, she's lying about her birth date and her birthplace. There's no record of a Rachel Goddard being born on that date in—"

"Stop it. You're not even making sense." Tom strode down the hall to the kitchen, Billy Bob beside him. He reached for the dog's water bowl, intending to fill it, but saw it was already full.

"I gave him fresh water," Lindsay said from the doorway. "I took him out too, and I cleaned his feet and dried him off when we came back in."

Tom brushed past her and headed up the hall again. He didn't know where he was going. He ended up in the living room, staring out a window at the rain. He wondered if Rachel was out on the road now. Brandon would be right behind her, but if she tried to drive through standing water and spun out of control, Brandon couldn't do anything to prevent an accident.

Tom was aware of Lindsay entering the room, pausing somewhere behind him. "The rain's easing up a little," he said. "You can leave now."

"Rachel's turned you against me completely," Lindsay said to his back. "We can't even be friends anymore because of her. What hurts the most is knowing how wrong she is for you. She's going to hurt you, and I can't do a damned thing to stop it."

Tom turned to see Lindsay's stricken face. "Don't you get it? I want you to stay out of my life."

She bowed her head, hiding her face from him. Her voice was sorrowful and so soft he barely caught her words. "Do you know how much I love you, Tommy?"

"Lin, don't do this. You've got to let go, for your sake and mine."

"I can't remember a time when I didn't love you. There's never been anyone else."

"That's not true."

She raised her head to meet his eyes. Tears spilled down her cheeks. "Yeah, I've seen other guys, even slept with some of them. There's a guy in Roanoke who wants to marry me, believe it or not."

"Maybe you ought to think about saying yes."

"Tommy, I don't *love* him! I've never loved anybody but you. I always thought we'd end up together. That was my dream from the time we were teenagers, marrying you and having three or four kids. But then you just walked away, moved to Richmond without me, and next thing I knew, you were engaged to somebody else. You broke my heart, Tommy. I almost didn't survive that."

The sight of her in tears because of him caught at his heart and shamed him. "Come on, Lin, what's the point of rehashing it now? It's late, it's been a long day and we're both exhausted. My head feels like somebody's beating on it with a tire iron. I want you to leave now."

She continued as if Tom hadn't spoken. "After your parents and Chris and Carol died in the accident, I heard about you breaking up with that woman because she wouldn't come and live out here in the sticks. Then you came back to me, and I thought you'd finally realized we belonged together. We'd get married and have a family. I waited *years* for you to ask me, but you wouldn't even talk about it. You were just using me till somebody better came along. Rachel took you away from me before I even knew she existed."

Tears poured down her cheeks. Tom knew he was making a mistake, but he went to her. He pulled a handkerchief from his pocket and pressed it into her hand. As she wiped her face and blew her nose, he said, "I'm sorry I hurt you. I don't blame you if you hate me."

"I wish I could hate you." She gave a sad little laugh. "But I can't, that's my problem. I just go right on loving you no matter what you do to me."

"Aw, god, Lindsay—"

Then she was wrapping her arms around his neck, pressing her body against his. "Tommy," she whispered, her breath warm in the hollow of his throat, "I need you. I feel so lost and alone without you."

"Lindsay, don't—"

She drew his head down to hers. Alarm bells clanged in his head, but his body responded to her touch, to her soft kisses on his neck. She lifted her head, murmured against his lips, "I'm so in love with you, Tommy. I'll always love you."

She pressed her lips to his as her warm fingers caressed the back of his neck. A soft moan escaped her, and he felt her tongue in his mouth, stroking his.

Something in him snapped. *This is insane.*

He pulled her arms from his neck and pushed her away. "We're not doing this. I want you to leave right now."

The kiss had banished Lindsay's tears and erased the sadness from her face, and she looked back at him with a gleam of triumph in her eyes. Her voice was soft, gently teasing. "Do you think I can't tell when you want me? I know you, Tommy. I know your body as well as I know my own. You want me as much as I want you."

The rain was only a soft *tap-tap* against the window now. He had pushed Lindsay out of his arms, but he couldn't shut out the memories of the two of them together in his bed upstairs, in her bed in Roanoke, her legs wrapped around him as they moved in a long-familiar rhythm. An image of Rachel rose in his mind too, not the warm, beautiful woman he loved but the cold, judgmental stranger who had lashed out at him in Ben Hern's living room.

"Tommy," Lindsay said, "can you look me in the eye and tell me you don't love me at all anymore? Can you tell me to my face that you don't want me anymore?"

Chapter Thirty-seven

Unable to sleep, replaying the whole disastrous evening in her mind, Rachel sat cross-legged on her bed at three in the morning and wondered if she could repair the damage Lindsay had done to her life in the last few days.

The woman's malignant maneuvering had turned Tom against her with breathtaking speed. When Rachel thought of Tom, a bottomless hole opened up inside her, and she ached with a sorrow that felt like grief. At the same time, she was angry at him and at herself. *Why do I want a man who's that weak, that easily manipulated?* If Tom had loved her, Lindsay couldn't have come between them. If he didn't love her, she would only humiliate herself by fighting for him.

Now Lindsay, not content to take Tom away from her, was spreading around a twisted version of what she'd learned so far about Rachel and her family. Hearing Beck Rasey, a virtual stranger, say anything at all about her mother would have been shocking enough, and Rachel was horrified to have her private pain dragged into the open for a hostile crowd to gape at.

Maybe she should cut her losses and get out of Mason County. She would never fit in here.

If Lindsay got her obvious wish and married Tom, she would always see Rachel as a threat and wouldn't stop until she drove her away. If she probed deeply enough into the Goddard family's background, she could do extraordinary damage. Rachel wanted above all else to protect her younger sister Michelle from Lindsay's prying.

She had moved to Mason County because she'd wanted to be among strangers and have the freedom to ignore the past. But ignoring it didn't erase it.

She longed to see her sister, hear her voice, but Michelle was with her husband, many miles away in a Washington suburb. Rachel didn't want to call in the middle of the night and scare Michelle out of her wits.

Suddenly she thought of the photo album filled with all the pictures their mother had taken of her and Michelle over the years. The album was the only thing Rachel had kept from their family home when it was emptied and sold. During her first months in Mason County, when she'd felt lonely and cut off from everything familiar, she'd browsed through the pictures almost every day, often smiling with tears in her eyes as she remembered when each one was taken. She'd been drawn back to the album less and less in the last few months, because she'd been happy with Tom and her life here and hadn't felt the need to look backward.

She switched on a lamp, causing Frank to raise his head from his resting spot at the foot of the bed. He blinked twice, then settled back into sleep.

Rachel opened the closet and reached up to the shelf, where she kept the album. But all she found were the winter blankets, folded and stacked. Where was it? She groped around, shifted the blankets and a couple of sweaters, thinking the album had somehow been pushed to the back. She couldn't find it.

It was gone.

Chapter Thirty-eight

Dennis rose from his desk and handed Tom the autopsy report on Meredith Taylor. "Just came in. I looked it over. I don't think there's anything in it we don't already know."

"I'll read it later," Tom said, glancing at the cover sheet of the faxed report. "I want to get through the rest of her manuscript before Ragsdale's bail hearing."

"You still think you're gonna find something in that book that'll make a difference?"

"I've about given up hope," Tom said, "but I want to finish it."

"Good story?" Dennis asked with a grin.

"It's pretty sad. Those kids were so naïve I keep wanting to shake some sense into them. I guess idealism has its place, but it won't get you far in the real world."

"You're a hard man, Tom Bridger."

Tom retrieved Meredith's CD from the evidence room and took it to his office. He tossed the autopsy report on his desk and sat down at the computer. Waiting for the machine to boot up, he stretched and yawned. God, what a night. He'd slept a total of about an hour. But maybe his haggard appearance, added to the bruises around his eye and nose, would help persuade the judge that Scotty Ragsdale was too dangerous to release on bail.

He slid Meredith's CD into the computer and found the spot where he'd left off last time.

The story had moved into winter, and preparations for the following summer's outdoor play about Melungeon history occupied most of Chad's time. Although this young character bore little surface resemblance to the Cameron Taylor Tom had known, his behavior was unmistakable—sometimes selfish and manipulative, trampling on other people's feelings, at other times gentle and generous. Like Cam, Chad focused obsessively on empowering the poor.

Meredith had been merciless in detailing the humiliation endured by her alter ego in the book out of love for Chad. Watching Chad with Donna, the character who represented Scotty Ragsdale's older sister Denise, the Meredith character put her emotions through some pathetic contortions in an effort to see Chad as the innocent object of Donna's obsession.

Tom read on:

Chad was so patient with her. She was a simple mountain girl and needed a tremendous amount of help if she were ever going to develop the confidence to perform onstage before an audience. He spent hours with her, coaching her on how to speak lines naturally. She threw herself at him, and he used her adoration for the good of the project. She was so completely besotted with him that she would do anything he asked her to and was willing to take his criticism and work hard to please him.

But as the weeks passed, Meredith couldn't keep up the pretense.

He had spent the previous night with me, in my house, but he told me he couldn't come over that night. Too much to do, he said, without sharing any details. When I saw him drive off around seven o'clock, I almost followed him, but I resisted the urge. If I spied on him, what would that say about the level of trust between us? I believed he loved me and wouldn't lie to me. If he said he had work to do, I believed him.

Snow had started falling, adding to the several inches already on the ground. My little house was frigid, despite the coal fire in the potbellied stove. I had on my coat and gloves, but I still shivered as I stood by the window, watching and waiting for him to return.

I stood there for an hour, waiting. When I saw headlights approaching, my heartbeat quickened. The car turned into the yard of Chad's house, a hundred feet away. I smiled and tugged my scarf tight around my neck, preparing to run over and join him.

Then I saw her. Chad parked, and when he opened his door the dome light went on and I saw he wasn't alone. Donna opened the passenger door and got out. By then Chad had walked around to her side. In the dim glow through the open passenger door, I saw him slide his arms around her. They were locked together for what seemed a lifetime, while I stood rooted at my window, unable to tear my eyes away.

The narrative went on to describe her vigil, the shadowy movements she saw behind the curtains of Chad's one-room shack, the long evening that ended when he drove his visitor away and returned alone. Meredith didn't confront him. Instead, she asked herself what the other girl was giving him that he wasn't getting from her.

Reading that, Tom felt a clutch of guilt because he realized Lindsay had been asking herself the same question about him and Rachel. But he had no reason to feel guilty. He hadn't lied to Lindsay. He'd broken off with her months before he and Rachel became seriously involved.

He shook off thoughts of his own screwed-up life and concentrated on the story unspooling on his computer screen.

When she and Holly left for work, Rachel was still seething about the photo album's disappearance, but she tried to hide her anger from Holly.

She was sure Lindsay had taken the album. Who else would want it?

She felt as if Lindsay had stolen her memories when she took the only remaining link to Rachel's childhood. What did

Lindsay plan to do with the pictures? Rachel didn't even want to imagine.

If she forced a confrontation, Lindsay would deny everything, claim Rachel was persecuting her while she was going through a personal crisis. Rachel couldn't tell Tom that Lindsay had stolen something from her, not without proof. And Rachel's accusation might spur Lindsay on to even more devious and destructive actions.

That lying little bitch, Rachel thought, her hands tightening on the steering wheel. She was furious at Tom for being so gullible, for buying into Lindsay's act. His seven-year-old nephew could see behind Lindsay's mask. Why couldn't Tom?

Driving past the barn and stables, Rachel murmured noncommittal answers to Holly's chatter about the clear, cool morning ushered in by last night's rain. She hadn't told Holly what happened at the meeting, and she wouldn't tell her if she could avoid it.

They were approaching Joanna's house when Joanna ran to the edge of the farm road and waved her arms, signaling Rachel to stop. Noting Lindsay's car in the driveway, Rachel braked in the middle of the road instead of pulling over, and as soon as the window on the passenger side was down she leaned around Holly and called out, "We don't have time to come in."

Joanna waved that aside and hustled around to Rachel's window. "A friend of mine just called and told me what happened at that awful meeting last night. Honey, I am so sorry. I'm going to give Lindsay a piece of my mind."

"What do you mean?" Holly asked. "What happened at the meeting?"

Oh, great. Now she'd have to give Holly every revolting detail, and the girl's sensitive nature would have her fretting for days over it. "I'll explain later," Rachel told Holly. To Joanna, she said, "Don't worry about me."

"Well, I think it's unforgivable, and I'm sure Lindsay's to blame. I sympathize with her for losing both her parents, but that doesn't give her the right—"

"Let it go, Joanna. Please."

Joanna shook her head. "No. She has to answer for this. In fact, I'm not going to wait for her to get up. I'm going to wake her up and tell her what I think."

Rachel sighed. If Lindsay got a tongue-lashing from Joanna, she would take out her resentment on Rachel.

Joanna went on, "I'll bet she didn't come back last night because she was afraid I'd already heard and she didn't want to face me. So she snuck back in the house during the wee hours of the morning, probably thinking I wouldn't hear her."

The wee hours of the morning? Where had Lindsay been all that time? With Tom? An image of the two of them together popped up in Rachel's mind, and she felt breathless, lightheaded and sick.

"I hope she'll go back to Roanoke after the funeral," Joanna was saying.

Rachel pulled herself back to the here and now. "When is the funeral?"

"She told me yesterday the bodies are being released today, so it shouldn't be long now. She has an appointment at one o'clock to make arrangements with the funeral home. Unfortunately, that leaves *me* to deal with those damn goats. I've found somebody to take them, but he wants me to deliver them, so I have to spend my afternoon wrestling them onto a truck."

"Oh? What time will you be taking them?" Rachel asked.

"Well, right after lunch is what I'm planning on. Twelve-thirty, one. Why? You want to come and help?"

"Sorry, I'll be too busy in the middle of the day," Rachel said, her mind already skipping ahead. If she rearranged her afternoon schedule, she could clear an hour, get back here while both Lindsay and Joanna were away from the farm, and search Lindsay's room for the photo album.

Chapter Thirty-nine

Tom glanced at his watch. Ragsdale's bail hearing was set for 1 p.m. A dozen minor things had interrupted his reading, but he could get through the rest of Meredith's book by then if he skimmed.

He doubted this was a finished manuscript, because some of the latest pages he'd read seemed hurried and sketchy, as if she meant to go back and fill them out in another draft. Those pages were also boring as hell, because they concentrated on the VISTA campaign to force the county to send snow plows up every narrow road, paved or unpaved, in every hollow in Rocky Branch District.

Tapping the mouse button with one finger, Tom moved through all that material without reading it closely. He slowed when the story became personal again. On the night of a heavy snowfall, Meredith and Celia/Karen met with Chad at his house to discuss new developments in their plans for the Melungeon play. But VISTAs weren't the only people present. Chad had brought Donna, the local girl, home with him again, and Meredith wasn't happy about it.

The story continued:

How much more was I expected to endure? Why didn't Chad see that he was tearing me apart? Donna touched him, leaned against him, and when he sat on the bed she sat next to him and glued her hip and leg to his. I waited for him to push her away, but he didn't. She complained about being cold, and snuggled closer to him.

I was standing by the stove with Celia, watching Chad and Donna. I couldn't help saying to Donna, "If you're cold, you should come over here by the stove. Or put your coat back on."

She gave me a self-satisfied little smile. "I'm nice and cozy now, thanks."

Chad laughed.

Then he delivered the final blow to my dignity. Donna had to go home early so she could finish a paper for school the next day. She expected Chad to drive her. But he said he had to stay and iron out a few details about the play with Celia.

Donna pouted. She acted like a little girl who's been told she can't have a treat. "Cha-a-a-d," she whined, clutching his arm and leaning against him, "can't you spare just a few little minutes for me? How am I going to get home?"

Chad looked at me. "You can drive her."

A terrible sense of betrayal overwhelmed me when I realized he knew exactly how much he was hurting me. He was trying to prove that he could make me do anything he told me to do, and that included providing taxi service for the girl he'd been sleeping with behind my back.

I don't know where I found the nerve, and the truth is I was shaking inside, but I looked him in the eyes and said the one word he'd never heard from me before. "No."

Chad stared at me for what seemed an eternity. Then he got up and stood so close that I could feel his breath on my face. "Take her home," he said, very quietly.

Celia and Donna were watching us. I felt tears filling my eyes and I hated myself for being so weak. "Take her yourself," I said, even though the last thing I wanted was for him to be alone with Donna. Once I'd spoken my brave words, I didn't have the confidence to let my refusal stand. I had to justify it. "It's snowing too hard and my car doesn't have good tires."

He narrowed his eyes and I could tell he was furious with me. "You're from upstate New York," he said. "Don't tell me you don't know how to drive in the snow."

"Why can't Celia take her?" I couldn't just say I didn't want to and leave it at that. I had to go on seeking his approval.

"I told you, Celia and I have things to work out together."

I looked at Celia, who looked back with a tiny, self-satisfied smile on her face.

I had a choice between leaving Chad alone here with Celia or insisting that he and Donna go off alone.

Chad pulled my coat out of the pile on the bed and held it up. I thought of all the things I should say, but I didn't say any of them. I wanted to snatch my coat away from him and stomp out and go back to my house, but I didn't. I slipped my arms into my coat and buttoned it up. Donna, still pouting, put on hers.

Donna kissed Chad—a quick little peck, but it was enough to make my heart constrict.

Donna wouldn't shut up in the car. She recovered from her pique over Chad refusing to drive her home and talked nonstop about him. "He's not like these boys around here. He's so smart, and so educated, and he's got so many great ideas. He makes all the boys around here look stupid and lazy."

The car was pitch black and I couldn't see her. I held tightly to the steering wheel and tried to concentrate on driving. The snow was falling so heavily that I couldn't see the road anymore. The windshield wipers couldn't keep up with the snow, and they made an ominous groaning sound as they scraped the glass.

"Chad's goin' places," Donna said. "He'll be an important man someday."

"And you think you're going to be part of his life?" I asked.

"Yes," Donna answered proudly. "I will be."

"What makes you so sure?"

"I love him, and he loves me."

I couldn't take it anymore.

"Shut up!" I screamed. "You're out of your mind if you think he cares about you. You're nothing but a stupid little hick."

"Ha!" Donna said. "I guess you think he loves *you*. Well, I happen to know the only reason he paid any attention to you was because he feels *sorry* for you."

"You don't know anything," I said. "He's just using you. You're nothing but a slut."

"Don't you dare talk to me that way!" Donna cried. "I'm gonna tell Chad what you said. He loves me. He told me so. He's *mine*."

I braked so hard that Donna screamed.

I couldn't control myself. I was out of my mind with anger and resentment and pain. I put the car in park.

"What's the matter with you?" Donna yelled.

I jumped out and left the door open so the dome light would stay on. I went around the car and felt for the handle of the passenger door. I opened it and reached inside and grabbed Donna's arm.

"Have you gone crazy?" she cried.

I had both my hands around Donna's arm and I was pulling her out of the car. I'd never felt such strength before.

I yanked her out and she fell onto her knees on the snow-covered road.

I pulled her to her feet and pushed her away from the car. She screamed and started beating her arms at me. I pushed her again, and she stumbled into a big pile of snow by the side of the road and fell again.

I got back in the car and made a U-turn. I drove away and left Donna on the dark road in the snow.

I told myself I had left her close enough to her family's house that she could walk home. I was sure she knew her way around, even in the dark.

I returned to my own house. I added coal to the stove, for all the good it would do with winter blasting through a million cracks in the thin walls. I crawled into bed in all my clothes, including my coat and boots, and I pulled the blankets over me and cried for hours.

I didn't care if Chad and Celia called me a coward and a quitter. I was going home as soon as I could get out of this place.

Eventually I cried myself to sleep, and I didn't wake up until the next morning when someone banged on my door. It was Celia. She barged in as soon as I unlocked the door, and Chad was right behind her. The storm had passed and the sun was shining, sparkling on the fresh snow in the yard.

"What's going on?" I asked, groggy from too little sleep. I combed my fingers through my hair, concerned even then about how I looked to Chad and hating myself for caring.

"Donna's family's looking for her," Celia said. "She didn't make it home last night."

"What?" I said, confused. "But I—"

Chad gripped my arm tightly, his eyes boring into mine, and pulled me farther away from Celia. He spoke in an intense whisper. "Where did you let her out?"

I whispered too. "Near her house, just up the road—"

"You left her right in front of her house, do you understand? You saw her walking toward the house."

"I—I—" I couldn't string together words. I could feel Celia watching us.

"Nobody can blame you," Chad said, his voice now strong and certain. "You were right in front of the house, and she was walking toward the house, so you thought she was home safely and you headed back."

I couldn't tear my eyes from his. I was mesmerized, as if every bit of inner strength I had was draining away and he was filling me with his will, his determination.

I heard a car door slam outside, then footsteps on the porch and a knock on the door. Celia went to open the door.

Chad leaned close and whispered to me, "The local politicians are just itching for an excuse to scrap the poverty program. If anything happened to that girl because of a VISTA—"

Celia opened the door and Donna's sixteen-year-old brother, Larry, was standing there. Tears ran down his face.

Celia stood back and motioned for him to come in. For a moment nobody spoke. Larry wiped his face with his sleeve. Finally he said, "They found her. The deputies found her in a ditch by the road, curled up like a baby and all covered with snow. She froze to death."

He burst into sobs.

I couldn't breathe. I felt as if cold fingers were strangling me. What had I done? I never meant to hurt her.

Celia watched Larry silently, but Chad was watching me. I knew what I had to do. The only thing I could do.

I went to Larry and placed a hand on his shoulder. "I'm so sorry," I whispered. "If I'd known there was any danger, I would have driven all the way up the driveway to the house before I let her out. But she said it was okay, we were right in front of the house and she didn't want me to go up the driveway because the car would probably get stuck. Maybe somebody else came along after I drove away, and she...I can't imagine what happened. Oh, Larry, I feel awful. I'm so sorry. If I could go back and—"

"It's not your fault," he said. He laid his head on my shoulder, and I patted his back while he cried like a heartbroken child.

In that moment I surrendered my dreams for the future and began a lifetime of atonement.

The manuscript ended there.

Chapter Forty

At 1 p.m., the side door of the courtroom banged open and Scotty Ragsdale shuffled in, handcuffed and flanked by the Blackwood twins. The deputies steered him to a chair at the defense table. Ragsdale shot a belligerent look at Tom and Brandon in the front row behind the prosecutor, but he ignored his parents sitting directly behind him.

In a courtroom that could hold 100, the Ragsdales were the only spectators other than Tom and Brandon. Irma Ragsdale blotted her tears with a crumpled tissue. Beside her, Carl sat with his jaw clamped tight, staring at the back of Scotty's head. Tom imagined Carl asking himself for the millionth time how they'd ended up with a son like this.

Following Tom's advance orders, Kevin Blackwood unlocked the plastic cuffs when Ragsdale was seated, and Keith grabbed the prisoner's right arm and clicked his wrist into the metal cuff dangling from a bolt on the table.

Irma Ragsdale whimpered and reached across the railing that separated her from her son. The Blackwoods stepped between them, and her husband pulled Irma back onto the bench. "They don't have to chain him up like a dog!" she wailed.

Jeff Fuller, the young lawyer at Scotty's side, swiveled in his chair to lodge a protest with the prosecutor. "Is it really necessary to handcuff my client in the courtroom?"

Raymond Morton, the longtime Commonwealth's Attorney for Mason County, swung his head around in a long, slow glide and gave Fuller a raised-eyebrow *Are you talking to ME?* look. After a moment he said, "Yes." Then he returned his attention to the papers on the table before him.

Fuller's cheeks flushed deep red and he faced forward again without another word.

Brandon sniggered, but Tom had too much sympathy for the older Ragsdales to laugh at this situation. In the past, they'd hired the best attorneys they could afford for Scotty, but they'd apparently run out of local lawyers who were willing to get involved in a lost cause. This time, with Scotty facing charges of assaulting two police officers and possible murder charges looming in the near future, the Ragsdales had scraped the bottom of the barrel and come up with Fuller. He was borderline competent at best and had spoken with his client for a total of three minutes before the hearing.

The Ragsdales had always bailed out their son, but today Tom hoped the judge would set the amount so high they wouldn't be able to swing it. He wanted Scotty to stay in jail. Meredith's manuscript—if it recounted actual events—provided a credible motive for Ragsdale to kill both Meredith and Cam Taylor. The man had obviously loved his sister, and if he'd somehow discovered after all these years that Meredith caused her death and Cam helped her cover it up, Ragsdale would have lashed out. Armed with a new knowledge of past events, Tom believed he could wring the truth out of him if he had Ragsdale in custody.

"All rise," the elderly bailiff intoned, sounding as if he were stifling a yawn.

Judge Angus Buckley took his place and frowned over his bifocals at the defendant. "My lord, Scotty, I thought you'd cleaned up your act and started behaving like a man."

Fuller leapt to his feet. "Your honor! Is it really necessary to—"

"Oh, sit down," Judge Buckley said. "Let's get on with it."

After Ragsdale entered his not guilty plea and the judge advised him of his rights in the court system, they moved on to the bail hearing.

"Your honor," the prosecutor said, rising, "the defendant is a suspect in three murders. When Captain Bridger and Deputy Connelly visited his home to question him, he attacked both of them. As you can see, they're still recovering from their injuries. At the time of the attack, the defendant was under the influence of drugs and was brandishing an ax. Only the deputies' quick action in subduing the defendant prevented far more serious, and possibly fatal, injuries."

Tom heard a whimper of protest from Irma Ragsdale. Her husband hushed her. Scotty slumped over the defense table, his head down.

"As you know, your honor," the prosecutor continued, "Mr. Ragsdale has a long history of drug abuse. And the recent assault was the second time he has tried to harm Captain Bridger."

When Fuller's turn came, he reminded the judge that Ragsdale had stayed clean for several years, ran a one-man woodworking and restoration business that supported him, and had lifelong ties in the community. "He realizes how disappointing it is to his family that he allowed his grief over the death of a close friend to pull him back into bad habits," the lawyer concluded, "but it was a temporary setback, and he is determined to resume living a productive life. He poses no risk of flight and is not a threat to anyone in the community. I'm asking that you release him on his own recognizance into his parents' custody."

Tom barely listened. He was busy plotting his strategy for drawing a confession from Ragsdale. The man was so volatile right now, with so much preying on his mind, that one poorly chosen word could ruin any chance of getting him to talk.

When the arguments concluded, Judge Buckley studied Ragsdale long enough to make him squirm under the scrutiny. At last the judge said, "Scotty, I don't want to believe this slip-up means you're falling back into your old patterns, but common sense tells me it's highly likely. And on top of those misgivings, I take a dim view of anybody attacking an officer of the law."

Tom nodded, relieved that things were going the way he wanted. Then Irma Ragsdale stood and spoke directly to the judge. "Please, Angus, just let us take him home. We'll make him stay with us, we'll get him some help, I promise we will. It's just killing me to see him in jail."

The judge sighed, and he looked so sympathetic that Tom felt compelled to interrupt. Getting to his feet, he said, "Your honor, if you'll allow me to speak—"

"Hold on, Tom," the judge said, raising a hand. After another long look at Scotty Ragsdale, he said, "I'm setting bail at $200,000."

Carl Ragsdale gasped, and a cry of distress escaped his wife.

"The usual restrictions apply. Court is adjourned." Ignoring Fuller's cries of protest against the high bail, the judge swept out of the courtroom.

Tom stood to leave, satisfied with the outcome. While the Ragsdales tried to find the money to free their son, Tom would get a confession out of him and charge him with three counts of felony murder.

Chapter Forty-one

By the time Rachel got away from the animal hospital, it was past one o'clock, and she was afraid she'd blown her chance to search Lindsay's room. Lindsay's car sat in the funeral home parking lot when Rachel drove by, but how long had she been there and how soon would she leave?

Rachel sped out of town and made it to the horse farm in less than twenty minutes. As she turned into the farm road, she debated whether to park in plain view outside Joanna's house, so any employee who passed would wonder why she was there in the middle of the day when Joanna and Lindsay were absent. If she hid her vehicle, on the other hand, and someone saw her stealthily entering or leaving the house, she might arouse even greater suspicion. Both possibilities fed her guilt about doing this behind Joanna's back. She was sure, though, that Joanna wouldn't approve a search of Lindsay's room and belongings, and she didn't want to lose this opportunity to find the photo album.

Rachel bypassed the paved driveway in favor of a dirt track on the far side of Joanna's house that led to a big tool shed in the back yard. She parked behind the shed and hustled toward the house, feeling as if a million eyes were watching.

Her hands shook as she inserted a key in the lock. Joanna had entrusted her with keys to the front and rear doors in case she ever needed to get into the house in an emergency, but Rachel doubted the current circumstances were what Joanna had in mind.

Inside the kitchen, Rachel closed the door and leaned against it, letting her racing heart slow down. So far, so good, but she couldn't even guess how much time she had before either Lindsay or Joanna returned. She hurried along the hallway and up the stairs. When she reached the second floor, she paused, watching dust motes float in sunlight at the far end of the hall, listening for sounds from behind the closed bedroom doors. She heard nothing. The silent emptiness of the house spooked her a little, and she scolded herself. *Stop wasting time. Get moving!*

She entered Lindsay's room, closed the door, and walked straight to the dresser. Yanking out the drawers one by one, she ran a hand beneath a jumble of panties and bras. God, what a mess Lindsay left her belongings in. Rachel hated the feel of the slick fabric against her own skin because it had touched Lindsay's most intimate places.

Nothing there.

Moving fast, she searched the bureau, which was empty, and the closet, where she found only a few tee shirts, a pair of jeans, and a pair of black gabardine slacks.

Damn it, where did she put it? Unless Lindsay had hidden the photo album in her car, it had to be in this room. Wiping her sweaty palms on her slacks, Rachel turned in a circle, looking for more hiding places. Her gaze came round to the bed.

Rachel dropped to her hands and knees, lifted the bedskirt, peered under. Nothing there either. She sat up, drew the bed's coverlet and top sheet out of the way, and shoved her hand and half her arm between the mattress and box springs. She felt all the way up, then back down again on that side of the bed. She moved to the other side and repeated her blind search.

Halfway down, her fingers collided with something solid. She grabbed it and pulled it out. The photo album's green leather cover had *A Book of Memories* embossed on the front in gold.

"Yes," Rachel whispered, hugging the album to her breast. She felt as if she'd snatched something precious from a fire.

But was the album intact? Had Lindsay removed pictures, perhaps to use in tracking down information about Rachel's family?

She flipped through the pages, watching her sister and herself age from small children to teenagers to young adults. The pages were still full, the photos where they should be. She allowed herself a sigh of relief, then scrambled to her feet. She had to get out of here. She didn't know how much longer—

The door opened.

"What the hell?" Lindsay exclaimed.

Rachel froze.

"What are you doing in my room?"

Lindsay started forward, and Rachel instinctively tried to step back, but she bumped against the bed, lost her balance, and sat down hard. Infuriated by her own awkwardness as much as Lindsay's self-righteous outrage, she jumped to her feet and held up the album. "I was looking for this. It happens to belong to me."

Lindsay halted, staring at the album, and a flush rose to her pale cheeks. "I don't even know what that is."

"Your fingerprints are probably on every page. Did you think I wouldn't realize who took it? I don't know what sick and twisted reason you had for stealing a photo album, but I never doubted for a minute that you had it."

Lindsay tilted her head up to meet Rachel's eyes with her own hard glare. "You're crazy. You brought that here to plant it, didn't you? You're so determined to turn Tom against me, you're so afraid he's going to come back to me—"

"I think you're dangerous, but I'm not afraid of you," Rachel said, trying to believe the lie.

A sour little smile formed on Lindsay's lips. "Well," she said, "you should be. I haven't figured out exactly what you're hiding, but I know it's something big, and I'll uncover it sooner or later."

An involuntary shudder moved through Rachel and her throat closed up as if a hand gripped it. *Leave. Just take the album and go.*

She was moving past Lindsay when Lindsay's cell phone rang.

"Get out of my room," Lindsay said, at the same time pulling her phone from her pants pocket. Keeping her eyes on Rachel, not checking the display, she pressed a button to answer the call.

Rachel was almost through the doorway when she heard Lindsay's gasp. Pausing, she looked back.

Lindsay, pale-faced and open-mouthed, seemed to have forgotten Rachel was there. "But—but how—" she stuttered. "I don't—I can't believe—"

What on earth had happened? Another murder? Rachel went cold inside, waiting for Lindsay to say something that would tell her what was going on.

Lindsay's gaze jumped around the room but didn't seem to focus on anything. Her breath sounded harsh and fast and she swayed on her feet as if she were about to faint. For a second Rachel's instinct to help overcame her loathing for the woman, and she moved forward to steady Lindsay.

Lindsay's eyes widened as they locked on Rachel. "Get out! Get out of here!"

She shoved Rachel toward the door. Rachel shook Lindsay off and stepped into the hall. "What's wrong? What's happened?"

"*Get out!*" Lindsay pointed down the hall. "Now!"

Clutching the photo album, conscious of Lindsay watching, Rachel strode toward the stairs. She rounded the corner and, knowing she was out of sight, paused on the top stair. Lindsay's door slammed shut.

Rachel peeked around to make sure Lindsay was in her room, then she crept back into the hallway and tiptoed to the door. She had to find out what had shocked Lindsay so profoundly. *Oh, God,* she prayed silently, *don't let it be Tom. Please don't let anything happen to Tom.*

On the other side of the door, Lindsay sounded agitated, frantic, her voice higher and louder than normal. "Where are you? I need to know where you are."

A pause.

"No, I won't," Lindsay said. "I promise I won't. Tell me where you are! I'll come right away, I'll bring everything you need."

Another brief silence.

"Which McClure house? What are you talking—" Lindsay broke off, apparently interrupted by the caller. A moment later, she said, "Where Pauline McClure lived? But it's all boarded up. How did—Never mind. I'm coming. I'll get some things together and come right away."

Rachel jerked back from the door and hurried down the hall, going as fast as she could without making any noise. She shot down the stairs and out through the kitchen door. In the yard, she broke into a run. She didn't feel safe from detection until she was behind the tool shed where she'd parked. Waiting beside her vehicle, she listened for the sounds of Lindsay's departure.

Five minutes went by. In her mind Rachel went over Lindsay's half of the mysterious conversation again, searching for clues to its meaning. Something important had happened. Something that had knocked Lindsay for a loop, shattered her cool, disdainful self-assurance. Rachel still thought it was most likely that someone else had been murdered. But who? And who was Lindsay going to meet at the empty, closed-up house that Holly had inherited from her dead aunt?

Rachel heard a car door slam, an engine revving, a squeal of tires. She waited a couple more minutes to give Lindsay a head start. As she climbed into her SUV to follow, one clear thought formed in her head: *This is crazy.* But she intended to find out what Lindsay was up to. Nobody else would do it. If she reported this situation to Tom, he would think, at worst, that Rachel had lost her mind. At best, he would think she was inventing things out of a jealous desire to make trouble for Lindsay.

She set off toward Pauline McClure's house, forcing herself to drive slowly so there would be no chance of Lindsay spotting her.

Chapter Forty-two

"We're stealing your dog," Darla Duncan called out when she saw Tom coming down the hall toward his office.

"Uncle Tom!" Simon cried, and he launched himself at Tom. Billy Bob, liberated from Tom's office, hustled after the boy, panting and drooling.

Tom stooped to hug his nephew. "Don't give Billy Bob any candy, okay?"

"I won't, I promise." With a mischievous grin, Simon added, "But he might steal some from me."

Coming up behind him, Darla tousled her grandson's black hair. "Well, I guess that means *you* can't have any either."

Simon groaned and made a face.

Suddenly remembering something Rachel had said the night before, Tom asked Darla, "Do you mind if I talk to Simon for a second?"

A few months ago, she would have bristled at being excluded, but her easy agreement was a sign of how far they'd come in building a better relationship. "I'll take Billy Bob out for a visit with the nearest tree before we get in the car."

Taking his nephew's hand, Tom led him into the office. He lifted Simon to the desk and sat beside him. "Listen, champ, I want to ask you something. Promise you'll tell me the truth, the whole truth, and nothing but the truth?"

Laughing, Simon nodded.

Might as well be blunt about it, Tom thought. He'd get a more telling reaction that way. "Did Lindsay do something that upset you? I don't mean just the last few days, but back when she was my girlfriend."

Simon's cheerful expression had dropped away the second he heard Lindsay's name, and it was replaced by fearful uncertainty. Rachel's words had been in the back of Tom's mind since the night before. *Haven't you ever wondered exactly why your nephew can't stand being around Lindsay?* Tom wasn't blind—he knew Simon didn't like her, and that was yet another reason why he'd broken off the relationship. But Rachel seemed to be implying that Lindsay had done something specific to turn Simon against her. He doubted Rachel knew anything about his nephew that he didn't. But the look on Simon's face now told Tom that he had, in fact, let something get past him. *A hell of a detective you are,* he thought.

Simon squirmed, hunching his shoulders and staring at the floor.

"Hey, now." Tom squeezed the boy's shoulder. "You know you can tell me anything, don't you?"

Simon swung a leg forward and back, banging his heel against the desk, and mumbled something Tom didn't catch.

"What's that?"

With obvious reluctance, Simon raised his eyes to meet Tom's. "She said you'd be mad at me," he whispered. "You'd say I was making it up, and you wouldn't want to be my uncle anymore."

Jesus Christ. What would make Lindsay say such a thing to a little boy? "Hey, I'll always be your uncle," he told Simon. "You're stuck with me. I love you, champ, and there's nothing you could tell me that would make me mad at you. Nothing. Understand?"

Simon hesitated, his gaze searching Tom's face. "You sure?"

"Never more sure of anything in my whole life," Tom said. He pulled Simon into a hug. "Come on now. Whatever this is, I think it's been bothering you a lot, and I want to help."

Simon buried his face against Tom's shirt. "She told me I was in the way," he said, his voice muffled. "She said you just wanted to spend time with *her* on the weekends, and I was always in the way and you didn't really want me around. And I told her that wasn't true, and she—she *hit* me. She slapped me."

For a minute Tom couldn't speak. He wasn't sure what he'd been expecting, but it was nothing this outrageous. He hugged Simon closer and kissed the top of his head, forgetting for the moment that the boy thought he was too big to be kissed by anybody but his grandmother. Right now he was a very young child, baffled by the behavior of adults. "I wish—" Tom had to stop to clear his throat. "I sure wish you'd told me about that right after it happened, champ."

"I couldn't!" Simon cried. He pulled back so he could look up at Tom. "She said she was real sorry, she didn't mean to do it, but if I ever told you, *ever*, she'd say I was lying, and you'd believe her 'cause grownups always believe each other and not little kids."

"Listen to me," Tom said. "I'm glad you told me. I believe you, because I know you're honest and you don't tell lies. You're a real big, important part of my life, understand?"

Tears glistened in Simon's eyes, but he nodded.

Tom smoothed the boy's unruly hair. "You're my best bud, right? Huh?"

Simon gave Tom a tiny smile, the beginning of confidence returning to his face.

"Hey, come on," Tom said. "If you're gonna grin, make it a real one. Do I have to tickle it out of you?"

He tickled the boy's ribs and at last Simon broke into a broad grin.

◇◇◇

A few minutes later, with Simon and Billy Bob in the car with Darla and headed for a nearby lake to feed and terrorize the ducks, Tom began printing out the last chapter of Meredith's unfinished book. He had to act fast. If Ragsdale's parents raised the money to get him out of jail, Tom would lose a big psychological advantage.

He expected Ragsdale to refuse at first to read the manuscript pages. After he did, he probably wouldn't admit they contained the truth about his sister's death. Tom could hear him already: *You wrote this yourself. You're trying to trick me. I'm on to you.* But Tom believed that if he kept up the pressure, Ragsdale would break sooner or later.

While the pages printed, he took a closer look at the autopsy report on Meredith, another weapon he could use to break down Ragsdale's defenses. Tom skipped to the medical examiner's conclusion and read that first. Meredith had suffered both a gunshot wound and blunt trauma to the head, either of which could have killed her. The damage done by the fire made determination of the exact cause and time of death impossible, but her lungs were clear, which meant she had stopped breathing before the fire started. "Thank heaven for small mercies," Tom muttered.

He turned back to the first page of the report, which contained details about the general condition of the body as well as the degree of damage to skin, hair, skull. Her internal organs were intact and healthy. The joints of her fingers and knees showed early signs of degenerative arthritis. Her lumbar spine had been fused at L4-L5 with a bone transplant, indicative of a herniated disc.

Tom frowned. A spinal fusion? That was major surgery with a long, painful recovery and rehab period. When did she have it done? No doctor in Mason County could have performed the surgery, which meant Meredith had gone elsewhere—for weeks, maybe months. Had this happened when he was working for the Richmond Police Department? That was a reasonable explanation. But Tom's mother had delivered a stream of in-depth reports on the lives of Mason Countians, including the Taylors, during those years, and he didn't recall her mentioning that Meredith had serious surgery. Maybe she'd told him and he'd tuned it out. It wouldn't have seemed important to him at the time.

Lindsay could fill him in. But he didn't trust himself to be civil with Lindsay right now. Who else would know? Joanna McKendrick. She was the only person in Mason County who had remained close to Meredith through all the Taylors' ups and downs over the decades.

At this hour, Joanna would be out working on the farm. Tom pulled his personal notebook of phone numbers from a desk drawer and found Joanna's cell number. When she answered she sounded winded and harried.

"Hey, it's Tom," he said. "Did I catch you at a bad time?"

"Oh, no. It's a wonderful time. I'm out at Hank Russell's place. He's taking these damn goats off my hands, but I had to deliver them. I'll tell you, getting a bunch of stubborn goats onto a truck is not my idea of fun. But it's gonna be a *lot* of fun to drive away and leave them behind."

"I'm sorry to interrupt, but look, I just had a quick question for you. Do you know whether Meredith ever had spine surgery?"

Joanna was silent a moment before answering. "Spine surgery? What on earth makes you ask that?"

"I can't tell you right now, but I need to know. Did she ever have a spinal fusion?"

"Good lord, no."

"You're positive?" Tom's mouth had gone dry.

"Yeah, I'm positive. Do you have any idea what's involved in the recovery from that kind of surgery?" Joanna said. "I mean, it just takes over your whole life. My brother had a herniated disc removed and his lower spine fused, and it was three months before—"

"So if Meredith had it done," Tom broke in, "you would have known about it?"

"Well, of course I would've. Tom, what's this about?"

"I'll tell you later. I'll let you get back to the goats."

Tom dropped the receiver back into its cradle, then pulled his case notebook from the top desk drawer, his mind swirling with speculation and half-formed thoughts. Was it possible he'd been staring at the truth all along without seeing it? He needed answers, he had to finish this, set things right.

He thumbed through the notebook for Ben Hern's home number.

Angie Hogencamp answered.

"It's Tom Bridger," he said. "Let me talk to Hern."

"Do you have news about his mother?"

"I need to ask him a question. Put him on, please."

"No. I won't."

"What? Angie—"

"I'm not going to let you badger him anymore."

"Put him on the line, Angie. I don't have any time to waste."

"No!"

But in the next second Tom heard the scuffling sound of the phone being removed from her hand. Then Hern said, "Hello? Who is this?"

"Tom Bridger. I've got a question for you."

"What is it now?"

"Has your mother ever had spine surgery? A spinal fusion?"

The silence stretched out. Tom imagined realization washing over Hern in a hot wave, the same way it was hitting him. When Hern spoke again, his voice had gone flat. "Yes, she did. My mother had a spinal fusion. You've found her, haven't you?"

Chapter Forty-three

Rachel pulled onto a dirt track through the woods a few hundred feet from the McClure property entrance. If passing motorists looked up the narrow path, they might see her vehicle, but she counted on most drivers keeping their eyes straight ahead.

She grabbed her birdwatching binoculars from the glove compartment and climbed out. Like Ben's property, the McClure place was secluded, the house set far back and screened from the road by trees and shrubs. She would have to get close enough to see what was going on around the house without exposing her presence to anyone who glanced toward the woods.

She still believed the shocking news Lindsay received by phone might have been a report of another murder, and she wouldn't be surprised to see deputies' cars parked outside the house, uniformed men standing around while Dr. Gretchen Lauter, the medical examiner, bent over the body of—who? She would know soon enough.

Stashing her sunglasses in her shirt pocket with her cell phone, she wondered why Lindsay had been called to the scene of a murder. She had seemed stunned by the phone call, as if it concerned someone she cared about, but Tom wouldn't want her on the scene if somebody she was close to had been killed. If it hadn't been a report of another murder, what had shocked Lindsay so profoundly?

Stop speculating and find out, Rachel told herself, irritated by her own circular thoughts. She waded into the undergrowth in the dense woods.

After a refreshingly cool morning, the day had heated up, and a couple of minutes of fighting off clingy vines and sticky brambles left Rachel dripping with perspiration. The sweat attracted the inevitable gnats. She batted them away with one hand while shoving aside vegetation with the other.

She could hardly believe she was doing this, and she wouldn't want anyone to know she'd gone to such lengths to snoop on Lindsay. She cringed at the thought of Tom's and Lindsay's reactions if they discovered her lurking in the woods. But she was here now, so she might as well take a look and satisfy her curiosity. Then she had to get back to work. Her late afternoon schedule at the vet clinic was booked solid, and she'd already been gone longer than she'd planned.

She glimpsed the house through the trees up ahead. Abandoning her battle with the gnats, she raised the binoculars. Vegetation blocked her view of the yard and the first floor of the house, and all she saw were the roof and the second story. She had to get closer.

Letting the binoculars dangle from their strap around her neck, she used both hands to brush aside evergreen branches. When she was about a hundred feet from the edge of the woods, she raised the binoculars again.

The driveway and the overgrown yard were empty. No cars, no people. The big brick house—the McClure mansion, most people called it—looked closed up tight, its windows covered with boards that had long ago weathered to a silver-gray.

Odd. Rachel was positive she'd heard Lindsay correctly. *Which McClure house? Where Pauline McClure lived? But it's all boarded up. Never mind. I'm coming.* Had Lindsay been here and gone already? Or had she parked her car behind the house?

Careful to stay well back where she couldn't be seen, Rachel circled the yard, pushing through the tangled carpet of weeds and vines in the woods. The birds, she noticed, had fallen silent, and several squirrels chittered furiously from branches above her, probably reacting to Rachel's intrusion. Nothing strange about that, but the longer she slogged through the woods, the creepier this situation felt. Unspeakable things had happened on this property. In these woods.

Rachel had driven out here the previous January, soon after Holly learned she would inherit her aunt's fortune and house. They had planned to take a look inside the house, but when they arrived Holly refused to get out of the car. They'd left after a couple of minutes, with Holly declaring she would never live in that awful old place and wouldn't care if it crumbled to the ground.

Why would anyone choose this as a meeting place? Because it was isolated, seldom visited, and couldn't be seen from the road. That meant a clandestine meeting. Rachel was glad she hadn't come upon another murder scene, but she was more curious than ever about Lindsay's mysterious rendezvous.

The squirrels were going crazy, ratcheting up the volume of their raspy, scolding calls. Rachel stopped and peered into the tree branches above her, wondering if the squirrels were following her from tree to tree.

Something slammed into the back of her legs and knocked her to her knees. *Oh god, what, who—*

A brown mutt appeared, panting in her face. Startled, relieved, bewildered, Rachel whispered, "Where did you come from?"

The dog jumped her again, planted its feet on her shoulders and licked her face. Pushing the animal away, Rachel realized this was one of her patients. She hadn't seen the dog often, but it was too unusual to forget, with floppy beagle ears and long setter legs. Grabbing its collar, she checked the name tag. She was right. This was Cam and Meredith Taylor's dog.

"Cricket?"

A mistake. At the sound of her name, the dog began barking, a joyful, celebratory sound, loud enough to send the squirrels into a frenzy again. Loud enough to be heard at the house, if anyone was there to hear.

"Hush, hush. Be quiet."

Cricket let out a string of happy yips and bounced around Rachel, inviting her to play.

"Shhh, hush," Rachel whispered again, with no effect. Had someone found Cricket and asked Lindsay to come and pick her up? But why the McClure property? And why had Lindsay reacted to the call with such obvious shock?

"Cricket! Come back here!" A woman's voice, calling from the yard around the house.

The dog barked in answer.

Rachel got to her feet and steered the dog toward the house. "Go! Go back."

"Cricket!" the woman yelled.

Cricket moved a few feet toward the voice, then turned and, wagging her tail, barked at Rachel to invite her along.

The woman appeared at the edge of the woods, her face in shadow.

Get out of here, now. Lindsay was either around somewhere or soon would be, and Rachel wouldn't be able to explain her own presence. "Stay!" Rachel ordered the dog. Then she took off, back the way she'd come.

The dog stayed right behind her, barking, enjoying the game of chase. And the woman was on their trail, shouting the dog's name, gaining ground.

Rachel's right foot caught in the tangled undergrowth and in the next instant she pitched forward. Her binoculars, strap and all, sailed free into the brush, along with her sunglasses. She landed hard, face-down. Thorns stabbed her cheek. Cricket stood over her, barking.

Rachel pushed herself up, tried to yank her foot loose, but a thorny vine bit into her ankle. Something tickled her skin and she spotted a daddy longlegs crawling up her arm. Shaking it off, she leaned down, desperate to rip the vine from her foot. Thorns pricked her fingertips.

It was too late. The woman had moved closer and stood thirty feet away among the trees. "What are you doing here?" she demanded.

Rachel straightened, staring at the woman, seeing her clearly now.

Meredith Taylor.

She looked ill, her skin pasty and her eyes bloodshot, her blond hair tangled and her loose shirt and pants soiled, but this was Meredith Taylor, beyond doubt.

"You're alive," Rachel blurted.

Meredith's face was blank, her body perfectly still, yet the air between them hummed with tension. "What are you doing here?" Meredith asked again.

"What happened to you?" Rachel asked. "Why are you— What's going on?"

Meredith stepped closer, her eyes cold and flat. Rachel felt the first tremor of fear. She wanted to back away, but with her foot entangled she had no choice but to stand her ground. Sweat rolled down her spine, her cheek stung where thorns had pierced it. The dog sat at Rachel's feet and watched with interest.

"Mom?" Lindsay called from the edge of the woods. "Did you find Cricket?"

The dog barked when she heard her name, and Rachel and Meredith both swung their heads around.

"Mom? Where are you?"

With a happy yelp, the dog loped off in Lindsay's direction.

"Over here," Meredith answered her daughter.

Rachel didn't understand what was happening, but she wasn't going to stand there and hope for answers. For a second Meredith took her eyes off Rachel to glance at Lindsay, and Rachel grabbed the chance to dig her cell phone from her shirt pocket. She pressed speed dial for 911.

"Stop that!" Meredith snatched the phone from Rachel's hand. She pressed the button to turn it off, drew back her arm and flung the phone into the woods.

Rachel watched helplessly as it disappeared in the undergrowth.

"Mom!" Lindsay exclaimed, coming up beside her mother. "Why did you do that?"

Flicking her gaze between mother and daughter, still trying to wrap her mind around the reality of Meredith standing alive before her, Rachel fumbled for words. "Lindsay, what's going on here? Everybody thinks—Your mother—"

"She was kidnapped," Lindsay said. "Scotty Ragsdale's been holding her prisoner here."

"Was she the one who called you a while ago?" But if Meredith had a phone, how could she have been a prisoner?

"What the hell are you doing here anyway?" Lindsay said. "Did you follow me?"

"I thought there was another murder. I wanted to find out—"

"Let's take her to the house," Meredith said. She caught Rachel's arm and shoved. "Go on."

Rachel lurched and almost fell before she regained her balance. "I can't. My foot's caught."

"Oh, shit." Lindsay knelt and began tearing at the prickly vine.

Rachel stooped to help. "Lindsay," she whispered, "what—"

"Be quiet." Lindsay's voice was barely audible. "She's diabetic, her blood sugar's screwed up, she's not thinking straight. Just play along, and it'll be okay."

"What are you telling her?" Meredith yelled. "Stop talking to her. Let's go!"

Rachel looked up and her breath strangled in her throat. Meredith held a pistol, pointed at Rachel.

Lindsay leapt to her feet. "Mom, you don't need that. Everything's going to be all right. We'll tell Tom what Scotty did and everything will be fine. Give me the gun, okay?"

Lindsay held out a hand to her mother. Rachel rose slowly.

"No." Meredith shook her head.

"Mom, come on now," Lindsay coaxed. She stepped in front of Rachel as if to shield her.

She had a telephone and a gun? Rachel thought. *How could she be a prisoner?*

Meredith spoke to Lindsay in a tone of mild rebuke, as if she were explaining an obvious point to a stubborn child. "I can't let her go. Not after she's seen me."

Fear squeezed Rachel's chest and made each breath a painful struggle.

"It doesn't matter," Lindsay said. "It's all over. Scotty can't hurt you anymore. Give me the gun, Mom."

"I can't let her go!" Meredith raised the pistol, aiming beyond Lindsay at Rachel's head. "She'll tell everybody."

Lindsay grabbed her mother's arm just as Meredith squeezed the trigger. Rachel ducked. She heard the sharp crack of the shot, and the bullet slammed into a tree inches from her head.

Dizzy with relief, rigid with fear of what might happen next, Rachel kept her eyes on the pistol while Lindsay and Meredith scuffled and grunted. The dog jumped around, barking in her excitement.

Meredith stomped on Lindsay's foot.

"Damn it!" Lindsay yelled and let go of her mother's arms. Grimacing, she hopped on one foot.

Meredith still held the gun. "All right now, you're going to mind me and do what I say. We're all going in the house."

Without another word, Lindsay crouched again and tore the vine away from Rachel's foot. Rachel tried to catch Lindsay's eye, to get some idea of what she was thinking and planning, but Lindsay didn't look at her.

When Rachel tugged her foot free, Lindsay rose and walked away toward the house with the dog beside her.

"Don't even think about running, Dr. Goddard," Meredith said, sounding calm now. "Don't test me."

Knowing that anything she did might make Meredith pull the trigger, Rachel had no choice but to walk out of the woods with a gun at her back. Her thoughts fractured, images of herself lying dead mixing with a flood of questions. How could Lindsay's mother still be alive? Who had died in the fire? Ben's mother?

At the thought of Ben's grief, tears welled up in Rachel's eyes. She caught herself, realized how insane it was to let her mind wander. Her life was in danger, right here, right now. *Focus.*

Lindsay's car was parked in the back yard next to a garden where daisies and daylilies bloomed in a forest of weeds. Rachel walked past the car and stopped at the back steps. Glancing up, she saw an open door and an empty, shadowy space beyond.

If she went into that house, Rachel knew, she would never come out alive.

"Go on, Rachel." Lindsay's voice was quiet, pleading.

Say something. Stall. Fear held Rachel's throat in a vise and she had to force the words out. "Did you know your mother was alive all along?"

"No. I didn't, I swear."

"Shut up, both of you!" Meredith snapped. "Lindsay, stop talking to her."

"That was her calling you at Joanna's, wasn't it?" Rachel asked. "You were surprised. Shocked."

"I told you to shut up," Meredith said.

Something hard jabbed Rachel's lower spine and sent a streak of pain down one leg. The barrel of the pistol.

Meredith planted a hand on Rachel's back and pushed.

"No!" Rachel spun and flailed at Meredith, kicked at her knees, grabbed for the gun, but Meredith evaded her like a wisp of smoke that couldn't be captured.

"Stop it!" Meredith screamed. She drew back her arm and cracked the gun butt against Rachel's cheek.

Stunned, Rachel dropped to her knees. Everything went dark for a second before she was able to focus again. Blood pooled in her mouth.

Through a haze of pain she heard Meredith say, "I'm the one with the gun, and I'm the one making the decisions. Lindsay, get her up."

Lindsay grasped Rachel's arm and dragged her to her feet. A wave of dizziness and nausea overwhelmed Rachel, and her knees folded under her. She sank onto the bottom step and hung her head. Blood dripped from her mouth and spotted her white athletic shoes.

"I said get her up."

"Okay, Mom. All right." Lindsay gripped Rachel's arm again and pulled her upright.

Rachel pressed a hand to her throbbing cheek. Gagging on the taste of her own blood, she stumbled up the steps.

They entered the kitchen. Beyond the rectangle of light that spilled through the doorway, Rachel picked out a refrigerator and range in the shadows, and the outline of a boarded-up window over the sink. On a counter she saw what looked like food, a white jug, a loaf of bread. She saw nothing she could use as a weapon. But she had to find a way to free herself. She couldn't wait for Lindsay to talk her mother back to sanity.

"I know exactly where to put her," Meredith said, "while we decide what to do with her."

"You don't have to put her anywhere," Lindsay said. "Come on, Mom, you need to eat some more. Have some juice and finish your sandwich, okay?"

Meredith didn't seem to hear her daughter. She pressed the gun to Rachel's temple and pulled her by the arm into a hallway, toward the stairs. Pointing to a small door under the stairs, she told Lindsay, "In there. Open it."

"Mom, no. Please don't do this."

"Open it."

"Okay, okay." Lindsay flipped the latch and swung the door open on a small, black hole beneath the stairs.

"No!" Rachel cried, struggling to get free, blood spewing from her mouth. "No!"

Meredith rapped the gun against Rachel's head and Rachel fell to her hands and knees, fighting to stay conscious. Meredith crammed her into the storage space. The door closed and the latch clicked into place.

Chapter Forty-four

"It all makes sense, it ties together." Tom paced around the conference room table, and the sheriff and prosecutor swiveled their heads to follow him. Every minute he had to spend explaining the situation was wasted time. He wanted to get rolling, but everything had changed and he had to bring his boss and the prosecutor up to speed. "Meredith is alive and Scotty knows where she is. He's been saying he has to get out of jail, he has somewhere to go, he has commitments. My bet is he's taking care of her, supplying her with what she needs while she's hiding."

Sheriff Willingham ran a hand over his bristly gray hair. "Well, I admit it looks like it might be Karen Hernandez who died in the fire—"

"It *was* her," Tom said. "She had a spinal fusion. Joanna McKendrick and Ben Hern both confirmed that. If it wasn't her in the fire, it was a hell of a coincidence that some other woman who'd had a spinal fusion just happened to be in the Taylor house Friday morning—at the same time Karen Hernandez disappeared."

"But that doesn't mean Meredith's alive," Willingham said. "She could be dead and we just haven't found the body yet."

Tom leaned on the table between Willingham and the prosecutor, who faced each other. "Meredith's wedding ring was on the corpse. Whoever put it there wanted everybody to believe Meredith was dead. Somebody went to the trouble to hide Karen Hernandez's car. They didn't do a very good job of it, but they managed to throw us off for a few days. Somebody also called the

Taylor house with Karen's phone *after* the house burned down, so it would look like she was still alive and we wouldn't question the identity of the corpse. Who, besides Meredith herself, would want to fake her death?"

Sheriff Willingham wore a sour expression, as if he'd been asked to swallow something he couldn't stomach, but he blew out a sigh and said, "Yeah, I guess it does make sense. You think Meredith killed all three of them—her husband and Karen Hernandez and Lloyd Wilson?"

"With Scotty's help, yeah."

"And you think she's still around here somewhere, still in the county?"

"Seems that way to me, considering how Scotty's been acting. If all this happened without premeditation, and I think it did, then she doesn't have any money. She left all that expensive jewelry in her safe deposit box—if she'd been planning this, she could have sold the jewelry and had a stash of money to finance her own disappearance."

Raymond Morton, the prosecutor, frowned and shook his head. "If Meredith really was responsible for Scotty's sister dying, why would he help her do anything? Why would he be her friend, or lover, whatever he was?"

"He didn't know the truth. I don't believe anybody except Meredith and Cam knew why Denise Ragsdale didn't make it home that night. Karen might have suspected, but she didn't have any proof. And if she'd never voiced her suspicion to anybody, never confronted Meredith or Cam about it, she probably didn't realize Meredith was afraid of her. It looks to me as if Karen's visit to Mason County to see her son was what set everything in motion."

"Meredith felt threatened," Morton said.

"Right. She'd lived with this secret a long time, and Karen was the only other person who suspected the truth and could have exposed her. The worst thing Karen could have done was turn up on Meredith's doorstep, but Karen apparently didn't know she was in any danger. That's my theory. All we know for certain is that Karen went to see Meredith Friday morning and ended up dead."

Morton nodded. "Now what? I assume you're going to shove the truth in Ragsdale's face and try to make him give up Meredith."

"He's not going to believe it," Willingham put in. "He's got too big of an emotional investment in his relationship with her. He won't believe he's been wrong about her all this time."

Tom dragged a chair out from the table, its legs scraping across the tile floor, and sat down. "I'll make him believe it. Sooner or later he'll spill the whole story and tell us where she is."

A cell phone buzzed in the pocket of Morton's suit jacket. He pulled out the phone, answered, and listened without comment. When he ended the call, he told Tom, "You'd better try to make that sooner rather than later. His bail's been posted."

"Aw, Christ. How'd his parents come up with that much money?"

"They didn't. They came up with 10 percent and went to a bondsman this time. They're about to spring Scotty, so if you want to question him, you'd better go do it right now."

"You know," Tom said, "we could make this work to our advantage. Let's hold up his release for an hour, blame it on paperwork, keep him in custody long enough for me to tell him what I've found out. If he doesn't believe Meredith was responsible for his sister's death, or he's not sure and he needs proof, he'll want to hear either a confession or a denial straight from her. He'll lead us to her."

"On the other hand," Morton said, "if he does believe it, he might decide not to go near her. He might want to let her rot, wherever she is."

Tom shook his head. "If she's still around, he'll go to her, I'd bet on it."

Rachel didn't have enough room to stand up in the dark space under the stairs. She sat with her knees drawn to her chest, breathing in hot, stale air, and fought the urge to vomit. Waves of pain radiated from her cheekbone, intensifying with the slightest movement of her jaw. She had let the blood drain from her mouth so she wouldn't swallow more of it, and the front of her shirt felt sticky against her chest, but at last the bleeding had stopped. The metallic smell of blood mingled with the odors of mold and her own sweat.

Why didn't I fight harder? Why did I let this happen? Even as Rachel berated herself, she knew she'd had no choice. If she'd kept fighting back, she would already be dead.

Where were they now? Rachel strained to make out what Lindsay and Meredith were saying but caught only fragments of their agitated exchanges, as if they were moving around, in and out of her hearing. She mopped her face with the hem of her shirt and leaned her ear against the door.

"...give me back my phone so I can call 911," Lindsay said. "You look like you're crashing again. You need a doctor."

"No!" Meredith said. "...not calling anybody...don't understand..."

"Then help me understand. Explain it to me."

They both seemed to move farther away, and for a couple of minutes Rachel heard only the indistinct murmur of their voices. Meredith must have taken Lindsay's cell phone, too. Rachel felt herself drifting perilously close to despair as she let go of the hope that Lindsay would summon help.

Something scraped against the door, a shadow blocked the light at the bottom. In a panic Rachel scrambled backward until she hit a wall. Then she heard a snuffling noise and realized Meredith's dog had found her.

"Cricket, no!" Meredith yelled. "Get away from there!"

The dog whined, the shadow disappeared.

"Mom, try to stay calm," Lindsay said. "You'll make yourself sicker."

Rachel curled her hands into fists, nails biting into her palms. *Think, think! There must be a way to get out of here.* But her freedom, her life, depended on Lindsay now, and Lindsay seemed as helpless against Meredith as Rachel was.

◇◇◇

With Scotty Ragsdale's paperwork conveniently misplaced and half a dozen deputies on standby for a possible surveillance and arrest operation, Tom waited alone in the conference room for the Blackwood twins to bring the prisoner over from the jail. He drummed his fingers on the pages he'd printed from Meredith's novel and mentally reviewed recent events, reassuring himself that his theory made sense.

He was sure he'd figured out most of what had happened, but one thing continued to niggle at him: Who had gotten into Rachel's cottage and turned on the gas without leaving any evidence of a break-in? It must have been somebody with a key, but Joanna was adamant that no extra keys were floating around.

Wait a minute. Tom's fingers stilled as he tried to recall exactly what Lindsay had said the night before. Something about keys. She'd been explaining why she still had a key to his house although she'd returned the one he'd given her.

You remember how I was always losing keys and Mom had to make sure we had extras. That was it. But why would Meredith have a key to the cottage in the first place?

Tom pulled his cell phone from his pocket and called Joanna again. When she answered, he said, "I need to know whether the Taylors ever stayed in the house where Rachel lives now."

Joanna was silent a moment, then said, "I guess you won't tell me why you're asking that question either."

"Sorry, I can't. But it's important."

She sighed. "Meredith and Lindsay stayed there for a few days, a long time ago. Lindsay couldn't have been more than thirteen or fourteen at the time. Meredith and Cam had some kind of spat, I don't remember what it was about, and I suggested they get a little distance from each other. I guess it helped, because Meredith and Lindsay went back home. Tom, what—"

"Thanks." He hung up.

A few minutes later, Scotty Ragsdale slumped in the same conference room chair where the sheriff had sat not long before.

Resting his cuffed hands in his lap, he fixed his gaze on the tabletop and refused to look at Tom, who sat across from him. The Blackwood twins stood guard behind Ragsdale.

"How are you feeling, Scotty?" Tom asked.

"Like you give a damn," Ragsdale muttered.

"Well, I do, believe it or not. You're going through a rough time. Worst time of your life, maybe—except for when your sister died."

Ragsdale jerked his head up. "My sister's death is none of your business."

Tom let that go for the moment. "Your sister was friends with Meredith, wasn't she?"

"What about it?" Ragsdale shifted in his chair, tapped one foot on the floor. "My folks been by yet? They should've come up with my bail by now."

"I'm sure they're working on it. What I was about to say is, we found a lot of CDs in Meredith's safe deposit box when we opened it, and most of them have book manuscripts on them."

Ragsdale narrowed his eyes, making the bags under them more pronounced. "You went through her stuff? Why?"

"We have to examine everything in a murder case. There could have been something there to point us to the killer."

Wary now, Ragsdale watched Tom but didn't respond.

"Anyway," Tom went on, "like I was saying, we found a bunch of discs with her writing on them. And one of them stands out. It's different." He paused and leaned forward over the table. "Did you know Meredith was writing a book about her experiences as a VISTA?"

Ragsdale drew in a deep breath and released it, his shoulders rising and falling, and he seemed to relax a little. "Yeah, she told me about it. She said she was going to write the truth. What it was really like."

"Didn't you read it? I know the two of you shared your writing."

Ragsdale shook his head. "She said it was just for herself. Things she had to work out for her own peace of mind. She didn't want anybody to see it." He threw a scornful look at Tom. "She sure as hell wouldn't want *you* to read it."

"Ah," Tom said, hoping he sounded surprised. "That explains it, then. Why you didn't hold it against her. You didn't know the truth. Or maybe you knew, but you forgave her?"

"What the hell are you talking about?" Ragsdale was starting to fidget, flexing his shoulders, squirming in his seat. "Forgave her for what?"

Tom sighed. "I guess you really don't know. I hate to break it to you, after you were friends with her for so many years."

"Break *what* to me? You know what I think? I think you're jerking me around."

Tom looked down at the printed sheets in front of him on the table. "I was going to let you read this, but maybe that's not a good idea after all."

"Read *what*, damn it?" Ragsdale jumped to his feet, but the Blackwoods were on him in an instant, shoving him back into the chair. "What is that? Just *tell me*, for god's sake. Cut the bullshit."

"It looks like the last chapter Meredith worked on before she died. At least, it's the last backup she made. It's the chapter about your sister's death."

Ragsdale's mouth opened, closed again.

"If what she wrote is the truth—Well, I believe you have a right to know. That is, if you think you can face it."

"You're full of shit, Bridger. There's nothing Meredith could have written that I'd be afraid to read. I lived through it, remember?"

"All right then." Tom turned the pages to face Ragsdale and slid them across the table.

Ragsdale used both cuffed hands to pull the papers closer. He leaned over and began reading. Tom settled back in his chair to watch Ragsdale's reactions.

The first pages of the chapter brought a sour smile at one point, a shake of the head at another. As he neared the end, his face went slack and pale. By the time he finished, he sat rigid in his chair, staring at the last page, all emotion blasted off his face by shock. The sound of his rapid breathing filled the quiet room.

At last Ragsdale said, "It's fiction. She decided to...She must have decided to get away from the truth. Give it more dramatic conflict."

"But you said she was writing down some things she needed to get off her mind," Tom said. "And, you know, I've checked out a lot of the other incidents and people she wrote about, and it all seems to be true. Of course, I can't check out her story about your sister's death because the only people who knew about it are dead now."

Ragsdale's gaze flicked to Tom, then away. "It's not true. I don't believe it."

"Well, maybe that's for the best," Tom said. "That you don't believe it, I mean."

A minute passed in silence, Ragsdale rocking back and forth in his chair, Tom studying the stew of emotion on the man's face. He looked like he wanted to cry. He looked like he wanted to hit somebody.

"I've gotta get out of here," Ragsdale blurted. "Where the hell are my folks? What's taking them so long to post my bail?"

"I'll go check on it," Tom said. "See if they've been by yet."

He walked out in the hall, closed the door behind him, and gave the thumbs up to Dennis Murray, who was coordinating the tail on Ragsdale.

Tom waited a few minutes before he returned to the conference room.

"You're in luck," he said. He reached for Ragsdale's hands, unlocked the cuffs. "Your bond's been posted and you're free to go. These two deputies can give you a ride back to your place."

Chapter Forty-five

Rachel shook her head, wincing at the burst of pain from the movement, willing herself to stay alert. The heat and stale air inside her dark little prison made her woozy, fear exhausted her, and she longed to surrender and slip into unconsciousness.

How much time had passed? She had no idea. The staff at the animal hospital would worry when she didn't return for her appointments or answer her phone. They would call around, trying to find her. But would they call Tom? Even if they did, he would never think to look for her in Pauline McClure's abandoned house.

She had only herself to rely on. She couldn't count on Lindsay to help her. If Meredith decided to kill her, she would have to open the door. Rachel would get one last chance to save herself. She had to be ready. But how could she escape from a woman with a gun?

You can do it, Rachel told herself. *You can.* She went over everything she'd learned in the self-defense class she'd taken two years before. *Use your feet. Bite. Use your fingernails. Go for the eyes. Grab her hair. You can do this.*

Rachel heard Meredith's voice again, strengthening and fading like a bad cell phone signal. "…Scotty's idea…forced me into it…left me here…in love with me, he wants me to go away with him."

"You're saying he did it all?" Lindsay asked. "You didn't kill anybody?"

"Of course I didn't! I'm not a murderer."

"All right then. Let's call Tom. You can explain everything to him."

"No!" The rest of Meredith's answer was too faint to make out.

Don't walk away, Rachel silently begged. *Come closer, come closer.*

Lindsay said something Rachel couldn't make out, then Meredith's voice became clear again. "…know how hard your father was to live with sometimes. He thought I might inherit something when Dad died, and we'd have enough to keep the paper going. He was furious when I didn't get a cent. Then he thought I'd get a lot of money when Aunt Julia died, because she'd helped me before. Cam blamed me when she left all her money to charity. He said I should have sucked up to her when I knew she was dying."

"But she left you all that jewelry. I've seen it, Mom. It's worth a fortune. If you wanted to leave with Scotty, why didn't you just sell the jewelry and take off?"

"I wasn't sure what I wanted. I thought I might just leave by myself and start a whole new life. If Cam or Scotty knew about the jewelry…I wasn't going to turn it over to either of them. Whatever I got for it was *mine,* not theirs."

"But you let Scotty believe you were going to leave with him? The two of you were making plans?"

Meredith's answer was a mumble.

"Why did Scotty kill Dad? And Karen Hernandez, and Lloyd Wilson—Why did Scotty do such a crazy thing?" Lindsay sounded as strung out as her mother, close to breaking. "Was he the one who tried to kill Rachel?"

Rachel shifted, sat straighter, flexed her cramped legs. The sound of her own labored breathing echoed in her ears.

"Yes," Meredith said. "He went over… the house fill up with gas, then set it on fire…would have exploded."

"How did he get in?" Lindsay asked.

"I gave him a key, God help me. We used to meet there sometimes at night, before she moved in."

"Why did he want to kill Rachel?"

"She saw him in the woods with Cam. He had to get rid of her."

I didn't. I didn't see anything.

"According to Tom," Lindsay said, "she didn't see anything,"

"That's what Tom wants you to believe. She saw Scotty, and she told Tom."

"Then why didn't Tom arrest Scotty?"

"Because he knows I'm alive too. He's pretending to believe I'm dead, but he's really searching for me so he can lock me up. Scotty must be staying away because he's afraid Tom will follow him. But he's coming back, he'll find a way—"

"Scotty's not coming back. He's in jail. He got high on meth and attacked Tom and Brandon Connelly. He's been locked up ever since."

"Oh, no. Oh, dear god."

"Mom, if you're innocent, why—"

"Of course I'm innocent!"

Rachel heard nothing more for a moment and thought they'd moved away. When Lindsay spoke again, her voice sounded weary, placating. "Okay, I didn't mean to upset you. We don't have to talk about it anymore. We need to get more food into you. Do you have your testing supplies with you? Let me check your blood sugar."

Rachel couldn't hear the rest. She leaned her throbbing head against the door. *Please, Lindsay, get your phone away from her and call Tom. Do the right thing for once.*

◇◇◇

Tom braked hard at the fork in the road, and Brandon pitched forward in the passenger seat, straining his seat belt.

"Where the hell did he go?" Tom motioned at the choices ahead of them. "I should've stayed closer behind him."

Everything had gone smoothly until now. Kevin and Keith Blackwood had dropped Ragsdale off at his house, and the minute they were out of sight Ragsdale jumped into his car and tore off in the opposite direction. Tom and Brandon had followed in the sheriff's personal car, an unmarked green sedan, and the Blackwoods and Dennis Murray trailed in Sheriff's Department vehicles.

Tom blew out a breath and grabbed the radio from its hook. When he raised a signal and connected with the two cars behind his, he said, "We lost him at the junction of Albemarle and Dunkirk. Brandon and I are heading east. The rest of you head west. Let me know if you catch sight of him."

He swung the car onto Albemarle Road. "You know whose house is out this way, don't you?" he asked Brandon.

"Oh, yeah. Meredith could hide there for a long time without anybody seeing her."

◇◇◇

What's happening? Rachel was sure she'd heard—*Yes!* There it was again, a man's voice. She couldn't make out words, but a man was in the house. Who? She didn't care. She had to take a chance.

She pushed herself to her knees and banged her fists on the door. "Help me!" she screamed. "Help me! I'm locked up in here! Help!"

"What the hell—" a man said, close enough now for Rachel to hear him clearly. "What's going on?" Heavy footfalls approached.

"In here!" Rachel pounded on the door. "Under the stairs! Let me out!"

"Who is that?"

"No, don't open it!" Meredith cried.

The latch clicked. Rachel shoved the door open and tumbled into the hallway on her hands and knees. Meredith's dog trotted over to her, tail wagging.

"What's she doing here?" the man exclaimed.

Rachel scrambled to her feet. The corridor was dim, shadowy, but so much brighter than the dark space she'd escaped that she blinked, trying to make her eyes adjust. The dog huffed and sniffed at the blood stains on her slacks. "Meredith locked me up. She was going to kill me. Help me, please help me."

But when Rachel looked up at the man's face, she realized she had made a terrible mistake. This was Scotty Ragsdale, Meredith's friend. The man who tried to kill her and Holly.

"We have to get rid of her," Meredith said.

He scowled at Rachel, then at Meredith. "If you think you can get away with doing it like this, you're crazy."

Meredith exploded. "Who are you calling crazy? She wouldn't be a problem now if you'd done your part right. How could you dump me here and desert me, with nothing but dog food—I could have died while you were off getting high."

"Shut up!" Ragsdale roared. He swung his arm and struck Meredith in the face so hard that she staggered backward.

Meredith let out a wail. The dog howled.

"Stop it!" Lindsay cried. Rachel hadn't spotted her before, but suddenly she was there, beside her mother. "Leave her alone!"

"What's your daughter doing here?" Ragsdale demanded. "How many more people did you tell?"

Rachel backed away, into the empty, darkened dining room. If she could get to the kitchen while they were distracted, if she could get to the back door—

"Why did you hit me?" Meredith sobbed.

"Did you kill my sister?"

"What? What are you talking about?"

His sister? Rachel didn't understand what he was accusing Meredith of. She didn't care. She had to get out of here. She kept moving backward. Where was the pistol? Who had the gun now?

"I read what you wrote." Ragsdale loomed over Meredith, his hands fisted at his sides. "I read it in your own words, telling how you pushed Denise out in the snow in the dark and left her to freeze to death. You wrote it all down, every detail."

"Scotty, no, you don't understand—"

"Karen guessed, didn't she? That's what she was about to tell me. That's why you shot her, to stop her from telling me what you did to my sister."

"Scotty, please, let me explain—"

"You played me for a fool," Ragsdale said. "I let you drag me into this mess, I almost killed those two women for you, I shot Cam, I shot that old man—And all the time, you were lying to me, laughing at me."

"No, Scotty, no. Please, please listen to me—"

"I ought to kill you right now." Ragsdale lunged at Meredith.

The gunshot exploded through the empty rooms. Rachel froze, watched Ragsdale fall to his knees, clutching his abdomen. Meredith stood over him, gripping the gun with both hands, disbelief and astonishment on her face. "Oh, my god! Scotty!"

Panting, Ragsdale folded forward, his head almost touching the floor, then he tilted sideways and collapsed.

Meredith knelt beside him, one hand on his head, like a frantic mother with an injured child. "Scotty, I'm sorry, I'm so sorry, I didn't mean to. I need you! You have to help me—"

"Mom," Lindsay said, "he needs a doctor. You don't want him to die, do you? Let me call 911."

Meredith pointed the pistol at her daughter. "You don't understand! You're just like your father."

"Mom, no, please—" Lindsay raised her hands, and they shook so violently that she might have been waving at her mother.

Rachel spun and ran, through the dining room to the kitchen. She flung the back door open. Outside. Sunshine. Birds singing.

The dog rocketed past Rachel, bumping her legs and almost knocking her off her feet. She grabbed the door jamb to regain her balance, then she started after Cricket, toward freedom.

Meredith's voice stopped her. "If you move one more inch, I'll shoot you. Get back in here."

A second later Rachel felt cold metal pressed against the back of her neck.

"Lindsay, get hold of her," Meredith said.

"Mom—"

"*Get her.* Do what you're told."

Lindsay appeared beside Rachel, her movements jerky as a robot's. She didn't meet Rachel's eyes, but caught her by the arm and pulled her back into the kitchen.

Stay calm, Rachel told herself. *Don't panic. There has to be a way. There has to be. Wait for it. Watch for it. Be ready.*

Lindsay let her go and stepped away. Meredith reached for Rachel's arm. With one hand Rachel grabbed Meredith's wrist and twisted, with the other she chopped at the hand holding the gun.

For a second Meredith's arm dropped, but she held onto the gun. Rachel struck her arm again, at the same time she dug her thumb into the nerves at the base of Meredith's other hand. Meredith screamed and her face contorted with pain. Then she raised the gun again, aimed at Rachel's head. She shoved Rachel away and held her injured wrist against her body, grimacing as she tried to flex her fingers. "You little bitch. I'll kill you right now."

"Mom, wait!" Lindsay said. "You don't want to leave her blood in the house. We've already got Scotty to clean up after. You ought to take her out in the woods. We could bury her and she might never be found."

Rachel stared at Lindsay, at the yellow hair glued to her cheeks with sweat, her trembling hands, the frantic gleam in her eyes, and she couldn't tell whether Lindsay was trying to buy time or trying to help her mother get away with murder.

It didn't matter. Meredith intended to kill Rachel regardless of what Lindsay said or did. Something broke loose inside Rachel, and she felt rage boiling up, swamping her fear.

"Will you help me dig?" Meredith asked Lindsay. "I can't do it alone. And we might have to bury Scotty too." The gun drifted away from Rachel.

Now!

Rachel sprang forward, caught Meredith's hair with one hand and yanked her head back. She thrust out her other hand and scraped her fingernails across Meredith's eyes, digging in with her nails. Meredith screamed. The gun fired and a window shattered, raining glass into the sink.

Rachel clawed at Meredith's eyes again. The gun clattered to the floor as Meredith raised both hands to her face.

Rachel and Lindsay both dived for the gun at the same time. Rachel got to it first, seized it and turned it on Lindsay.

Meredith sank to her knees, hands over her eyes, keening.

"Mom! Oh, god." Lindsay knelt beside her mother.

Rachel raised her voice to be heard over Meredith's wails. "Give me a cell phone. Yours, hers, I don't care."

"Why aren't you leaving?" Lindsay said. "Run, get out of here while you can."

"I'm not going anywhere. Give me a phone, Lindsay."

Lindsay dug into Meredith's pants pocket, came out with a cell phone.

Rachel snatched it and pressed 911. "This is Rachel Goddard. I'm at Pauline McClure's old house on Albemarle Road. Someone's been shot, another person's hurt—Send an ambulance, send the police, tell Tom Bridger—"

She was still trying to explain the situation to the operator two minutes later when Tom burst into the house, gun drawn, with Brandon on his heels. Rachel gaped in disbelief. All she could say was, "But I just called."

"Tommy," Lindsay cried, "thank God you're here!" She scrambled to her feet and rushed toward him.

"Stay back." Tom pointed his gun at her.

"Tommy." Lindsay sounded as hurt and bewildered as Meredith had after Ragsdale struck her. "I'm not part of this. I didn't know she was alive until today, I didn't know about—"

"Shut up!" Tom's gaze jumped from Rachel to Meredith and back. "Where's Ragsdale? We heard a shot. Who fired it?"

Tom was right there in front of her, but Rachel couldn't quite believe he was real. She kept the gun she held aimed at Meredith, in case she was imagining things. "Meredith shot Ragsdale," she said. "I think he's unconscious—or dead."

"What are you doing here?" Tom peered at Rachel's face. "Aw, god, what have they done to you?"

"Meredith hit me with this gun." The pain in Rachel's cheek had been a distant throb in the last few minutes, but now it roared back full-force. "She made me come in the house, she locked me in that hole under the stairs—"

"I tried to help Rachel," Lindsay said. "I really did. Please believe me, Tommy."

"That's true," Rachel said. "She tried to protect me."

"We'll get all that sorted out later." Tom motioned to Brandon, pointed at Meredith. "Cuff her." Then he held out a hand toward Rachel. "Want me to take that?"

"Oh." She looked at the gun in her hand. "Yes. Yes, please." When she handed Tom the pistol, Rachel felt as if she had surrendered a crushing burden.

Brandon stood above Meredith and rolled her onto her stomach. When he jerked her hands behind her to cuff her wrists, she raised her head and let out a long scream. Blood ran from both her eyes.

Rachel's stomach lurched at the sight of what she'd done. She backed up until she hit a wall, then she let herself slide down to sit on the floor.

Meredith's dog slunk in through the open kitchen door and sidled over, her tail between her legs. Rachel pulled Cricket close and pressed her face into the dog's shaggy coat.

Chapter Forty-six

Scotty Ragsdale lay flat in the hospital bed, his eyes focused on the ceiling, and didn't seem to notice when Tom walked in.

"Hey, Scotty." Tom switched on the portable recorder he'd brought and placed it on the over-bed table.

Ragsdale's gaze drifted toward Tom, down to the recorder, then back to the ceiling. "Didn't take you long to get over here."

"I didn't want to give you time to change your mind about talking to me. We need to get this done today. Right after your arraignment tomorrow morning, an ambulance is going to move you to the regional jail. They've got a sick bay where you can recuperate."

"Doesn't matter to me where I am," Ragsdale muttered.

"Your folks told me you fired your lawyer. The judge appointed one for you, and he'll be in to see you before you're arraigned."

"If he's going to tell me to plead not guilty, he can save himself the trip. I just want to plead guilty and get it over with."

"That's between you and him. You ready to answer some questions?"

Ragsdale's eyes shifted to Tom again for a second before he turned his head toward the window. "How is she? Meredith. Where is she?"

"You don't need to know where she is." Meredith was also hospitalized, on the floor above this one, and even though both prisoners were guarded by deputies, Tom was afraid Ragsdale might try to get to her if he knew she was so close. "She's doing okay. Talking a lot. She claims you were responsible for everything that happened—you killed Karen Hernandez, and Cam, and Lloyd Wilson—and you forced her to go along with it."

"I didn't kill Karen." Ragsdale's mumbled words were barely audible.

This was the first statement of any substance that Ragsdale had made since coming out of surgery two days before. "Were you there when she was killed?"

Ragsdale stared out the window at the brilliant blue sky for so long that Tom was tempted to prompt him for an answer, but at last he turned his head on the pillow and met Tom's eyes. "Yeah. I was there. I didn't kill her, but I saw her die."

"Tell me the whole story, Scotty, from the beginning."

"I loved her," Ragsdale said, his voice thick with emotion. He swallowed hard and went on. "I loved Meredith for a long time before—I was just a friend to her for a long time."

Ragsdale fell silent, as if he were lost in thought or memories. In the corridor outside the room, a cart rattled past and the intercom alerted a doctor to a waiting phone call. Tom prodded Ragsdale, "But things changed? You became more than friends? Did that happen recently?"

"Couple of years ago. She thought Cam was fooling around with other women. I don't know if it was true, but Meredith believed it. She was fed up. We started talking about leaving, going somewhere together."

"San Francisco?" Tom asked, remembering Scotty's incoherent rambling when he was high on meth.

"Yeah. We had this picture of ourselves living near the water, writing and having a lot of writer friends." Ragsdale gave a bitter little laugh. "A big stupid fantasy."

"Why didn't you go?"

"Money. Meredith was afraid to take off without much money, and no idea how to support ourselves."

"Why didn't she sell the jewelry her aunt left her?"

Ragsdale's eyes snapped toward Tom. "What jewelry?"

So he hadn't known. Tom almost felt sorry for the poor bastard. "We found it in her safe deposit box. If she'd sold it, she would have had enough money to live comfortably for a long time."

Ragsdale's face contorted with anger. "God damn her and her lies!"

He struggled to sit up in the bed, but Tom pushed him back against the pillow. "Take it easy now. Get hold of yourself. Just tell me what happened."

For a couple of minutes Ragsdale stewed in his fury, his fists clenched on the blanket and his breath coming in ragged gulps. Tom waited for him to calm down.

When he spoke again, Ragsdale got to the point without any further nostalgic glimpses of the past. "She got upset when she heard Karen was here to see her son. I didn't know why she cared. I thought maybe she was ashamed to have Karen see how she was living, her and Cam, because Karen was this rich successful lawyer. But she didn't have to see Karen. She didn't have to invite her over for a visit. Just knowing Karen was around really had her on edge, though. Then Karen showed up at the house that morning."

"You were already there when she arrived?"

Ragsdale nodded. "Meredith tried hard to get me to leave, but I could see she was upset, and I wasn't going to leave her in that state. She tried to act cool, but she was just about to fall apart. I didn't get it. Karen was being nice, all smiles. She said she came to see Cam, but it was okay, she'd deal with Meredith instead. She said her son was being pigheaded, and he didn't know she was coming over there, but she just wanted to give Cam what he needed and be done with it. Then Karen pulled out a check, already made out, and said, *I hope this will be enough to put an end to it. I don't want my son to be bothered again.*"

"What did Meredith do?"

"She looked like she just wanted to drop through the floor and disappear. Her face turned red and she started shaking, trembling. Then she grabbed the check and tore it up and threw it in Karen's face. She told her they weren't beggars and they didn't want her money. And Karen just blew up. She said, *Well, you'd better talk to Cam about that, because he's been begging me for money and trying to blackmail my son, and we're not going to put up with it anymore.*"

"Do you think Meredith knew about the blackmail?"

"No, she didn't have any idea Cam had gone that far."

"What happened then? After Meredith tore up the check?"

"They started yelling at each other and Karen said Meredith was a fake, acting like she was so pure-hearted. I didn't know what she was talking about, but she said there was something Meredith did when they were VISTAs that she always wondered about, and she wanted Meredith to explain it in front of me, since I'd be interested too. I didn't know what she meant at the time. But I know now."

"She never got to the point of spelling it out?"

"No. Meredith started screaming at her to shut up, and everything went nuts, I remember the dog was barking, and— Next thing I knew, Meredith had Cam's gun in her hand, and she shot Karen."

Ragsdale paused, closed his eyes, and released a long breath.

Tom let him rest for a moment, then asked, "What happened then?"

When Ragsdale continued, he sounded weary, defeated. "After she shot Karen, Meredith fell apart. She couldn't stop crying."

"Did you ask her why she did it?"

"Sure I did. She lied to me, I know that now, but I believed her then. She seemed so broken up about it. She said she had an illegal abortion when she was a VISTA, and Karen suspected something but never knew for sure. She said she felt guilty all those years... *haunted* by it, she said, knowing she killed her first baby. She begged me not to hate her. But I didn't care. Why would I? But the way she was carrying on, I believed it was eating at her and she just snapped because Karen was about to make her own up to it."

"How did the two of you decide what to do next?" Tom asked.

"She wanted to leave, dump Karen's body somewhere, ditch her car, and keep on going. But there was some blood on the floor and probably hairs and fibers. She knew a lot about that kind of stuff from Lindsay, and she said we'd never be able to get rid of it all, and the police might come there asking questions when Karen was reported missing. I thought this was our chance, Meredith was finally willing to go away with me, and I wanted that to happen. I came up with the idea of putting Meredith's ring on Karen's finger, then setting the house on fire so everybody would think Meredith was dead. She could hide somewhere, and after a few days we could take off."

"Why did you kill Cam?"

"He knew about Meredith and me. I think he even knew we were talking about leaving together, but he never thought Meredith would do it. He never believed she was capable of doing anything without him. We were afraid he'd figure out what happened if he heard Karen had disappeared and I took off too. We knew it wouldn't be long before Karen was missed, because she had people expecting her to be at work, and her son would be trying to get in touch with her."

"So you decided on the spur of the moment to kill Cam too?" Tom could imagine Meredith and Scotty in the little house, facing the reality of what she had done, running out of options, desperately groping for a way to save themselves. "Did Meredith shoot him?"

"No. I did. I did it for her, like the fool I am. She helped me so much, she was always there when I needed her, and I thought, finally, this was something I could do for her."

Murdering her husband. Quite a gift. It took some effort for Tom to keep his expression neutral.

"Everything started moving so fast," Scotty went on. "I think back on it now, and it's just a blur. Meredith called Cam on his cell phone and found out where he was and when he'd be heading back to town, and I went over there and waited for him to come along. I flagged him down and made him get out of the car and go in the woods. And I shot him. He was laughing at me when I pulled the trigger."

"Did you see Rachel Goddard at the edge of the woods?"

"I saw somebody standing there looking straight at us. I didn't know who it was until later."

"What happened after you shot Cam?"

"I went back to the house. While I was gone, Meredith—Jesus, she took a hammer and smashed Karen's face in, she said she had to break the teeth so Karen couldn't be identified. We dragged the body into the kitchen by the door so we could get out fast when the fire started. Meredith poured kerosene right on Karen's face and her body, just doused her with it. We took Meredith's medicine and some food for her and the dog, and we got rid of the Jaguar before I drove her out to the McClure house to hide."

"We found Karen's jewelry with Meredith's things at the McClure place," Tom said. "What did you do with her other belongings? Her laptop, her luggage?"

"Threw them in the river."

"And after that you decided to get rid of the witnesses? Rachel Goddard, Holly Turner, Lloyd Wilson."

"I had to try. They saw me. They could put me at both places. I couldn't understand why you kept waiting to arrest me. I figured if they weren't around to testify—I was just trying to protect myself. You can't tell me you don't understand that. Anybody would do the same thing, wouldn't they?"

Tom didn't trust himself to attempt an answer.

◇◇◇

Tom hurtled down the farm road in the dusk of early evening, mentally rehearsing his speech to Rachel. This would be the first time they'd had a chance to talk privately since he'd found her at the McClure house.

I love you, he'd say. *I want a life with you, and I hope that's what you want too. But we have to be honest with each other. If you don't trust me enough to—*

He passed the stable and Rachel's cottage came into view. *Oh, Christ.* Ben Hern's black Jaguar sat in Rachel's driveway.

Tom slammed on the brakes and idled in the road, debating whether to turn around and leave. Hern was probably having dinner with Rachel and Holly. He might be planning to stay for hours. Tom would be an intruder, unwelcome.

But no, he wouldn't leave. He was here because he loved Rachel and he wasn't going to stand by and let her walk out of his life without trying to win her trust. And if being with her meant accepting Ben Hern as her friend, so be it. He might have to go out of his way to overcome Hern's resentment—being accused of murder was hard for most people to forgive—but he would make the effort. Hell, they might end up liking each other. Maybe they could play basketball together. Go fishing.

Yeah, right. Maybe he'd get lucky and Hern would go back where he came from.

He parked his Sheriff's Department car on the road in front of the cottage instead of pulling into the driveway. Wouldn't want to block Hern in and keep him from leaving.

From the passenger seat he grabbed a paper bag containing some things he'd brought for Rachel. As he climbed out, Hern emerged from the house with Rachel behind him. They spotted Tom and stood on the porch watching him approach.

Rachel was a slender silhouette with light spilling across her back from the open front door, her face in shadow. Tom couldn't tell whether she welcomed or dreaded his presence.

Hern surprised him by sticking out a hand as Tom mounted the steps. "Tom," Hern said. "Good to see you."

First names, huh? Okay. "Ben." Tom shook his hand. "How are things going? I know it can't be easy right now."

Hern broke the contact, stuck both hands into his pants pockets. "I'm leaving for New Jersey in the morning. That's where most of my mother's family is. We're having a memorial service up there in a couple of days."

Tom wanted to ask if Hern's plans for the future included leaving Mason County permanently, but he kept silent.

"Are there any new developments you can tell us about?" Rachel asked. "Have you been able to question Ragsdale yet?"

"Yeah," Tom said, glad to slip back into professional mode. "I can't go into detail about it, but he intends to plead guilty."

"That's good to hear," Hern said, nodding. He added with a little laugh, "I'd say the Taylors' dog is the only one who's profited from all this. She seems to like living with Joanna."

"It's Joanna's dog she likes," Rachel said. "I think Cricket and Nan have a best friends forever thing going on."

"Yeah, that's good," Tom said. Was Hern ever going to leave and let him talk to Rachel?

A brief awkward silence followed. Then Hern said, "Well, I guess I'll see you both when I get back."

Rachel hadn't yet looked directly at Tom. She stood with her arms folded, watching Hern leave, and Tom felt the way he always did when she withdrew into herself—shut out and frustrated. For once he refused to dwell on that frustration, and he countered it with all the good memories she had given him. Her rich, warm laughter, her gentle way with sick and frightened animals, the bond she had formed with his nephew Simon. The passion of their lovemaking.

"I brought you something," Tom said, holding out the paper bag.

Rachel took it and looked inside. "Oh, my gosh." She pulled her cell phone from the bag and turned it on. "How did you find them in that jungle?"

"I didn't. I gave Brandon and the Blackwoods the day off yesterday, and they spent it searching the woods at the McClure place. They found the binoculars without much trouble, but it took them a few hours to spot the phone."

"I don't know how I'll be able to thank them, but I'll think of something." Rachel looked up at Tom, the light from the doorway exposing the purple bruise on one cheek. "Have you heard a prognosis? For Meredith, I mean."

Tom hesitated, wishing he didn't have to answer the question. She would hear it from somebody, though. Might as well be him. "She's lost the sight in one eye, but she'll have some left in the other. The doctors aren't sure how much."

Rachel pressed a hand to her mouth. Tom wondered how many times the image of Meredith's bleeding eyes had risen up in her mind, the same way it had in his.

"You acted in self-defense. You did the right thing."

Her humorless little smile came and went in an instant. "You might have to repeat that several hundred times before I start believing it."

"As many times as it takes." Tom brushed his fingertips across her bruised cheek. The brief contact pierced him with longing. He wanted to hold her. He needed to hold her.

Rachel lowered her head so that her hair fell forward, obscuring her face. "Will you tell me something? Was Lindsay with you the night of the meeting? Was she at your house?"

"She showed up there, yeah. We had it out, I told her there was no chance of us ever getting back together. And I made her leave." Tom tilted Rachel's chin so he could look into her face. "What have you been thinking? That I was sleeping with her again? I thought you knew me better than that."

Rachel's solemn eyes searched his face. "I was beginning to feel as if I didn't know you at all." She added in a near-whisper, "You probably feel the same way about me."

Tom hooked his thumbs in his pockets to keep himself from pulling her into an embrace and telling her he knew all he needed to know, nothing else mattered. It did matter. It always would. "I think something happened in your life that you want to keep hidden. Something that's caused you a lot of grief." He paused, choosing his words carefully. "It's not the secret itself that bothers me, because whatever it is, you're still the same person. What kills me is that you don't trust me enough to confide in me."

The silence that followed was broken only by the chirping of crickets. Tom looked out into the gathering darkness and wondered if he'd just sealed his fate, destroyed any chance of rebuilding their relationship and having a future with Rachel.

He'd spoken the truth and he didn't regret that. How could love ever be enough if they didn't trust each other too?

At last Rachel spoke, her words halting. "I'm not protecting myself. I haven't done anything wrong. Something happened to my sister and me when we were small children, and we didn't learn the truth until a few years ago. There are others involved— innocent people who don't deserve to be hurt. If it all came out, it's the kind of thing that might get a lot of attention, and it would turn their lives upside down. I promised my sister I would never let that happen."

"Hey," Tom said, forcing a grin, "I wasn't planning to put out a press release. Regardless of what you tell me, I won't betray your confidence. I love you, Rachel. I want you to trust me."

Rachel placed the bag containing the phone and binoculars on the floor. She reached out and pulled one of his hands from his pocket. Twining her fingers in his, she moved closer and leaned her head on his shoulder. "I've missed you, Tom," she said. "I've missed you so much."

He wrapped his arms around her and drew her tight against him. "Oh, God, Rachel, it's so good to hold you. I feel like it's been a lifetime."

"It might take me a while," she said. "Telling you about my life. I didn't find out the truth about my family until a few years ago, and I've gotten used to keeping it all a secret. Talking about it is going to feel very strange, and it might take a long time to tell you everything."

"I've got all the time in the world."

Rachel ran a finger over his lips. "Can you stay with me tonight? Holly's spending the night with her grandmother. We have the house to ourselves. We can—"

A hoarse meow cut her off. Rachel and Tom both looked toward the doorway, where Frank sat inside the screen door. When the cat had their attention, he meowed again, turning up the volume, giving it the urgency of a command. Somewhere behind him in the living room, Cicero squawked, "Hello, come in. Hello, come in."

"Well," Rachel said, "not *entirely* to ourselves."

Tom laughed, and his laughter seemed to erase the last traces of doubt from Rachel's eyes. She smiled up at him, that intimate, sexy smile he hadn't seen since this nightmare began.

A few days ago, happiness had shimmered in the distance like a mirage, an unreachable fantasy. But in the end, it was as simple and real as this—a bossy cat, a noisy bird, and Rachel in his arms, smiling.

Author's Note

Readers unfamiliar with Rachel's background will find the entire story, told in her own voice, in *The Heat of the Moon*.

To receive a free catalog of Poisoned Pen Press titles, please contact us in one of the following ways:

Phone: 1-800-421-3976
Facsimile: 1-480-949-1707
Email: info@poisonedpenpress.com
Website: www.poisonedpenpress.com

Poisoned Pen Press
6962 E. First Ave. Ste. 103
Scottsdale, AZ 85251